Nancy Livingston was born in Stockton-on-Tees. She has worked as an actress, a cook, a musician, an air stewardess and as a production assistant in television. Her radio plays have been broadcast in Great Britain and abroad. Her first novel, a murder mystery entitled *The Trouble at Aquitaine*, was published in 1985 and she has also written two further crime novels, *Fatality at Bath and Wells* and *Incident at Parga*. *The Far Side of the Hill* is Ms Livingston's first family saga, and the sequel, *The Land of our Dreams*, will be published by Futura in 1989.

Nancy Livingston lives with her husband in a two-hundred-year-old house in Nottinghamshire.

NANCY LIVINGSTON

The Far Side of the Hill

Futura

A Futura Book

ISBN 0 7088 3684 4

Reproduced, printed and bound in Great Britain by
Hazell Watson & Viney Limited
Member of BPCC plc
Aylesbury, Bucks, England

Futura Publications
A Division of
Macdonald & Co (Publishers) Ltd
Greater London House
Hampstead Road
London NW1 7QX
A member of Maxwell Pergamon Publishing Corporation plc

ACKNOWLEDGEMENTS

My grateful thanks for all their help to;
Mrs C Copeland, Senior Assistant, Darlington Reference
Library, Miss V Redhead, Senior Assistant, Darlington Lending
Library, Mrs J Campbell, Archivist, Darlington Branch of the
Durham County Record Office.

CHAPTER ONE

Beginnings

The peninsula was remote and very beautiful. Men had lived there for centuries. They'd fought to possess it and their successors often found souvenirs of battles washed up on the sands after winter storms. There were never any reminders of the women who'd loved them, no broken pieces from children's toys; only tokens of war.

This was strange for the land was gentle, full of legends about the strange Megalithic cairns, about the standing stones; but in the midst of gentleness were sharp reminders: the Viking hill forts and Stone Age remains of Celtic Chieftans.

After bloodshed between the clans, the English came and took away minerals from beneath the soil. Then they emptied the land of people, dragging Highlanders from their homes, setting the thatch alight, pulling apart stone and turf walls until there was nothing but charred circles left to show where an entire community once lived.

A few remained, clinging tenaciously, refusing to accept that this was God's will (for Ministers were in the habit of equating

Him with the ruling classes). They re-established their right to
the crofts while at the Big Houses, built with all the certainty of
Victorian self-righteousness, the English returned to enjoy what
could never be destroyed, a magical landscape of sea and sky
surrounded by distant hills.

(i)

In one settlement on the eastern tip of Kentra Bay, a small boy
lugged an empty bucket up the slope to the spring. He moved
quickly to keep warm. He'd been asleep five minutes earlier
when his mother roused him but there wasn't a moment to lose.
So many things had to be done before he set off on the greatest
adventure of his life. His brother John was already up, helping
Father bring in peats for the fire, feeding the hens, taking the
beasts to the grazing, but then John was ten, a responsible age:
Davie McKie was only eight.

As he unlatched the door, cold air made Davie blink.
Outside, the mud was firm under his bare feet. It was early
September but already there were ground frosts most mornings.
Not hard, like those in the mountains, but sharp enough to kick
the sleep out of a boy.

Davie pounded up the track. Five hundred yards to the
spring, downhill all the way back. Sweet water that had never
run dry, the source of life here since time began.

He could see others moving now. Alla's married daughter,
making her way along the track to see to her father's breakfast.
Alla still grieved for his son, killed with the rest of the gang
building the new railway line. It was a tragedy right enough,
Davie had heard the men discussing it, but this was the age of
progress, of steam. Dynamiting was dangerous but when the
line was finished, a man could travel from Fort William to
Glasgow and from there, all the way to London! It was an
incredible thought for a boy who'd yet to see a train.

When the bucket was full he made his way back slowly.
Overhead in a clear sky he could see the golden rim of the sun
rising above the hills: it would be a grand day!

Inside the croft the dog sensed the excitement and hid, not

wanting to be outside where he belonged. There weren't many places of concealment, even for a dog; the one room was full to overflowing. Davie and John slept in the cupboard beds, built into the walls on either side of the fire. On the hearth was the hob where Jeannie, their mother, did the cooking and heated the water. Above, on a narrow shelf that stretched the width of the croft, all their most precious possessions were stored. It was dark, apart from the firelight, but the family could find what they wanted on that shelf, by reaching out a hand. In pride of place was the oil lamp, never used if a rushlight would suffice.

For furniture, there was a bench along one wall. In front of it was a table with stools for Jeannie and Davie. Beside the fire were the only chairs. Beyond the door, beneath the one small window, was a rickety box covered in oil-cloth on which Jeannie prepared their food. All the way round the walls, in any remaining space, their belongings were stored: pans waiting for the tinkers to come and mend them; bits of sacking which everyone used to protect themselves from the weather; spare tackle and tools; all the detritus accumulated by a family sharing a room for years. Above, from the beams, anything that could not be stowed hung on nails.

Built onto the end wall of the croft was a lean-to where Alex and Jeannie slept, surrounded by wooden tubs that contained flour, oats, salt and sugar. These were replenished twice a year when the supply boat called from Fort William.

Nothing was new when Alex brought his bride home nearly eleven years ago. How could it be on a labourer's wage of nine shillings a week and that uncertain during the winter? Jeannie hadn't known much about her bridegroom either. At the Big House where she was third housemaid, 'followers' were strictly forbidden. She would have risked losing her place if it had become known she had one, and her 'character' – which would have been disastrous. Her mother warned her about that when, at fourteen, Jeannie was turned out to go and earn her living.

With seven brothers and sisters at home, she never expected to return. Unable to read or write, speaking only Gaelic, she had no other prospect than service at the Big House. The Minister provided her with a piece of paper on which he'd written her name and date of birth. This Jeannie handed to the

11

housekeeper, from Glasgow, who didn't understand the Gaelic.

If Jeannie wept at her fate, she wasn't alone. Four other girls from the crofts shared the same attic bedroom. It smelt of urine because Jeannie's predecessor had been so homesick she'd wet the bed, but no one suggested replacing the mattress.

For the next two years she rose at six and began cleaning, dusting and polishing the first of five large rooms. When these were done, she scrubbed first the front steps of the house, then kitchens, sculleries and pantries. She had no identity as far as the owners of the house were concerned. If one of that family appeared, Jeannie was expected to flatten herself against a wall until they'd passed. After a turbulent, noisy but loving home, she lived and worked in limbo. Her presence was never acknowledged unless she failed to curtsey deeply enough.

Out of a wage of seven pounds nine shillings a year, Jeannie was expected to clothe herself, provide for her old age, and send money home to help her parents. By sixteen, she no longer wondered why some women ended up penniless and on the parish; she knew. They weren't any different: they were old or sick, no longer capable of work. This thought haunted the dreams of these girls in the attic. There was only one escape.

Jeannie first saw Alex among a group of beaters waiting patiently in the rain for the gentry to come out with their guns. She recognized him as one of the many workers on the estate, hired during the summer and laid off in winter. He was several years older than herself. She'd heard of the McKies. She knew that Alex's father had died as a rebel years ago but that was all.

Jeannie herself had learned what it was to feel rebellious. Two years in service had hardened her. That, and the mistress's trick of leaving coins under the carpets, to ensure Jeannie cleaned beneath and to test her honesty. They were usually half-crown coins, silver representing nearly a week's wage. It was cruel temptation but each time she found one, she handed it to the housekeeper, burning with indignation.

Outside in the rain, the fair-haired Alex saw the girl stare. She was thin, dark hair tucked under her cap, with an anxious look about her. She'd been on her way across the yard when she'd paused. They were only feet apart but to move and converse would've been against the rules. Jeannie hesitated a fraction longer before continuing on her way to the pump. On an impulse, Alex McKie followed and began working the handle. She looked up from her pail, and blushed.

During the next three years, they seldom met for longer than a few minutes at a time. As Jeannie couldn't read, Alex took to leaving flowers for her at their special trysting place. It was enough. They had an 'understanding'. When, after morning service one Sunday, he murmured, 'Will I speak to the Minister?' she had only a few seconds to decide her future. Even as she loitered, the head housemaid called out sharply.

It meant losing the security of employment. As the wife of a labouring man, her future would be bleak. But she would be free! Alex had a croft, surely they could survive? Jeannie didn't hesitate. She squeezed his hand then hurried to take her place in the crocodile of servants.

On the morning of her wedding, after she'd scoured the front steps for the last time, Jeannie put on her hat and listened submissively but without understanding, to the housekeeper telling her how stupid she was. One of the other girls who had sufficient English, stood at her side to ask for the precious 'character'. It was an insurance, should Alex fall sick and Jeannie need to earn for both of them.

During the lonely walk to church she had plenty of time to consider her folly but when she saw Alex, his hands full of flowers gathered from the hedgerows, she set down her bundle in the porch and walked proudly into church beside him.

(ii)

A year later, although childbirth was as bad as she'd feared, Jeannie was even more convinced she'd made the right choice. It didn't matter that she'd married a stubborn man – in the Highlands to be stubborn was to survive – she'd also married a man with enough sense of poetry, he could reach out and touch the moon! And what ambition! Not for themselves, it was too late for that, but for their children.

Alex had been away when Jeannie's pains began. Her neighbour heard the cries, helped her back into the croft and made her comfortable. There was nothing more she could do. No doctor or midwife lived anywhere near, nor could the crofters afford them. Each woman did her best for her friends knowing her own turn would come. Some survived, some did not. The most the women could hope for was a spring baby. Like the lambs, they stood a better chance of growing strong before the next winter.

When Alex returned that evening, Jeannie had been in labour eleven hours. He sat beside her, wiping away the sweat, trying to distract her. 'They were saying in Salen there is a new law passed by Parliament. All children are to be educated now. Our son will not be allowed to work in the fields until he is ten years of age because of the education.'

'Oh, it's to be a son, is it? And were they telling you that in Salen?' She tried to smile but a wave of agony swept through her. The pain of her grip frightened him.

'Of course it's a son, Jeannie my love.' Oh God, let it be over soon!

The next time she shrieked, the neighbour told him he must leave. Outside the night was very dark. Alex waited in the warm steamy byre. 'Dear God, don't let her suffer so!'

The neighbour prayed too, silently. She was frightened Jeannie might die. She'd helped at other birthings that had been straightforward. This time was far more difficult. She felt clumsily, to see if the cord was round the baby's neck. Her man would be home by now, wanting his dinner. 'Come on now Jeannie McKie, push harder!'

Out in the byre, Alex whispered to Jupiter, low in the sky, 'Boy or girl, our child will have the education. He will be the equal of any man's son,' and began to calculate the cost. For naturally, although it was now the law, one had to pay for the privilege.

(iii)

It wasn't easy. From 1875 to the end of the decade, farm prices fell every year. Alex's wage fluctuated alarmingly. There were four disastrously wet summers too, one after another until Jeannie began to fear for their survival, never mind an

14

education. But Alex was stubborn as usual and continued to save. She proved she could match such tenacity with her own remarkable thrift.

After so many lean years, if she didn't bother to thank her Maker for his most bounteous gifts, at least he'd answered her most urgent prayer. There were only two children. She and Alex were spared the nightmare of her mother's existence.

Both boys were healthy too, Davie gloriously so. But when the neighbour put that baby in her arms, two years after John's birth, Jeannie was startled. 'Where on earth does he get that red hair?' she asked. The neighbour sniffed.

'Well, Jeannie McKie, only you can tell us the answer. And will you listen to that noise! You'll not need bellows any more if he keeps that up.' Jeannie hugged her second son tenderly. Let him yell. There had been too much meekness in the Highlands.

(iv)

John knelt in front of the fire and spooned porridge onto two plates. He'd inherited his mother's thin build but his father's strength of purpose. Life for John McKie would always be a serious matter. And he understood enough of poverty now to ensure nothing was wasted. This morning not a drop of porridge was spilt. Apart from her thinness, John had Jeannie's anxious eyes. They were a lighter grey and slightly myopic. Nor was his hair as dark or his cheeks as bright. Altogether he was a much paler boy.

At the other end of the room, the door burst open and Davie stood there, glowing. 'It's going to be fine, John. Will you take a look? A really grand day!'

'There will be time enough to see it. Come and get your breakfast. We do not want to be late.'

Alex waited until the last bit of bread had wiped the plates clean. Neither boy spoke. They daren't look at one another, they were afraid. Had father forgotten? Or, much more likely, had there not been enough money?

Then Alex rose, opened a cupboard and reached to the top

15

shelf. 'You are to look after these, Davie. They cost me three-pence ha'penny and are to last you, mind.'

'Aye, father.' Davie was so brimful he nearly choked.

'John's only cost me threepence,' Alex grumbled.

'That was because they didn't have the laces, Alex,' Jeannie said quickly. 'You could not expect to pay the same with the laces.' She could see Davie was near to tears. She couldn't bear for him to break down, not today. Alex put the boots in front of Davie and the family gazed contentedly at the utter perfection: secondhand boots, well patched and studded with nails, the laces neatly threaded, the leather polished by Jeannie to a chestnut sheen. Holding his breath, Davie put out a finger to stroke an immaculate toe. His very own boots!

Jeannie busied herself, wrapping oatcakes in two pieces of cloth. 'You are old enough to see to your own food, Davie. Don't lose it on the way.' There was one final ceremony. Alex took down from the shelf a cracked tobacco jar and counted out twopence to each of his sons.

'Education is a privilege, Davie, never forget that.'

'No, Father.'

'Stick at your lessons like John and I shall be content. Now be off with you.'

Outside, high above, a kestrel hovered. Beneath the two dots that were John and Davie moved forward but the bird wasn't interested. Columns of smoke rose from the crofts and evaporated in the sunlight. The bird spiralled lazily in the air currents. Suddenly there was a slight twitch in the bracken and he spotted it. His wings trembled as he manoeuvred into position then snapped shut as he dived. They heard the scream. Davie stopped. 'Did you see? He got a rabbit, I think.'

'Come on. It's a fair way yet.'

Davie obeyed, reaching every so often to finger his talisman, the boots, swinging by their laces round his neck.

'You must try and remember everything I've told you.' John had more of Jeannie's air of anxiety about him this morning. He peered at Davie from beneath the brim of his cap and frowned.

Immediately Davie felt guilty. When John looked at him like that he knew he hadn't been concentrating hard enough. 'Suppose you go through it again, John,' he said, placating

16

him. 'I don't want to let you down.' John sighed. It was very worrying being responsible for another, frailer human being.

They walked on steadily. Davie watched the sun rise above the moor. Ahead, trees marked the edge of the loch. Behind were the purple-blue hills of Moidart. In a couple of miles they would reach Acharacle. Yesterday, when he hadn't a care, Davie had gone across Kentra Bay with one of the fishermen to his favourite place on the sands. He had run, scuffing the grains, listening to the sand 'singing' to him. This was the place where occasionally, he'd turned up relics of battles. Once it had been a part of a sword. He'd taken it home but Alex had told him sternly never to bring it inside the house. Davie didn't understand why.

John stopped speaking. Davie's heart sank. He'd let his attention wander again. John was always warning him about that, but the day was so beautiful – couldn't John see that? Without seeing anything John said, 'I'm thinking it would be better if we used the English from now on.'

'I haven't many words yet,' Davie protested.

'Which is why you must practise. Now then, that is – the sky. This is – my hand.' Davie mouthed the strange sounds.

(v)

On her own Jeannie needed to celebrate. Luxury was a simple matter. Once the washing was done, she'd heat more water and have a bath. They took it in turns once a week in the tub in front of the fire but today she'd be extravagant and indulge herself. Jeannie chuckled over her wickedness. What a thing on a Monday morning with all the work waiting to be done.

There'd been three baths at the Big House, massive porcelain ones framed in mahogany, but the servants weren't allowed the use of them. For them there was an earth closet behind the stable block and when they wanted to wash, they had to carry water up to their rooms.

As she'd polished and scoured, Jeannie could smell her own sweat. The crowded attic was full of the odours of its inhabitants, past and present. To be clean was wonderful! Since

17

her marriage she'd revelled in the opportunity to enjoy soap and water whenever she chose. If her sons didn't share the same ecstasy, never mind. Please God, they'd never have to humble themselves in service, either of them.

Today garments spread farther and farther along the hedgerow as Jeannie walked to and fro with the washing. It had been such a gamble all those years ago, marrying a man she scarcely knew. There had been bad times when she nearly buckled under the harsh life but Alex's strength was always there to steady her. In the early weeks too, the gap in their ages made her shy of him but when he held his son in his arms for the first time, the love in his eyes . . . Jeannie hugged herself, remembering. With Davie, Alex's joy and ambition grew fiercer. That's when he'd confided in her for the first time. What an effort it had been to achieve his great ambition but now, both the boys would be safe. With an education they could travel beyond the reach of the Factor's hand. She and Alex would rarely see them once they left the peninsula – Jeannie closed her eyes to that cloud on the horizon. She told herself sturdily it was the price every mother had to pay; nothing could be allowed to spoil her happiness today.

She undressed with care; many of the fastenings were loose, the fabric was so worn. Jeannie smiled as she remembered Alex's tales of fashionable ladies in Fort William, with skirts that fitted so smoothly, the shape of the figure could be seen. She was puzzled rather than shocked; how on earth did they keep warm in the winter? Her skirt was thickly gathered against the cold. Stockings were too expensive so she wore an old pair of Alex's socks on her feet.

'Today,' she whispered, 'I wouldn't swap places with any of them. Not even the Queen in Balmoral!' Then she laughed at her foolishness. Standing naked in front of the fire and talking to herself? Come, Jeannie McKie, this will never do! Picking up the rag and the soap she began to scrub herself methodically. Perhaps one day her boys would live in a house with a tap! She hoped so. It would make the sacrifices of the last ten years worthwhile.

Not that Alex was doing too badly now. The demand for labour to build a further extension to the railway had pushed up wages in the area. There had been harsh words from the estate office of the Big House, accusing crofters of being greedy. An extra shilling a week could price them all out of a job, they were warned. But everyone knew there were fewer people here now. The bad harvests, the potato famine and now the demand for seven pounds a year rent for a croft meant that of course people were leaving. There wasn't enough to feed and clothe their families. The coming of the railways meant that men could reach the new industries in the south.

After the clearances, there'd been a lull in the exodus from the area. Labour was still needed to a certain extent, to enable landowners to pursue their way of life, but transport had changed all that. A man was no longer limited to the distance he could walk in a day. Apart from rail there were steam packets calling regularly. And when the young men and women moved farther afield, few returned. To Jeannie it seemed as if she and Alex would be the last generation to live here.

Those that had gone had found work in Glasgow, some in English factories. There'd even been those who'd gone to Nova Scotia, America and Australia. Jeannie had accepted that John and Davie would leave from the moment they were born and was glad. There was nothing left for them here but servitude. But Alex wasn't content for his sons to end up in some factory. He had made plans – oh, such plans! Jeannie shivered as she thought of them, and because the water was cold.

She towelled herself, dressed, and began to wash her hair. She stooped over the tub. When she was first married and still wore corsets, tightly laced, she could never have bent so easily. But after so many lean years, Jeannie no longer needed them. She always wore them on Sundays of course. None of the women would dream of going to church without their stays! As she retied her apron, she looked up at the sky. Davie was right, it was a perfect day.

(vi)

After four miles the boys left the road and went down a track. By a gate, a diminutive figure waited, standing courteously when he saw them. 'Good day, John, Davie . . . ' He spotted something and his eyes widened. 'Man, you've got boots!'

Realization was swift. From wee Georgie's expression, Davie understood that what hung round his neck was more than a sign of his new life, it was a symbol that separated him from those less fortunate. He saw the gap, how it would grow to a chasm between him and his friend, and went crimson at the hurt he knew the precious boots were inflicting.

'You knew Davie was to be a scholar, too?' John shared the same embarrassment but it made him unnecessarily severe. Wee Georgie nodded. Of course he knew. He took the slate John held out and stared at it blindly. He also recognized that he was doomed to stay where he was.

Georgie's parents like other crofters had clucked and shaken their heads over Alex McKie's ambition for his sons, prophesying failure yet here they were, already on their way.

To break the mood John began to instruct swiftly, referring to the slate and showing how to make the shapes using a stick in the dust. It was a twice-daily ritual and it grieved both him and Georgie that progress was slow. 'These are all the numbers between one and twenty. If you can learn them by this evening, maybe tomorrow I can show you up to a hundred,' he urged.

'I will do my best. It's not easy on my own.' John nodded sadly. Wee Georgie had application but he lacked encouragement.

Back on the road again, John was angry. 'If that mother of his were not so feckless, Georgie would be with us today.' Davie stayed silent. It was true, but he liked Mrs Hamilton, always laughing, with ribbons in her hair. He wished their mother could afford ribbons too, her hair was even prettier.

He sighed. He'd heard the condemnations often enough. Georgie's mother was a spendthrift who could be tempted by any packman who chose to call. If it was a fine day, she'd leave her work to walk on the hills, which was where Davie often met her. He sighed again. Those carefree days were behind him now. He didn't argue with John about Mrs Hamilton. If he could avoid it, he never argued with him.

For the last two miles Davie gave John his full attention, repeating the new English words and savouring the warm turf beneath his feet. As they stood on the summit of the last slope and looked down, each saw their own vision of paradise. For

John it was the small grey building with its shingled roof, that sat comfortably in a dip beside the loch. Tall fir trees and wild rhododenrons sheltered it on one side. Behind were the school teacher's living quarters and the outhouse and privy. In the yard in front of the building other children were assembling.

Davie saw only the bleached silvery rocks covered with lichen framing the sparkling water. He watched the way sun and cloud dappled the landscape, shadows emphasizing the golden light. He let out a deep sigh of pleasure.

'Aye, Davie, a grand sight.' John was pleased with him. Davie was showing proper respect for this temple, this gateway to their future. 'Right then, we can put our boots on now.'

(vii)

Inside the temple, the high priestess looked at herself in the mirror. Helen Shields was a tight-lipped woman of thirty-three. Next door in the schoolroom she could hear the monitor setting out chalks and cleaning the blackboard. Helen thought of the screech of those chalks on the slates and already her head began to throb. Soon the bell would be rung, the shuffle of feet begin as, outside, her pupils formed up into a double line, ready for inspection. There was no escape; there never would be.

Helen stabbed the collar of her blouse with a cameo brooch as she muttered her daily invocation for courage, 'You've made your bed my girl, now you must learn to lie on it.'

It had been a long journey for her, from the shabby, genteel English vicarage where appearances mattered above all else. She still hadn't grasped the fact that here on the peninsula, while there were fish in the lochs, peat under the turf, these people could survive. She saw only their poverty and it frightened her. Perhaps because it reminded Helen of the abyss into which she too could fall, should she fail.

It wasn't conscious cruelty that made her scold a girl vigorously one morning for coming to school in a badly torn skirt, it was fear that poverty was getting the upper hand. When next day, the girl appeared in a garment that was over-large, it never occurred to Helen that this was the only other skirt in the

21

croft, that the girl's mother would now be working outdoors in nothing but her petticoat and shawl.

During her early days, Helen Shields had expressed surprise to the Minister at the lack of footwear among her pupils. He preached on the subject, admonishing his congregation. Within a couple of weeks, all the children had boots, as old, ill fitting and patched as those on Davie's feet today, but every child had a pair. If she'd had any notion of the sacrifices made to provide them, Helen would have been ashamed. Naturally, once out of her sight, the children took them off. They'd only been bought to please her. To wear them would have been utter folly.

The monitor rang the bell. Helen could delay no longer. She stiffened her back, assumed her severest expression and swept outside, ready to begin.

The pupils filed past, two by two. Many of the girls had rough sacking aprons to protect their clothes. When she'd first been appointed here, Helen had imagined eager middle-class children in attractive straw boaters, like those with whom she was familiar. Reality was different: now she was surrounded by tam o'shanters, ancient caps, ragged shawls. From beneath, bright eyes looked at her expectantly.

'Good morning, Mistress Shields.'

'Good morning, Katriona . . . Effie . . . '

Inside the small lime-washed room, Helen took her place behind her desk. 'You may sit.' Thirty stools scraped the flagstones. Thirty pairs of arms folded across thirty chests and sixty eyes stared out front as she opened the register and prepared to call out the names. There was an interruption. John McKie, grasping Davie by the arm, marched forward to stand in front of her.

'Yes?'

'If you please, Mistress Shields, this is my brother who is to begin his schooling today.' Davie scarcely dared breathe as Helen looked him over. Suppose she rejected him, what would he do then?

Helen Shields saw perspiration on the child's face and wondered what ailed him? She frowned over his ragged trousers. Those were the ones John McKie had worn last year, they were nearly through at the seat. And what hair!

'What is your name?' The boy looked so white she feared he was about to faint. When he spoke it was with the slow sibilance that was common to all of them in the Highlands, softening and lengthening the English words.

'My name is Davie McKie, Mistress Shields.'

'How old are you, Davie?'

'Eight years . . . old.'

'And why have you come?' She never normally asked this but she wanted the boy to look up at her. When he did, she saw the blue eyes were intense.

'For the education.' He thrust the two pennies at her, out of anxiety she might refuse. Helen took them, thanked him and entered his name and date of birth in the register. As she drew a line underneath, John beamed with satisfaction and Davie let out a huge breath of relief.

'We will make a start. Take Davie to sit beside you, John. Now pay attention, all of you. Hector Cameron, stand up please. Take the Bible and read the text for today.'

Lessons proceeded briskly but when she'd first arrived it had been a different matter. The children had no idea of discipline. Their first teachers, hastily recruited following the new Act, were ex-governesses, accustomed to very few pupils. The crofters' children had never sat indoors for hours at a time in their lives. It was very difficult for them to accept this.

Helen Shields was of a very different metal to her predecessors. The children sensed it and she made sure they didn't forget. She had enough personality to hold their attention and she knew they wanted to learn. It was up to her to make them understand they could only achieve this by listening in silence. Those who refused to do so found their parents had been informed their money was being wasted, and suffered accordingly. The Minister was surprised Helen herself had so little use for the cane but she told him in her opinion it had never brought satisfactory results. If any of the older boys 'cheeked' her or grew too bold, she only needed her tongue to reduce them in stature.

The greater part of her pupils soaked up knowledge like sponges. To cope with their varying abilities, Helen began each day with a lesson for all, then divided them into groups with an able child in charge of each. She gathered the slower ones round her desk to make sure they didn't fall behind. It wasn't ideal but it was the best she could do unaided. Those who were bright were given a quiet corner and extra work. She saw to it that every child had a turn with her during the day.

Helen never had any idea how long her pupils would stay at school. By law they were supposed to be there until their thirteenth birthday but if money were short or an extra pair of hands needed, a pupil would disappear. As it was, on Mondays, several girls had to stay at home to help with the washing.

As she herself gradually came to know the true value of their twopences, Helen tried to give equal worth in return. No child ever left her school without being able to read and write in English and do simple arithmetic. They knew an outline of history, as approved by the School Board, and they had a knowledge of geography. Girls learned how to patch and darn, to turn sheets and make neat buttonholes. The Minister was emphatic that they must acquire all such skills necessary for going into service. Helen Shields compressed her lips and held her peace. She would fit any bright child for something better; it was up to them whether they accepted the challenge.

(viii)

By the end of the morning, one or two heads had begun to nod. Helen called an early break. They sat at their desks and unwrapped food while the monitor took round a pitcher of water from which each of them drank. Helen spoke sharply to the sleepiest boy. 'Willy Henderson, can you not stay awake today?'

'Beg pardon, Mistress.'

'Did you not sleep last night?'

'Until the milking, yes, Mistress Shields.' Helen remembered the family were farmers with a small herd.

'Doesn't your father usually attend to that?'

'He is away with the sheep.'

When Helen looked blank, several voices hastened to explain.

'It is the market this week for the spring lambs – '

'They have all gone to Fort William – '

'Please Mistress, my father has gone as well.' Helen stared at them severely until they subsided.

'One at a time if you please. Now, Willy Henderson, you weren't doing the milking at this time last year, were you?'

'No Mistress, my brother was. But he's gone to be a fisherman with my uncle at Arbroath. I do the work at home now when my father's away.' Helen considered briefly. Willy Henderson was tolerably bright; she might achieve results if he could stay awake.

'You must ask your mother to do the work instead, or one of your brothers. I cannot have any slackness while you're in school.' She raised her voice. 'That applies to everyone here, is that understood? You come to me to learn.'

Heads nodded. Their mothers would cooperate. Every parent, every boy and girl knew the sooner they mastered the education, the sooner they could leave the peninsula.

When classes finished that afternoon, Helen found Alex McKie waiting to speak to her. She could see how anxious John was about the meeting. He stood at his father's side to act as interpreter.

Helen had first met Alex when he'd brought John to school, wearing an old-fashioned frock coat that was green with age. He had on the same coat today because he was on official business. In Helen's eyes, he looked comical. When John asked deferentially if his father 'could have a wee word', Helen indicated they would move outside so that the monitor could finish scrubbing the floor.

Alex was a big man with a weathered complexion. Close to, Helen was much more aware of his masculinity. She sat abruptly on the low stone wall, leaving him standing, in an attempt to enhance her authority. The coat no longer made her laugh because of the powerful nature of the man inside it. She was apprehensive as to what might be coming. The three of them waited respectfully for her to indicate she was ready. Helen pulled herself together and nodded that they might begin.

'My father would not wish to be a trouble but would be asking a question.'

'Yes, what is it?'

'It is the Latin. Would you be having the Latin?'

Had she heard aright?

'Why does your father want to know that?'

25

'Davie and I will need it to pass the examination for the university.'

Helen was stunned.

'John, I don't think I quite understand?' Her tone communicated her meaning to Alex. He spoke emphatically and John translated.

'It has already been decided that we will both go to the university, Mistress Shields. My father has spoken to the Minister to find out what was necessary. He told us about the Latin and about the examination.' Helen was still so flabbergasted she didn't know what to say.

Her silence worried them, Alex particularly. He muttered and John grew even more anxious. If Helen couldn't teach them Latin, they would have to go back to the Minister. It would mean confessing their plan for he was bound to ask questions this time. So far Alex had avoided telling him about the university. All he'd done was to ask, innocently, how a man went about preparing himself for such an establishment. The cleric had been only too pleased to dazzle McKie with his own achievements. In doing so, he'd told Alex all he needed to know.

The crofters were aware that the Minister was in complete agreement with the Big House in disapproving any attempt by them to rise to the middle class. He preached at least three times a year that the meek would inherit the earth, but that that earth was not any part of Argyllshire was implicit. Besides, as Alex now murmured to John, if they had to ask the Minister for lessons, he was bound to ask more money than the lady teacher.

Helen struggled with her incredulity. That these two ragged boys, sons of this labourer – it was ridiculous! Whatever ambition she had for her brighter pupils never reached these giddy heights! She cleared her throat. 'Does your father realize that to attend university costs a great deal of money?'

This time Alex was vehement. 'My father says kindly do not concern yourself with that. He has spoken to the Minister about it. He has come here prepared to pay what is needed for the Latin.'

It was a put-down but who was she to interfere? Money was men's business. There must be a source of wealth among the McKies that she knew nothing about. As regards Latin, Helen

26

had a smattering of the classics but not enough for Alex's purpose. 'Please explain that I can teach you a little, John. I have studied Latin. But Davie cannot begin for some considerable time. He must first learn English.'

John translated and Alex's brow cleared. It was better than he thought. He was about to speak when Helen added thoughtfully, 'I'm almost certain you will both need Greek as well as Latin. Did the Minister say anything about that?'

The three withdrew for a moment's consultation. Helen sat, staring unseeing at the loch. How could this family possibly hope to . . . ? It was all nonsense, they must realize it. Alex wanted extra status for his sons, a commendable desire, but that's all it was. And in another three years when John was at the end of his schooling, that would be the end of it.

She heard them return and turned to face them.

'We have decided that Davie and I will learn the Latin together,' John announced. 'I will teach Davie extra English every night so that he can keep up. And I will make sure he learns the Latin too because I'm a good scholar.' It was said without boasting and was, Helen acknowledged, an honest claim. John was the most conscientious member of the school.

'My father will find out about the Greek,' John went on, 'but we will begin the Latin now, please. We will learn as much as you are able to teach us . . . ' He paused and Helen was alert. What was this? 'As you only know a little, Mistress Shields, my father is prepared to pay one penny extra for each of us for the lessons.'

They waited for her reaction. Privately, Alex had been prepared to go as high as a penny ha'penny but he wasn't going to throw his money away. He might still have to ask the Manse for help if the boys were to reach the necessary standard.

Helen was grim. It was her own fault if these people took her at her word. She should know them better by now – but only a penny a week! She knew very well that if she refused, the Minister would discover and want to know why. He was Chairman of the School Board and she'd claimed at her interview to know the classics.

'Tell your father I will teach both of you Latin to whatever standard he requires,' she said icily. After all, what was three years of it? She should be able to cope with that. 'But if he also

27

wishes you to learn Greek, that will be another penny, making a total of fourpence a week each.'

Alex was far too careful to let the school mistress see how relieved he was. The Manse would've demanded sixpence at the very least. He seized her hand and gave her his carefully prepared phrase. 'A bargain, Mistress Shields.' He put a small parcel wrapped in sacking on the wall beside her. Inside, something moved.

'That is a crab for your supper,' John told her. The deal had been struck. All three insisted on shaking hands before wishing her goodnight and starting off on the eight-mile journey home.

Helen stood watching them. It took another movement in the sacking for her to come to her senses. She had agreed to teach two barely literate boys enough Latin and Greek to reach university standard! Thank heavens it was just a whim of Alex McKie's. The sooner it was over, the better. All the same, she was terribly rusty, even for beginners.

Helen went indoors, put the crab in the brown stone sink and sent the monitor home. She banked up the fire, trimmed the lamp and went through to the tiny bedroom where she kept her trunk of books. She found her Latin grammar. If she began revising immediately she could just keep ahead of them. Alex had been very firm that he expected lessons to begin next day. 'I shall need plenty of extra books,' Helen told herself, 'there goes the first tuppence. And what about Greek? I shall be in debt before I'm finished. Then there's the actual work . . . ' She had to keep at least one lesson ahead of John.

Back on the croft, the evening tasks finished, Alex sniffed the air and decided it would be a cold night. The beasts were in the byre and the dog had sneaked inside the croft. It lay, head on its paws, puzzling at the family's strange new behaviour.

Although the meal was finished they had resumed their places at table and the lamp had been lit. John had been surprised when his mother joined them but Alex insisted. 'We both want to learn the English.'

The ten-year-old faced his class. 'We will begin with words for everyday things. This – is a table. It begins with the letter T . . . ' Chalk squeaked on the slates, breathing became heavy; in his corner the dog brooded.

Two hours later they could name most of the objects in the room and write the words. Jeannie couldn't get her tongue round the sounds but she was satisfied. She copied the last letter from John's slate onto her own and looked at it: FLOUR BIN. She'd been keeping her flour in one all these years and had never known before.

John was white with fatigue but satisfied. 'Tomorrow we will learn the words for things outside,' he began when there was a soft tap at the door. Alex slipped outside, and voices conversed softly.

Jeannie smiled. 'It's Alla. There must be a cloud across the moon.' Alex returned and picked up his coat. Instantly the dog was awake, moving beside him like a shadow.

'Go to bed,' Alex told them. 'Maybe there will be fish to sell tomorrow at the Big House.' He grinned at his wife. 'It's only right that they should help pay for the education.'

(ix)

The lamp in the school mistress's room was extinguished now as Helen prepared for bed. She undressed by the warmth of the fire, folding two flannel petticoats, woollen stockings and tweed skirt before nerving herself to hurry into the cold bedroom. Her cotton nightgown, although voluminous, offered no protection against draughts. She pulled a Paisley shawl round her shoulders. It was the one luxury she'd allowed herself when she'd been appointed mistress here. Its rich pattern soothed her.

She sat toasting her toes as the last ember sank into ashes, then remembered the Greek. And the letter to her old governess. With a groan she got out of her chair, re-lit the wick and took the writing slope down from the shelf. Wiping the nib she began:

Dear Miss Milne,
You will no doubt be surprised to hear from me so soon after my last letter but I need your advice . . .

Thirteen years previously, when Helen Shields was twenty, she decided to leave home and earn her living. It wasn't a sudden decision, it had come about gradually. Helen was the fourth daughter of a parson, all of them without a dowry, but worst of all, she was the ugly one.

Although it was a time when women were pushing back frontiers, demanding the right to use their brains, most of those women came from wealthy backgrounds. Such wealth gave them the confidence to withstand parental opposition. Helen Shields had to rely on obstinacy. To be the daughter to an impoverished gentleman narrowed her choice of career still further.

Her three pretty sisters clung to the notion that marriage was the only option. Hadn't their mother impressed this idea on them since birth? But as they progressed through their twenties – indeed the eldest was teetering on the brink of twenty seven – they were in danger of drifting into a poverty-stricken old age, trying to maintain respectability in the eyes of the congregation if not of an all-seeing God.

Helen tried to warn them of the danger, to think of the future but they turned their minds resolutely away with increasingly shrill cries. But Helen couldn't ignore the truth herself. Whenever she looked in the mirror there was the sallow skin, the long plain face and hair. To use the curling tongs was futile. After a few minutes, any curls went limp. Helen settled instead for braids wound into a tidy bun. As for clothes, hers were straightforward. Her sisters' low necklines and frills embarrassed her.

So did their behaviour. Whenever an eligible man appeared, these three pretty women fluttered to greet him, competing with each other to pour tea and simper. Helen became increasingly conscious of the sniggers among her father's parishioners. She tried to tell her mother but Mrs Shields was incredulous. Her three elder girls were charming and who could blame them for seeking out 'Mr Right'? Helen shouldn't criticize; she should be searching, too.

Finally Helen rebelled, most of all against her Saviour, who had given her nothing but foolish, snobbish parents and an uncertain future. But having faced up to the idea that He had, she knew it was up to her to change matters. She would leave home and earn her living. Her mother ridiculed the idea, her father forbade her to mention it again. Work? Like some common woman? But after a few days, he changed his mind.

30

Helen was so dour, forever prophesying doom about their finances. Without her, with his three pretty girls fussing over him, life would be so much more pleasant. Yes, he thought, he might allow himself to give in.

Helen didn't leave immediately; she had to prepare herself and there was no urgent necessity. It took a push from fate to expedite matters.

(x)

The Reverend Mr Shields had begun his professional life with an adequate income and a small inheritance. He'd then made the error of marrying a woman dedicated to squandering both. When his daughters were small they were surrounded by servants and luxury. As they grew older and the vicarage emptier they became aware of what was happening, but their mother insisted they need not worry: rich husbands would seek them out, providing they were accomplished.

The three older girls dedicated themselves to becoming accomplished; there was nothing they weren't prepared to acquire except perhaps a little learning. They could speak phrases in French, sing arias in Italian, so why bother with mathematics?

When Helen was born there were only two servants and a cook. Much of the silver had been sold, discreetly, to pay debts. Later in life, Helen could only remember her mother as a querulous woman giving to weeping when quarter day came round.

It wasn't that Helen found learning any easier than her sisters, but she recognized its worth. The elderly governess who'd replaced the fashionable tutors encouraged her and Helen responded. She didn't compete with her sisters in pokerwork or playing the piano, but then she didn't try.

She rose before the rest of the house to work at her books and when the three other girls tired of frittering away the governess's time, she and Miss Milne began again in earnest: history, geography, mathematics, French and English were all necessary. Classics she studied with Mr Standing, a retired schoolmaster, using money set aside for dancing lessons.

By the time Helen was eighteen, Miss Milne declared herself

satisfied. 'You know when I first began, my dear, I had to work without payment, just for my food and lodging. Children and servants knew this and despised me for it. But there was no other choice for women in my station in life.' Miss Milne sighed. 'It's wonderful how times have changed. So many openings for women now. Imagine, Helen, *you* could end up in charge of a school!' They smiled at each other.

'If I can be independent, that will satisfy me. Were I to stay on here,' and Helen shrugged, 'I'd end up like my sisters. When Father dies and his income with him, what will happen I dare not contemplate. But as they refuse to concern themselves, neither shall I.'

'You do not think you will marry? At eighteen Helen still had hope but she was honest. 'No, Miss Milne, I don't think so.'

They worked in silence for a while. Helen put down her pen and stretched cramped fingers.

'You think I am ready to apply for a post?'

'If you feel confident, then you are. But I would leave it a little longer, to be quite certain. And remember when you do apply, you have one great advantage.'

'What is that?'

'You are the daughter of a cleric. My father was only a journeyman.'

'I don't see what difference that makes?' The governess stared at her sadly.

'You will, my dear, once you are out in the world. In the eyes of many people, it matters a great deal. Never forget to mention it when you apply for a post.'

Thinking about this afterwards, Helen found the implications distasteful, but the date for leaving home was deferred indefinitely. Now that her education was officially over and Miss Milne had left, Mrs Shields made claims upon her. As Helen was good at mathematics, why should she not make herself useful and take over the housekeeping?

At first reluctant, Helen was very worried indeed when the true state of their finances was revealed. She tried to interest her father but he flapped his hands and retreated into his study. Helen followed him there. 'You must listen, Father. If we continue like this we shall end up having to sell the furniture! We've been overspending for years.'

'Nonsense! Your mother always managed. Why cannot you do the same? Such a fuss – it's completely unnecessary. And unpleasant.'

'Father, it is serious or I wouldn't have troubled you. Mother has had to pledge your salary up to six months ahead. What will happen when you retire? There are no savings in the bank, nothing.'

A ripple disturbed the Reverend Mr Shields' calm. 'Perhaps we should retrench, just a little.' He looked at the shelves of books. 'We could always sell some of those,' he suggested vaguely, 'I seldom refer to them nowadays.' And having made a gesture he sat at his desk to indicate the interview was over. Now it was up to Helen.

She took him at his word and retrenching was severe. Her mother whimpered when subscriptions to fashionable journals were cancelled. Her sisters complained much more loudly when told there would be no dress allowance that autumn. After nearly eighteen months' scrimping, when Helen finally managed to balance income against expenditure, no one thanked her. They despised her for being so pleased about it.

When she thought she'd plugged every loophole, Helen began to make plans for saving towards her parents' old age. Foolishly, she told her mother. And when Mrs Shields understood there was a small surplus in the bank, she and her daughters indulged in a spending spree. Convinced they'd been so good, so *restrained* for so long, they ordered a mass of furbelows without which, they told themselves, life would be insupportable.

At the end of the month when the bills arrived, Helen found herself shaking with anger. That they could be so stupid! She shouted at her mother as she'd never done before and hated herself for losing control. Mrs Shields flooded the study with her tears and at the end of the day, her father warned Helen if she behaved in that way again she would be made to leave home. Fate then gave her another push.

At this same time, Mr Shields engaged a new curate. Mr Giles was a middle-aged widower, called late in life to the ministry following his wife's death and his inheritance of her fortune. Having enjoyed matrimonial comforts for many years, this widower intended to enjoy them again as soon as possible and

33

was agreeably surprised to find a wide choice conveniently to hand. At least, so he presumed.

Unaware of his inheritance, the three pretty sisters did not simper at him over the tea-cups. They considered curates, especially balding ones over fifty, not worth the bother.

Mr Giles proposed to the eldest, Euphemia, and was dismissed. He tried Victoria who was extremely curt. He decided to ignore Sophie because of her tiresome giggle and considered instead, Helen. She was ugly; it followed therefore that she would be grateful. He considered the situation carefully. Helen was capable, she was better educated than the others and could instruct his two children, thereby saving the expense of a governess. Provided one ignored her looks, she was very suitable. And did those looks really matter? Privately Mr Giles acknowledged he no longer needed passion, he required serviceability. He made his decision.

Helen was accosted in the pantry whilst trying to decide if the butcher's bill could be deferred again. Astonishment reduced her to silence. This the impetuous lover interpreted as consent. Unfortunately he then made the mistake of congratulating Helen on having more sense than her sisters.

She was confused. The price of cutlets, the mention of 'comfortable circumstances' whirled in her brain. She excused herself to consider her answer and for a few moments her heart beat wildly. That she should be the object of a man's desire! But Euphemia and Victoria met her on the stairs. They wanted to know what Mr Giles had said and whether Helen's proposal varied in any particular from their own. They laughed and ridiculed, finally they left her. By then Helen knew beyond a doubt she was not loved, she was more a final expedient.

Perhaps because she'd faced reality so many times recently, she didn't immediately refuse Mr Giles. He could give her security, he'd promised as much. He could banish for ever the spectre of poverty, the need to earn a living. To Helen alone of all the sisters, he'd hinted at his private wealth. The thought of that security tempted her. But alas, although she was ugly, Helen also was only twenty and even ugly women over thirty have been known to be silly, to prefer hope to reality. She refused him. She pushed a note under his door thanking him but regretting her inability to accept. She sent a message she would not be down to dinner and alone in her room, Helen wept. When all the tears were shed she knew the time had come to leave.

She took work where she could at first, as assistant in a ladies' academy then as governess to various families. For the first time she understood Miss Milne's warning. Neither a servant nor one of the family, she was ostracized. Once she even had to share a bedroom, with one of the maids. She shrank from the enforced intimacy. At the vicarage she'd always had her own room. But Helen wouldn't give up, she couldn't. Occasional letters from Sophie hinted how desperate the situation at home had become.

After several years as a low-paid teacher, Helen saw the advertisement for a school mistress in this remote part of Argyllshire. Her own school! It seemed like a dream come true. When she applied, she remembered her governess's advice and mentioned her father's profession.

She was alarmed to find many gentlemen applicants waiting to be interviewed but she needn't have worried. Behind the mahogany door, discussion among members of the School Board was to the point.

'Miss Shields has sufficient experience and we can offer her thirty-five pounds per annum less than any of the men.'

'Aye but, Minister, d'you think a woman is up to the work? We've had our failures before, remember. And she'll not have come across children like these, not in England. Look here . . . ' A finger stabbed a line on Helen's application. 'She taught young ladies at an academy for gentlewomen!' The Minister pursed his lips.

'I doubt if she'll have trouble, that one. I would not want to cross her, would you?' There were grins among the all-male selection committee. 'Well it's either her, or finding more money for one of the men, gentlemen?' Thus was Helen selected.

Full of joy she wrote to Miss Milne.

This will, I'm sure, bring fulfilment. There are only twenty-two pupils on the register at present because work for their fathers has been scarce. Many could not afford to pay the children's fees. However the railway is being

35

extended in this part of Scotland. This means prospects are much improved – and the school inspector has promised to visit any absentees, although I doubt if it will do good, not when one sees the poverty here.

But the sooner these people learn how their children will benefit from schooling, the better it will be for everyone. I anticipate a full turn-out when we commence next Monday. The Minister has promised me he will preach on Sunday, urging his flock to send their children.

I wish I could bring myself to like him for he is one of the few people I shall meet regularly in my post here. His manner is most unpleasant. I fear he regards himself as my intellectual superior! A base assumption, I assure you! He makes a great parade of his 'university education' but none of it seems to have stayed with him. You taught me to hold my peace when confronted by fools but I have to confess I find it difficult!

I know you will share my joy when I tell you my income will be sufficient. I can face the future without fear provided I do not fail here. To be truly independent at last – the knowledge helps keep me warm on cold evenings – and it can be very cold up here.

God bless you for your unfailing support over the years.

I remain, yours most sincerely,

HELEN SHIELDS.

That was three years ago and marked the end of Helen's youth. What followed was a slow realization that achieving her goal also meant isolation. Wherever she'd lived and worked before there had been other women with whom she could discuss trivial, inconsequential matters. Here she was denied female company; within the peninsula was no social equal apart from the Minister and her antipathy towards him had increased. Discussions about bright pupils often ended acrimoniously, Helen's ambitions for them clashing with the Minister's firm conviction that crofters' children must be kept in their place.

At the beginning, overcome by loneliness, Helen wondered and sometimes hoped that those at the Big House would include her when they left cards. They chose not to. Word had reached them that Helen was the daughter of a gentleman and they had made their money in trade. What was worse, the schoolmistress had the reputation of being stiff-necked. That fierce expression which so impressed the School Board made her sensitive nouveau-riche neighbours fearful of being snubbed.

Did Helen ever regret her rejection of Mr Giles? Many, many times during that first winter in Scotland when icy flagstones combined with the warmth of the fire to set her chilblains tingling. She was no heroine, and he could at least have provided carpets and security in her old age.

There was one morning too when she felt ill but had to struggle into her clothes because there was no one else to take her place. As 'Mrs Giles' she could have stayed in bed and been cosseted, Helen thought resentfully. She was sick several times that day, rushing outside to retch but returning to the classroom to carry on. That evening brought a small consolation; she found gruel ready on the hob, prepared and left for her by the monitor out of loving concern.

There were moments of joy too, as she'd anticipated. One came when, at the end of her first year, the Minister examined each pupil and pronounced himself satisfied. Perhaps best of all was the day when one boy found work as an apprentice in Inverness. Amid the rejoicing, Helen could see how much this meant to every child. Now they knew what was possible, each would strive even harder to follow in his footsteps.

What Helen hadn't learned to accept over the years was the love of her pupils. Shy offerings of flowers left on her desk were treated as specimens for dissecting, not to be put in a vase. She'd grown from ugliness into a plain, passionate advocate for work. The only rewards she'd had out of life were through hard work. This was the message she drummed into them, plus a sense of responsibility. If she told any they had done well – and they looked at her with shining eyes – Helen turned away fearing they might slacken. She couldn't allow them to relax, there was still so much to do.

Now, in the increasing chill of her room she bent over her letter to Miss Milne.

Yet again I take the liberty of asking your advice. Today I had an extraordinary request from the father of two of the younger boys . . .

Next morning, John raised a delicate matter. He'd been worrying about it ever since Mistress Shields spoke yesterday. 'Father, it will take a great deal of money for the university.'

'It will.'

'Did the Minister say how much?' The Kirk was not only the voice of authority, it was their only source of information.

'He said what it had cost his father to send him. The exact amount. Of course he did not guess what we are planning.' John nodded, relieved. His father had told him this before but he wanted reassurance. He now asked the most delicate question of all. 'There will be enough, will there, Father?'

'If I keep my health and strength, God willing, there will be.'

Whether the Almighty approved Alex's methods of supplementing his income, none of them questioned. There was contempt throughout the peninsula for the ghillies the gentry brought with them from the lowlands. If the lobster pots were not full, nor the game plentiful, no one here would enlighten the men from the Borders.

The Minister knew but then he enjoyed a bit of fresh salmon. When one appeared on his table he didn't enquire how it had got there. He offered up a longer Grace instead: tacit acknowledgement that the fruits of the earth were unevenly distributed in the Highlands. If the gentry had invited the Minister to dine more often, or even attended his church regularly, he might have felt obliged to tell them what was being taken from their river.

As for Alex, he had no qualms. He offered his catch for sale to the Big House because they paid better, and fished from the opposite bank to the landowner's own.

Miss Milne's reply disturbed Helen. She read the letter through a second time while her pupils took their midday break. Retired now, Miss Milne was living modestly in Bath and knew several other ladies with similar backgrounds. They had pooled their knowledge and the result was now in Helen's hand.

First there was a long list of necessary books.

Although if it were my problem, my dear, I would send off for the first two and see how the boys progress. Do you not think it likely they may be unable to sustain the effort required? It is such a massive step, perhaps their father does not comprehend how great? Nor do you say whether you think the sons are of the same mind? Had you not better discover this before going any further?

Then followed more information. Helen was told she must write to the universities to discover what was required, that there would be oral as well as written examinations. Finally, Miss Milne ended by listing useful addresses where syllabuses could be obtained.

Helen summoned John to her desk. 'Tell your father I'll visit him this evening. There are a great many matters to be settled before we go any further with the Latin.'

'Yes, Mistress Shields.' He and Davie would have to hurry home. Alex would need time to shave and put on his suit. Georgie would not get a lesson tonight but there it was. John sighed over neglecting a friend.

Helen had never walked so far before. Until today she'd only a sketchy notion of where the McKies lived. On the way she rested, looking down on the crofts that fringed Kentra Bay. There weren't many. No doubt the clearances had affected the area. A breeze wafted the tang of the sea but Helen was oblivious to it. She was examining the narrow cultivated strips of land on which each home stood; not much there to support a family.

Beyond the McKies' dwelling, two heifers and a cow munched the thin grass, swishing angry tails against midges. Beyond the homesteads, on the hills, were the inevitable sheep cropping better pasture. Not the property of anyone here of course but owned by the Big House. The Crofters could only graze on their own bits of land.

Alex emerged and shielded his eyes as he looked at her. Once again Helen became aware of his strong personality, that might dominate her own. Telling herself not to stand any nonsense, she walked down the final stretch of track. He was wearing that terrible old coat again; he might have changed into something better once he knew she'd be visiting. He held open the gate. 'Good evening, Mistress Shields. It is a fine evening, is it not?'

With a shock Helen realized he'd spoken in English! 'Mr McKie, I didn't know you'd been having lessons?' He raised a deprecating hand.

'Only with John.' He couldn't conceal the pride. 'His mother and I have but a few words yet. Won't you step inside, please.'

Helen walked into a room that had been the living quarters for generations of McKies. She thought she'd never been anywhere so impoverished. It was dim, the only window deliberately small against the weather, the walls creamy grey with years of smoke and cooking. The glow of the fire leavened the gloom, and the kettle hissed gently on the hob.

The table had been moved to the centre in her honour and the best cloth put out, still creased from its box. The boys had decorated it with flowers but as usual these were wasted on Helen. She saw nothing but deprivation from the warped doors that didn't quite conceal the cupboard beds to the belongings stacked everywhere.

Two chairs were set beside the table. Alex gestured she should sit. Helen moved with care, trying not to trip over anything. By the fire, Jeannie McKie was tongue-tied. For the past half-hour while she'd swept and tidied for such an important visitor; she'd rehearsed a greeting over and over again. Now she couldn't get the words out!

'How d'you do,' Helen was smiling graciously. 'I'm very pleased to meet you.' Was the woman a deaf mute? Why hadn't the boys warned her?

Jeannie was nearly in tears. She opened her mouth but what came out was a pitiful gasp. Helen's voice reminded her of those at the Big House and terrified her. Privately Helen was wondering how old Mrs McKie was. Thirty perhaps? She looked nearer fifty in those clothes. What a pity she'd let herself go. With her hair up she'd be reasonably handsome but not with that unkempt mane hanging down her back.

In despair Jeannie murmured in Gaelic, which Helen couldn't

40

understand. She noticed how few teeth Mrs McKie had and again the neglect saddened her.

John was shining with pride. 'My mother is bidding you welcome to our home,' he told her. It was good that Davie had persuaded mother not to wear her shawl. In the firelight, her dark hair was so beautiful.

The boys sat together quietly. They had on clothes more ragged than those they normally wore. It shocked Helen to think what they came to school in was their 'best'. Conscious of other eyes watching, she discovered a sheepdog in the darkest corner, his head between his paws, noting her every move.

In her swift glance round the room, Helen tried to find some evidence of comfort but there was none. Each item had its purpose; there was no frivolity. With her narrow experience she couldn't begin to understand that here, where money was so much less plentiful than at the vicarage, Alex saw it as a tool, to be used to maximum advantage. If any object could be made to last, why replace it? Clothes and furniture were the appurtenances, not the stuff of life itself.

Davie put a glass of water before her. Helen sipped without realizing they wanted her opinion of it. They knew it was the sweetest water in the world but they needed her to confirm it. Helen used the drink to gain a breathing space. In the few minutes since she'd entered, her ideas had somersaulted. She'd imagined Alex, with his huge ambition, to have private means. Instead she was sitting in one of the poorest homes in the peninsula. It didn't do to let such thoughts show but it made her task that much more difficult.

John sensed Helen's withdrawal. It was a frightening thought, but was the bright shining bubble of his future about to burst? Why had she come? If she refused to teach them, there was no one else. For the Minister would surely be scornful if he learned of their plans! Sitting beside Davie, John could scarcely breathe. Helen cleared her throat.

'It is about the university, Mr McKie.' Alex nodded that he'd understood. He looked at John to make sure he was ready to translate. His son was very pale. 'It will mean an enormous amount of work,' Helen went on. 'For the boys as well as myself.' Again Alex nodded and murmured something to John.

'My father assures you we will do all that is needful, Mistress Shields. And I promise too, for Davie and me.' Beside him, the red curls nodded vehemently.

'But what about the money? It costs so much to go there!' Helen couldn't help it. It might not be her concern but she couldn't help looking about her. Alex was puzzled by the look. Was something lacking? Had they not made the teacher feel welcome? He half turned to his wife who stumbled in her eagerness to put freshly cooked oatcakes in front of Helen? Davie leapt to refill the glass.

When Alex spoke it was with dignity. 'The money will be found. There is time enough yet.' The woman surely didn't expect him to count it out in front of her? She might be English and mistress of a school but there were limits! Nor could he understand why she kept on about the money. He'd explained, hadn't he? She knew he'd been to the Minister? Alex didn't want to risk Helen going to the man, she might let something slip, but he'd yet to find out why she'd come here this evening. To soothe her, he repeated, 'There is some time yet.'

'Six, seven, perhaps eight years, Mr McKie. I think it will take that long.' There was a pause then she blurted out, 'I cannot guarantee it, Mr McKie, for either of your boys.'

She'd puzzled him again. He gestured at the cakes but she shook her head. 'I cannot guarantee that either John or Davie will get to university.'

'Whyever not?'

'They might not be able to – might not achieve . . . ' It was even more difficult than she'd anticipated. Alex was leaning forward now, as anxious as John. Both his hands were clenched with the effort of making her understand. John translated in frightened snatches.

' "They will work . . . They will work as hard as ever you require of them." Indeed we will, Mistress Shields! "They will not have to work in the fields" – my father is saying he and mother will do all that so we may study. He means it; we do too. We have all given our word!'

Helen was overwhelmed both by the heat and the stifling emotion filling the room. Alex was speaking again. A terrible thought had crossed his mind. When he asked a question, John went crimson. Helen waited but there was no translation.

Alex's voice rose. It was sharp, demanding an answer. John stared at the table, unable to meet her eye.

'My father would know . . . if it is you . . . if you are – unable – to help us?'

'Unable to teach, d'you mean?'

'To teach us sufficient. He is asking if *you* cannot reach the standard . . . that is necessary?' John finished in a whisper. Helen's mouth set in its grimmest line. It had done so too many times since she left the vicarage and now the creases were permanent.

'Tell your father not to worry, I shall manage. But John, you and Davie must answer me this: do you both want to go? Think carefully before you reply. It will require so many sacrifices from all of us, you must both be very, very sure.'

'What is she asking this time?'

'Whether we both want to go, Father.'

This time Helen had foxed him completely. Alex sat, clicking his teeth at the incomprehensible question. Had the woman lost her wits? And was his investment safe? He'd already spent sixpence on the Latin. Words failed him. He looked at John to reply.

'It will be our only chance, Mistress Shields. If we stay here there is only labouring work – '

'John, I had no intention of suggesting . . . Of course you must leave!' To stay on the croft was for Helen the most ridiculous idea of all.

'But it is not enough that we find ordinary work. We know if we go to the university, we will have a proper life. We will become qualified . . . ' John pleaded with force. He turned to Davie, lapsing into Gaelic so that his brother understood. Davie was confused. He'd never seen John so upset. His mother too was nervous. All of them begging Mistress Shields and she as fierce as when you got anything wrong in class. He desperately wanted to placate her. Davie stood up suddenly and dashed outside without saying why.

Alex was pouring out words so that John could scarcely keep up.

'We own nothing. We rent the croft. If we fail we can be turned out. There's no security – Father wants us to have that when we're old, as he has not.' Alex clutched at her hand.

43

'Please!' he said in English. Across the room Jeannie McKie recognized the word and moved forward timidly.

'Yes, please,' she repeated softly. Helen was trapped. With her free hand she reached for the glass but it was empty. John dashed with it to the bucket by the door. Helen gulped a mouthful of water and declined the offer of oatcakes for a third time.

'Thank you but I must be leaving. There's much to do . . . to think about.' She smoothed on her gloves and Alex towered above her.

'You will help?'

'Yes, Mr McKie, I will.' He went to take her hand again but Helen slipped past, suddenly nervous that he might touch her. 'What do the boys intend to study at university?' She asked the question simply to divert Alex but he smiled – a great beam of warmth in her direction.

'Medicine. They're both to be doctors.' It was game, set and match but he hadn't finished with her. As she moved outside in a daze, John followed. 'My father is asking if we are paying sufficient for all the books? He does not wish to be in your debt.'

'Tell him not to concern himself.' Helen's sole desire was to escape but if she continued like this she'd end up poorer than they were. Davie had gone ahead of her to open the gate. He held out his hand shyly.

'Don't give her that!' John was shocked and protested in Gaelic, 'That's your best treasure,' but Davie insisted.

'It is a gift,' John explained reluctantly. 'My brother found it in the sands. It must've belonged to a warrior.'

Helen looked at the bronze buckle in her palm.

'The Minister offered Davie money for it,' John sighed with regret, 'but he wouldn't part with it. Now he wants you to have it because he wants to go to university.' He stared at Helen covertly; he was beginning to share some of his father's doubts. Until today she'd been the rock on which he could rely but this visit had shaken him. He wanted to make a gesture, to seal the new pact and reassure himself but found he couldn't. 'My best treasure is a book by Sir Walter Scott but I haven't finished with it yet.'

Behind her veil, Helen's eyes were wet. 'Never part with a

book, John, not while it can be of use to you.' She turned to Davie. 'My best thanks for your best treasure,' she whispered and walked swiftly away up the track. They watched her go.

'I hope yon woman doesn't let us down John, I do indeed.'

'I'm sure she won't, Father, not now she understands.' All the same, his goddess's reputation was a little tarnished.

It was a long walk back but Helen needed every yard to regain her composure. One short hour had produced emotions she didn't know existed. They threatened to engulf her; her heart pounded erratically, she couldn't control her tears.

On her way to the croft she'd seen herself as the bearer of bad tidings. She had believed that once the McKies learned how impossible the task was, they would agree, reluctantly no doubt, that such plans were unattainable and that would be that.

Instead they'd worn her down and she'd capitulated. There could be no going back now, she'd pledged her word. But how on earth would she manage? Could she reach the standard required, let alone teach those two boys? And what about money? But Helen put that worry from her mind. Alex McKie had assured her twice it was none of her business. He and the Minister could sort it out between them.

One fact was obvious: the McKies saw none of the difficulties because they'd no clear idea what was involved. For them it was a simple, shining vision: doctors! Had any of the family ever even met one? Judging by Mrs McKie, she hadn't had much medical care.

Striding along between the sliced banks of peat, Helen railed at herself for giving in. Nothing but work for years and years and all for fourpence a week extra!

Ahead of her the sunset was crimson and gold but Helen didn't see it. What occupied her was the dread that either John or Davie might fail. She would be blamed! She thrust a hand in her pocket and found Davie's gift. It lay in her palm: a bronze buckle that had once fastened some Norseman's cloak or maybe the strap of his helmet. Delicate inlay outlined the rim. Davie's best treasure, probably worth more than anything else in the croft but given spontaneously, out of love, in return for a future.

Alone with the sunset, Helen broke down completely, sobbing her heart out at the roadside, for herself, for the boys and for the long hard years ahead.

She was taxed to the utmost, day after day. Evenings were spent in preparation and as the boys progressed, Helen rose with the dawn to fit in more work before school.

Sometimes when she prepared for bed, Latin, English and Gaelic would be whirling in her brain like autumn leaves but she picked up her books once more. John and Davie would be there in the morning, tasks complete and eager for more.

Help came from an unexpected quarter. Mr Standing, the schoolmaster who had taught Helen the classics, sent a packing case full of books. Helen was astonished at his generosity but her reply was cautious; did Mr Standing require remuneration?

He wrote emphatically that he did not. He was bored and he was offering help with her two promising pupils – did Miss Shields accept or did she not? Helen found herself smiling. These curt phrases were exactly the ones she used when annoyed. She took up her pen and wrote a straightforward answer; she accepted his offer with gratitude and enclosed essays handed in by John and Davie that morning, for assessment. They were returned within a week, the mistakes ringed in red ink and with Mr Standing's comments. 'Very ably written,' he'd put on John's but under Davie's last sentence, 'Bravo! Ask Miss Shields to lend you some poetry. E Standing.' Also enclosed was a foolscap sheet addressed to Helen. On it he'd drawn up a five-year plan for teaching the boys mathematics.

Helen felt as though warm arms had reached out to support her. She wasn't alone. Miss Milne would always be the friend in whom she could confide but from henceforth Mr Standing would be her mentor. There could be no slackening nor falling off in standards where he was involved. For the first time since she'd begun Helen began to believe that Alex's ambitions might be realized.

She settled before the dying fire to read the essays for she'd been too busy the day she'd sent them. The subject had been An Ordinary Day. John had described his meticulously; the walk to the school (seven miles, two furlongs), the number of pupils and arrangement of desks, what he'd eaten and the subjects he'd studied, then the evening at the croft, helping his father bathe the house cow's sore udders.

Davie might not have been at school at all, so much had happened to him on the way. He wrote of the smell of autumn, the changing colours in the morning sky; the mysterious way clouds rolled down from the hills, never twice the same; and finally of the wide-open eyes of a dead kestrel he'd found in a ditch.

Helen stared into the embers. John would always be a worker, beavering away at every problem until he'd found the answer. Not clever in her opinion so much as tenacious, which was just as good. He'd never give up and he'd always be reliable, but Davie had a gift.

She got up stiffly and went into her bedroom. There were shelves there now, not stained and varnished but made by one of the parents from silvery driftwood washed up in Kentra Bay.

She looked along the row of titles sent by Mr Standing. He'd claimed to be so familiar with their contents he no longer needed to read them. Helen selected a volume of Burns. Under 'Ex libris Elias Standing' she wrote, 'Given to Davie McKie in recognition of his excellent essay, November 1880'.

(xiv)

The Minister was cool when Helen tried to discuss the boys' education. Alex had been insistent she divulge as little as possible but she had to confess any additional lessons to the Board.

The Minister smiled. 'Latin and Greek is it? Whatever next!' Helen took this to be a question.

'Mathematics, English and history to university standard – ' She broke off because the man was roaring with laughter. She could see the unhealthy gums and the fur on the back of his tongue.

'University! How ludicrous!' Another fit of humour gave Helen pause to consider how very little Alex had in fact revealed. 'I suppose nothing concerning the McKies should surprise me.' The Minister was mellow now. 'They are an outlandish family as I'm sure you've discovered.' Instead of agreeing. Helen decided as he was in an amiable mood to press for an additional earth closet now that pupil members were increasing.

The Minister was immediately grave. Additional capital expenditure had a ritual all its own and further discussion of the McKies was at an end.

Word spread that the teacher would give extra tuition to those who could afford it and other fathers began to appear, asking if their children could have 'the Latin'. For them there was no thought of university, simply the desire to enrich their children's lives, but for Helen, the twopences began to accumulate.

Then John produced another request for additional lessons on Saturday mornings. Helen was annoyed because these days were hers to do as she pleased and she'd planned to make a vegetable garden. The children knew of it. As their part of the bargain, they offered to work her land and their parents would supply plants and seeds.

On the first Saturday, when a load of manure arrived and tools appeared in the outhouse, she felt guilty. Her pupils were so generous, she must do something extra in return. More exercise books were needed but her polite request was turned down by the Board. Helen grew bolder. Next Sunday, in front of the congregation, she deplored loudly that several pupils had had to 'cross' their pages because they'd run out of paper.

The Minister was furious but within a couple of weeks Helen was able to assure the school, now totalling thirty-four pupils, that new books would be available next time the steam packet arrived from Fort William.

Victory made her confident. But next time Helen overreached herself. The weather was bitter and many children were without adequate clothing so she wrote without a second's thought to the Big House, inviting them to make a donation.

The lady of the house, Mrs Manners, had been waiting for an opportunity to teach the school mistress a lesson. Mrs Manners imagined herself slighted. On leaving the post office one day, Helen had failed to see the lady sitting in her trap, waiting to be acknowledged. It wasn't rudeness, simply that Helen's thoughts, as usual, had been elsewhere. Anyone other than Mrs

Manners would have overlooked the matter, but Mrs Manners was a grocer's daughter and she knew Helen was the daughter of a gentleman. Her answer to Helen's request was as follows:

To Miss H Shields, school teacher,
c/o The School House.
Madam,

I am charged to reply to yours of the third ult addressed to Mrs H Manners. Mrs Manners desires that in future, no requests for charity be sent. She cannot think of any way she can be of service. She has many calls upon her and already subscribes to the Church Missionary Society both here and in England.

Regarding your enquiry for 'warm clothes', Mrs Manners desires me to say she is sending under separate cover a basket, but that she cannot be expected to answer further appeals nor does she require either you or your pupils to write and thank her.

Mr and Mrs Manners will be distributing their usual rewards at the Village Sports on the occasion of their son's birthday in July and trust both you and your pupils will attend.

I remain, Madam,
WHG DUGDALE,
STEWARD.'

It took Helen a moment or two to grasp this, so confident had she been of success. When she did, she flushed with temper. She and the monitor, Cissie, dragged the basket into Helen's room.

Cissie was an established part of the school now and at Helen's insistence, recognized by the Board. She cleaned the classroom and living quarters and her mother did Helen's laundry. In return, Cissie received a free education. When the school expanded sufficiently, she took over teaching new pupils the alphabet and their first painful lessons in English. She also took it on herself to warn them of Helen's moods. She saw the storm signals now and didn't say a word as they untied the rope and lifted out layers of newspapers. Underneath, the basket was full of a selection of aprons, stockings and underwear, torn, yellow with age and of the poorest quality. Helen exploded.

'What disgusting . . . ! How dare they send me such rubbish!'

'I don't think there's much wear in these, ma'am.'

'There isn't, Cissie, not a scrap.'

'Perhaps this chemise? If I mended – '

'I forbid you to touch it. Leave everything where it is and bring me the scissors.'

Cissie watched as Helen snipped savagely. Blades crunched through buckram and whalebones, stained, frayed cloth and webbing belts. Most she hurled onto the fire. Buttons bounced off the flagstones like pebbles as she sheared them off. At the finish, still very angry, Helen flung aside the scissors. Cissie paused in gathering up the buttons. 'Is it all right if I keep these, ma'am? They might come in useful.'

'Certainly.'

'Thank you – '

'Don't thank me, Cissie, don't thank anyone for this – insult!' Helen took a deep breath to calm herself. 'I'd like your mother's assistance in the matter.' She pointed to a pile of squares of cotton she'd chopped out of the aprons, 'D'you think she can boil or bleach these? I want them all to be conspicuously white.'

'I'm sure she can, ma'am.' Cissie knew better than to ask why. She began to coil the rope methodically. 'At least this basket will come in handy. We can use it to hold turves for the fire.'

'That basket is going back whence it came, the rope with it,' Helen replied sharply, 'and my letter will be inside.' She was sufficiently composed again to take a sheet of her most expensive paper. Unconsciously, she too remembered she was the daughter of a gentleman and it made her straighten her spine.

To Mr and Mrs H Manners,
Glen Orchy House

Dear Mr and Mrs Manners,

My thanks for your great kindness in acknowledging my letter and the magnificent gift which accompanied it today. Mr Dugdale writes that you do not wish your munificence to be mentioned but pray allow me to thank you on behalf of my pupils.

Never before have the children had such a fine collection

50

of rags. They are able to clean their boots, polish their desks and, in some instances, enjoy the comfort of a soft cotton handkerchief during this bitter weather. True, most of them come to school without coats, which can increase their dependence on handkerchiefs. Nevertheless they are all extremely happy to learn that the Church Missionaries can rely on your generosity.

We all look forward to the distribution of those magnificent rewards made to sports winners on your son's birthday.

I remain, Mr and Mrs Manners,

Yours most respectfully,

HELEN SHIELDS.

Yes, she thought, that just about covers it. Would the reference to 'soft cotton' be obvious enough? Cotton was the basis of Mr Manners' fortune. She rang the bell and Cissie reappeared.

'I'd like the basket returned to the Big House, Cissie. My letter is inside.' Helen hesitated. What she really wanted was a much wider circulation but she couldn't possibly say so. 'It is a letter thanking Mrs Manners for her kindness.' A wide smile spread across Cissie's face.

'Shouldn't that go by way of Mr Dugdale? Wouldn't that be proper?' Helen pondered. She couldn't see any objection.

'My mother does Mrs Dugdale's laundry too, you see,' Cissie went on innocently, 'And that Mr Dugdale, he rattles on. Doesn't keep anything from his wife, so I've heard.'

'As long as that basket ends up at the Big House, that's all that interests me,' Helen answered firmly.

It went a circuitous route. Cissie's brothers explained to everyone they met there was a time-bomb inside the basket. They asked at the lodge if they should continue on with it up to the House – and heard the groans as Mr Dugdale read the letter. Most of the community knew about it before it was laid in front of Mr Manners the following morning.

By that time Cissie and her mother had been extremely busy. Steam rose from their outhouse as rags were bleached, possed and boiled as never before. When that was done there was much coming and going so that throughout the peninsula, all those who wanted one had a white cotton square. Some peeped from breast pockets, others were tied to neckerchiefs. Alla wore his pinned to his hat like a cockade. And when Helen made her way along the street, people turned, nodded and winked before patting their bit of cloth.

And Mrs Manners? She was perhaps the only person who actually needed a handkerchief that day, when she explained to her spouse why she'd behaved like that – she hadn't intended to snub Miss Shields, not really. She'd merely dropped a hint that respect should be shown where respect was due.

Mr Manners cursed his silly wife as she'd never been cursed before. Thanks to their schooling, many more of the staff understood what he said to her. And because the Highlanders couldn't bear to let a good joke slip away, whenever Mr Manners went for a stroll, he usually met someone coming in the opposite direction, fiddling with a rag. After a week, he'd had enough. He and his wife cut short their holiday to return to London.

In July, convinced everyone had forgotten, young Manners rose to present silver threepenny bits and sixpences, and lead his father's tenants in three cheers for her Gracious Majesty. Halfway through the opening sentence, somebody sneezed. It was amazing how quickly contagion spread. Within seconds, trumpetings, sniffles and thunderous hootings were heard all over the sports field. Everywhere people held white cotton squares to their noses.

Helen told Cissie it was disgraceful but her words lacked conviction. She realized as she acknowledged greetings wherever she went that she'd cast her lot in with these people and their children. She had a responsibility, they looked on her as their champion. It was no use pretending she might one day be invited to dine in polite society; a glass of water and an oatcake were all that she could expect.

Her invocation as she looked in the mirror took on a new meaning. 'You've made your bed my girl, now you must lie on it.' But she added as she pinned on her cameo brooch, 'This is where you belong.'

52

CHAPTER TWO

John

'I think it is high time we checked their progress.' Helen was
outside shelling peas. It was a Saturday and Alex was astride her
roof repairing the shingles. He was paying with his labour this
month because wages were low again. Many other fathers did
the same. Helen didn't mind. Her rooms were less spartan as a
result. The chairs in her parlour had been re-covered, a stove
installed in the schoolroom which the children stoked night and
morning from October to April and there were rag rugs on the
bedroom floor. Her vegetable patch was flourishing. 'John is
nearly seventeen, isn't he? Yes, it's high time indeed.'

'Would it mean going to Fort William?'

'No, I don't think so.' Helen shaded her eyes as she looked
up at him. 'I'm told they're expecting visitors at the Manse. Old
friends of the Minister, coming for a walking holiday. One of
them is supposed to be a university professor and the other's a
grammar-school teacher. If it's true, I'll try and arrange for
them to give the boys an oral examination.'

'How much will it cost?' The perennial worry. Helen shucked

the last of the peas and threw the pods into a bucket kept for pigswill.

'Leave all that to me, Mr McKie. I will deal with the Minister.'

Alex looked down, at the tinge of grey in the bun, the thin line of hair on her upper lip. The school mistress moved stiffly as she straightened up. That knee of hers that nobody was supposed to know about was giving her a bit of trouble nowadays. Deal with the Minister! And she would. She might be ugly but she was a powerful woman, yes indeed. Alex clicked his tongue softly in admiration.

John burst into the croft a week later. 'It's all arranged. She says three good lobsters for the Minister will pay for everything. We're to be at the Manse at eight sharp on Wednesday, Father.'

At sixteen John was tall and still very serious. He wore glasses with steel frames now, bought second-hand from a stall in Fort William. His hands and feet were too big for his thin limbs but whenever Jeannie tried to fatten him, he grew taller instead.

Davie was much like Alex. Perhaps because he took pleasure in using his strength, he'd put on muscle. He was catching up with John, which made Jeannie sigh. She could no longer pass on John's trousers.

(i)

In the study they stood rigidly to attention, sniffing rich smells of beeswax and blackleading, antimacassars and dusty velvet curtains. They'd heard about the Manse but this was the first time John and Davie had penetrated this far, to see for themselves. It was so full of things! Here was wealth and comfort they didn't know existed.

'That colour on the walls, John. Is it paint, d'you think?'

'Painted paper. Look, you can see where the strips join. Fancy having dark green paper on walls!'

'There are six chairs. I've counted.'

'What would any man want six chairs in one room for?' Their whispers grew bolder as their wonder increased.

'That fender – like gold!'

54

'It's brass, Davie. Marie Cameron polishes it, she told me.'

'What must the other rooms be like?'

'Like a palace,' said John simply.

'Has the Queen got six chairs in her rooms, d'you think?'

'Maybe more.' Overwhelmed by that thought, Davie fell silent. Then the door opened and his cup of happiness was full. The two gentlemen who entered were wearing knickerbockers! Thick tweed ones with matching socks. Davie had only heard about them from his father but now there were two pairs right in front of him – and spats! One of the gentlemen had spats, and gold rims to his spectacles. Wait till he told them at home! The two pairs of eyes took in every detail greedily. They would have to tell Miss Shields, wee Georgie, Father and Mother . . .

Professor Bennett was anxious to get the business over. He was on holiday. He'd come here to get away from work. When his host first mentioned the business, the professor had refused point blank. Then came the embarrassing revelation that the Minister had already committed both of them. Naturally his guests expected him to untangle them from the situation but there'd been mumbling about a school mistress who kept pestering him, an over-ambitious father . . . Nothing had been said about three lobsters so this morning the professor still felt annoyed.

He settled himself behind the desk, oppressed by the old-fashioned room. Those windows hadn't been opened for years and outside the day was as fresh and crisp – damn, damn, damn! 'This won't take long,' he muttered. His friend Kemble nodded in agreement, flung himself into a chair and rested spat-clad ankles on the fender. Davie was amazed that anyone should be allowed to do such a thing.

The Minister entered, wiping his beard, bringing in the fragrance of devilled kidneys. John swallowed. It felt like an age since he and Davie had eaten their porridge.

'Here we are.' The Minister was almost jovial. 'Introduce yourselves.' The boys stood regimentally straight, eyes to the front.

'How d'you do. My name is John McKie and this is my brother, Davie.'

'Right. I'm Professor Bennett and this is Mr Kemble. How old are you both?'

Some considerable time later, Professor Bennett became aware his buttocks were numb. He snapped open his watch – Heavens! Nearly midday. He looked at Kemble, now leaning against the mantelpiece but his friend shook his head.

'Yes, we've covered the ground thoroughly.' The professor half spoke to himself. 'Ring the bell if you please.'

Sweat stood out on Davie's forehead – would he be failed because he couldn't see one? Then he noticed the handle beside the fireplace, went over and tugged at it. In the distance he could hear the jangle. John cleared his throat. 'My father would be wishing to know . . . ' he began but Professor Bennett shook his head.

'We'll be in touch with your teacher, that's the way we do these things.' He looked again at Kemble, 'The remarkable Miss Shields, eh?'

'Remarkable indeed,' Kemble smiled. 'Never ask at a Viva, old chap,' he told John, 'It isn't "done".' He saw the strain on the two young faces. 'Perhaps a hint?' he murmured. In his corner, the Minister said not a word. Bennett pursed his lips.

'You may tell your father you've done well.'

'Very well indeed,' added Kemble but this was too much enthusiasm.

'You've some way to go yet,' the professor warned, 'Now cut along, the pair of you.'

(ii)

They floated above the ground. They could hardly get through the school door in their excitement. Words tumbled out, English and Gaelic, and Davie's hair was a tangled red mass as he hurled his cap in the air. 'Done very well!' he shouted. 'Some way to go but done very well *indeed*!'

Helen had heard enough. The rest could wait. They'd explode if they stayed indoors. 'Go home and tell your parents. I'll visit in a day or two, when I've spoken to the gentlemen.'

The Minister would send her word. Or perhaps the visitors would like to see her school? Helen was immensely cheered by this thought. Yes, they were bound to come, they'd be

56

interested. 'We'll give the schoolroom an extra turn-out,' she told Cissie, 'We may have visitors.' But no one came.

Days passed and the two Englishmen were seen boarding the ferry back to Glasgow. Helen was puzzled but far too proud to go to the Manse. The School Board was due to meet. Perhaps the Minister wanted to tell them the good news first and then hand her the report? Yes, that would be it; he wanted to be the one to congratulate her. She was disappointed not to meet the professor and his friend but what mattered most was that report. If she had to possess her soul in patience, then so be it. The intervening days could be spent in sweet anticipation.

The sad truth was that Professor Bennett had intended visiting her but the Minister prevented it. That fateful morning had brought a terrible revelation. For years the Reverend McAlister had scoffed at the McKies' ambitions; naturally he'd been expecting the boys to fail. He had hugged himself in anticipation. Afterwards he would dampen forever Alex's hopes: there would be no more talk of 'university education' among the crofters.

Until the business of the handkerchieves, the Minister had held sway in the peninsula. His opinion was the one sought and he'd enjoyed the power this gave him. He'd been prepared to exercise his authority over Helen. Being a frail woman, she would naturally turn to him for guidance, or so he had thought. But Miss Shields considered the minister a shallow, vain creature and her contempt was ill concealed.

Neither had she any finesse with the male ego. After spurning his advice, she made no attempt to soothe his vanity. Also, it had to be admitted, the Reverend McAlister had come to fear the school teacher. More than once during their clashes, she'd made him look a fool in front of his congregation and the Minister was not a man to practise forgiveness.

Thus when questioning began that morning in his study, he sat in a corner to observe the boys' defeat. Pretending to examine Mr Gladstone's proposed Home Rule Bill the minister waited for John or Davie to make their first mistake. He was taken aback by their quiet self-possession but told himself it was the result of Alex McKie; such a father was bound to teach his sons to be obstinate.

Gradually the tempo of questioning quickened and the

Minister lost interest in the fate of Ireland. He couldn't believe his ears; these two – tinkers – were falling over themselves in their haste to answer. Kemble quoted something the Minister thought of hazily as the Bard but here was Davie McKie shouting the rest of the speech. Much good would that do in a proper Viva! He heard Kemble suggest the words might have a secondary political meaning for a Jacobean audience and here John McKie began to dispute with conviction, line by line. Suddenly the Minister began to feel ill.

Jealousy choked him. In this room where windows were kept tightly shut against fresh air and sunlight, he could smell more than the staleness, he could smell success and it was heady. What he could taste in his own mouth was failure.

Later, as the professor and Kemble laced up their walking boots, the Minister declared he was too ill to accompany them; he had a headache. He was also bitter at hearing Helen's praises.

'The woman must be exceptional,' the professor repeated for the umpteenth time.

'Personally I can't wait to meet her,' said Kemble.

'Oh, I doubt whether there'll be an opportunity for that!' Mr McAlister couldn't restrain himself. 'Not if you're to enjoy the fresh air during your holiday,' he finished lamely.

'You must persuade her to come to the Manse,' Professor Bennett said firmly. 'Oh, by the way, might I borrow your shooting stick? The ferrule has broken on mine.'

'Take it, take it.' The Minister couldn't wait to shut the door on his guests, his head was splitting so.

'Sorry you're not joining us.' The professor looked at his old friend critically. 'Take a Sedlitz powder, do you the world of good. Ready, Kemble?'

(iii)

With only a few days remaining, it wasn't difficult for the Minister to invent excuses why Helen Shields didn't appear but he was forced to listen to their admiration at his dining table.

Alex's lobsters disappeared slowly and with them, the

marvel at two boys so mature for their years. 'Judging by their poor appearance, McAlister, I'm astonished the family can afford to send them to university. Are there sufficient funds?'

The Minister refused to meet his eye. He wanted more of the brandy-flavoured sauce but his stomach felt bloated. 'That is not my affair,' he answered shortly, 'I've not discussed it with McKie.'

'But surely . . . !' Kemble looked at him in astonishment. 'Would it not be a kindness to do so? They will need advice, if they lack money, as to scholarships and so forth.'

The Reverend McAlister gave up the battle and put down his fork. 'They are a quarrelsome family. If and when they decide to apply to me for help, I will do what I can.'

There was an imperceptible exchange of glances between the other two. 'D'you not consider, McAlister, a hint as to the probable cost?' the professor asked delicately. 'And the ways and means available, should they be needed?' The Minister realized he must deflect their criticism.

'I'm fairly certain that McKie has discussed the matter with Miss Shields.'

'Of course. How stupid we are!'

'Naturally, she'll advise them,' Kemble agreed. And Mr McAlister saw no need to tell them that the school mistress hadn't been to university herself. His sense of grievance overcame him.

'McKie is not a church-goer. His wife attends twice on Sundays, as do the boys, but he chooses to appear only at Morning Service. How can I be expected to help a man like that?'

Bennett examined him properly for the first time; how prim the mouth had become. In the years since they'd been up at Edinburgh together, his friend had turned into a very finicky soft of chap.

'I don't think you should let that influence you,' he ventured. 'It's the boys who are unique, not their father. We cannot fail them surely, McAlister?'

'Hear, hear!' cried Kemble.

The Minister didn't want to lose his friends. He managed a smile. 'You're right, both of you. Those boys are a sacred trust and deserve our help. I will make sure your comments are passed on and on their behalf, I thank you for all you've done for them. And now,' he continued quickly, 'we've yet another local delicacy to tempt you with; a blaeberry tart. The fruit is gathered from the moor beyond the village.'

Mr Kemble saw himself as a man with a mission: after supper, he would be the one to seek out the McKie croft and speak to the family. He would tell them about scholarships and bursaries and in after years, the boys would look on him with gratitude. But the shining gold pastry and velvety blue-blackness satiated him. He would go tomorrow, he told himself. Alas, that day it rained and the next and the day following that. It was still raining when he and Bennett caught the ferry on their way back to Glasgow. Being English, neither realized rain is something to be ignored in the Highlands.

(iv)

Nothing was said during the School Board meeting and Helen was confused. Afterwards, she invited the Minister to take tea. Again she waited. Eventually she said, 'Mr McAlister, I'm sure you're aware why I wished to speak to you. I need to know the verdict on John and Davie McKie.' The Minister tried to bluster.

'I understood you to be offering me tea, Miss Shields – '

'As soon as the kettle boils, you shall have it but please, answer my question. What was your friends' opinion of the boys?'

By way of answer he removed his spectacles and rubbed the sore spot on his nose. When he spoke, she was astounded. 'Mistress Shields, are you quite certain you are teaching those boys sufficiently well for them to reach the standard required by a university?'

'I beg your pardon! I understood the professor confirmed beyond a doubt that both were doing very well indeed!'

'Ah yes, but . . . ' and the Minister gave her a smile, for now there was no one here to contradict him. 'But he also stated categorically that John and Davie have some way to go.'

'Davie is only fourteen.' Helen spoke automatically, gripping the arms of her chair. What had happened? Had the boys been mistaken? 'If I may write to the professor myself – ' but the Minister jumped in quickly. 'That is unnecessary. I have reported faithfully and I trust, Mistress Shields, you do not doubt the word of a man of God?' There was a dreadful sincerity in the question for he was terrified she might press him further but Helen had been brought up to be obedient. Although bemused, she fell silent.

'If that is all they said . . . ?' she asked at last, wistfully. He didn't reply. 'I shall continue to do my best . . . To educate them to a much higher standard.' Relieved that the crisis was past, Mr McAlister could afford to be magnanimous.

'I'm sure you will. When I first heard of this project all those years ago, I didn't remonstrate yet I feared for your health even so. She will do her best, I thought, and what if she crumbles under the strain?' Helen stared at him incredulously. He'd never expressed the slightest concern before.

'Yes, you may look like that Mistress Shields, but it's true. I even spoke to the Board. "We are allowing those crofters to impose", I said, "do you not consider I should reprimand them? Tell them they ask too much of one frail woman".' He expected gratitude but Helen tried not to let her lip curl.

'How fortunate you did not misrepresent the situation. I'm as strong as a horse, Mr McAlister. You may inform the Board I shall continue teaching "those crofters" any subject within my power. I shall certainly do my utmost to ensure John and Davie achieve their goal.'

Damn the woman! Why could she never be grateful? Her reference to misrepresenting the facts unsettled him. 'I shall play my part,' he assured her, 'So far you have carried on alone but now I shall visit the McKies and report what was said.'

Helen nearly argued but decided she didn't have the right. She'd been so confident but apparently she'd been mistaken. The Minister had witnessed the examination, it was only right that he should tell Alex. However unsatisfactory, it was the correct solution. 'You may tell them I will try harder in future,' she sighed, humbling herself in front of her enemy, 'for I intend we shall get there, in the end.'

It was several days before the Minister made his promised visit. During the long walk he told himself constantly that it was for the boys' own good they be not praised too highly. By the time he reached the croft, he'd convinced himself completely.

In this state of mind he gave his version of events. John stared, wide-eyed, but didn't speak. It wasn't the truth but how could he contradict the Minister? Almost as an after-thought Mr McAlister consoled Alex with the thought that had the boys been up to standard, it wouldn't have been any use; universities cost too much money.

Alex roused himself, reminding him of the conversation long ago before the boys had begun attending school. It was the Minister's turn to stare. 'When we talked of the time when I was a student? But that was twenty years ago!' Alex was puzzled: what difference did that make?

'All the difference in the world! Prices have increased, McKie, added to which I didn't mention the additional cost of lodgings, books, membership of clubs. Life at a university is more than study, it's communion with fellow human beings – it is comradeship.' But Alex couldn't be tempted into a discussion of the social aspects. Without looking at John, he asked if Mr McAlister would be kind enough to discover the total cost nowadays and let them know.

As he was leaving, Jeannie forced herself to be bold and demanded to know if either of the gentlemen had thought well of her boys. Reluctantly, the Minister admitted that they had. It wasn't much but it helped her sad heart. When he'd gone, she washed and put away the one good cup and saucer before creeping off to the privacy of the byre. All that work, all those years and years of it . . .

Alex didn't give up without a fight. He spent weeks trying to devise new ways of earning money for it was against his nature to submit. He even went to Fort William in search of better paid work. The boys watched his departure in silence and Alex could scarcely face them on his return, so great was the disappointment.

Finally, when there was nothing more than could be done, John went to Helen with a message. 'My father would like to come and see you, Mistress Shields.'

'Yes, of course. Tomorrow evening?' John had grown taller lately but he hadn't broadened out. Under the jacket, the shoulders were painfully thin. His face, level with hers now, was pale. She looked at him covertly; was he still worrying about the examination?

Alex was outside at the appointed time. She invited him in and he and the boys trooped through to the parlour and waited for her to make the tea. Silently Alex handed over his customary gift and the crab scuttled about in the sink. Helen filled the cups and they drank in silence. Alex was a little stouter these days she thought, but like John he was terribly pale. What on earth had happened? Suddenly, she was afraid. Putting down the cup she asked, 'What is it?'

'There isn't sufficient money.'

'Oh, no!'

Alex went crimson with shame and the boys stared at the floor. Helen was so appalled, at first she couldn't speak. She knew if she tried she'd burst into tears. Her body shook as the torrent of emotion built up inside – she'd have to say something or she'd burst!

'Mr McKie, why? After all these years . . . Surely you'd some idea what it would cost?'

'It's not my father's fault!' Davie was on his feet, shouting at her, 'Mistress Shields, it cannot be helped, it's because of the Minister – '

'Hush, hush,' Alex chided, 'We cannot blame Mr McAlister, he didn't know of our plans.'

'Oh, come, the whole peninsula knew!' Helen was harsh. 'Forgive me if I sound impertinent but everyone knew what was intended. Oh Mr McKie, I'm so very sorry!' For she put aside her own disappointment as he raised his face, made so old by defeat. 'Please, isn't there some way?'

'I've tried, indeed I have.' Alex stared at his hands as if their strength had failed him. 'I even asked Mr McAlister if he knew of a way but he said there was none. I asked if his friends . . . ' His voice shook as he remembered the scene. 'I well nigh begged the man . . . He told me it was my own fault for having such grand ideas . . . I've done all I can, I tried everything before coming here tonight, lassie . . . ' The word slipped out and Alex didn't even notice, but it nearly overcame Helen.

'I'm sure you did. Have some more tea.' The necessary pause gave her time to recover. 'I've often worried about it over the years. I always assumed Mr McAlister had advised you properly

63

at the time.' She wanted to comfort him. 'No one could have done more for their children than you and Mrs McKie.'

It scarcely covered a lifetime's ambition lying in ruins but it was the best she could do. John said quietly, 'We cannot blame the Minister entirely, Mistress Shields. When he told my father the fees, he didn't know then why we were asking, otherwise he might have warned us.'

As usual John was being scrupulously fair but Helen's rage flared up. That arrogant, bigoted fool must have guessed why he was being asked! John was still speaking. 'Apart from the fees, there's lodging, books and so forth, double what we were expecting. Whatever we do, we cannot manage it.'

What careful discussions must have taken place before they came here tonight. Exhausted by their disappointment, Helen felt she couldn't move. A lump formed in her throat but she choked it away: these two, their faces as bleak as their father's, needed her help.

'So what is to happen?'

'After the harvest, I will leave for England. From now on, I must earn my living,' John replied. 'The Minister has promised to help me find a position.' Helen's lips tightened: the very least the man could do, she thought.

'Davie will stay at school,' said Alex, 'with what John can send us, what I can put by, my wife too. She's knitting mufflers for the ladies and gentlemen who come on walking holidays. Alla sells them for us at the ferry – we're all trying, Mistress Shields. Please God there will be sufficient when the time comes for Davie – '

'But it's John that should go to university!'

She couldn't help it, it burst out of her. Davie's talent had bloomed but John would have made such an excellent doctor. Hadn't she been nurturing him for it all these years? In the dreadful silence that followed, he spoke, his voice weary and drained of all emotion. 'I have promised my father that if ever I have a son, when the time comes he *will* go to university.'

Helen clung to the sink. Tears poured down her face but if she let go to wipe them away, her legs wouldn't hold her. They stared at her back, listening to the plop, plop . . . as the drops bounced onto the brownstone. This was awful, like watching Jericho crumble. Alex twisted his cap as he attempted to express his feelings. 'I would like to thank you for sticking to your side of our bargain. Everyone knows it wasn't quite as Mr McAlister would have it, the boys were doing fine. Maybe not perfect but good enough. If I'd been able to find the money, they would have managed it.' There was no reply.

'Mind your fingers on yon crab,' Alex whispered finally, 'he's a wicked devil.'

(v)

When they'd gone and she'd recovered a little, Helen poured out her troubles to Miss Milne. A letter to Elias Standing was too difficult just now but her own governess would understand. The reply came by return.

> My dear Helen,
> Your letter filled me with such sorrow not only for the boys but for yourself. I can well understand your bitterness but remember, my dear, how much those two will depend on you for comfort. John will need your strength and advice to face his new life, whatever that turns out to be. Be loving and caring toward him. How I pray that the younger boy may have his chance when the time comes.
> Yours most affectionately,
> GERTRUDE MILNE.

(vi)

Helen did her best to prepare him. At the croft one Friday evening she said, 'In an English city, it's possible to pass an entire day without seeing a blade of grass.'

Jeannie thought she'd misunderstood. When Helen assured her she hadn't, she asked, 'What do they have instead of grass, just the peat?'

'Not even that. Pavements and buildings cover the land.'

'How do they breathe? The people who live there?'

'They get used to it as I'm sure John will. He'll make an excellent businessman because he has such application.' She smiled encouragingly. 'Is it to be London then?'

'Aye. The wages are much higher there, so they say.'

'And the prices, don't forget that.'

'I'll be careful,' John managed a grin. 'I've had as much practice as most people at that. And mother is preparing plenty of food for me to take.'

'See that he eats hearty before he goes, Mrs McKie. He must put on weight. The winters in England can be very trying and the fogs are a disgrace.' Mother and son, who'd never seen anything thicker than mist, tried to imagine one.

'There is one more thing,' Helen frowned because it was delicate, 'John will need a suit, a good one.' Worry left John's face. Behind the spectacles, his eyes were once more eager.

'I'm to have one, Mistress Shields. Father has arranged it with a tailor in Fort William.'

'A – new suit?' Helen asked diffidently.

'No but it has years of wear in it yet,' Alex assured her, 'It's being altered to fit John at present. You'll see him in it before he goes.'

'I shall look forward to that.'

'And a greatcoat,' John leaned forward, 'And a proper gentleman's hat – what d'you think of that!'

'Without your old cap, John, I shan't recognize you.'

'Oh, you'll be seeing that again right enough. Davie is to have it when I go.'

(vii)

It was a hot summer day when John visited in his finery. Helen had received a letter that morning but she wouldn't allow it to spoil John's happiness. He stood before her in a tweed suit thick enough to withstand an Arctic winter and a hat that rested on his ears. The greatcoat hung over his arm as he rotated slowly, a proud if sweaty peacock. 'What d'you think?'

'Turn again so that I can see it properly. Yes . . . yes, very smart indeed, John.'

'Shall I put on the coat?' Perspiration trickled down his face.

'Why not spread it over that chair where we can both see it.' He stroked the fabric lovingly.

'It has a shoulder-cape, d'you see, to keep out the rain. Both the cape and the coat are lined. Mother says no sleet will penetrate all that material.'

'I'm sure she's right.' Excitement at the new clothes animated John for the first time in weeks.

'Those are genuine horn buttons, the man told Father. Oh, Mistress Shields, if you knew what all this has cost! There were shirts, too . . . '

'They are fine clothes, John, most impressive.'

'Good enough for England?'

'Certainly. Sit down. We're using the best china today, in honour of your new elegance.' These were a few pieces of Spode Helen used when teaching about the English pottery towns. John recalled her description of huge chimneys and belching smoke. He might see them at last, in England! His eyes glowed; if it wasn't the university at least it would be an adventure.

'Would you like to take off your jacket? The weather is extremely warm.'

'Oh, no! that won't be necessary.' He sat, hitching up the new trousers. Helen tried not to smile as she whisked muslin covers off the milk jug and scones.

'There's a package beside your plate . . . from Mr Standing. A bequest, John. He died about a month ago, apparently, that's why we haven't heard from him.' A cloud threatened to blot out the day. John ran a finger along the wrapping.

'Did he know?'

'No. I didn't bother to write.' She took the solicitor's letter from her pocket to refresh her memory. 'According to his executor, he'd been warned by doctors the end was near. He died content, we must be thankful for that.' John untied the string and Helen sent up a heart-felt prayer that nothing inside would distress him.

It was a small picture. John exclaimed with delight. 'Paris,' he said, examining the inscription. There was a note attached to the back. After glancing at it, he passed it across the table without comment.

' "To be given to John McKie," ' she read, ' "May it hang

67

over his mantelpiece when he is a student, as it once did mine, and bring the same pleasure.'' '

'I'm glad he didn't know,' said John flatly. She pushed the plate of scones in front of him.

'Eat up. Try not to brood.'

'I've had an answer to my application.'

Helen read this very carefully indeed. With Mr McAlister's backing, John had applied for the position as clerk in an ecclesiastical stationers in Southampton Row. The reply invited him to attend for an interview.

'It sounds – satisfactory. It might lead to better things,' said Helen helplessly. They had ended up in Mr McAlister's hands after all. 'Keep up your Latin and Greek,' she urged. 'You never know . . . ' But in her heart she did and the waste of this young life made her wretched.

(viii)

John and Davie started out at dawn. They borrowed Alla's donkey to carry the trunk and the herring barrel. Excitement buoyed John up as he hugged his mother and father and set off along the track, looking back every so often to the small doorway and the two figures silhouetted by the lamplight.

When he and Davie arrived at the jetty, it was raining, the fine, soft rain of the Highlands. They were bubbling over by then so that they failed to notice Helen, standing in the shadows to see John leave.

Davie lifted the trunk on board, slapping the tight cording he'd spent so many hours helping to fasten. 'Well, John, that'll be safe enough, I reckon.'

'It will. Thanks again, Davie.'

'Watch yourself mind, when you get to Glasgow.' And Davie shook his head again at the immensity of it. 'London, just think of it!'

One of the boatmen saved John from breaking down completely. 'Away ashore if you're not coming,' he told Davie. The gangway was hauled on board. Leaning over the rail John found it necessary to be very severe.

'Mind you stick at your lessons,' he called, 'And I'll do my best to save enough.'

'Aye, aye . . . ' Davie was suddenly hoarse.

The paddle turned slowly at first as *The Pioneer* eased away gently before gathering momentum. Smoke poured from the stack. There was a brief toot and the ferry set off down Loch Sunart through the Sound of Mull and Loch Linnhe, up to Fort William.

Davie waved until it was out of sight but John never looked back; he daren't. Had he done so he would've seen Davie crying too as the mist separated them for the first time in their lives.

(ix)

John peered through the steamy window of the ticket office in Glasgow. 'A single to London, third class, if you please.'

'Two pounds one shilling and tenpence.'

'What!' It was nearly double what he'd been expecting and all his spare money had been sewn inside his coat for safety. Behind John, other travellers began to shuffle their feet. 'How far can I go for one pound two shillings and fivepence?' The clerk stared superciliously.

'In a southerly direction would that be, sir?'

'Yes, definitely.'

'There's Darlington.'

'Where's that? Is it an important sort of town, would you say?' The sophisticated Glaswegian considered.

'Yes, I would. For the north-east of England, that is.' He slid the map under the glass. 'That's it there, in heavy type.' The density settled the matter.

'I'll take a ticket.' Thus was the future decided.

John buttoned the pasteboard inside his innermost pocket. A porter directed him to the platform and he perched on a milk churn. Inside the waiting room he could see people standing about; one was reading from the Bible chained to the reading stand. John wanted to venture in but he was too nervous. Mr McAlister had warned that Sodom and Gomorrah were as pale shadows compared to Glasgow or London. Well, he was nearly

69

clear of Glasgow and he wasn't going to London, not yet.

He was exhausted by the noise; a couple of days ago he'd never seen anything more exciting than farmers' waggons on market days but this was another world! There was a wooden sign slotted in beside the platform number: next train – Darlington. It had a ring to it. No doubt there'd be opportunities if he worked hard enough and he would work hard, yes indeed. It was only temporary. A staging post on the road to London.

(x)

The engine thundered in, billowing steam. He tried to climb the high step into a third-class carriage but the guard stopped him. 'What's in yon barrel?'

'Herring.'

'It'll have to travel in the van then. You cannot take a barrel of fish into a compartment, the ladies would object to the smell.'

John was desperate. There was six months' supply of food here; he hadn't taken his eyes off it since he left home.

'I'll not part with it.'

'Then you must go in the van, too.' So John crossed from Scotland to England, jolted from side to side in the open-slatted waggon on the end of the train. Instinct prompted him to request a rebate on his ticket but the guard refused him.

North Road Station, Darlington, wasn't very welcoming. Bursting at the seams with traffic and soon to be replaced by a brand new station at Bank Top on the Victoria Road, all was shabby and bustling. Drops of rain hissed as they fell in the hot mantles of oil lamps, making white flames smoky blue. In the gloom, passengers descended from the wood-seated second-class and even less comfortable third-class compartments and walked up and down to ease cramped limbs. Lordly ones were assisted out of first class and porters hurried past pushing mountains of luggage. The hansom drivers leaned over the rail, calling and tipping their hats to potential customers; everywhere was noise, smoke and steam.

John stumbled along the platform towards the light,

70

clutching his trunk and barrel. Now that he'd finally arrived, he was terrified. There were warning shouts for those passengers about to re-embark and a porter called, 'Are you for this train, sir?' John shook his head and the guard blew his whistle. 'If it's the connection for Stockton you want, sir, you'll need to cross the bridge.'

'No, I'm for Darlington. D'you know where I might find lodgings?' The porter looked him up and down.

'Just stay there a bit.' He disappeared inside a doorway. For an instant John had a glimpse of gas light and men in uniforms before the porter reappeared with a person of some importance, the Deputy Station Master. He stood under the sizzling lamp, the gold watch chain adding to his dignity. Like the porter he examined the thin man before him, hidden inside the vast coat.

'Yes, young man?'

'I'm seeking lodgings. Not expensive, just a room would do, where I can look after myself.' The Deputy Station Master obviously decided in John's favour for he turned to the porter and asked, like any ordinary mortal, 'Is tha' Aunty Annie's back room to let?'

'It might be.' His Aunty Annie was particular. It didn't do to take her opinion for granted. John attempted to clarify his requirements.

'Is she – your aunt – is she a God-fearing woman?' The porter stared then spat into his palms, rubbing them together.

'My Aunty Annie – if she was took tonight – and if St Peter refused to let her in, I'd black his eye for him.'

'And I'd black the other for 'im an' all,' added the Deputy Station Master, settling the matter.

The porter hoisted the barrel onto his shoulder and John followed, sagging under the weight of the trunk. The man called out a stream of information which John could scarcely understand in the strange accent. 'We're at sixes and sevens, night and day in Darlington just now. The new station's nearly ready, up at Bank Top, but we're having a "do" here first. And they're building a plinth – there's going to be an engine put up there next month – *The Locomotion* herself. What d'you think of that? You've heard of *The Locomotion*, haven't you? World famous, she is. It'll be a great sight. There's going to be a

71

proper ceremony, a procession. They never stop celebratin' in Darlin'ton nowadays! Come on, I'll show you summat else. Only a bit out of our way.'

The streets were black with rain. John's ankles ached from slithering over the cobbles but he followed blindly. His spectacles were blurred and he concentrated on putting one foot in front of the other, the greatcoat swirling round his legs. The two of them went along Northgate into High Row where the porter stopped.

'There. D'you see? A statue to Joseph Pease – see the panels round the bottom here . . . showing what he's done for people. As far as Darlin'ton's concerned, he's done more for this town than any man, you cannot deny it.' John didn't. 'Are you here for the celebrations then? When they open the new station?'

'No, I've come to earn my living.'

'Well, you couldn't ha' come to a better place. Right then, come on. It's a bit step farther to Aunty's place.'

The thought of a haven at last made the rain less wet and cold. John followed the porter closely, trying to understand. 'It's a really modern house, is Aunty's. A walk-in parlour, like, but we'll be using the back. Very particular about her parlour, Aunty Annie is. Mind you, she lets her lodgers use it. Her terms is very reasonable . . . and the house is spotless.'

They left the yellow gas lights of East Street and splashed down an alley. John's nose told him there were ashpits and privies behind the walls on either side. He kept to the centre of the narrow lane.

'It's so modern, there's even a tap in each of the sculleries in this street,' the nephew told him proudly. It was the first time John had seen a terrace. He looked at the winding ribbon of it, the chimneys stark against the night sky. It was an alien landscape. Then the porter pushed open a wooden door and led the way across a yard. Up two stone steps, he tapped on another door which opened immediately. Light and warmth flooded out. 'I've brought tha' a lodger, Aunty. Is tha' back room vacant?' John walked inside.

72

It was several days before Helen had any news. Davie told her that a letter had finally arrived and his father invited her to come and read it. 'But it's not what we expected. John isn't in London.'

Classes were about to begin, there was no time for questions. Had she misheard? If he wasn't in London, had there been an accident? She would have to be patient. Tonight there were several matters she wanted to discuss.

In the croft the best cloth was spread as usual and the precious envelope beside her plate. Alex urged her to read it but Helen first examined the postmark. 'Darlington? What on earth's he doing there?' She unfolded the two sheets of paper.

> C/o Mrs Beal,
> Coburg Street,
> Darlington.
> Dearest father and mother,
> You will see from the address I am not yet in London. Please don't be concerned. You will find Darlington on the map in the north-east of England. I have had to stop here due to the cost of the ticket but have since had time to have a good look round and can assure you Darlington is an amazingly prosperous place. There are many horse-drawn trams, all of them full of people! But there is no need to waste money riding on one for it is easy to walk – everywhere there are pavements!
> I am staying with Mrs Beal temporarily. She assures me there are plenty of opportunities in Darlington just now. I occupy an enormous room, on the *first* floor! It is ten feet by eight feet three and a half inches and I have it entirely to myself. The rent is one and ninepence per week in advance to include washing, use of front parlour PM and blacking for boots. There are four persons lodging in the front room on the first floor, all from Ireland working in shifts. As two get up so the next two take their place in bed, which is convenient. All are rivetters in the new locomotive sheds. Mrs Beal and her daughter sleep downstairs in the kitchen.

The rent is expensive but this is a modern house with a tap in the scullery! I'm assured every house in the street is the same, can you imagine it?

I have written to the stationers in London to explain my change of plan. I will apply to them again as soon as I am able to continue my journey.

This evening I have an appointment with a Mr Gordon, a Scottish trader known to Mrs Beal who arranged it when she discovered I needed work.

There is no Mr Beal. Mrs Beal said he had 'moved on' but I'm not sure whether this means he is dead or living elsewhere. She was crying as she spoke of him so I could not press the matter.

Please give my respects to Mistress Shields and show her this letter as it will save the cost of a stamp.

Yr. obedient son,,

JOHN MCKIE.

Post Scriptum: tell Davie I miss him.

Helen gazed at the letter long after she'd finished it. A Scottish trader. It had come to that after all the effort. It was no use grieving, however. She must reassure everyone here.

'It will be a good way to earn a living, I'm thinking,' said Alex anxiously. 'If John works hard and gains customers – he'll never cheat anyone.'

'Of course he won't, Mr McKie. I'm sure he'll make a success of it.' When he could've been a doctor . . . Helen pushed the thought away. 'I am concerned about another matter. Davie's future. It occurs to me that he may not be suited to medical work.' Alex and Jeannie were puzzled.

'It was settled years ago they'd both be doctors,' said Alex.

'Is it not a good profession for a man?' asked Jeannie softly.

'Excellent, in the right circumstances. But Davie's is a different temperament from John's. I think we should consider other possibilities.' This was a new idea for Alex. Davie looked at her anxiously.

'D'you mean I cannot go to university?'

'Of course you can. But I will arrange for you to visit a hospital first, to see whether you are inclined for the work.'

'I should like that, Father.'

'We'll see, we'll see.' There had been too many changed plans lately. Alex wasn't to be rushed over this.

The family watched respectfully as Helen set off. They did not offer to accompany her along the way. They knew she would have a stick hidden nearby and would want to retrieve it. The slight touch of arthritis in her knee had become a nagging ache sometimes. Helen refused to admit it even existed but she carried a stick for safety and would have been shocked to learn the whole peninsula knew of it.

(xii)

Outside an office on a first floor in Darlington a row of tired men waited. They leaned against glass partitions or squatted beside battered valises. Some had coughs. It had been wet for days and they'd been outdoors most of the time. They greeted each other listlessly. John climbed the last few steps before he saw them. One or two stared back at him. No one spoke. He hung back, not knowing quite what to do.

Feet pounded up the stairs behind him. Mr Gordon walked past, brisk, tough, in a check suit and curly-brimmed bowler. He didn't waste time, time was money. 'Higgons, Fortescue, Brown, Tyler – in that order. You can wait, Chadwick. And who the Dickens are you?' John looked round nervously to check whether it could be anyone else.

'John McKie, sir. I have an appointment.'

'I'll see you after I've seen Chadwick.'

'But my appointment was for seven o'clock.' There were shocked sniggers along the line. Halfway into his office, Gordon checked and spun round.

'I said – after Chadwick. Take it or leave it.' Frightened but dignified, John replied, 'I will await your pleasure, sir.' The door closed on Gordon and Mr Higgons.

An hour later there were only the two of them left. Waiting didn't agree with Mr Chadwick, he'd begun to shake. 'Haven't got a drop of something have you, old chap?' John was dumbfounded.

'Surely this is a Temperance Hall?'

'What's that got to do with it? I need a bit of something,' Chadwick shivered again, 'Terrible week. People on short time – it's not that they won't pay, they can't, some of 'em.' Mr Chadwick indicated the office door. 'You won't catch Gordon believing it, though. He'll be out for blood when he sees my books.' He was interrupted by a violent attack of coughing which made John edge away.

'Here,' Chadwick was struck by an unpleasant thought. 'Why are you seeing him?'

'I have an appointment.'

'I know that. What I'm asking is – why? He don't need anyone, not at present, he's got no books for sale. You're after mine, ain't you?' His voice was suddenly urgent and his face very close to John's. 'He's trying to get rid of me, isn't he? The bastard! Well, I won't let him. I'm a married man, got two kiddies – '

The door opened and Gordon stood there, arms akimbo. 'Right, Chadwick, you can come in now.'

Chadwick hissed a final, 'You won't get away with it!' before walking jauntily toward his employer, saying with awful jocularity, 'Amazing wet weather we're having, Mr Gordon. I told the wife, summer's come back, that's what it is.'

It was a short interview and didn't give John time to recover. It sounded as though Chadwick were pleading. 'Married man, two kiddies . . . ' the phrase echoed in John's mind. Then the door opened and Chadwick re-emerged. He blundered past John, in tears. Gordon's voice was sharp. 'Well? What are you waiting for?' Taking a deep breath, John followed him into the office.

It was a small room, thick with smoke, for Mr Gordon believed in a good cigar. Wicker skips were everywhere, spilling out their contents; moleskin trousers, woollen stockings, shirts, nightdresses, sheets and blankets, switches of suiting and lengths of cambric. On shelves, boots and stacked caps alternated with bales of lace curtaining and calico.

'So you want to buy a set of books, do you?' Mr Gordon was seated behind his desk, 'What was the name again?'

'John McKie.' He saw a pair of heavy ledgers but he didn't understand. Gordon opened one and fingered the page lovingly.

'These are worth gold, John McKie, pure gold. Here's a

family for instance, Montrose Street, number forty-seven. Doing very well, buying from us for years. No risk, not with two boys working in the Rolling mill. One's about to get married, see. Here's a note of it. Always make a note of happy events, John McKie, births, marriages or deaths. We do a nice line in mourning.' Gordon flung out an expansive arm. 'But when it comes to setting up home, we can supply everything this young man needs; sheets, tablecloths, aprons for his intended – '

'I can see you have an excellent range, Mr Gordon.'

'Nothing but the best. But it needs to be sold. These goods don't leap off the shelves. People have to be tempted, they need to be convinced that what we offer is value for money.'

'I'm sure that it is, Mr Gordon.'

'So how much are you prepared to invest, hmm?' He indicated the ledger with his cigar, 'These represent a valuable clientele from which you would reap the benefit.'

'I didn't realize I would be expected to – '

'You didn't think I'd give away a set of books! Why, I know nothing about you.' John fumbled in an inside pocket.

'I have a letter from my school mistress – ' and blinked at Mr Gordon's reaction.

'School mistress! You'll be the death of me, John McKie! Twenty-five quid, take it or leave it. And your word you'll work for me for five years.'

'Five years!' John didn't know which shocked him the more.

'Plenty of others wanting these ledgers.' John had a confused memory of Chadwick.

'But – five years?'

'Shall we say six? After all, you're very young. Very – inexperienced. I'm correct in assuming this would be your first employment, am I not?'

'I cannot afford twenty-five pounds.'

'I'm being generous!' Mr Gordon flung wide his arms, 'Tender-hearted to a fault. What's money with the goodwill I'm offering? Have you got the money?'

'Yes.' John couldn't dissimulate. Gordon's chair crashed into an upright position behind the desk and he stretched out his hand.

'It's a bargain.'

'Not – entirely.'

'You won't find better terms elsewhere, not without experience. And I don't believe in bits of paper. A man's word, John McKie, that's what counts.'

'Oh, I should require a proper agreement.' Helen's teaching on this point had been thorough. Gordon's eyes narrowed.

'Look, why not settle the matter? If you hand over the money I can give you the ledgers and you could begin tomorrow morning.'

'You haven't told me what wages I could expect.'

'Wages? I don't pay wages. You earn commission, that's the way for a trader. The mark-up is eighty percent and I take sixty of it. You won't find better than that, not with quality goods.'

'I need to consider the matter, sir.'

'Now, listen . . . ' Gordon leaned across threateningly. 'If you're not here first thing tomorrow with the money, the offer's withdrawn.' John remained silent. 'Oh, get out!' said Gordon irritably.

Footsteps receded. Drat the boy, he could have done with that money tonight. But he'd be back; the youth was too green to do anything else. Anticipation of bank notes lying on his desk top made Mr Gordon salivate and he reached for the brandy bottle hidden in a drawer.

(xiii)

At the presbytery, visitors before breakfast were rare. The maid knocked on the study door. 'A young gentleman to see you, Mr Wingford.'

'Can't it wait?'

'He begs pardon, not having made an appointment, but says the matter is urgent. He wants your advice, sir.' Had John but known it, this was the most likely way to Mr Wingford's heart.

'Advice, eh? Well, send him in – but call me the minute my food is on the table.'

'Yes, sir.'

John was at his most formal. He advanced, hat tucked under his arm, hand outstretched with his letters of reference. Mr Wingford read them. 'Now, in what way can I advise you, Mr McKie?'

78

'On a matter of business, sir, concerning a Mr Gordon of whom you may have heard. I am contemplating becoming one of his traders and it is a question of investing money. A very large sum indeed, otherwise I would not have troubled you.'

Mr Wingford made a steeple of his fingers and pursed his lips. 'I have heard of him but I never advise on matters of business, Mr McKie. Such wisdom as I possess is confined to spiritual matters. However . . . Concerning Mr Gordon – who is not a church-goer, Mr McKie . . . ' John looked grave and waited, ears finely tuned to every nuance. 'My *opinion*, not advice d'you understand, would be that any investment needs to be receipted. Evidence, Mr McKie, worth its weight in gold on occasion.'

'Thank you, sir.'

'Not that I want it known I said so.'

'I am honoured by your confidence, sir.' The smell of bacon wafted under the study door and Mr Wingford became brisk.

'I don't suppose you know many people in Darlington as yet? Perhaps if I furnished you with one of my cards? There is much confusion in the town at present, due to the railway celebrations . . . There we are. A man needs a reputable introduction, hmm?' John put the card in a very safe pocket indeed.

The maid arrived to show him out and Mr Wingford asked casually, 'Elsie, does a Mr Gordon call below stairs?'

'One of his traders does, sir, and at some of the other houses in the street,' which gave John another valuable piece of information. He arrived at the Temperance Hall out of breath but with confidence restored. Gordon looked pointedly at his watch.

'I'm sorry to be late, sir, I've come from the presbytery.'

'What?'

'Mr Wingford was kind enough to see me. The maid there was telling me about some of your customers, among his congregation.' John's face glowed with enthusiasm. 'I'm hoping to meet them next Sunday, that is if we can conclude our business this morning, Mr Gordon.'

The man studied the glowing tip of his cigar. John was no longer defenceless; Mr Wingford had considerable influence in Darlington. The pause made John bold. 'There is one matter, however, that of the area near Montrose Street where I believe

79

you intend I should work? According to my landlady, the population there is sparse . . . ' Gordon stared but John returned the look steadily. 'Which, under the circumstances, means that a premium of twenty-five pounds is too high and twenty percent commission too little – '

'The devil it is!'

'Twenty-five percent is the least I can consider, and not more than twenty pounds for the books.'

At this, Gordon's lip curled; the ledgers weren't worth more than ten. John McKie wasn't so clever after all.

'Twelve months' trial at twenty percent,' he snapped.

'With respect, six months.' John continued to hold on to the four white banknotes. 'And concerning our contract, Mr Wingford was able to help me there, too. He has told me to apply to Barclays Bank, mentioning his name. They will draw up an agreement for us.'

Gordon bit on his cigar. He'd have to capitulate. Either that or risk having Wingford discover he'd refused to sign, thereby losing his Presbyterian customers. The voice from the pulpit boomed far and wide over Darlington. Inexperienced John McKie might be but he was learning fast. 'When may I expect to see this – contract?'

'Tonight, Mr Gordon.'

'Then that's when you can expect to have these books.' John's face fell; a whole day wasted!

'May I not pay half the money now so that I may begin immediately?'

'Are you sure Mr Wingford would approve?' The sarcasm was lost on John.

'Oh, yes. He believes in hard work, he said so.'

Gordon's fingers itched to feel those banknotes. He wanted to pocket them and deny the fact afterwards but John McKie had invoked the protection of the church. 'Oh, take the books, drat you. And the list of goods and prices. You're to meet Robinson in the King's Head at one o'clock. See that you're familiar with all our lines by then.'

'Yes, thank you very much, Mr Gordon!' John was so enthusiastic he didn't notice the trader insisting that their bargain was for the full six years but the phrase was firmly inserted into the subsequent contract. Only then did John realize what he'd committed himself to but it was too much to expect he'd be a match for Gordon.

(xiv)

When she learned what he'd done, Helen Shields was desperate. It was a sense of guilt that made her cry aloud, 'No, not six years!' She'd failed him, he hadn't been able to stand alone. John had fallen into the first trap that had been laid for him.

Secretly, Helen hadn't given up hope that somehow there would be a miracle and John become a doctor. It was her own upbringing and outlook that kept the blinkers in position. She was the daughter of a gentleman; she wanted John to join her, to be of the same social class. He'd been educated for it, she'd seen to that. Once he was embedded in trade, they would be separated.

There was another worry: that his good nature and honesty would make him sorry for people, allow them too much credit. Here Helen's fears were groundless. John understood poverty, it had been his experience since birth. He could judge to a nicety just how much any of his customers could afford.

'As there are few houses at the edge of my area,' he wrote, 'Mr Gordon has agreed that I visit many surrounding villages and farms, to add new names to the books. Such journeys are not popular with the other traders as they are some distance from Darlington but a wee walk never bothered Davie or I!'

John was describing light-heartedly journeys of over twenty miles in all weathers but Helen didn't know. She only sighed over his letter; surely clerical work in an ecclesiastical stationers would have been preferable to this?

'I've had to look for other ways of supplementing my income as it would be foolish to draw on my remaining capital. Mrs Beal knows of many local children whose parents want them coached in reading and writing. No Latin or Greek, alas, but at least I earn enough to pay my rent. Mr Wingford has also been most kind. He hints there may be an opening as a Sunday School teacher eventually.'

Helen snorted. Sunday school teachers worked for no pay.

Why waste time doing that? But John was far-seeing: such a position would give the ultimate seal of respectability in the eyes of the women, his potential customers.

'I am often fortunate in having many hospitable customers who offer refreshment. I think it is because I'm the first trader to visit some of the outlying farms. On those days, with a hot drink inside me, I can go all day without needing to spend a farthing on food. Also I can often purchase fresh eggs for Mrs Beal, which are much appreciated.'

Helen was baffled. Such enthusiasm for the incidentals of life: had John lost his sense of purpose entirely? She failed to understand he'd transferred all his fervour to the business. Regrets were forbidden. He must do well for Davie's sake. Nor did Mr Gordon's other employees understand such single-mindedness but they didn't have John's goal. If Davie were to have his chance, there wasn't a minute to waste.

He was out of the house, the vast coat buttoned against the wind, before Mrs Beal had lit the fires. As he tramped along muddy lanes he recited his new litany; the collar and boot sizes of his customers. Before a month was out he knew them all. He learned their habits as well and set himself the mathematical problem of the best use of his time. Afterwards, he asked Mr Gordon's permission to hand over his takings only three times a week: the other evenings could be better spent when he knew his customers would be home from work.

Twice a week he went farther afield, to the villages of Sadberge and Long Newton. If trade was slow, John didn't mind. It would take time for them to become used to him. He'd already sold a pair of linen sheets to one farmer's wife and never failed to mention her delight to the rest. Teaching the children of Coburg street had added their mothers to his books, too.

On Saturdays, he waited at Bank Top station with the other traders for the arrival of their supplies. The wicker skips were heaved onto the handcarts and wheeled through Darlington to the Temperance Hall where each man parcelled up his own orders. Most left them there until Monday but John spent the afternoon delivering. If his customers wanted a new shirt to wear to church on Sunday, he made sure they had one.

Mr Wingford's introduction opened the door of the Mechanic's Institute in Skinnergate. Never one to miss an opportunity, John offered to help catalogue the books they were donating to the new free library. He managed to leave word that he was available for such thankless tasks – and that he could supply top-quality moleskin trousers at very competitive rates.

Mr Gordon was scornful but John didn't care. He was becoming known in Darlington. Not only that, he was building a reputation. Mr Wingford approved of him; it was 'safe' to allow John in the kitchen to sell to the maids. Mistresses of houses told each other about the new trader. By the time his probationary period was over, John was established and both he and Gordon knew it.

Mr Wingford's well-thumbed card had pride of place on the mantelpiece beside Mr Standing's picture. If the Church had failed John in Scotland, in England it had redeemed itself. Occasionally on Sundays, John had a twinge of conscience, for transgressing a rule he'd observed since childhood, that of reading nothing other than the Bible or *The Pilgrim's Progress*. On Sunday afternoons it had to be admitted, John now studied accountancy. Was it trespassing on the good nature of an Almighty who'd replaced Mr McAlister with Mr Wingford? John shut his eyes to it. All he knew was he needed to study.

The bank manager had hinted accountancy might be useful. In an emergency one Sunday morning when John had acted as sidesman and carried the plate, the manager had noted the demeanour, the speed at which the collection was added up and pointed out that in Darlington – booming with trade – bookkeepers were in short supply. John took the hint. Even if he would be leaving for London eventually, an additional skill would be useful.

After a year John heard a rumour in one of the many kitchens he visited. The master of the house, a Quaker, was opening a new warehouse behind Widdowfield Street. John respectfully asked for an interview. The Quaker was doubtful. Yes, he'd need an experienced bookkeeper eventually but at present, the business was in its infancy. John staked his claim: would Mr Richardson grant a second interview once he'd obtained his certificate? The Quaker agreed. It didn't commit him but it gave John a goal and time, especially on Sunday afternoons, became precious.

He wrote weekly to his parents and once a month to Helen Shields. In letters to her, John poured out his fears as well as his hopes but her replies were often cool. If Mr Richardson sounded a better prospect as an employer than Mr Gordon, what did it matter? Neither offered a proper career. Once she made a mistake of referring to his lost career in medicine; she wounded his lonely heart far more than she realized and it was two months before he could bring himself to write to her again for of course John had regrets he couldn't stifle. They came thick and fast during the first frightening weeks in Darlington. He was still young enough to weep and to feel hungry. At night, when the tempting smell of the herring barrel overcame him, he let the tears flow. The croft seemed as far away as the cold moon outside his window. He pulled himself together. What was the use of weeping when, with a bit of study, he could become an accountant? And if he could ignore his stomach in order to make the barrel last longer, his fortitude might overcome his misery, or so he hoped.

CHAPTER THREE

Davie

Davie tried to apply himself to study but without John it was less easy. There was no one urging him to 'keep at it', no one to consult over insoluble problems. It wasn't that Davie slackened, but he turned more and more to subjects he preferred. Helen understood. In her eyes Davie had moved out from beneath John's shadow and was finding his true identity. But he wouldn't make a doctor, she was sure of it.

It was nearly two years before she managed to arrange a visit to the hospital at Inverness. In that time Davie had grown so much it was making life difficult. Apart from being tall he was her oldest pupil and this added to his self-consciousness. John had never worried but then his whole being had concentrated on his goal. For Davie it was different. With university still uncertain, his attention wandered. Helen worried occasionally about the direction it was taking. More than once she'd seen him with his arm round Morag Cameron's waist. She wondered if Alex was aware of it.

In Inverness, Helen and Davie waited in the panelled entrance hall. The hospital was impressive enough outside but in here, surrounded by newly varnished wood, shining floors and an antiseptic atmosphere so full of purpose, it affected both of them. A nurse, starched from the pleats of her bonnet to the tip of her apron, took Helen's letter and creaked off with it. Thank goodness Davie had lost some of his exuberance. On the train he'd behaved abominably, full of excitement at his first journey, noisy, stumbling clumsily over other passengers jammed so tightly along the wooden seats.

There was too much of Davie altogether, Helen told herself. He'd insisted on fiddling with one of the lamps. He'd seen a gentleman tip one with his umbrella to increase the size of the flame, so Davie must needs do the same, spilling hot oil on those below. Helen was furious.

Davie subsided but only for a short time. He caught sight of a book a young lady was reading and tried to engage her in conversation, which brought a severe reprimand from the young lady's mother. By the time the train arrived at Inverness, Helen Shields was exhausted.

Once inside a cab she delivered a sharp lecture to induce a mood of penitence and, she hoped, concentrate Davie's thoughts on the ordeal ahead. If he was to be shown all aspects of hospital work, Helen could imagine how gruelling that might prove.

When the nurse returned to conduct them both to the Superintendent's office, Helen shook her head. This time, Davie would be on his own. She reached for her crochet work and settled down to wait.

Davie walked eagerly beside his guide, his feet squeaking on the polished linoleum. They would begin, he was told, with a visit to the general wards, then men's surgical. After that, if the surgeon gave permission, Davie could sit in the gallery to watch an operation. Afterwards some first-year students would be attending a lecture in the mortuary – a lecture, Davie interrupted! Could he sit and listen with the rest? The guide looked at him sardonically. If Mr McKie was that interested, he could even handle the cadaver.

They paused beside a wooden container and the man lifted out two pads of gauze sprinkled with carbolic. He handed one to Davie. 'Cover your nose with it, you'll need to in here,' and opened a ward door.

Davie never attended the lecture in the mortuary; he collapsed in the gallery during an operation to amputate an old woman's leg and lay there until two of the porters climbed the stairs to drag him away. Back in the entrance hall a nurse placed a bucket beside him and raised her eyebrows eloquently. If Davie needed to be sick again, he must at all costs avoid soiling the linoleum.

Helen waited. There was no trace of exuberance now. 'It was awful, Mistress Shields. I'd no idea what it could be like . . . so brutal! Some in there – they've given up hope. You can see it in their eyes.'

'Davie, you were seeing people for the first time who were very ill. Of course some of them looked poorly –'

'No, it was the pain, Mistress Shields! Some of them were crying out, they couldn't help themselves.' Helen was about to speak again but thought better of it. Let Davie get it out of his system.

'The stench, too . . . the nurses do their best but they cannot prevent all of it. I couldn't bear to touch people the way they do, ordinary people though they are. I felt . . . ' And he swallowed, remembering. 'There was one old man – they were changing his dressing. I stood there to see them do it – his flesh was suppurating! I had to leave . . . It was shameful, but I could not stay,' he mumbled.

Helen folded her crochet briskly. 'Then our visit was not without purpose. It is why we came here after all. We must make other plans for your future.'

'John will never forgive me!'

'Of course he will, when he understands. I will write and explain after it's decided what's best for you. But first, we'll have some tea.' He looked so despondent that she added gently, 'It's not the end of the world, you know.'

Davie roused himself, staring at bustling figures, each hurrying past with a sense of purpose. 'It's the end of my father's dream,' he said simply. 'That's the worst thing of all.'

She found a smart tea shop to try and give a little sparkle to the day, and ordered currant cake when she discovered Davie had never seen dried fruit before, but he stuck to bread and butter, preferring to keep his slice for Jeannie. 'She'll be so disappointed, you see. I want to take her something.' A little impatient, Helen tried to turn his thoughts in other directions but he wasn't yet ready. 'My father and John will decide what's best,' he replied apathetically and Helen had to curb her impulse to shake him.

He recovered a little during the journey home, remembering how pretty some of the nurses were and how terrified of the matron.

'They said she was a real tartar. Why, she was even worse than – ' Davie stopped and blushed. Helen had no idea what he'd intended to say. As they parted at Salen she told him she would visit the croft when Alex was ready to discuss the future.

'I'd like to help in any way I can, Davie.' She was determined there wouldn't be any mistakes this time but she still didn't have the right to take the initiative, that must be left to the McKies. Alone in the school house, Helen waited anxiously.

(i)

Perhaps they should have realized Davie would seek consolation. He was no longer a boy, not in the eyes of many young women. Helen made that discovery for herself, several weeks after the visit to Inverness. She and Cissie were in the schoolroom where Helen was marking books.

'Here's a naughty thing!' Helen held up an exercise book disapprovingly, 'Davie McKie has used the back of this to scribble in Gaelic.' Cissie got up painfully from her scrubbing.

'That's not like him . . . why would he do a thing like that? Oh . . . it's a poem, ma'am. Davie's written a poem.'

'Well, why couldn't he write in English and in the proper book?' Cissie chuckled. Helen was immediately alert. 'What is it?'

'I'm thinking Morag Cameron has a lot to answer for. This is a love poem, Mistress Shields.'

'A what!' Helen had never had any trouble like that before, her pupils were far too young. Davie still was, in her opinion. 'Morag Cameron . . . ? Isn't she still abroad with the others?' Morag had moved from the Manse to the Big House and was now part of the household the Manners took with them on trips overseas.

'Yes, it says here she's in Monte Carlo,' Cissie agreed. 'They've been writing to one another, seemingly.' She put the exercise book back on Helen's desk, 'It's private, that poem,' she said primly.

'Nonsense! It's written on school property.' Helen stabbed the first verse with her finger, 'Kindly oblige me by translating it.'

Cissie hesitated. Sometimes the school mistress could be obsessive about the McKies. She'd been very difficult to please after John had gone to England, she still carried on about it although John was doing well by all accounts. Now she was fixing on Davie. Why had he been so foolish as to leave love messages lying about! Reluctantly Cissie began, ' "Dh, fhalbh mo chruinneag – "'

'Never mind the Gaelic. English will be sufficient.'

'At the beginning he is saying "My beloved has departed and left me . . . " It's a lament, if you were singing it. Then he goes on to say how she took ship at Salen for Europe . . . ' Cissie scanned the lines, wondering how much to reveal. 'He says the Glen is cheerless . . . "Hope and consolation have departed" because "The light of my eye has gone overseas".' Helen's mouth had settled in a familiar tight line and Cissie paused.

'Go on,' Helen insisted. 'There's more to it than that, I can see there is.'

'Davie is saying he had a letter from Morag, a sincere letter, telling him there was sunshine and a thousand boats at Monte Carlo but her greatest wish was to be with him, climbing up to Loch-Laga . . . ' Cissie sighed over the sentiment. No one had ever said that to her. 'The last lines are about how he says she thinks of him . . . how sad he is – "All the lads are dejected" –

' "S'na gillean uile trom fo' churam, O's beag ar duil g'um faie gu brath iad",' Cissie quoted defiantly, ' "Maybe never again shall we see them" – it's a lovely poem, Mistress Shields.' But there was no room for romance in Helen's soul.

'He should never have written it! We'll keep this matter to ourselves, Cissie.'

'Very well, Mistress Shields.'

But Helen showed the poem to Alex. 'I fear this changes things.'

89

'Mmm?' Alex looked up slowly, his mind still savouring the Gaelic.

'I've made enquiries,' Helen went on. 'The Manners family are returning from Europe within a week or two. It follows that Morag Cameron will be returning with them.'

But Jeannie murmured something softly so that Helen couldn't hear. She knew of her son's weakness for the girl but she also knew, from Morag's mother, that the girl had been offered a place with another family in France and was likely to take it. Jeannie murmured how glad she was that this was so.

'Aye, aye,' Alex was irritated, 'One of you at a time, lassie. My head's spinning with it.' Helen attempted to press her own case.

'I don't think it would be a good idea for Davie to be here when Morag returns,' she said fiercely. 'We must nip this affair in the bud. If Davie is to make progress, he must work harder. I feared his enthusiasm was fading, now I know why.' She waited expectantly. Alex read a few more lines.

'It is a fine poem he has written.' Helen was scandalized.

'He's too young to be writing verses like that!'

'Maybe so . . . Aye.' Alex could remember how he'd felt years ago, waiting at the trysting place for Jeannie. 'Well, this needs thinking about, right enough. I will have a word with him. Will I walk a bit with you along the road?' he asked hopefully but Helen wasn't ready to leave.

'Has it been decided what career Davie is to take up?' she asked. Alex frowned.

'Not yet. We are still considering it.' Seeing she was about to speak again he added hastily, 'Aye, you are right. We must decide soon.' Helen swept the offending exercise book back into her bag. 'We are both very honoured that you should be so concerned.' He was anxious to placate her.

They watched Helen march off and Jeannie asked softly, 'What did Davie say in his poem?' Alex chanted the lament.

Dh, fhalbh mo chruinneag 's rinn i m'fhagail,
Dh, fhalbh mo chruinneag 's dh, fhag i 'n duthaich,
Chan eil duil gu'n till i 'n drasda,
Dh, fhalbh mo chruinneag 's rinn i m'fhagail.

90

In some ways, Alex agreed with Helen but for different reasons. He did not see the affair with Morag as serious. He was as thankful as Jeannie that the girl had been tempted to remain in France but he was under no illusion that Davie's affections would not turn elsewhere. His second son had a tender loving heart: if not Morag, then another pair of fine eyes would beguile him eventually.

Helen worried over Davie's academic standards but Alex took pleasure in watching his son develop in other ways. The croft was full of laughter when Davie was there. Jeannie sang about her work and the evenings were often spent telling stories round the fire, stories of the old times, the legends. It was slack behaviour for a young man hoping to reach university, but then Davie wasn't likely to go, was he? Alex sighed out of resignation and despair.

It wasn't simply that Davie wasn't a true scholar, it was again a question of money. It would take at least another five years to save enough – and Davie couldn't wait that long. The poem had proved it if nothing else had. And the spark of ambition, so strong in Alex, had been passed in full to John. He'd inherited his father's drive. If those hard early years were to mean anything it would be in the future, with the next generation. They had laid the foundations and Alex would continue to strive, but he knew in his heart it wasn't for Davie's sake. The lad would have his chance but whatever it was to be he must decide it for himself.

He talked to Davie that evening, while they unravelled the nets.

'Are you prepared to wait and study while John and I work to save what is needed? You'll be seventeen next birthday. I fear you'd be twenty-one or two before we could manage it.' Davie coloured deeply.

'I hadn't thought it would take so long,' he admitted.

'Aye, well, there it is. We cannot manage it sooner. John hasn't had it easy – '

'Father, I'm not complaining!'

'I know you're not, son. But I think you're nearly done with schooling?' Davie nodded, near to tears.

'I've failed you. You, John and Mother – '

'No, of course you haven't. There's no failure here. What we must decide is what you're best suited to, as Mistress Shields said. I will write and ask John his opinion. He sees so much more in Darlington.' Descriptions of that town filled their minds so much they scarcely remembered it was only a staging post on the route to London.

After negotiating with Gordon, John replied. When she learned of their decision, Helen Shields was angry. She wrote to her old governess.

> What I cannot understand is how it has all dwindled to this. After all we've been through together, all the battles, it's as though the McKies have been brow-beaten. They're behaving like crofters after all. There's no ambition left. Whenever Davie does decide to leave, I shall not be at the pier to see him go.

(iii)

Had she witnessed the meetings between John and Gordon that led up to the decision, Helen might have thought differently. The years had left their mark: it had been a period of development in which John hadn't wasted a single day. When he faced Gordon across the desk he was no longer a gullible fool. He had learned how to deal with his employer.

First there was the matter of money. John no longer waited each evening in the Temperance Hall. He demanded to be trusted, paid his takings into the bank instead and handed Gordon receipted accounts. Such an arrangement made the trader uneasy. He was a man who liked the feel of money. To see gold and silver on the desk top brought saliva in the way food never could. But he didn't refuse. John pointed out how foolish it was to risk being robbed and that prospect worried Gordon even more.

Then there was John's industry. He hadn't become a shirker like many of his predecessors. He was out in all weathers, working harder than Gordon himself. At first it was a joke among the others: why wear yourself out when it wasn't your own purse you were filling? Why bother bicycling so far in the rain? For John had increased his round yet again.

He was never in the King's Head to hear the laughter. For John, money spent on drink was the ultimate folly. Far better use a lunch hour visiting employees at a woollen mill, or the hospital on Greenbank Road where certain female staff had half an hour's leisure to spend their wages. John's order book was always full when it came to holland and calico for aprons.

By arrangement with Mr Wingford, John also visited any patients who were members of the congregation. It was mutually beneficial. It enabled the Minister to pass on glad tidings from the pulpit, or hurry to Greenbank himself if the signs weren't promising. And John increased his custom among the bedridden. He'd taken the precaution of presenting his introduction to Matron first and she let it be known that young Mr McKie came with the blessing of the Church.

Gordon couldn't understand it: he was accustomed to men who considered themselves trapped by his terms, who became disillusioned, worn out by the drudgery. Most of his employees sought refuge in drink, borrowing against future income so that they ended up permanently in his debt. He welcomed it. It bound men to him. But he had no hold over John. What was worse, John had a contract.

Occasionally Gordon tried to goad him. He was never seen in any of the eating houses, not even Hunter's cocoa palace, so what did he live on? Fresh air? John refused to be drawn. Visiting his customers, he would accept the offer of a hot drink but never a plate of food, however tempting. He'd decided early on that his reputation mattered more than his stomach.

And if Gordon was puzzled as to how much John saved and what he did with his time, he was none the wiser. The trader didn't know of the lessons given in Coburg Street or the Mechanics Institute. Mathematics were John's speciality and apprentices from the locomotive sheds were eager to learn. During the daylight, John rendered unto Caesar that which was his but at night he used the time for his own benefit.

This evening he sipped a very small measure of Mr Gordon's brandy before broaching the delicate matter of Davie's future. Not that Gordon knew John had a brother, not yet. In some matters it was prudent for his employer to know as little as possible of John's private circumstances.

He shook his head at the offer of a refill but watched the trader top up his own glass. Gordon was in a mellow mood.

'Well now, Mr McKie, from now on you'll be earning commission at an increased rate, as I promised when we exchanged contracts . . . ' Gordon never failed to refer to this irritating piece of paper, 'Now that you've completed the necessary preliminaries – '

'I think you said sixty percent for you, forty for me, Mr Gordon.' John was anxious to get on.

'Did I indeed? So I did.' Gordon leaned back, his shoes propped up on the desk as was his habit. 'And that satisfies you, I trust?'

'Yes indeed, sir.' Privately John thought the mark-up excessive and the division unfair but he'd also learned when the truth was not expedient. In time he proposed to make changes, but not yet.

'Should you wish to re-invest your increased earnings with me, John McKie . . . ?' Gordon began half-heartedly but John shook his head. Blast his eyes! Young McKie would no doubt have it all worked out, down to the last farthing. 'Only two and a half more years, John McKie?' Gordon attempted to make the question a joke but thoughts of what John might have planned for the future secretly worried him. Suppose this stripling set up in opposition? By God, he'd crush him! Gordon shook off his imaginings and poured another brandy.

'I would like to discuss a matter of business, Mr Gordon.'

'Oh, yes?' Gordon was upright immediately.

'Those areas outside Darlington where I have established new trade. They were villages where no one had visited previously,' John emphasized.

'Well, what about them?'

'From now on I should like to consider them my own area. I would continue to buy stock from you of course, but wish to sub-let the area.' Gordon squashed his cigar flat. John noted the waste automatically.

'That's your game, is it, John McKie. That's what you've been hatching all these months – '

'Please, Mr Gordon! It is because I wish to offer myself to you for the two vacant areas within Darlington, and discuss other streets where I believe we can do better.'

'Which would those be?' John named several of the poorest streets. Gordon pondered. It would mean foregoing two extra premiums if he let John take those vacancies, but in return he knew John would increase trade. As to the other streets, they were Tyler's, but he wouldn't object. Lazy, drinking on the sly, Tyler probably hadn't visited them in a twelvemonth. John said quietly, 'I plan to bring in from those streets the same amount of business I have brought from the new villages.' It was a bold guarantee. Gordon stared at him.

'How on earth could you? When will you have the time? You can't cover that new area on your own?'

John didn't reply. He wasn't prepared to divulge his plans unless he was forced to. 'Tyler should have worked up trade in those streets by now,' grumbled Gordon, 'I'll have a word with him.' But John wanted to head him off that idea.

'I'd be prepared to go there in the evenings, when families are back from work.' They were discussing streets built for factory workers, houses bursting with people where as one man rose from a bed, another occupied it.

'It's risky, going after dark. What about the take? It's my money that we're talking about – '

'I'd go to the bank, Mr Gordon. I think I've proved that I can be trusted to do what is sensible.'

It annoyed Gordon even more to be reminded of it. He preferred a man with failings, a weakling made him much more comfortable. Tyler was one but then Tyler didn't bring in much profit.

'We'll see,' he temporized, 'I'll think about it. Ask me again in a couple of weeks.' But Davie's needs were pressing.

'I would prefer to begin as soon as possible, if you please.'

'What if I refuse?' John had his answer ready.

'With much regret I should inform my customers in the villages that I would be back when my contract with you was at an end. It would mean you could offer the area to someone else but not many enjoy the fresh air as I do.'

It was audacious but calculated. John was pitting his energy against any stranger Gordon might choose to hire, if he could persuade anyone to walk that far. Suddenly Gordon was tired of the game.

'I shall hold you to what you promised, John McKie. The same amount of business from Tyler's streets as you brought in from the villages, right? You can have both those areas without further premium because I'm a generous man . . . but we'll leave the villages to rot for a while.'

'Thank you, sir.' John was eager to be gone. He'd no intention of neglecting anything but now was not the time to reveal Davie's part in his scheme. He hurried downstairs, for he had another important appointment outside the town. As the door shut behind John, the trader saw he hadn't even finished the small amount of brandy he'd poured for him. For some reason, this annoyed Gordon most of all.

(iv)

In the Quaker's house, the cook was answering her master's questions concerning John. She was as solid as her pastry was light. She stood facing her master, elephantine legs set squarely apart.

'When he first visited, he'd a recommendation from Mr Wingford else I wouldn't have let him in the door, not after t'other talleyman.' The Quaker understood. One traveller had been invited in, had charmed sixpences off the maids and had never returned. Enquiries revealed a trail of sorrowful girls throughout the country but nothing more. It was a cautionary tale and John McKie was the first to be allowed over the threshold since.

'You are satisfied with Mr McKie, cook?'

'Yes, he's most obliging. And trustworthy. Nothing is too much trouble, neither. When I wanted . . . ' The cook had been about to describe whalebones for corsets but recollected to whom she was speaking. 'When I needed a particular item, Mr McKie sent to Middlesbrough before he found some the right quality. He even helped Minnie Davies at High Staunton farm when her old cow was calving and there's not many as 'd do

96

that. She didn't buy nowt, she's too mean, the old – woman. Her husband took two pair of stockings instead. Said he wouldn't feel easy if he didn't.' The Quaker stuck to the point.

'Does he sell much here?'

'Not but what they can afford and he's most careful about it. Never lets anyone overstretch, however much they want summat. And he won't tek nowt. When I wanted to give him a bit mutton for tea one day, he said he couldn't without doing summat in return. That's when I remembered the place cards, Master.'

She looked at him in triumph. Mr Richardson was baffled.

'For the dinners, sir, when you and madam have guests. My eyesight troubles me over they little cards.' Her sight was excellent but using a pen meant sweat and anguish for the cook. 'He allus does 'em for me now, sir, when he calls. They're a credit to your table.'

The Quaker was silent because he hadn't noticed. Slightly offended, cook said stiffly, 'Madam is pleased with them anyways, sir. And Mr McKie won't tek more'n a cup of tea in return.'

The clock chimed nine and he thanked her. As she made to leave the woman had an uneasy thought. 'There's nowt wrong is there, Master, with Mr McKie?'

'Nothing that I know of, cook. So far I've only heard good reports of John McKie.'

John knocked at the front door because it was an official visit. Once inside the study he was nervous. 'I come with a request, Mr Richardson. I don't know if you will think it presumptuous.'

'Neither do I until I know what it is.'

'At a previous interview we discussed your new warehouse behind Widdowfield Street.'

'We did.'

'On that occasion you suggested I study accountancy . . . ' John fumbled inside his greatcoat and put the precious vellum in front of the Quaker. 'My first certificate, sir.'

'So soon! I congratulate thee.' John blushed with pleasure. 'And dost thou intend to continue?'

'Oh yes, indeed!' The Quaker stared.

'Do I misunderstand, John McKie? I thought thou already hadst secure employment?'

'But only for two and a half more years. It is the future that concerns me, sir.' He couldn't remember a time when it didn't.

The Quaker sat for a moment or two contemplating the fire before he asked, 'What *are* thy plans? For the future?'

John hesitated; so far he hadn't discussed them with anyone. If he spoke them aloud, might they not disappear? 'Thou must be frank with me,' said Mr Richardson quietly.

'I hope in time, to start in business for myself.'

'And meanwhile thou needst to do all thou can to amass capital?'

'Yes.'

There was another silence. The study was half in shadow. Butterfly gas mantles were turned down and an oil lamp burned on the desk. Gazing into the flame, the Quaker began to describe how the warehouse fitted into his business. Now that the coastal trade in coal was firmly established, the community of Friends was exporting farther afield to northern Europe. 'Heavy engineering, steel and iron, John McKie, there's none can touch us for quality, not even the Germans. We import in a smaller way and that's where the warehouse comes in.'

Mr Richardson leaned back in his chair. 'Trade has grown faster than any of us thought possible . . . When thou consider what it was like here twenty years ago.' John nodded. He knew that without Quaker money financing the railways, Darlington might never have risen to such prominence – if only he could become a part of it!

'In two or three years, I may have need of a confidential clerk,' Mr Richardson said cautiously, 'who will run my business when I travel abroad, but . . . ' Seeing the look of hope, he raised a warning hand, 'Whether that man will be thee, John McKie, will depend on whether thou canst prove thyself capable.'

'Oh, I will! You have my word.'

'I have one man already working in the warehouse. Thou wouldst need to begin as his assistant.' Mr Richardson looked at him thoughtfully, 'Would that suit thee?'

'Would it be an indentured post, sir?' Nervousness made John croak. Every penny was invested, he couldn't afford to pledge a large sum.

'It would not. Equally, there would be no guarantee of a firm

98

position. I cannot guarantee that trade will continue to grow.'
John nearly smiled; how could such an impetus slow down?

'I am willing to take the risk, sir, if you will give me the opportunity.' The Quaker stared at the thin, eager face; an honest man unless he was mistaken.

'I'll make a bargain, John McKie. In return for three hours' work every Saturday morning at the warehouse, thou wilt take proper meals when thou visit my cook and the maids. Will that suffice until we make other arrangements?'

'It will indeed, sir, it'll suit me fine.' All those pies, those steaming bowls of soup – the prospect of sampling them nearly made him swoon!

'One thing thou must learn straight away, if thou art to work among the Society of Friends. We are plainspoken people.'

'Yes, indeed. Thank you, Mr Richardson.'

John's cup overflowed. Confidential clerk! Only a few years and he could look forward to that – he'd never expected to reach so far in such a short time. His hands trembled as he tucked his precious certificate back inside its scroll. He'd begin studying for the next grade that very night. Such marvellous prospects, he could scarcely believe his good fortune.

He flew back to Coburg Street. His letter to the family that night was ecstatic.

The future is better than I could have dreamed possible. I am sufficiently well established to take on Davie as my assistant (although I haven't yet revealed that to Mr Gordon) but best of all is the prospect ahead of us.

A trader's life is arduous but with me beside him, Davie will make a success of it.

In the croft, Alex nodded over this phrase. That is what Davie missed just now: John's firm hand under his elbow.

Truly I think we can be thankful for our blessings. Pray that we continue in good health which is necessary for us to succeed. Davie will need a premium of £20 for Mr Gordon even though he will be working for me, for that is the way of the man. He will also need a good suit and a heavy coat like mine. The winds here can be bitter. If he can bring oatcakes and herring too, it will help considerably.

Next, John discussed with Mrs Beal whether Davie could be permitted to share the small room. In his eyes there was plenty of room provided they were careful. 'He is my *younger* brother after all,' John pointed out.

When Helen Shields, still full of anger, had finished her outburst to her old governess, she wrote another letter to John. It was composed when her disappointment had reached its peak:

> Although unsuited to medicine I had always assumed Davie would pursue a proper career. That, I understood, was why you were sacrificing yourself. Nor had I finally given up hope that once Davie was established, you too would look for a situation worthy of your talents.
>
> All those years when Elias Standing and I did our best for you – are they to be completely wasted? Are you really serious when you suggest Davie becomes a tradesman like yourself? Pray consider again before committing him to similar servitude.
>
> I have never reproached you before, John, but I consider you owe me some return for those years of effort.
>
> I remain,
> Yrs. affectionately,
>   HELEN SHIELDS

(v)

Inside the small room, the atmosphere became very bleak. John sat on the edge of his bed, cold as ice. In one page, Helen had destroyed the love he'd held in his heart since he was a boy. She had been the person he'd always been able to turn to but now that was finished.

How cheaply she held his achievements! No mention of the certificate, the first tangible qualification John had obtained. He couldn't understand it. He re-read the two paragraphs, each sarcastic phrase stinging him.

He had worked as hard since coming to England as he had in her school – couldn't Mistress Shields understand that? And

100

he'd done so alone. He'd aimed at the same goals of excellence; how was it possible he'd failed? But whichever way John tried to interpret Helen's words, he failed to understand the gap between middle-class aspiration and trade.

Dawn came at last and John rose, determined not to waste any more time brooding. He stared at the roof opposite. The school mistress had told him he owed her a debt: well, he'd repay it one day, he didn't know how yet but he'd repay one hundredfold. No one would ever accuse him of being beholden. He stood by the window to look at the first page again. Helen had referred to Davie's 'instability'. No doubt she was referring to Morag. John sighed. He could deal with that problem once Davie was here in England but he wasn't looking forward to it.

Alex had told him of the poetry, of Davie's charm and the way girls looked at him. John shook his head. He'd had no trouble with women, nor would he behave so foolishly. It would be years before either he or Davie could afford anything as costly as matrimony.

He was still depressed when he set off on his rounds. Mr Richardson had lifted him so high, given him such hopes: Helen Shields had reduced them to ashes. She'd made one suggestion in her letter of a different career for Davie, that of teaching. A new education act was being talked of, to provide free education for every child. Many more teachers would be needed.

John stood still on the empty, wet cobbles. Free education! All those pennies so carefully put by. The effort it had taken! But it was right, he told himself. If only it had been free then, when Georgie Hamilton could have benefited. The last he'd heard, Georgie was a labourer on the estate.

He waited for the street sweeper to finish before crossing briskly. There, but for the grace of God . . . He, John McKie, would not waste the advantages his father had given him.

But would Davie be happier as a teacher? He worried away at the problem. He mustn't deprive Davie of his chance, if that was what he wanted. More letters were exchanged but Helen's remained unanswered. John couldn't yet bring himself to write to her.

The school mistress had been equally caustic to Alex but he hadn't told John the whole of it. He and Jeannie sat meekly, while the harsh voice berated them. 'A trader – like John!' She filled the croft with her scorn. The dog crouched as far away as he could. Alex tried to placate her.

'Just think of the start you've given the boys. You'll be proud of them yet, I promise you.' Helen didn't hear. Davie, with his fine imagination, to end up selling things! The upbringing that conditioned her every thought couldn't accept this: she'd been hoping to turn John and Davie into gentlemen.

(vi)

The remaining weeks of term passed quickly. Davie attended as usual but Helen held herself aloof. On the final morning, she found a small package on her desk. She guessed who'd put it there but swept it aside. She was still hurt. Her suggestion that Davie consider teaching remained unanswered. How could the McKies treat her like this!

When Davie approached to take his final leave she actually turned away and pretended not to see him. She could feel his shock and bewilderment. She listened as his footsteps went away, nearly crying aloud with disappointment.

She sat a long time at her desk. The monitor, Cissie's replacement, called goodnight and closed the door. The small kitten one of the children had wished on her miaowed plaintively for its supper but was ignored. Eventually, unwillingly, Helen found the package and unwrapped it. Inside the small box was a tiny iridescent brooch, a mother-of-pearl butterfly bound with gilt wire to a pin. There was a note, in Davie's best hand.

Dear Mistress Shields,

The shop assistant said this was very fashionable and that Her Majesty often wears one similar in her bonnet. It comes from all of us, with our deepest respects and sincere gratitude.

Yrs. obediently,

DAVIE MACKIE.

And Helen sat alone with her bitterness.

John was waiting on the platform of the new station, at Bank Top. He straightened his shoulders. There was plenty to be proud of here, so much gleaming black and gold, green and cream, everywhere bright, new and not a speck of dirt the length of the platform. No doubt about it, Darlington reeked of prosperity. The train, symbol of everything the town stood for, thundered towards him.

Davie stepped out of the waggon and looked round eagerly. He recognized the thin, spare figure but what a difference! My word! Apart from his dark jacket and trousers, John had a stiff peaked collar, black tie, a cap, a waistcoat – and a moustache! Davie took in each detail greedily. He looked like someone from the Big House!

Davie was delighted. He grabbed John in a bearlike hug, laughter ringing through the station, 'John! You're a proper businessman!'

John's first reaction was astonishment followed by alarm. Alex had written that Davie had 'filled out' but not by how much. This was a giant nearly lifting him off his feet. How on earth would they manage in the bedroom? And the clothes! John was dismayed by the patched, worn jacket. They would have to visit Mr Fawcett. It would mean more expense but Davie must be fitted out properly. He nearly sighed but was stopped by the beaming face and unruly red hair.

It flooded back: his loneliness, his sense of isolation, all the hardship of being in a foreign land. None of it existed any more, all dissipated by the warmth of Davie's smile.

'Oh, I am glad to see you,' John spoke impulsively in Gaelic, 'Welcome to England!'

They followed an extremely small boy with a cart down the steep slope. Davie's possessions were piled onto it despite his protests he could carry everything. John gave him his first lesson in 'appearances'. People might notice: everything must be done correctly from now on. John bowed to the station master. The magnificent figure bowed back. Davie was immensely impressed. He followed the diminutive figure obediently. 'Besides,' John whispered, 'the cart only costs a ha'penny.'

They entered by the front door, stepping directly into Mrs Beal's parlour. In front of the fire a table was laid: matching cups and saucers on a white cloth accompanied by thin slices of bread and butter. Davie whistled through his teeth, he couldn't help it – this was how gentlemen lived. And John had a room here! John was satisfied. He'd debated long and hard about this additional expense but it had been worth it.

'I will just see Mrs Beal and ask her to put the kettle on, then we will go upstairs.' Davie stood, examining the wonders of the parlour but taking great care not to move lest he shatter any knick-knacks. There were china dogs, fringed covers concealing the legs of the furniture, starched covers to protect the upholstery, glass covers protecting dried flowers – all so fragile!

John returned and, negotiating the two doors between parlour and staircase, Davie carried the barrels up to the first floor. 'Mother sends her dearest love . . . she thought two barrels would see us through the winter. There are plenty of oatcakes in the trunk.' Staggering under the weight of it, John was enthusiastic.

'If we go carefully, they will.' He paused in front of the door to his chamber. 'This is the back bedroom which we are to share.' He inserted the key. 'I will show you round.' Davie squeezed inside the doorway. He knew every detail from the letters but it would have been tactless to say so.

'My, it's a grand room, John,' he breathed, 'I can see that it is.'

'There are many points in its favour,' John admitted and proceeded to demonstrate them: the brown oilcloth, the painted walls and varnished door, the engraving of Dante's inferno above an empty fireplace, now filled with red paper to simulate warmth. 'Coals are extra and I find I keep quite warm enough without.'

'Oh, so do I, John. It's a very warm room. I can feel it from here.' Davie fanned himself frantically. John looked gratified and moved on to describe the furniture. The pitch-pine cupboard, the chest of drawers and wash-stand jammed along the walls, the metal bedstead with John's thick coat neatly folded for additional warmth. Finally he moved to the window and gestured, 'The view.'

104

Davie stared at wet tiles and chimney pots. 'A fine town,' he ventured but he'd missed the point.

'Look beyond,' John urged. Davie stretched on tip-toe. 'Can you see the hills?' Davie narrowed his eyes and used his imagination.

'I think so.'

'Beyond them is London.'

Davie was amazed. 'Just over there? Why, we could walk it!'

'Not quite. It's another two hundred and thirty-seven miles. Approximately. But it's in that direction.' Immensely impressed, Davie took another look.

From below a voice called that tea was ready and John asked gravely, 'Would you like to wash your hands?' He'd saved this last, best treat till now and lifted the cover of the wash-stand. Inside was the *pièce de résistance*, a floral bowl half full of water. Beside it in a dish was a small piece of yellow soap. Davie was dazzled by the luxury. 'How does the water get in there?' John pointed to the jug standing in a china basin beneath.

'They don't have buckets here because there is a tap downstairs in the scullery. Whenever she wants water, all Mrs Beal has to do is turn it on!' John couldn't keep his poise, but still got excited at the thought. 'I tell you, Davie, you won't believe it until you see it. And in the mornings, Mrs Beal's daughter brings each of us a jug – of *hot* water, to wash and shave. You pour it into that basin and when you've finished, you lift up that plug and let it fall back into the bowl for them to clear away.'

John's letters had told them of this miracle but Davie hadn't believed it until now. 'Water inside a house!' he murmured, 'Like the Romans had . . .'

'And the privy is only a small step across the yard,' John assured him. 'We go through the scullery to get to it. Outside's where we black our boots. She is very particular.' As they descended the steep stair, he murmured a caution in Gaelic. 'Do not mind if you cannot understand Mrs Beal. They haven't mastered the English here in Darlington.'

While Davie consumed the entire plate of bread and butter, John described the town. There were approximately thirty-three thousand people living here now, for the place had expanded wonderfully thanks to all the engineering works. Most men worked in the locomotive sheds, building and repairing the engines, but there were foundries too. 'At night you should see the glow of the furnaces, Davie. It's a grand sight!'

There had been a recent debate at the Mechanics' Institute: Darlington, it had been agreed, had a much healthier climate than the towns nearby. 'Not like Middlesbrough. They've had bad times there with the cholera. We can be thankful our trade isn't based there.' John took such matters seriously. With a system of weekly payments he needed to be sure his customers would still be alive next time he called.

'You'll be meeting the other lodgers. All of them work in the boiler shops except Mr Murphy. He's in the brass foundry. Neck fifteen and a half.'

'D'you supply all of them with shirts?'

'Not yet,' John replied regretfully, 'but one day, Davie, one day.'

After tea they tramped through the town. The wind had risen and Davie had only a muffler to wrap round his throat. 'There wasn't a coat big enough in Fort William. Maybe we'll find one here?'

'We'll call on Mr Fawcett on Monday,' John shouted. 'He is an undertaker and can buy up complete wardrobes. His prices are very reasonable.' Davie's laughter rang out.

'Why, John, wherever will he find a dead man the same size as me?'

Battling up Priestgate, John paused to point at the magnificent building on the corner of Crown Street. 'It's the new Free Public Library, Davie.'

'A library? It's too grand, surely! You mean – we can go inside?'

'Not now. There will be queues right round the reading room, for the newspapers from London. Ten minutes, that's all the time allowed for reading them. They have to be strict. I'll tell you what though, Davie.' Heads bent against the wind, they struggled on up the street. 'It's as grand inside as it is out. Edward Pease donated ten thousand pounds to found it – and there's over five thousand books been donated so far.' Davie's whistle was blown away. 'I helped catalogue some of them,' John shrieked.

Up Tubwell Row and past the covered market they went. 'Open on Mondays. We do our shopping there as late as possible, when things are cheap. And that great clock keeps excellent time. I set my watch by it.' He was dismissive of the 'five lamps'. 'Men stop here when they're full of drink, preaching revolution some of them. Take my advice and ignore them.'

They paused to admire Edward Pease's statue before dodging through the line of cabbies in front of the King's Head. 'There's more money wasted in there than anywhere else in Darlington,' John yelled and Davie nodded. He wanted to see inside but was wise enough not to say so.

Along Northgate they stopped outside St George's. 'It's always full for morning service. The Sunday School, where I teach, is in the basement. Then there's the Dorcas Society, run by the ladies. We will attend any of their fund-raising events, Davie, because they're our customers.' And Davie nodded obediently.

He wanted to see inside the theatre but John kept him moving. 'It's another grand building but it costs money for a ticket and we've none to spare, not yet.' In Skinnergate, their eyes watering with the gale, John paused in front of the pillared entrance of the Mechanics' Institute. Davie could no longer hear. When John's lips moved, he nodded enthusiastically but that was all. Up Greenbank as far as the hospital so that Davie could admire that, then, chilled to the bone they hurried back along Widdowfield Street past the warehouse, slithering over the cobbles in Station Road, past the gas works in John Street, dodging the street sweeper on the corner of the Haughton Road. 'He's the seventh I've counted!'

'It's because of the horse trams,' John screamed proudly. 'First thing in the morning you can scarcely cross the road, it's so busy. We'll ride on one some day.'

Back in the small bedroom, Davie's teeth chattered as he began broaching the first of his barrels. On the landing they could hear Mrs Beal's daughter going past with a scuttle of coals for Mr Murphy. 'We could have a fire too if you like, Davie. It's a cold night, I cannot deny it.'

'No, no.' Davie was loyal. 'I'm nearly in a sweat with all the walking we've done. I think I'll take my jacket off for a while, if you've no objection.' Manfully he hung it over a chair and John saw for the first time how patched his shirt was.

107

'We'll have to get you more than just a coat. You'll need to wear wing collars as I do. All businessmen wear them in Darlington.' They were quieter now. The news was told, the excitement fading slightly. They were slipping back into the easy companionship they'd known since childhood. 'I told Gordon for the first time yesterday that I planned to have you as my assistant. He's being difficult because I insisted you be indentured for three years, not five. When he sees the money in front of him, no doubt he'll agree.'

John spoke with more confidence than he felt. Gordon had been very difficult indeed. It was only John's assurance that Davie would bring in as much trade in three years as any other man in five, that swayed him. But Davie had never yet sold a pair of stockings! John nearly shuddered as he thought of it. He would teach Davie but supposing his brother had no aptitude for the work!

'On Monday, when we meet Gordon, leave all the talking to me, Davie. There are plenty of men looking for work in the town just now so we cannot take risks.'

'Whatever you say, John.'

It was the moustache, Davie decided, that made John look so much older. At first he'd thought it was the formal clothes but now he'd grown accustomed to them and could examine his brother closely, he could see the changes. Despite spending so much time out of doors, John was still pale. He'd grown, he wasn't far short of Davie in height, but he was much thinner. His hair lay in two flat wings against his skull. In the past, Davie had attempted to copy him but it was no use. Plastered with water, his curls sprang up against as soon as they dried. Perhaps he could grow a moustache, though? Or a beard? Which lassie was it who said a beard would be the very thing . . . ?

John was looking severe and the deep frown lines creased automatically. 'We've so much to do. Three years isn't long. That's when we'll no longer be in Gordon's employ.'

Davie asked curiously, 'What happens then?'

'If all goes well and I become confidential clerk to Mr Richardson, we will open our own business with you as manager.' Davie was bowled over.

'That's a great idea!'

'See here, this is the way we go about it.'

The most amazing revelation of the day had arrived. John cleared everything from the table and spread out his account books for Davie to examine. It was a testament. Here every hour of labour was recorded, every coin spent and not saved – the story of its loss accounted for, misdemeanours underlined in red as a warning. When John had been tempted by fruit on a hot day, when he'd purchased a newspaper instead of using the reading room. 'It was to read about Mr Gladstone's new bill,' he admitted, 'to see for myself whether it was true.'

'The Crofters' Act, you mean?'

'Aye.'

'Oh my, what a fuss at the Big House when that was passed,' Davie shook his head. 'They called us all manner of things, revolutionaries, communists – what is a communist, John?'

'I don't know. I'll look it up next time I'm in the library.'

'Father said it had come too late. I think he's right. It's too late for us, anyway. We'll not go back, will we John, even though we have the right to the croft when father dies?'

'Who can say?' John was more cautious. 'We'll not give up the croft, that's for sure. Maybe we'll put a tenant in, to uphold the right. It's been dearly bought. Anyway, look here. I didn't waste the newspaper completely.' And there it was, folded between the thin blankets for extra warmth.

Davie felt ashamed. He had a little store of money, some earned from the sale of fish, some from working in the gardens of the Big House. But he'd spent some of his! He confessed immediately. John already knew about the brooch and had contributed – but a book of poetry? 'You already have the works of Burns.'

'This book contains poems by Tennyson.' John shook his head. 'I also bought some ribbons.'

'For Mother?'

'No.'

John was wide awake. 'I hope you've not been wasting money on Morag Cameron?'

'Morag?' Davie was puzzled, 'She's been gone for ages, hadn't you heard? I doubt whether she'll come back to the glen.'

'Then who, for heavens' sake?'

'Esther Richie. She's got the sweetest blue eyes. I found some ribbon exactly the same shade – '

'Davie, listen to me.' John pushed aside his accounts and faced him squarely. The face was guileless but John might have been addressing a criminal, so terrible was his tone. 'We've got to thrash this matter out, right from the start.' Davie didn't help. He sat there, smiling helpfully. 'I had hoped you'd got over such foolishness. Father thought you had once Morag went away.'

'I was very fond of Morag,' Davie agreed happily.

'But you'll be meeting young women every day from now on,' John thundered, 'women with blue eyes, married women!' He lowered his voice, mindful of other occupants of the house. 'You'll be selling them – garments!' John had a comprehensive knowledge of ladies' underwear, greater than that of most husbands but he never allowed himself to consider the *purpose* of the apparel. He knew the quality by fingering the material and the price by the amount of lace trimming; the connection with the female form he put from his mind.

'When we visit the houses, and talk to ladies and their maids, we have to be trusted,' he hissed. 'Our livelihood depends on it!'

'I'm looking forward to meeting them,' Davie assured him.

'But don't you understand what I'm saying? There can be no – no intimacy – with any of them. Not one. Is that clearly understood?' Davie's bright countenance fell slightly.

'I can chat to them a wee bit? Maybe recite a poem?'

'Only a short poem.' John was firm; time was money. 'Only if they particularly request it of you and . . . on condition there are always two persons present besides yourself. Remember that, Davie. If you forget yourself, lose your head only once, we're done for!' It was a dreadful warning, the voice of Jove himself. Davie was abashed.

'I never meant any harm, John. Those lassies at home, it was very pleasant talking to them. I think they enjoyed it, too.'

'No doubt, no doubt, but you're a businessman now and you mustn't forget it.' And because tomorrow was Sunday, John cleared away his accounts and took down the Bible and Pilgrim's Progress. 'It's past midnight. We'll get in bed and then we'll read for a bit. It's warmer that way.'

Davie effaced himself as best he could while John washed his collar, placing it next to the spare one on the mantelpiece. Then he brushed his suit, placed the trousers under the mattress and pulled on his nightshirt over the woollen combinations. The truckle bed was beneath his own and he wheeled it out, saying sadly, 'Mrs Beal thought this would suffice. I'd told her you were younger, you see. I fear you'll have to have mine, though.' John sighed. It was a comfortable bed and he'd enjoyed sleeping in it. Davie agreed apologetically. He managed to undress without treading on John. As he sat on it, the bedstead creaked ominously. John said anxiously, 'Try not to fling about when you get into it, Davie. I doubt the frame will stand it.'

They said their prayers and blew out the candle. Davie got out of bed once to take a final look at the hills which concealed London. The wind had blown away the smoke from the hundreds of chimneys and the stars were bright. 'How long before we leave here?'

'I'm in no hurry. There's money to be made in Darlington provided we work hard enough.'

'But we will go eventually?' Davie was surprised.

'Oh, yes, when the time is right.' John closed his eyes and Davie scrambled back into bed.

'What's she called?' he whispered into the darkness.

'Who?'

'Mrs Beal's daughter? The one that brings the hot water in the morning.'

'Emily. Now you go to sleep, Davie!'

CHAPTER FOUR

Other beginnings – Charlotte

In her cashier's cage in Armitage's, a grocery that sold the choicest ham in Darlington, Mrs Armitage gazed down fondly at her great-niece behind the butter counter: dear Charlotte! Today was a private anniversary; seventeen years to the day since Mrs Armitage's prayers were answered and Charlotte's mother Jane had arrived on the doorstep with the baby girl.

Poor Jane . . . Mrs Armitage's immense bosom and tight bodice quivered with emotion and strain. How desperately ill she'd been and what an unnecessary journey she'd had to New Zealand and back, for it had begun a mere ten miles away in a pit village where there had been no work.

Nothing unusual in that. Men had been laid off many times before but on this occasion the coal owners had shut the pit to force a drop in wages and miners, already on the breadline, refused to accept their terms. Jane's husband, Joseph, had been one of them.

Throughout the Durham coal field it was stalemate as owners sat it out, confident the men's spirit would break, but for once the miners discovered a solution. One of them had seen a poster on a wall in South Shields: 'Men wanted in New Zealand. Miners needed for the gold fields of Hokitika.'

Arguments split the village apart. Older folk didn't want to leave, Jane said and Mrs Armitage could well understand why not. New Zealand was on the other side of the world and for a village where most hadn't travelled more than a few miles from the house in which they'd been born – what courage to contemplate such a voyage! And for gold! To an unemployed pitman in 1877 that thought was intoxicating.

An elderly widow helped them make a decision. 'Old Lotte,' Jane had called her. When the coal owners closed the pit they'd also stopped payment of her meagre pension, then turned her out of her cottage for failing with the rent. Lotte had been too proud to ask for help. It was when her neighbours saw the bailiffs taking away her few sticks of furniture they realized what had happened. Jane and Joseph were distraught; Lotte had been a mother to them since their own parents died. The old woman listened to their protests with a faint smile and interrupted Joseph, 'Nay lad, I didna' tell thee for what could tha ha' done? Thee and Jane, tha've got nowt, same as meself.' She shushed Jane's weeping. 'Don't tek on, remember the bairn,' and to Joseph again, 'I'll not stop, pet. I've got a bit walk in front of me today.' She added quietly, 'I'll niver be a burden. A've not been afore, a'll not be now. And listen, both of ye – on ya' own ya'll manage but with me as well, it'd be impossible.'

'You're not going to the workhouse, Lotte!' The old woman put up a hand to stop Joseph's mouth and tried to ignore the horror in his eyes.

'A'can still work for ma living, Joseph Forrest, a'can still scrub floors for that's what a'll have to do in theer, a've got me strength yet,' and the young man whose arms were tough from the coalface hugged the arthritic wreck tenderly.

'You've got the courage for it, our Lotte, I'll give you that.'

Jane gave her bread and as a gift, a faded shawl that had once belonged to her mother. Lotte was delighted with it. 'Cherry red, ma favourite colour! A'll have to fight the men off when they see me in this, pet!' Then she gave them a last, fierce piece of advice, 'Leave here. There's nowt worth stoppin' for, niver

113

was. An' Jane's going to have that bairn so look to the future. New Zealand's got to be a better place than this.'

Jane kissed her for the last time. 'If it's a girl, she'll be named after you, Lotte.'

The following day there was another shock. The coal owners sent out notices: any man who had not reported back for work by 24th December would be dismissed and evicted from his home along with his family.

Those pieces of paper nailed to each cottage door convinced the waverers and for the remaining bitter weeks of that autumn, the villagers walked the countryside like gypsies, selling everything they possessed apart from the clothes on their backs and household necessities, to raise money for the voyage.

On their last night in England, they piled up wood in the village street, doors, banisters – any furniture that hadn't been sold – and on top of the pyre they flung the eviction orders. It was the finest bonfire there'd ever been, Jane told Mrs Armitage, but as excitement died along with the embers, everyone knew there was no turning back.

They'd set off at dawn up the old north road, fathers carrying the sacks and women the babies. It was dark before they'd crossed the Tyne bridge and saw the ship for the first time. That's when courage nearly failed, for the small cargo vessel was old with patched sails; surely destitution would be better than facing the oceans in that? As they waited nervously on the quayside, Joseph and some of the other men went on board and returned with a final item of bad news. The captain had asked to see their supplies of food and declared there wasn't enough. The voyage would take longer than they had supposed.

'Some of them began to cry when Joseph said that,' sighed Jane, 'Grown men, an' all. For we'd no money left by then.'

'What did you do?' asked Mrs Armitage.

'What could we do? There was only one thing left to sell. Joseph held out his hand, for he knew I'd understood, and I gave him my wedding ring.'

'Oh, my dear!'

Other women had followed suit, all except one who declared she would not go. Mr Armitage asked what had happened to her and Jane answered sadly, 'Last we saw of her, she and her

114

husband were walking back the way we'd come, in the sleet. They must've ended up like old Lotte.'

There was silence for a while. In the snug comfort of their room above the shop, Mr and Mrs Armitage had stared into the fire and and given thanks that they'd never had to make such a choice.

The voyage had been as long as the captain described and far worse than the villagers had imagined. They were herded together in one of the two cargo holds, men, women and children, each family divided from the rest by blankets nailed to the bulkheads. Then, after a storm when possessions rolled about chaotically, the tubs of flour and barrels of drinking water were firmly lashed down in the centre of the hold, cutting still further the available space.

'There was no privacy, not even what we'd known in the pit cottages. People got upset over every little thing, they were that close together,' said Jane. 'At first, what with the weather and everyone being ill, that was bad enough but when we'd gone a bit farther, where it was hot and there were flies, that was terrible! It wasn't so bad for the men. They could roll up their sleeves but there was nothing we could do.' Mrs Armitage understood; for a woman to undo the neck of her gown wouldn't have been seemly.

'What about – your baby?' she asked gently for Jane had looked so pitifully weak she was anxious for the tale to be finished.

'The captain told us right at the start there was no way he could guarantee we'd get to New Zealand before it was due. He'd got trading to do on the way, you see, and there were the winds. It was an old boat, he couldn't risk putting up too much sail. I wasn't too worried because Nelly was with us – she was always midwife in the village – but then there was the accident, to Joseph . . . ' The soft voice faltered and finally stopped as Jane wept. Mrs Armitage reached out to comfort her.

'My dear, not if you don't feel strong enough.'

'I'd rather tell you everything, then you'll know.'

It had happened during a squall in the southern ocean. The miners were on deck working alongside the crew, preferring the danger above to the foetid wet hell that their wives endured. Suddenly, the guardrail broke. One wave too many crashed down and it splintered like matchwood. A member of the crew, Sven, making his way forr'ard, reached for a support no longer

115

there. A sheet of water obliterated the deck and when it drained away, he'd disappeared.

Immediately the crew went into action, bringing down the main, turning the ship into wind. The lookout shouted himself hoarse, keeping an arm pointing steadily in Sven's direction. The miners stared out to sea, rubbing the wet from their eyes. The gap was widening with every second. 'He'll not make it,' said Joseph and beside him the others agreed. 'Come on,' Joseph urged, 'we've got to give him a chance.' They lashed a rope round his waist and he grabbed one of the cork life jackets.

The captain leaned from the wheelhouse and shrieked above the wind. 'I don't think Sven can swim!' Another wave smashed down, half drowning them and Joseph cried out in fear, 'Jesus God, I don't think I can, not in this lot!'

'When they told me about it,' Jane whispered, 'they said Joseph seemed to get a hold of himself after that for he turned to them and asked quite calm-like if the rope was fast and they were ready then he climbed on the rail and dived over the side.'

'How brave!' murmured Mrs Armitage, in tears. On the other side of the fire her spouse nodded in sorrowful agreement.

It had seemed an age before the miners saw Joseph surface and when they did, they'd begun cheering but one had steadied the rest and they'd started to pay out the rope, hand over hand as Joseph fought his way through the turbulence.

In the warm room, with no other sound but the slow tick of the clock, Jane had described a scene the Armitages could hardly comprehend. 'One of the men on that rope told me how it was . . .'

Terror had kept Sven afloat, the man said, but when he saw Joseph he acted like a wild thing, tearing off the life jacket the miner tried to pull over his head and clinging to his rescuer instead. Both arms wrapped round Joseph's shoulders. The lookout saw what was happening and screamed at the crew to haul in as fast as they could. The skin burned from their hands as they tugged and heaved.

The double weight finally reached the side and Sven gave a last hysterical thrust in an effort to reach the rigging lines. Sailors pulled him on deck but Joseph hung limply from the line making no attempt to save himself, battered against the side by the waves. When they managed to haul him aboard, he was dead.

The captain had ordered the body to be taken below and Mrs Armitage's eyes widened in horror, 'Not into the same hold?'

'There was nowhere else,' Jane replied simply, 'but when I saw his poor dead face . . . ' Tears ran unchecked. At her knee, the toddler implored Mammy for a cuddle and for a time, mother and baby rocked together in grief.

'So that's where Joseph lies,' said Jane eventually, 'somewhere in that great ocean. It was a Christian burial, Nelly told me.'

'My poor dear sister . . . ' Mrs Armitage's bosom heaved again, this time in memory of the dead Beatrice, 'She never saw her son after they quarrelled, you know.'

'No,' Jane agreed, 'and Joseph could be as stubborn as his mother. He never took me to meet her because of that quarrel. He only told me a long time afterwards that his mother had a married sister in Darlington.'

'A jewel,' said Mr Armitage suddenly, feeling the description inadequate, 'a treasure. *Sans pareil*.' And his spouse bowed her head graciously, in acknowledgement. She looked at the child, now peacefully sucking her thumb, 'Poor dear Beatrice, fancy never meeting her grand-daughter. Was Charlotte born on that terrible ship?'

'No. My pains began when we were nearly there. Someone told the captain. He came down to the hold himself. I heard him telling Nelly he'd do everything he could to make land in time. He'd been that upset over Joseph you see . . . then I heard Nelly say I shouldn't be having a baby at all, that I was too small . . . '

'Anyway we reached land and they tried to be gentle. It was a bright morning, I remember that, and I was lying on a beach. There was this man – I didn't know who he was, a sort of doctor – one of them had run into Hokitika to fetch him, he was there beside me telling the captain he'd have to kill me to save the baby and the captain was shouting and swearing, saying he'd got to save the both of us, and the pains were terrible by then . . . So the doctor did what he had to . . . ' Jane shuddered, eyes closed and Mr Armitage gripped the arms of his chair. 'Mercifully, I don't remember much after that,' she whispered.

'Next thing, I was in this house. It had wooden floors and

you could feel every footstep through those floors. Nelly and the other women were there. I could hear them talking though they thought I couldn't. They thought I was going to die but I could hear the baby crying so I knew she'd survived.' Jane broke off to kiss the child passionately. 'And when I knew that, I couldn't let go, could I?' she murmured. 'Not when I'd got her to look after?'

Mr Armitage was a man of very little stature but tremendous heart. He was at his best in a crisis. He rose to his feet and cleared his throat. 'We have listened to a history so harrowing, it is almost beyond comprehension. And of suffering . . . !' He shook his head at the enormity of it, 'But Mrs Forrest has been spared – and must be nourished. Sustained. For she is above all things – a mother.' He bowed in tribute, rang the bell and told Bertha to bring the port. 'May I, as a lesser mortal, a mere male of the species, also recommend a bowl of broth?' Jane smiled wanly.

'I'll try. I don't seem to be able to keep food down nowadays.' Mr Armitage gave orders firmly: the very best butter spread on the thinnest slices of bread to tempt the invalid. He glanced uncertainly at Charlotte, 'And whatever is wholesome for the infant,' he concluded. Bertha was female, she would understand. He returned to his chair as Jane was finishing her story.

'When I'd recovered enough to take notice, most of them had got over the disappointment and had begun making plans.'

'Disappointment?' asked Mr Armitage.

'Why, yes. By the time we got there, there was no more gold. They didn't need miners any more – Hokitika was a ghost town.'

For Mrs Armitage, the day Jane arrived also marked the end of a journey but one that had taken her only as far as Newcastle. There, a few days previously, she had sat in a Consulting Room facing a specialist across his desk. He had shaken his head. She had looked at him in disbelief, bosom a-quiver, setting the jet buttons shimmering.

'No chance at all, Mr Simpson Vance?'

'None, I fear.'

'But – why?'

'I'm afraid – your age is one reason, dear lady.'

The large woman sat up sharply. 'But I'm the same age now as I was on my first visit. Older in fact. By ten weeks.' The fashionable doctor examined the exquisite blotter on his desk.

'That is so, yes,' he murmured to the tooled leather.

'Then kindly explain why I have been invited to waste my money on ten further visits?'

The gentleman was accustomed to gratitude even if it was undeserved. 'Mrs Armitage, you asked for my help.'

'But you enquired my age on the occasion of my first visit. You knew then you would be unable to help. That didn't stop you taking my guineas!' Indignation made the jet tremble. She rose. 'Mr Simpson Vance, I find you – a charlatan!'

A starched attendant came swiftly in answer to the urgent bell. She held open the door and Mrs Armitage swept outside; Boudicca about to leap into her chariot. But it wasn't the Romans she faced on her return that afternoon, it was her husband.

Gold lettering informed passers-by in Skinnergate that Mr Armitage cured ham and bacon on the premises, stocked a selection of the world's choicest teas and was at all times, eager to oblige. It was perhaps not surprising, as he carried out all that he promised, that Mr Armitage was the owner of a prosperous business.

When his spouse was seen alighting from the station cab, he snapped his fingers. The boy put down the bucket of sawdust and ran to the door. He stood to attention as the proprietor's lady entered. There was a chorus of greeting. Mrs Armitage bowed to regular customers, not too low of course but judging intimacy to a nicety. To any whose account had over-run the three month limit, she nodded far more distantly, causing agitation in more than one breast. In a stately manner she proceeded toward the baize-covered door which led to the back premises. Mr Armitage excused himself to a customer and hurried after the Junoesque figure, a tug following a battleship, and held open the door. 'Thank you, Mr Armitage, I will order you tea.' She inclined her head graciously and the door closed behind her. A small sigh ran through the shop.

'A remarkable woman,' the customer confided to Mr Armitage.

'Remarkable,' he agreed solemnly. 'And,' his voice sank to a conspiratorial level, 'one of the loveliest of her sex, in my opinion.' Ham was sliced and wrapped; the patron departed.

Upstairs in her front drawing room with its bow window over Skinnergate, Mrs Armitage waited until the maid had set down the tray and lit the spirit lamp. 'You may tell the master tea is ready, Bertha.' The girl withdrew. Then, alone, Mrs Armitage allowed the tears to fall. They gushed over the jet, spurting copiously with each heave of the magnificent chest. A lace handkerchief was applied but was quickly saturated. Emotion prevented her searching for another. Fortunately Mr Armitage arrived equipped with a large red silk one.

'There, there . . . ' he said several times, 'Don't upset yourself, pray don't, Mrs Armitage.' She gushed again and he waited until the convulsion had passed. 'It isn't the end of the world, beloved,' he said.

'It is for me,' she replied and he was silent.

The water boiled for a long time before it was poured over the best Darjeeling. So little was left in the kettle, there was scarcely enough for two cups. Mr Armitage recognized a crisis and rang again for the maid. 'Fetch another ounce and refill that kettle, Bertha.'

'Yes, sir,' she whispered and fled. The routine had been broken; her world was threatened.

During his over-long absence, the shop buzzed with rumours.

'Very ill, I believe.'

'A specialist in Newcastle . . . '

'Really? How dreadful!'

'So I've heard.'

Faces were composed to receive the worst possible tidings. Mr Armitage re-entered his shop with a grave countenance. He consulted the watch on his heavy gold Albert.

'We will close five minutes early this evening,' he announced, 'Mrs Armitage is indisposed. Nothing serious.' He looked round the circle of faces and repeated the words, then added, 'I believe she requires my company to make herself easy.'

Approval, satisfaction, was immediate. Only indisposed! Nothing serious – what a relief! The empire was safe. And the bolts were pushed home, the stiff blind lowered at nine fifty-five precisely.

Once she had changed out of her 'best' and was comfortable in cerise cashmere with boned collar and bustle, Mrs Armitage was able to enjoy a strengthening bowl of beef tea. The storm had passed. Melancholy alas, remained. 'I was hoping to give you an heir, Mr Armitage.'

'I know, my love, but it doesn't matter.'

'It does to me.'

'It's God's Will, beloved.'

'It was a waste of five guineas!' she retorted.

A little surprised, he took another sip of port. 'I'm sure the consultant did his best, my love. And he was recommended.'

'Fiddlesticks! It's a conspiracy. Doctors!' The contempt would have made Hippocrates wince. 'He said it was my age!'

Her husband was astonished. 'But you are only thirty-nine!' She bit back the word 'Forty' and was mollified. How easily he lost count. But Mr Armitage did even better. 'To me, beloved, you will always be twenty-five,' and even the most prosaic of women must enjoy those words, spoken as they were with utter sincerity.

A fresh scrap of lace was applied to her eyes. The bosom heaved but this time it was a mere tremor. 'Mr Armitage, you are a flatterer!' Satisfied, he stood and opened the tantalus.

'A glass of port, Mrs A? It will restore your spirits.'

(i)

On Sunday the congregation at St Cuthbert's were relieved to observe that Mrs Armitage was completely recovered. The signs were there for all to see: both the beaver hat with the violets and the matching muff. Behind, bobbing in her wake, Mr Armitage nodded and smiled, acknowledging good wishes from customers on both sides of the aisle. 'Wonderfully well, yes . . . A remarkable woman.'

It was perhaps a trial for her that the sermon concerned the slaying of the innocents but so many weaker vessels were moved to sobs that her own discreet tears went unnoticed. It was during the walk home that the lady gave vent to inner feelings.

'If it is God's Will, Mr Armitage, then he moves in a very

mysterious way indeed. Why should he prevent me from bearing a child?' Her look heavenwards was thunderous. Mr Armitage knew it was not a moment for sympathy. Silently he held open the gate to the alley and offered his arm as they approached the back door.

Bertha was hovering in the passage behind the shop. 'If you please, mum, someone is here.' They looked round in the gloom. Did the glazed jardinière conceal a person? But Bertha had been trained. 'I asked her to step into the morning room, mum. Not upstairs. And I left the door open a crack, to keep an eye on the baby.'

The Armitages looked at one another, mystified, but as always, correct. 'If you will go up, Mrs A, I will interview this – person. You were quite right, Bertha,' he added. He waited at the foot of the stairs until his wife had turned the bend, David protecting Goliath, then he went into the 'morning room', more a storeroom behind the shop which had a name but was never used.

Sheer will power had kept Jane alive. As she lay in the wooden house, recovering so very slowly, she learned of the disappointment then the plans as the villagers faced up to the future.

The captain had advised them. After hearing their despair that first evening he told them if the gold was worked out, that was an end of it but New Zealand was still the land of opportunity.

'They need men, especially those with muscle.' He looked round the weary circle. 'Rest up a bit before offering yourselves.'

'Offering for what?'

'Sheep-farming. They always need men to help with that down on the plains.'

At first, the miners were indignant. They had a trade. They hadn't travelled this far to be labourers. One managed to sum it up for the rest. 'We planned it together, coming here. That was how we managed to come this far, by being in it together.' Other heads nodded: this was the crux of it. 'What you're saying is,' he went on, 'you're telling us to split up. Go off on our own. That could finish us.'

The captain had brought his old ship all this way. He'd made landfall where they wanted it though none had thought to thank him for it. Now he tried to put himself in their shoes. He began by describing the land about which they knew so little and they tried to understand. Until now their entire world had centred on the pit village.

He put the choices plainly. If any wanted to chance their luck in a town, he would give free passage to Christchurch or Dunedin. Those prepared to try for sheep, he'd take as far as the plains and, after refitting for the passage home, the final offer was a free voyage for any who would crew for him.

(ii)

A few months later, when the old boat had once again tied up at Hokatika, those who were left told the captain they would stay where they were, all except Jane. She was far too weak to offer for work. There was only one thing left for her to do and that meant returning to England.

The captain was frightened at the sight of her, so pitifully wasted and unable to walk without a stick. 'Why not stay, m'dear,' he urged. 'It'll not be easy, making passage, and you still need rest. Then there's Sven, willing to marry you to make amends. Will you not consider it? He'd not make a bad husband.'

But Jane shook her head. 'I've had one good man. That's more than most. I know I've not much time left but I'm not feared, for I shall be with my Joseph again. There's just the baby to see to first.'

'But what will happen to her, back in England?'

'Joseph had an aunty back home. He was too proud to beg when the pit closed but I'm sure he'd understand now. I want my baby to be with her family.'

When they set sail, Jane found she'd been given the captain's own quarters. 'Only the best for Joseph's wee girl,' he told her.

So Jane lay in his cot with Charlotte beside her, watching sea-dappled light make patterns on the tattered picture above their heads: a drawing of a pithead in a green field with a cuddy that had a leg at each corner.

She had dragged herself onto a train to Darlington and walked the last painful mile. Then she waited, nervously, for the Armitages to return from church. Mr Armitage, though small, had stared at her most severely. 'Yes?'

'Joseph Forrest was my husband. He's dead but this is his bairn.'

'Who?'

Dear God, after all that voyaging was this the wrong place after all?'

'Are you married to Joseph's aunty?' Jane faltered. 'He told me she worked in a shop.'

'I am married to a remarkable woman,' Mr Armitage was even more severe. 'And this is our Establishment.' Never a shop; it was the pinnacle of Mr Armitage's achievement. 'But wait one moment, if you please,' for the significance of Jane's words was beginning to dawn on him. This could prove momentous and must be shared with his Goddess. 'See that the child doesn't bring the cloth down.' Charlotte had discovered the bobble fringing on the chenille tablecloth. Jane stretched out a hand to restrain her and Mr Armitage disappeared. Outside, Bertha listened breathlessly.

Upstairs, the jet quivered under the strain. 'Are you quite sure she is who she says she is? Did you ask to see her lines?'

He was lost in admiration: what a woman! 'I fear I didn't think to ask,' Mr Armitage admitted, 'Shall I go down again?'

'What is it?' she asked. He was bewildered.

'Pardon, my love?'

'A boy or girl?'

'Oh . . . a little girl, I think.' And Mrs Armitage was not going to be ungrateful to Providence at such a moment.

'Ask Bertha to show them up,' she said.

So Charlotte was received into the bosom of her family and Jane watched as Mrs Armitage's stout arms reached out in welcome. Charlotte smiled to see the shiny buttons. Her tiny hands touched them for she was never shy. Her great-aunt kissed her and Jane knew her own journey was at an end. Joseph's child was safe.

She lingered only a few weeks more. Life had been too hard and she was in so much pain. She slipped quietly away while around her, all was anguish. Mrs Armitage was also very angry indeed. It was all the doctor's fault; he'd no business letting Jane die like that! The unfortunate man knew he'd be blamed from the moment he was first consulted. One glance at Jane's skeletal face and his heart sank; she'd lost the will to live. He tried to warn Mrs Armitage but she spoke tartly of excuses. He then attempted to explain to Mr Armitage but he was still convinced of the efficacy of beef tea.

Indeed, Jane was tempted with every delicacy, but it was too late. Her final effort was to thank the Armitages with a weak pressure of her hand. As Charlotte was held up for a last kiss, Jane managed to whisper, 'Be good now . . . ' before she ceased to breathe.

The doctor was at her bedside. If he'd been able to resurrect the corpse, he would gladly have done so. The wrath that descended on his head was terrible to behold. It was an hour before he made his escape and Mrs Armitage admitted defeat. She gave orders to Bertha to admit the laying-out woman and joined her husband in the sitting room. 'We must give Jane a decent send-off,' she told him. 'Beatrice would expect it of me.'

The horses were plumed and there were three carriages for mourners. All the shop assistants attended, provided with black gloves and bands. An announcement in the window, propped up on the stilton, respectfully informed patrons that the establishment would remain closed all day, and the doorknocker was draped in black ribbons. Mrs Armitage wore crêpe; Charlotte was swathed in the stuff. Word of the magnificence spread. As Mrs Armitage observed sadly, there was quite a respectable turn-out.

Her husband was downcast too, by the estimate, detailed by Mr Fawcett before the cortège departed.

'Nothing but the best, Mr Armitage, I assure you. Coffin, h'oak, not h'elm, four pounds and ten shillings. Underbearers ten shillings, hearse and pair plus two drivers, er . . . silk crêpe for scarves, gloves, cloaks for the use of, etc, cakes and wine, total altogether: ten pounds.

'Pall for the use of, one pound and my own humble fees, er five shillings. Making a final total of, er . . . ' But Mr Armitage was there before him.

'Sixteen pounds and five shillings,' he said automatically, his mind reeling.

'Quite so, Mr Armitage, er – quite so. All excellent quality, of course. And my best, er, service, at all times.'

Mr Armitage's sombre bearing as he followed the Sexton up the aisle was much admired. As he gazed at the man's back he couldn't help remembering that this was costing him an additional three shillings.

'You would have thought it was his own daughter,' was heard on all sides. Indeed, once or twice he thought so himself. After all, had she been, it couldn't have cost him any more.

So Jane was laid to rest with greater ceremony than she had ever known. When the wreaths were examined and admired, when the drawings of a marble weeping angel were exhibited, the mourners finished the ham and departed.

Later, in front of the fire, Mr Armitage contemplated – happiness. It had been worth it. Poor Jane. He wished she could have lived. If only she'd been strong enough to manage a little of his Invalid's Chicken Jelly, she might have turned the corner. But his spouse was herself again, no doubt about it. The crisis was past. No longer during the night did their bed shake with sobs when she thought of her barren state. Instead, from the deep cavity of her chest contented snores reverberated. If only Jane could have lived, too. Such a pretty, fragile little woman. Mr Armitage mused at the vicissitudes of life and admired the ruby glint of his port.

When his wife joined him, the nurse brought Charlotte to be kissed goodnight. 'You must call me Aunt Armitage,' the child was told. Fascinated by the tortoiseshell combs in the magnificent coiffeur, the baby appeared to listen intently, and those were in fact the first words she uttered.

(iv)

Charlotte's education began early at a nearby Dame School.

Mrs Armitage went to inspect it and to introduce the new pupil. After pleasantries, Charlotte was bidden to wait outside.

'I ought to explain,' Mrs Armitage confided, 'that although Charlotte is delightful, most intelligent – far beyond her little friends in ability in my opinion – she can be stubborn.' The Dame nodded sympathetically; she'd dealt with awkward children before.

As she was only four years old, Charlotte was taken every day by Bertha and her lunch handed to an older girl for safekeeping. Among the other little girls in the beginner's class, Charlotte's chin stuck out prominently. Her aunt had not exaggerated about her temperament. But after a tussle, when the Dame had had to punish her and Charlotte spent the day in the corner, a truce was reached. Lessons were over, the other children had left and she was told she might get down from the punishment stool. Only then did the first tear fall. The Dame realized what an effort of will that had taken for such a little girl. She kissed her, took Charlotte on her knee and together they went through the offending lesson until the child had mastered it. After that, schooldays passed without incident.

There were not many subjects. Each child learned to read and write using a copperplate style of loops and hooks that would stay with them for life. The dates of kings and queens sufficed for history, capitals and rivers of Europe for geography. When, due to unforeseen circumstances, Charlotte had to leave at the age of seven, she could read, express herself clearly and recite her times tables. 'You will learn everything else you need to know in the shop,' said her aunt between sobs, 'I want you beside me, dear.'

For that remarkable woman had been called upon to prove her worth. It was when the cup smashed against the brass fender that she realized all was not well. Mr Armitage hadn't cried out, hadn't moved, for the stroke had paralyzed him. The doctor was summoned and came with fear in his heart. He was relieved to be able to describe the attack as mild. Mrs Armitage couldn't believe her ears. What was mild about an infliction that reduced a man to a dribbling wreck? That twisted his face into such a ghastly smile?

The medical man tried to assert his authority, to frighten Mrs Armitage with tales of how much worse it might have been but decided against it. He had to admit once more to failure. There was absolutely nothing he could do.

So Charlotte was summoned by the breathless maid. She had already learned sufficient decorum from her aunt to take charge of the situation. 'We will walk back quietly,' she told Bertha, 'otherwise people might talk.' They arrived at the shop after the doctor had left and Mrs Armitage had regained her composure. Holding Charlotte's hand tightly they visited the stricken grocer. Despite her youth, Charlotte didn't flinch.

'We will manage between us, dear,' her aunt said. 'Pray go and ask Mr Collins to remain for a few moments after closing time.'

Mr Armitage's senior assistant bowed on receiving the message and at ten PM passed through the baize door. Behind him, other assistants went home whispering. They had seen the doctor's trap and there had been much speculation but no one knew what had actually happened.

Mrs Armitage poured tea into the second-best china cups and gestured to the absent master in the bedroom above. 'As you are probably aware, Mr Collins, I have very little faith in doctors.' He bowed and stirred in the sugar. 'Mr Armitage's complaint may take a little time to cure. We must all be patient.' Mr Collins bowed a third time. Long years of service in the 'Establishment' had rendered him the most discreet of men. Mrs Armitage found him a great comfort. She sipped and continued, 'We, that is Mr Armitage and myself, have decided it would be in order for you to assume the position of manager during his absence. In a temporary capacity, naturally.' Mr Collins recognized that his moment had come at last. He put down his cup, patted the moisture from his moustaches and declared he would be honoured to oblige.

For the next half hour they discussed the day-to-day running of the shop. Mr Collins knew who would be best employed on curing hams during Mr Armitage's absence, who on the buying of teas and coffee from the warehouses. They debated who should be promoted to take his own place now that he would be attending to important patrons. All was arranged to their mutual satisfaction and after expressing delight at a rise of two and sixpence, making a total wage of one pound, twelve shillings and sixpence per week, Mr Collins accepted a second cup of Darjeeling.

'There remains one other vacancy, madam, as I see it. A junior one. We have no one for butter and cheese.'

But the remarkable woman was ahead of him. 'I have decided that Charlotte will learn the business,' she said.

Standing on a box to reach the marble slab, Charlotte began. It was an age of slicing by hand. 'Two pennyworth of Cheddar . . .'

'One pound of best butter, a quarter of Wensleydale and a knob of lard, miss.' She sliced them all and enjoyed it.

Rising with her aunt at six every morning, standing behind the counter six days a week, Charlotte grew from a child into a young woman. Above her in the wooden cage overlooking the shop, her aunt wrote out the orders, checked the bookkeeping and 'kept an eye on things'. If the other assistants wondered at the length of Mr Armitage's illness their curiosity went unsatisfied. Charlotte never gossiped and Mr Collins hadn't got where he was without being utterly discreet.

Mrs Armitage remained the sole source of information concerning her husband's health. She was happy to describe his progress, to pass on his views about the weather, Mr Gladstone and the declining standards of morality among the working classes. If the doctor was surprised at his patient's loquacity he knew better than to say so. As a physician unable to offer a cure he understood perfectly his position in Mrs Armitage's eyes. His deportment was almost humble when he presented his monthly account.

The grocer did not improve. During the next few years he had a serious of strokes, each, though mild, more enfeebling. But his secret was kept. Between them Mrs Armitage, Bertha and Charlotte protected him from the world, sat beside him and read aloud every evening for half an hour. With the help of a visiting nurse, they washed and cared for his helpless body. Occasionally his wife thought she saw a smile of gratitude on the stricken mouth. She was satisfied and so perhaps, was he. He had after all, married a remarkable woman.

CHAPTER FIVE

Mary

Across the table in Coburg Street John sighed. 'She's sending another one down.'

'Anyone we know?'

'You might. Some cousin of the Hamiltons but I can't remember ever meeting her – Mary Hamilton?'

Davie considered. 'There were always too many cousins, according to Georgie. They lived out at Briaghlann – their father never had any work. Some of the children had a bit of schooling – Mary . . . Mary?' Davie shook his head. 'I can't recall her. One of the older girls was a cripple – '

'It would hardly be that one!'

'No. She would've gone into service, it was all she was fit for.' Davie began to clear the breakfast things. He could scarcely put faces to any of the old friends nowadays. It was only five years since he'd come south but the peninsula was a world away.

John frowned over the writing. 'Mistress Shields says she writes in haste but I wish she'd spared five minutes more. Oh, I give up!' He pushed his chair under the table, 'I've not got the time to spare today and that's a fact.'

The years had made John stern. Occasions when he'd denied himself in an effort to save for the future had hardened him. The shyness was suppressed so that others wouldn't take advantage but the effect was to make him appear dry and humourless. He'd grown even further from his roots.

These were turbulent times, with men constantly moving away from the land, seeking a toe-hold in the bursting industrial slums. When employers took advantage and lowered wages still further, there was an explosion of unrest. Last year alone thirty million working days had been lost in stoppages at work. John was loud with indignation now that he'd moved one rung up the ladder but Davie remembered their father, grey-faced with the effort of making ends meet. He held his tongue. Perhaps John was right. Maybe a pound a week was nonsense for a married man to expect. It seemed like riches to Davie, who was only allowed three shillings spending money a week by John.

He'd striven to fulfil John's hopes and didn't realize he'd exceeded them, nor was it part of John's creed to praise. But Davie's natural ebullience and his genuine liking for people made him popular in a way John's earnestness never could. From the first Sunday, the tall figure with the flaming hair and an infectious laugh was immediately spotted by the ladies in the congregation. John was alerted but he needn't have worried: Davie found it impossible to single out one amongst so many.

John watched the young women laugh and flutter like butter-flies around his brother and tried to puzzle out why. Was it that 'charm' their father had written of, was that it? He didn't understand what charm was. Sober by comparison, he waited patiently. None of it mattered so long as Davie and he were successful.

Before either of them left Gordon's employ, they'd worked up a considerable custom in Darlington that was entirely theirs. It was all part of John's plan for the future. The ever-expanding size of the town helped and eventually they needed assistance.

Gordon had no objection if they arranged matters themselves provided a premium was paid, so first one then a second young man made the journey south. After trying to interest them in a convivial glass or two and failing, Gordon washed his hands and left the Highlanders to their own devices. Each had a reference from Helen and each was proving to be a good businessman, so why worry.

The day his contract ended there was no way in which Gordon could persuade John to remain. His niche was ready at the warehouse. This time there was nothing more binding than a handshake between him and Mr Richardson but there was trust too, that could not be shaken.

In his new office, the businessmen that came and went, the sums that changed hands, would have raised eyebrows had they been made public. As well as the declining trades of wool and meat, the Quaker had invested heavily in the new Bessamer steel process. When he saw the size of that investment, John gave a silent whistle but he never spoke of it, not even to Davie. Confidentiality was a sacred trust.

He and Davie still lived in Coburg Street but not with Mrs Beal. He'd never admit it but it was the truckle bed that convinced John they should move. Taking a house, with a loan from Barclays, who had taken over Backhouses bank, was a risk – but not, John argued, if they sub-let as others did. That way they could recoup any outlay.

But the cost of bare essentials staggered him and he called a halt. Plundering precious savings was more than John could bear. They would pause and reconsider; sub-letting could wait.

(i)

Alex McKie's generation looked on sadly as the migration from the peninsula continued. They'd fought for years for the right of a son to inherit a croft. Parliament had now granted that right but how few sons remained! The lure of steady work proved too strong.

Helen Shields had also taken it on herself to find suitable places for her pupils outside the region. Her instinct was still to abhor 'service' – any pupils of hers could do better than that! Instead, girls were encouraged to become governesses or nurses in Inverness or Glasgow. The more adventurous travelled to England.

That was when John discovered he was expected to meet such young women as were due in the north-east and chaperone them at interviews. John sighed but complied. It wouldn't be proper for a woman to venture alone and wasn't he still in the school mistress's debt? Until that was repaid he would do as he was bidden.

His letters to Helen were far more formal nowadays. The camaraderie that had once existed was gone. John would never admit that his former idol had shortcomings, that her reference to 'what might have been' could still make him miserable, but there was a distance between them that was more than physical. Once his debt to her was discharged, he told himself, he would be free of Helen Shields at last.

He handed the letter to Davie. 'She writes that she depends on me to do what I can for this – Mary Hamilton – to "stand by her". Presumably she means at some interview. I can't make head nor tail of the rest of it. She doesn't say whether the girl intends going for nursing, or what. Simply that the impetuous Miss Hamilton insists on coming to England immediately and is due in Darlington this evening.' Davie smothered a laugh at John's annoyance: that anyone should dare treat his brother in such cavalier fashion.

'Maybe Miss Hamilton has something important lined up that cannot wait. Does Mistress Shields suggest where she is to stay? The interview, whatever it's for, will be tomorrow at the earliest. Coming from that family, I doubt the girl has two farthings to rub together but she cannot stay here, not with me away for two nights!' John didn't find this amusing, either.

'Of course she can't stay here. Apart from the impropriety, where would she sleep? We haven't got a spare bed.'

'She can have mine!' Davie flung his arms wide happily, 'She can keep it warm and well-aired till I get back!'

'I will enquire of Mrs Beal if our old room is to let,' John replied primly, putting an end to it. 'Now have you got time to make a few purchases? I think we ought to offer her tea.'

'What shall I buy?' John thought for a moment then wrote a careful list. He opened the small cash box in which he kept their housekeeping and gave Davie two shillings.

'She would come tonight,' he fussed, 'when it's my evening at the Debating Society.'

Davie swept the two coins into his purse.

'There'll be some change,' John reminded him.

'Yes, John.'

'Go to Armitage's. I went last week. Their ham is better and it's only a farthing a pound more. We can afford a farthing to give this Miss Hamilton a decent bit of ham.'

So for the first time, Davie met Charlotte, now standing without the aid of a box, dispensing cheese, butter and sugar under the fond eye of her aunt. He saw a slim woman of eighteen with masses of curly hair brushed into a chignon on top of her head. Sunlight showed glints of gold among the brown. The chin was prominent, it was true, but Davie was young. He noticed only that her eyes were very blue. They reminded him of someone else, he couldn't remember who. It didn't matter: they surveyed him coolly. He was about to present John's list when Mr Collins stepped forward and took it. 'Shall I, Miss Forrest? I can see you're busy. This way, sir, if you please,' and Davie was forced to follow.

Mr Collins handed the list to another assistant and Davie turned back to gaze at Charlotte. She did indeed have another customer. Davie had been so dazzled he hadn't noticed the chap before. He heard him begin to protest, 'I say . . . look here.'

'Yes, sir?' The tone was neutral but the demeanour was a little stiffer.

'You haven't weighed any of these, you know.' The young blade pointed nonchalantly with his cane; 'Mama's not payin' for short weight, I can tell you.' The doting mother hurried across, babbling nervously.

'Henry, please! It's not necessary to ask them to do that – '

'You will find we do not sell short in this Establishment.' The bell-like voice was no longer neutral but icy. Henry's mother tried to ease the situation.

'Miss Forrest knows what she's doing, dear. She is Mrs Armitage's niece.'

'I don't care whose demned niece she is, Mama. You're not payin' until all those items have been properly weighed.' In the silence Davie heard one of the other assistants catch her breath. Charlotte sounded perfectly calm.

'Mr Collins, the scales if you please.' The temporary acting manager moved swiftly. He snapped his fingers and the boy

134

rushed to take the various portions of ham, butter and cheese, placing each item one by one on to the scales. Mr Collins' husky voice, called the results.

'A quarter of parmesan . . . pound and a half best butter . . . three quarters of lard . . . pound of sugar loaf . . . pound and a half of ham.' He turned with relief. 'Everything full weight, Mrs Appleyard.' The mother was bright red with embarrassment.

'Thank you so much. Pray have them sent,' but Henry hadn't finished.

'I still say that young gel should've weighed 'em first.'

Charlotte had had enough. Reaching over the counter she took the cane from the grey-gloved hand. 'May I?' Balancing it on her palm she considered for a moment. 'Seven and one quarter ounces, Mr Collins.' In the shop the silence was profound. The boy took it from her, looking fearful.

My goodness, I hope you're right, thought Davie. As if it were fine porcelain, Mr Collins placed the cane delicately across the scale and began placing the weights on the opposite side. At seven ounces the needle began to swing. You could hear several intakes of breath as he added the final tiny nugget of brass. There was a quiver and the needle registered: the balance was exact.

Most gave a discreet sigh of relief but Davie laughed aloud, crying, 'Well done, lassie!' Charlotte quelled him with a look. She was not taking part in a circus! She returned the cane to its owner with her most gracious smile.

'You were right to insist, sir. I might have been incorrect.' Then she turned to Mrs Appleyard. 'I hope you are fully recovered from your cold. The weather this time of year, so inclement.' The lady gushed with relief.

'Yes indeed, so much better. Henry's down from Oxford. He can stay with us one more week then he has to join his friends in Switzerland.' Charlotte inclined her head toward him.

'I trust you enjoy the remainder of your stay, Mr Appleyard.' The young man thwacked the side of his boot with the offending cane and his mother hurried them both toward the door.

'My respects to your aunt,' she called. Mr Collins bowed them over the threshold.

Davie's order, neatly parcelled, was handed to him by Miss Compton. She was young and pretty and she smiled, but he never noticed. He went over to Charlotte. 'Well done,' he said again. She looked at him, blue eyes completely reserved. Davie wasn't giving in. 'I think you know my brother, John McKie.'

Charlotte remembered every customer who paid promptly. 'I believe we have had the pleasure.' Her tone was one degree less frosty.

'I'm Davie. Davie McKie.'

Charlotte, the perfect assistant, was also a woman.

'Pray call again.'

(ii)

John hurried into the scullery in Coburg Street and sluiced himself under the tap. Apart from the joy of opening the front door with his own key, this was the most luxurious moment of the day. A tap with a constant supply of water! He shared his mother's ecstasy at the experience. All those childhood days, filling buckets at the spring and, when the frost was thick, using a stone to break the ice. Those were over now that they had this miracle in their own house.

And Coburg Street was so modern! The very latest sanitary arrangements in the back yard, the privy with a purpose-built ashpit beside it. And the drains were excellent. There hadn't been one case of typhoid at this end of the town. Oh yes, he and Davie had made the right choice. He turned the magic on and off for the sheer pleasure of watching the cascade of silver explode in the sink.

The cold water washed away his irritation as he knew it would. He towelled vigorously, full of well-being, and selected a clean collar. He had to hurry, to meet the Glasgow train. He'd have tea with this Miss Hamilton then deliver her to Mrs Beal before going off to the glories of a debate at the Lit and Phil. Tonight he was opposing the motion that 'Anticipation brings greater happiness than Realization'. What nonsense! A man must work to make his dreams come true, only then would he know happiness. Anything else was a fallacy. Why were we put on earth if not to work – and to achieve. Oh yes, John could oppose that motion wholeheartedly.

As he struggled with his stud he looked at the kitchen table. Davie had done his best. They didn't yet possess a cloth so their assorted pieces of china stood on a sheet of red paper. In the centre on a white plate was the ham, flanked by a loaf and butter. Davie had put the receipt and change beside John's place with a note. 'I think we should shop at Armitage's more often. Back from Leeds on Thursday. Davie.' Gordon was having problems with one of his suppliers and Davie had been despatched to sort matters out.

On the station platform, John re-read Helen's letter. It irritated him yet again. Usually she gave such clear instructions; this time there wasn't even a hint of what had been arranged.

I trust you will do what is right and stand by Mary, John. I know I can rely on you to do your duty and do what may be necessary to help her. She has decided to leave for England immediately and there is no more time to arrange matters further.

His duty? Mistress Shields had never used that word before. Was it because of haste or was this occasion different? He wished Davie could have remembered something of Mary Hamilton. She must be a very distant connection of Wee Georgie.

Mrs Beal hadn't been pleased when he'd called. Gentlemen lodgers were one thing; a young woman was a different matter entirely. John protested. Miss Hamilton must be respectable otherwise Mistress Shields would never have sent her. Mrs Beal sniffed and John's reputation, so jealously guarded, nearly disappeared in that sniff.

And now the train was late; it really was too bad. He wanted to rehearse his speech once more before this evening. In the Lit and Phil there would be business colleagues. A man couldn't afford to make a bad impression. John stuffed Helen's letter back in his pocket and took out his notes instead. Silently, he mouthed the opening text. He'd managed to find several useful quotations and he intended using every single one.

As passengers alighted and straggled past the ticket collector,

John reached the climax of his argument. In his mind's ear he could hear the applause.

'Would you be John McKie? I'm Mary Hamilton.'

Shocked, he raised his hat. It was the cripple. She faced him, the club foot tilting her body, the worn cloak clutched as if to prevent the world seeing her deformity. John was horrified. What on earth was Mistress Shields thinking of? This young woman would be unemployable. He cleared his throat. 'Have you any luggage?' She indicated the old leather bag.

'Only this.' He signalled to the boy with the barrow. The sad little offering was put inside and the three of them set off down the steep incline. Neither of them spoke. Outside the house, the boy was paid and John unlocked the door.

'Please go inside and make yourself comfortable,' he said. 'I will have a word with Mrs Beal, where you are to stay.' Mary limped into the parlour.

Lace curtains had twitched when he'd first walked past, now they hung motionless. His former landlady sniffed again.

'You didn't tell me she was like that.'

'I didn't know myself,' John replied. It was going to be worse than he thought, to find employment for Mary. If anything, they were more tolerant in Coburg Street but if Mrs Beal took that attitude, he could imagine how it would be in smarter households. He sincerely hoped Mistress Shields had found a place and that tomorrow's interview, wherever it was, was simply a formality for Mary.

Hurrying home he found she'd put the kettle on the hob to boil. Without her cloak, the distortion her shorter leg gave was even more noticeable. She was plain too, he decided, and pale. She looked as if a good brisk walk would put some colour in her cheeks, then he remembered this was impossible.

'I have to leave shortly,' he told her. 'It's my evening for the debating society. I'm one of the principal speakers. After tea, I'll take you and introduce you to Mrs Beal. She has an excellent room which Davie and I used to rent.'

'Am I not to stay here then?'

He was offended. 'For goodness sake, how could you! With Davie away, too.' She turned away, crimson. He had a sudden awful fear. 'Have you not got enough money to pay Mrs Beal?

She only charges sixpence for the room and breakfast.' Silently Mary reached in her pocket and took out a purse. She emptied five guineas and some silver onto the table.

'I had seven guineas,' she whispered, 'but I had to pay for the ticket.'

'Of course,' John wondered why she bothered to tell him. 'You could hardly travel for nothing. I'm glad you saved enough to see you through until you find work.' He poured boiling water into the pot. 'Were you in service in Scotland?' She nodded and suddenly looked faint.

'May I sit down?'

'Yes, here . . . take this one.' John was annoyed. Because she was a cripple, he hadn't thought of her as a woman. She leaned back gratefully in the wooden chair. On the red tablecloth, her pile of coins glinted silver and gold. He glanced at her surreptitiously once or twice as he poured the tea. Was she lacking in her wits as well? Why on earth *had* the school mistress sent this one down?

He pushed a steaming cup towards her. 'Here, warm yourself. And have a bit of the ham, it's very good.' She looked at it and went even paler.

'I cannot afford it.'

He was angry. 'Now you listen to me, Miss Hamilton, I'm inviting you to eat so please don't be stupid. You've had a long journey and you look very tired. Please, be sensible. Have some nourishment.'

Her hand shook and the knife rattled against the plate, but he ignored that. Instead he reached in his pocket for his notes. He wanted to be word perfect with his quotations. Silently he tried a few of his polished phrases. Yes, there was a good ring to some of them. He'd score a few points over Simcox tonight. He got to the final phrase, stopped himself just in time from acknowledging the applause, and asked, 'Have you had sufficient?'

'Yes, thank you.'

'If you get your things, we'll be off to Mrs Beal. As I didn't know what you wanted I booked the room for a week but she'll charge by the day until you start your new situation.

Mary gave him such a beseeching look it made him uncomfortable.

139

'You have got a situation arranged, haven't you? Mistress Shields said nothing in her letter but I assumed she was leaving it to you to explain. If you wish, I will accompany you to any interview?' He waited for a reply but none came. 'Davie may know of somewhere,' he said uncertainly. 'He visits several big houses now. They're always needing kitchen staff.' And you certainly couldn't work above stairs, he thought, not with that limp.

He stacked their dishes in the sink as she struggled into her cloak. She waited as he put on his coat and carefully brushed the brim of his hat.

'I wondered . . . might I not work here, for you and your brother? As housekeeper when you have lodgers?' John stared and she went on, even more diffidently, 'It was your mother at the kirk. She was saying that was what you and Davie intended to do. I need a situation.'

'You mean you've come to England without one? Travelled all this way?' Mary nodded, her lip beginning to tremble.

'But what makes you think you could stay here and work for us?'

'I need somewhere to live. I'm going to have a baby.'

(iii)

At the Literary and Philosophical Institute, gas jets hissed importantly. Below, the elite of the town gathered, dignified and grave. Before any debate formality was uppermost. Afterwards when tea and Marie biscuits were circulating (the society was naturally teetotal), heat flowed upwards. An avalanche of talk was released over those cups. No one forgot his place, it was true. Young clerks rarely disagreed with senior colleagues, for a man had to consider his prospects, but many came perilously close to being reckless.

It was excitement generated by the debates that caused it and tonight's promised to be spectacular. The speakers were evenly matched. Silcox could present a sturdy argument but John McKie could keep going. Indeed he always did, right to the end, plodding, conscientious, with nothing left out. It usually took an extra half hour when John was a speaker. Yes, you needed strong tea after listening to McKie.

Tonight they were to be disappointed. When the opposer of the motion finally arrived he was ten minutes late. He appeared dazed. In the silence he fumbled with his coat and almost forgot to apologize. The Chairman was disgruntled, things weren't the same when he was young. Was Mr McKie ready? He tapped with his gavel and called the meeting to order.

John sat in a daze without hearing a word of Silcox's argument. Nor did he notice he was being called until his seconder nudged him violently. John rose. Faces looked at him expectantly. 'Mr Chairman . . . ' He'd taken out his notes but his hand dropped to his side and the notes slid to the floor. 'I was invited tonight to oppose my honourable friend. I find I cannot do so. I'm no longer convinced . . . that realization is for the best. A man must have his dreams . . . ' He stared at them vacantly as he whispered, 'Sometimes they're all he has left.'

Embarrassment made one or two shift in their chairs but they waited for him to continue. John's next words were so low, few of them heard. 'A man must also do his duty,' he murmured and slumped back into his seat.

The Chairman was bewildered. 'Is that it? Have you finished, Mr McKie?' John didn't look up. 'Am I to understand you've changed your opinion on the motion?' he asked more tersely. The bowed head nodded slightly. 'Well I don't know, I'm sure . . . ' He turned to the first speaker. 'That was the speediest reversal of opinion I've ever encountered. I must congratulate you, Mr Silcox. Nevertheless, this debate has to proceed.' He looked at the anxious young seconder. 'It all depends on you, Mr Parkinson. You will have to convince us without the aid of Mr McKie. You may begin.'

Mr Parkinson rose, smoothing his spiky hair, and the scent of cheap pomade drifted across the front rows. 'I am honoured to be called upon by you, Mr Chairman,' he began.

John didn't wait for tea. He slipped away leaving his colleagues to speculate. 'I sincerely hope . . . ' The Chairman was also under-manager at Backhouses, 'I sincerely hope that was a temporary aberration of Mr McKie's. I trust he isn't going to prove – unreliable.' It was doing him an injustice. The problem was, John intended doing his duty.

He believed he had no choice; that Helen Shields had demanded it of him in repayment for the debt. John's soul cried out in protest – dear God, no! but he never doubted for a moment that he'd understood what the school mistress wanted.

He walked about in the rain, arguments raging inside. 'It's too much,' he groaned, over and over, 'I can't do it!' But he knew he'd have to for it was his duty. It would release him for ever from Helen's bondage, into a far more terrible one. Exhausted finally, weighed down by so much emotion he no longer cared, he sat on a kerbstone. In the road a tram paused, picking up revellers. Snug inside, passengers stared at him; a lonely figure weeping as though his heart would break.

Until now John hadn't dared let his thoughts wander as far as matrimony. He and Davie had to become established first. During those early weeks, homesick for Scotland, he vowed he'd have a place one day, a home where a woman watched out for him, where warmth and comfort waited, where, above all, there was love. How John yearned for that! Love would be the flame which would warm him for ever, but not yet. Now Helen Shields had removed any chance of it. He had failed to become a doctor and this was her retribution.

He turned into the alley behind Coburg Street and stood outside the old lodging. *She* was in that room behind the dark window. Was she asleep? What did that misshapen foot look like – how could he be tied for life to that! To live with another man's child! John walked on to his own front door.

There was no pride any more, no joy at being under his own roof. He would have to share this with a cripple. He wandered about the empty rooms. They'd have to let one as quickly as possible with two more mouths to feed. He'd have to break into his savings to buy furniture – and where would they all sleep? It was so unfair – Mistress Shields was taking away his chance of having his own business.

He washed the tea things under the tap. The wonder of that was past now. He pulled up a chair in front of the dying fire and contemplated the future, discarding dreams one by one. There would be no love, no son destined for medicine, that was over, too. What would his parents think, or Davie? That he was a fool? No, Davie would never say that, but, neither would any of them understand. He'd never spoken to any of them about his feeling of guilt toward Mistress Shields.

With the first daylight, he opened the back door, shivering with cold. The last stars were fading and he whispered an appeal to them. 'Please . . . no!'

It was only seven o'clock when he knocked at Mrs Beal's.

'I'll see if Miss Hamilton is awake, Mr McKie.' John waited in the familiar parlour. Awkward footsteps descended the stairs. Mary opened the door but didn't venture into the room.

'Good morning. Mrs Beal said you wanted to see me?'

'I've something to ask, I won't keep you long.' She stayed where she was and they faced each other on opposite sides of the room. 'You are quite sure about the baby?'

'I saw a doctor in Inverness.'

'What about your family, do they know?'

'If he had, my father would've killed me.'

'Yes . . . ' In that small community it was hardly an exaggeration. Shame would reflect on all the Hamiltons but by saying so Mary had removed John's last hope. He tried to keep his voice steady. 'We will be married then. I will see the Minister this evening.'

She stared at him. What was he saying? She saw the pallid face with anxious grey eyes, a moustache to give it authority. He was proposing to save her from disgrace – this stranger? Mary was so shocked she couldn't speak. She wanted to cry out but clapped a hand over her mouth to stop herself. She knew nothing more about John than she'd heard in the kirk. All during the long, weary journey she'd prayed he and Davie wouldn't be cruel to her.

John broke the silence. He moved to the table, still keeping a space between them. 'This is a key to the front door. You can let yourself in. And some money. Perhaps you could cook us both tea if you feel up to it? Mrs Beal will tell you where to shop, where it's least expensive.' His voice trembled and he pretended to cough. 'I'm partial to a bloater myself,' he said gruffly. 'We could have that this evening.'

If she took her hand away from her mouth, she'd burst into tears, she knew she would. Above her hand, the eyes were very big in her pale face. They made John uncomfortable so that he tried to be kind. 'You do understand, don't you? There's no

143

need to worry any more. The baby will be looked after.'
Suddenly she was clinging to his arm.

'You cannot do it! I won't marry you, it would ruin your
whole life!' He was disturbed by her touch but managed to pat
her hand.

'Don't be foolish.' He spoke as gently as he could. 'It's the
only way I can help you, we both know that. I will be home by
eight o'clock.' He was about to leave when he remembered
something. 'I'll have to give the Minister your full name?'

'Mary Catherine Hamilton,' she whispered. He raised his hat
and was gone.

Upstairs in the room that had once been his, she lay on the
bed, shaking. Emotion stifled her; she had to take in gulps of air.
After a while she was so cold, she struggled upright, pulling her
shawl tight and rocking to and fro in agony. It was impossible to
believe anyone could be so kind. John spoke the truth when he
said there was no other way he could help her, Mary recognized
that now. She couldn't have stayed on as their housekeeper,
with a bastard child. But that he was willing to sacrifice himself?
She couldn't believe it! Tears rolled quietly down her cheeks.
He really had said those words: he'd told her they would be
married.

Into the empty chill of the room Mary whispered a vow of her
own: the rest of her life would be dedicated to serving John. She
went to the wash-stand, splashed cold water on her swollen face
and considered how to begin.

Helen Shields hadn't been hopeful when Mary approached
her but she'd always promised ex-pupils she would do her best
for them. Mary had visited the school house the day following
her appointment in Inverness. After listening to her request,
Helen wondered aloud if John McKie would know of a
situation, and Mary recalled the conversation between her
mother and Mrs McKie at the kirk. It brought the first glimmer
of hope. She didn't hesitate. The very act of buying a train ticket
dispelled thoughts of suicide.

And if at the end of the journey, John McKie refused to help,
if there was nothing but disgrace ahead of her, then Mary would
find some deep-flowing English river to drown her shame. Now,
only five days after that visit to the doctor, this good man had
promised to save her. It was a miracle! Mary fell on her knees to

thank her Saviour for John's existence.

As for John, he'd never felt so miserable in his life. Doing his duty brought no relief whatsoever. He broke the news of his betrothal to Mr Richardson and suffered his congratulations. When he left the office, he felt doomed. There was no way back. He went to the presbytery. 'I look forward to the pleasure of meeting Miss Hamilton,' Mr Wingford told him when the initial business was concluded.

Everyone would see her! John hadn't thought of that. He'd imagined Mary's life within the confines of Coburg Street, not in the town where he was known. And what about Sunday morning in front of the congregation? He would be an object of pity! The thought of carrying the plate, of meeting all those eyes – it would be humiliating.

'If Miss Hamilton is well enough, she will come,' John reddened at the small untruth. 'The journey from Scotland was tiring for her.'

It felt odd to be approaching his own house without a key in his hand but she must have been on the lookout, for the door opened as he reached the step. He entered the parlour. There was furniture!

In front of the fireplace was a round table. On one side was a horsehair sofa, on the other, two upright chairs. As he gazed at these, John's nostrils were filled with the smells of beeswax, carbolic, washing soda and very faintly, with bloater.

There was a pair of worn brown velvet curtains on the table and beside them, needles and thread. Mary had obviously been mending them while waiting for him. She'd gone into the kitchen and he followed, pausing in the doorway. She'd scrubbed every inch of this room, too. At the window were new lace curtains – Davie and he had never considered such luxury. A fire was burning and the grate had been blackened till it gleamed. In front of it now was a high fender.

'What on earth's been happening?' Mary lifted the pan lid and sniffed.

'This is wanting a few more minutes. Would you like to take a look upstairs? I've been making things ready for lodgers. Perhaps you could put an advertisement in the *North Eastern Independent*? Mrs Beal uses it.'

He went upstairs slowly. There was a narrow red drugget

covering them. Again he was assailed by clean odours. In the larger front bedroom were three iron bedsteads with mattresses and bedding. There were chairs, a wash-stand with ewer and basin and, in front of the polished fireplace, a square of carpet. Coals and kindling were ready for the match. Everywhere was so spotless! Slightly guilty, John realized neither he nor Davie had done anything to the house since moving in. He'd forgotten how hard their mother used to work at it.

On the landing he nearly tripped over the bucket and cleaning things left ready for the morning. Had she attacked the back bedroom which he and Davie shared? He opened the door apprehensively. It looked untouched. With mixed feelings he wondered whether it would be proper for Mary to come in here, into a bachelor's chamber? But there were other more important matters to consider first. He hurried down to the kitchen.

Mary was by the window with her sewing and seeing her like that he was too embarrassed to phrase his question. She filled the silence.

'I haven't quite finished but the house will be ready by the end of the week. You can put from next Monday in the advertisement.'

'How did you pay for all of it?' he asked bluntly.

'With my own money. Mrs Beal went with me to the auction rooms. We told them what was needed and how much I could afford. They were very accommodating.' John's face was white.

'That money . . . where did it – ? How did you come by it?'

She looked at him steadily although her voice trembled.

'It was my savings. The only money *he* gave me I used for the visit to the doctor and my ticket. In this house I have only spent what was mine.' He was so confused he couldn't thank her.

'John, if we are to be married, I need to tell you about it. May I do so now?'

'It's none of my business,' he mumbled. It was getting worse.

'It cannot be a mystery between us. I would rather talk of it now than later.'

'Very well. Then we need never discuss it again.' She took a breath and the words came in a rush this time.

'I've been in service at the Big House since I was thirteen, in the kitchen. Father thought it was a waste of money for me to continue at school, I must earn my living, he said. It was the

146

younger son of the family . . . ' She faltered but forced herself to keep going. 'I don't think you would've known him, he was away at university much of the time . . . ' She took another deep breath. 'He did it for a wager, he told me afterwards. His brother wanted to know how it would be . . . with a cripple. I would not have let him but he swore he loved me.'

John looked at her stupidly. Love? How could she have believed that? Mary saw and understood. She cried passionately, 'John, if you'd been as I am, if you'd seen people despise you all your life, you'd thank God for a man who said he loved you! You wouldn't stop and ask yourself if it was right or wrong, you'd give yourself, gladly. For love!' She spat the word out so scornfully, it made him wince.

'I know it was foolish. For five days, since I knew, I haven't wanted to go on living. If the only way to rid myself of the shame was to kill myself, then that was what I intended to do.'

'That's a sin!'

'Is it?' she asked wearily, 'I know I've been taught it. Men point to the scriptures and tell you about purgatory. I doubt whether any man knows what it's like, how desperate a woman can feel.' She shuddered, remembering. 'You saved me from wanting to kill myself, I know that,' she whispered but he turned away from the gratitude in her eyes. Thank God she couldn't read his thoughts.

Mary limped across to lift the pan off the hob, breaking the mood. 'Anyway, that's how it was, John. When I told him he gave me four guineas and said he'd look after me. Next day the housekeeper told me I must leave immediately. He'd complained to his mother the sight of me made him ill and that she must get rid of me.'

She put the plate in front of him and words of condemnation stuck in John's throat. What Mary had done was wicked but obviously Helen Shields hadn't thought so. No, the school mistress must have judged the man the guilty party. It took John several minutes to adjust to this idea. He made the effort. He was still unsteady amid the shifting moral arguments but he tried to be fair.

'What's done cannot be undone. It's the future that matters now. I had seen my own differently . . . ' He was on dangerous ground. 'That is to say, neither Davie nor I planned to marry

147

for some years. But that's no reason why you and I shouldn't
. . . ' Shouldn't what? Live as man and wife? Never! 'We'll
manage,' he finished lamely, 'but I wish you hadn't spent your
savings.'

'It was the least I could do. You are ruining your life for me!'
Tears were running freely.

'There, there,' he said helplessly, 'hush now.'

'Please, finish your bloater. Then I can clear away and go
back to Mrs Beal.'

'Where's your supper?' he asked.

'I ate earlier, thank you.'

'We could've had it together.'

'That is not my place,' Mary said firmly. 'I will not eat with
you or your brother. I'll look after the house, I'll work for you
all my life, but it will be as housekeeper, not mistress.'

'But you'll be my wife!' She shook her head sadly.

'You're a good man, John McKie, but I'll never be a proper
wife. It offends you even to look at me, I've seen it in your face.
I thank God for your kindness but you must let me do as I see
fit.'

He didn't argue. He felt relieved but hoped she couldn't read
that in his face. He tucked into his food and remembered he
hadn't told her about the wedding.

'It will be three weeks on Saturday, in the afternoon. I finish
work at one o'clock on Saturdays,' he explained, 'so it will be
more convenient. It will perhaps be better not to tell anyone
until afterwards,' he suggested awkwardly and she flushed
crimson.

'Yes, of course.'

It was his evening for teaching at the Mechanics Institute.
They discussed it and agreed Mary could stay until he returned.
Provided she was alone in the house, there would be no
impropriety. Besides, it meant she could finish the curtains.

When he returned at ten thirty she was ready to leave. She'd
begun mending sheets, turning sides to middle, for the first
lodger. A plate of bread and cheese was set for John and beside
it was the front door key.

'I found one for the back hanging by the sink. I'll use that in
future.'

Outside Mrs Beal's he offered his hand and remembered she

148

might need more money. Mary refused. 'You gave me more than I needed for the bloater. I'll give you an account tomorrow. Would you like mutton stew for your tea?' Walking back John reflected soberly that she seemed to be a good manager. The bedroom was ready to let; if Mary was prepared to cater as well, they could ask a reasonable rent. If only he didn't have to marry her!

Anguish came flooding back. He walked on, trying to tire himself. He needed to sleep after last night. Everywhere he passed couples out for a night stroll. Within three weeks, he'd be one of them: he'd have a companion. Could he bear to offer her his arm, have her limp beside him? He groaned at the thought. She wasn't planning to be his wife, she'd made it plain she'd never demand what he wasn't prepared to give, but a life without love? Helen Shields had asked too much.

(iv)

The journey to Leeds was Davie's first and an adventure. He'd been sent to sort out problems with Gordon's suppliers, especially the 'cut, make and press' tailoring firms. John reminded him that these were useful contacts for when they were in business themselves but such serious talk faded from Davie's mind as he dreamed the journey away. His mind was full of auburn-gold hair and what it would be like to encircle that slim waist. In short, he was dizzy with love.

For him alone in Leeds that day, the sun shone. His red curls were charged with energy as he strode through narrow streets, past smoke-stained buildings and narrow alleyways, enveloped in a personal cloud of happiness. He didn't notice the squalor nor the press of humanity. As long as a sliver of sky was visible to remind him of *her* eyes, it was enough to keep his mood buoyant.

The first firm he sought was in a basement. Round the entrance was a bewildering selection of plates and cards but eventually he found the name. An arrow pointed to steep stone steps. At the bottom, Davie pushed open the door.

Noise swamped him. In the low-ceilinged, confined space, a dozen men sat cross-legged, sewing as though their lives depended on it, as indeed they did: straining to see by the light of gas jets. Beyond them was a line of treadle machinists and further back still, grouped round a fire, were steam pressers. Two small boys darted among them, refilling irons from kettles kept boiling on the hob. The heat was overwhelming and most of the men were in shirt sleeves or vests. The steam pressers were half naked. Boiling water hissed and spat, machines whirred and above it all the tailors shouted to each other and at the two boys.

There was no space between the rows. Open skips stood ready to receive finished garments. Under tables and benches were bales of cloth. Occasionally one of the children scrambled to retrieve buttons dropped by the hand-sewers and was abused if he couldn't find them. It was a scene such as Davie had never witnessed before; the sight and smell of men on piece work, scratching a living. None of them looked up. Even if they noticed the rush of air, they ignored it, and Davie.

'Yes?' It was a short, middle-aged man, balding but with a rim of black hair. Like the others he only wore a vest, 'Yes, what you want, please?'

'Mr Rossi? I've come from Darlington, on behalf of Mr Gordon.' The Italian examined the business card. 'Come with me.' Davie followed, dodging half-finished garments hanging from overhead racks. The office was off the main room with nothing but a desk and two chairs, scarcely enough space for the two of them to sit. When the glass door too was shut, the air seemed cut off and Davie tugged at the buttons of his coat. 'We have some coffee, yes?' and without waiting for a reply, Signor Rossi leapt agilely onto the seat of his chair and tapped at a trap door above. It lifted a fraction. Davie saw a scarlet sleeve, a delicate hand and a large pair of brown eyes. There was an exchange in Italian. The manager stepped down but left the trap door open. 'She make good coffee, my daughter.'

Being in love, Davie hadn't eaten on the train. Now the aroma began to make his mouth water. He tried to itemize Gordon's complaints but Signor Rossi kept up a steady stream of excuses. Suppliers could not be relied upon, why only last week an entire consignment of trousers had to be re-made

150

because the thread was rotten. And as for finishers . . . He gestured derisively. Those men out there were useless, they lacked proper training and as for what they expected to be paid . . . He rolled his eyes to heaven. The smell of coffee was much stronger now. The Italian watched, judging nicely when the young man in front of him had ceased listening.

'You hungry?' he asked Davie suddenly.

'Oh no, I couldn't possibly – ' but Signor Rossi was already back on his chair.

'Hey, Maddalena, this handsome fellow is starving. How about tempting him with something, my darling?'

This time the brown eyes peered at Davie. Lustrous hair fell in wings, framing her oval face. She handed down steaming cups of coffee. 'That's very kind of you,' said Davie and Maddalena Rossi smiled. When she returned with a plate wrapped in a cloth, she gestured that Davie should take it. Not needing the chair, he reached up. Their hands brushed accidentally. Her skin was warm and soft. She smiled again.

'Please . . . you eat.'

'Thank you very much indeed.' John had warned him about accepting food, but how could he refuse such a lovely girl? She only wanted to be kind. Davie ate every crumb and drank his coffee in gulps. Signor Rossi looked pleased. 'She's a good cook my daughter, no?'

'Excellent!'

'Look, sir, you got other messages in Leeds? So when you finish them, you come back. All will be ready for you.' He took Gordon's list. 'Everything that make you unhappy in Darlington, it's all here?'

'Yes.'

He appeared to study the list intently. When he'd finished he asked casually, 'You work for Mr Gordon a long time?'

'Long enough. I shall be leaving as soon as my time is up. My brother and I are going in business for ourselves.'

'Your brother?'

'My elder brother, John. He makes plans for both of us.' And within a very few minutes, Davie had told the whole of it. Signor Rossi ascertained delicately that although John was a bachelor, it was unlikely he'd be visiting Leeds. He said even more emphatically, 'When you finish, you come back here this evening. Have supper with us. My daughter and me, it give us great pleasure.'

'Oh no, really, I – '

'Much pleasure!' The dark eyes were looking down at him through the trap door and the soft voice echoed her father's plea. Davie was overcome by their kindness.

The rest of the day dragged in a way that surprised him. Other suppliers weren't nearly so pleasant. He grew impatient. They hadn't had the problems the Italian had, with rotten thread and poor workmen. None of them offered him coffee. Why then weren't their suits up to the mark? He became more than a little censorious.

During the afternoon Davie began to check his watch more and more often. What dull chaps most of their suppliers were. And he had two more days of it before he'd contacted the lot. He sighed at the tedium that lay ahead. If only the evening would come.

By eight he was on his way back to the basement factory. He'd managed to find a woman selling flowers. They were poor specimens compared to those he used to gather for Jeannie, already shedding a few petals. Never mind, with a bit of ribbon they looked pretty enough. Maddalena was delighted with them. She peeped demurely over the edge of the posy. 'Very pretty . . . ' Davie was about to pay her a compliment but found himself thinking of blue eyes instead of brown ones. He hesitated and the moment was past.

They were in the room above the office. Signor Rossi had led him along an outside passage and through a narrow door. Davie tried to ignore the smells coming from rain-sodden piles of rubbish – why did no one clear it away? He stooped and entered.

He'd never seen a room like it. Instead of the usual dark wallpaper, these bare walls were colour washed a soft pinky yellow. Chairs had rugs and shawls thrown over them, great splashes of colour. Cushions spilled onto the floor like some Eastern palace. There was even a charcoal brazier to add to the illusion and the room was made snug by thick brocade drawn across every window or door. There was only one picture, a portrait in a heavy frame.

'Maddalena's sainted mother,' Signor Rossi told him piously.

What a fierce-looking woman, thought Davie. He tried to think of an acceptable platitude and turned, as if to make a comparison. The girl was still holding her flowers. She wore the same red skirt as before but her bodice was black and tightly fitting with a fichu of lace. It was an age when women avoided the sun and Maddalena's skin was like milk. Davie found it difficult to tear his eyes away but Signor Rossi was urging him to taste something.

'It is wine from where we live in Italy. Try it, dear sir.' Davie drank. He'd never tasted wine before. It stung his throat and they both laughed as he coughed. 'Gently, sir, gently. Don't drink it like beer.' Davie sipped more cautiously, letting it trickle over his tongue. He was convinced he'd never tasted anything so awful. 'Very nice,' he said politely. Signor Rossi grimaced.

'With the food, you try a little more wine. They complement each other. You will think of warm sunshine when it reaches your stomach.'

They ate at low tables by candlelight and Davie was entranced. Whenever his glass was empty, Signor Rossi refilled it. Maddalena had prepared chicken with spices. There were olives, strange cheeses and many, many toasts. Signor Rossi drank to him, to John and to their increasing prosperity, and whenever Maddalena lifted her glass it was as if a great red ruby rested against her white skin. Finally, to end the meal, Signor Rossi himself produced zabaglione with the rest of the bottle of Marsala to accompany it. By now Davie had overcome his initial dislike. 'Never tasted anything like this before!' he cried happily. He'd been saying so at regular intervals throughout the evening. 'Absolutely perfec' – oh, thanks very much.' Amazing how quickly a chap's glass became empty. These must be on the small size. He looked at his critically.

'You like music, dear sir? Maddalena will play for us.'

She sank down gracefully onto a pile of cushions and began to strum a mandolin. The melody filled Davie with melancholy and Signor Rossi produced yet another bottle.

Afterwards, Davie didn't quite know how it happened. One minute he was in his chair, the next he was beside her. It seemed ungracious not to stay there, especially when she smiled at him like that.

She stopped playing. Her father had disappeared. Davie

sipped the colourless new wine, so strong it made his eyes water. Maddalena was even closer now. He'd never seen skin like it, so white, and the veins, pale blue lines tracing the roundness right to the nipples. He'd never seen a woman's breasts before! He was far too hot. He wanted to take off his clothes, too. Her dress was undone, he could see it was. The candle guttered and she reached across to blow it out. The scent of her body nearly made him swoon! She took the brandy glass from his fingers and over her shoulder he saw the portrait, staring at him. Davie looked at Maddalena abruptly then back at the portrait. 'Why aren't the eyes blue? Either of you?' he asked. For an instant the girl resembled her mother, the same fierce mouth with compressed lips. It was fleeting but it startled him. She rose and extinguished the last remaining candle, leaving only the glow from the brazier.

'Wait here,' she whispered. 'I shan't be long.'

The sussuration of her skirts moved away. A curtain lifted and she disappeared into the room beyond. Davie struggled to his feet uneasily. How that portrait worried him. Standing there, fuddled, sweating, he had a sudden illogical thought: it was John's night for teaching at the Institute. He never knew why it came to him then but it was the only rational notion in his hot brain. He looked round wildly. On one of the tables was a water carafe. He dashed the contents over himself. Drops fell on the brazier, turning instantly to steam. He was full of desire but he knew he must get away.

Which curtain masked the door by which they'd entered? He dare not risk pulling back the wrong one. He remembered the trapdoor and stumbled across, sinking on his knees beside it. He tugged too vigorously; the balancing mechanism moved smoothly and Davie crashed through the opening onto the desk below.

There was no point now in worrying about the noise, all he thought of was escape. The office door opened easily enough. He stumbled across the room, ricocheting off tables and skips, tearing aside racks of suits. He could hear shrill cries in the room above – he found the outside door and fumbled with the bolts. It was locked! There was no other way out, even in his drunken state he remembered that much – it had to be through this door.

154

Davie flung himself at it again and again with all his strength. Maddalena was screaming now and he thought he could hear Signor Rossi, too. Suddenly, so that he almost jumped out of his skin, tiny hands seized him. In one of them he felt the cold shape of a key.

' 'Ere you are, mister!' It was one of the two small boys. 'It's too 'igh up for us to reach but it turns easy like!' To Davie it was all part of the nightmare. The hands guided his own farther up the door until he found the lock. In the blackness, the frightened whispers were urgent.

' 'Urry up, mister, 'e'll skin us alive!'

'We're coming wiv ya. 'E keeps us locked up in 'ere!'

The door opened and Davie didn't wait. He burst up the stone steps, out into the wet night, tripping over filth in the gutter. Two small shapes fled past him. Davie rose and staggered off in another direction. He wanted to give his rescuers a chance. He forced himself to run until the pain in his side hurt too much and he leaned against a wall to recover. He'd never felt so dreadful in his life, his throat and head were on fire.

There was a horse trough in the centre of the street. He stumbled across. His reflection wobbled across the surface of the water. 'Such a fool!' Gripping the edge he dunked his head once, twice, three times, gasping and choking. Wiping his eyes, he headed finally toward the town.

Later, when he'd retrieved his grip from the station and found cheap lodgings, Davie lay watching the stars through uncurtained windows. Did anyone in the world feel as ashamed as he did now? How could he ever look anyone in the face? How could he face John!

He remembered Morag and Esther. He'd never felt for them the way he did tonight, like a dog for a bitch. Alex had told him about lust. And drink. Davie's dry mouth wouldn't let him forget the latter anyway. But that his body should betray him like that made him shudder. How had Maddalena's dress come unfastened? Surely he hadn't done that accidentally? Oh to be safe in Darlington!

155

It was astonishing how a few hours' sleep helped a chap see things differently. Davie could scarcely believe it when he woke. He no longer felt guilty! He hadn't done anything to be ashamed of, or if he had, he thought guiltily, he couldn't remember doing so. Confidence evaporated a fraction. Surely he hadn't laid a finger on Maddalena's dress? It must have become unfastened by itself. Thank Heavens she hadn't noticed it, nor the effect it had had on him! What a relief he'd managed to get away before she realized the state he was in! How wonderful she'd chosen exactly that moment to go to her room.

It was embarrassing that he'd had to escape like that – and Davie thought worriedly about the two small boys. They weren't his concern, he decided. The main thing was to write a handsome letter to Signor Rossi, thanking him for the meal. He, Davie McKie, had nothing to be ashamed of and could look the world in the face. He leapt out of bed.

The next instant he was violently sick into his chamberpot. Oh, the aftermath of wine! He retched and groaned and swore he'd never touch it again. What a mercy he hadn't succumbed while he was still with the Rossis.

It was as he was eating a morsel of bread that the first few doubts about Maddalena arose. During the morning, with one of the shirt manufacturers, Davie let fall where he'd spent the evening. The man grinned knowingly. 'Met the fair Sicilian, did you? You want to take care, Mr McKie, the lady's desperate to be married,' he said, then he winked. It shocked Davie terribly. One never winked about a lady, surely? Was it up to him to defend Maddalena's honour?

He was kept far too busy during the rest of his stay and it wasn't until he was on the train that Davie had time to consider the remark properly. The more he turned it over in his mind, the way the words were said, the more he began to wonder about the whole sequence of events. They were approaching Darlington when an amazing thought occurred to Davie – had Maddalena actually intended – Great Heavens! And a few seconds later – By Jove! He couldn't wait to tell John.

That unhappy man was not looking forward to his brother's return. The thought of trying to explain destroyed John's concentration. He checked and re-checked his work. Thursday arrived. Davie would be there at suppertime.

In fact Davie had caught an earlier train so that he could call at Armitage's. It was with an enormous sense of pride that he strode down Skinnergate. Had he not visited the valley of temptation in Leeds and emerged unscathed? Well, almost. He'd already worked out what he was going to buy this evening: cheese. *She* alone worked on that counter so it followed she'd have to serve him.

She wasn't there! The bell jangled behind him with the force of Davie's entry but at her marble slab stood – Mr Collins. Davie's smile fell away, even the red curls drooped. Mr Collins was at his most obsequious. 'Yes, sir, may I be of assistance?' Self-confidence ebbed away. Davie shuffled his feet.

'The young lady, where is she?' he muttered.

'I beg your pardon, sir?'

'The one who guessed the walking stick.' Cold fear swept through him. 'She hasn't left, has she?'

When Mr Collins replied he was no longer obsequious.

'Miss Forrest? It is Miss Forrest to whom you allude, is it not, sir?'

'She's got – blue eyes.' Was there ever a more foolish reply?

'Ah yes, quite so. Miss Forrest is taking tea with her aunt and uncle at present.' Davie's sigh of relief lifted the doilies off the bowls of brawn. 'Now sir,' Mr Collins persisted, 'May I be of assistance?'

'No, thanks, I'll come again tomorrow. After tea. Oh, you could mention I called, if you would. McKie. Davie McKie.' But Mr Collins did not see himself as Cupid. He inclined his head dismissively, 'Good day, sir.'

So Davie arrived home ahead of John. The first surprise as he aproached the house was a discreet sign propped up in the parlour window: 'Vacancies. Bed, breakfast and supper for gentlemen.' He whistled in astonishment.

He experienced the same shock as John at the furniture. As

he opened the door to the kitchen, Mary called from the scullery,

'Is that you, John?'

Dear me, thought Davie, why is that Hamilton girl still here?'

Half an hour later he and John faced each other across the parlour table. The door to the kitchen was firmly shut.

'What are you saying!' Davie couldn't believe his ears.

'There is no point in discussing it. I intend marrying Mary and that's all there is to it.'

'All!' Davie couldn't keep his voice down any longer, 'You're going to throw yourself away on *her*?'

'Hush, she will hear you!'

'I leave you alone for less than three days and what happens?' Davie's finger stabbed in the direction of the kitchen, 'You meet a complete stranger and without knowing anything about her – except what you can see,' he added witheringly, 'you arrange to marry her? Are you out of your mind, John?'

'Don't shout. Please, Davie, don't shout.' John spoke in a whisper, his face pale, the eyes red from lack of sleep. Staring at him, Davie thought he was going to faint.

'What is it, man, are you ill?' John shook his head feebly, terrified the tears would come. Heavens, this would not do.

'I'm quite well,' he answered huskily, 'but it's no use asking any more questions. It's my business, not yours. I know you're worried about the future, and I'll do my best not to let it interfere with our plans.' He couldn't possibly tell Davie about the baby, not yet. As Davie opened his mouth to argue, John pleaded, 'I cannot explain any more, not yet. Please . . . !'

Anger surged in Davie. For the first time it was directed at John. After all the sacrifice, the prospect of owning their own business almost within their grasp – after all he'd gone through in Leeds! In retrospect that adventure had now become one of acute self-denial. Was all of it to be thrown away? And for what? Mary Hamilton would drag John down. Anger gave way to bewilderment.

'John, is it an old understanding? You didn't know her before, did you? You said you didn't – '

'That was the truth! But I'll not answer any more questions, Davie. I cannot! Please, don't let us talk of it any more.'

158

Davie replied quietly, 'You'll have to do better than that, John.'

There was a rap at the front door. Neither brother moved. The knock was repeated and the kitchen door opened. Mary limped through to answer it. 'Yes?' There was a quiet exchange on the step. Mary asked the caller to wait and half closed the door so that he couldn't hear.

'It is a young man from the foundry enquiring about the room. May I show him upstairs? He looks respectable.'

'Are we sufficiently ready?'

'I think so. I've nearly finished another pair of sheets.'

'Would you prefer me to speak to him?'

'No, John, thank you. I can manage . . . Would you like to come in, please?' She waited calmly for the caller to wipe his boots then led the 'way upstairs. Neither John or Davie spoke. The two came down again.

'We have agreed terms,' Mary told John quietly, then, 'This is Mr Nettles. Here is his reference. He would like to take the room from next Monday. This is Mr McKie . . . Mr Davie McKie.'

There was an apprehensive silence while John adjusted his spectacles and Mr Nettles' Adam's apple slid up and down anxiously.

'I shall need to write to this gentleman, Mr Nettles. Your supervisor, I take it? Care of the foundry?'

'Yes, Mr McKie. Yes, of course.'

'And you doubtless appreciate that room is intended for three persons, not one?' Mr Nettles cleared his throat.

'I have two colleagues, Mr McKie. They are not suited where they are at present. Perhaps, in a week or so, if I may bring them to see the room?' He wanted to test the cooking before committing his friends. John bowed. They settled a time between them when Mr Nettles could expect to move in and Mary showed him out.

'Supper is ready whenever you are,' she told them.

They didn't speak again until after Mary had left for Mrs Beal's. As they prepared for bed Davie tried again.

'Will you not even discuss it, John? There's so much I don't understand.'

'After Mary and I are married.'

159

'It'll be too late then and you know it. Have you said anything to Father and Mother?'

'Not yet.'

'They'll have to know!'

'Afterwards.'

'John, surely you haven't forgotten what an effort it was? What it cost Father? And all those years walking to school in bad weather, when we still thought you would be a doctor – '

'That's over!' John interrupted harshly.

'But we still have the rest of our lives. What about the future? You once told me it was possible for us to have dreams provided we set our minds to the task and worked hard enough.'

There was no reply this time. Davie stared across the darkened bedroom. John lay so still he couldn't even hear him breathing. 'You're ashamed of her, aren't you?' he said, puzzled. 'You don't like the way she looks any more than I do. You don't *love* her, do you?'

'No more!' John cried fiercely, 'Leave me in peace, d'you hear? I will explain afterwards, I promise, but not now.' It was a cry from the heart. They lay in silence, each pretending to be asleep, listening to the other's restless movements.

Never, never would he understand. John was so implacable, refusing to listen to reason. How could anyone marry without love? Surely John hadn't lusted after Mary – that was ludicrous! He hadn't got drunk and been seduced by a milky-white bosom. Davie sighed. How much older he felt suddenly, how much more experienced. Leeds was a thing of the past. If only he'd been able to share that adventure, but that was impossible. John wouldn't want to hear. My word, it had taught him something, though. If only John would explain!

(vii)

If John felt nervous about attending church on Sunday, he'd no idea of the fear in Mary's breast. She realized she'd be an object of curiosity. Unlike John, she knew what to expect. She'd endured it all her life. The first glance followed by embarrass-

160

ment as people turned away. The defensive manner they adopted when speaking to her. Worst of all was when they spoke loudly, as though she were lacking in her wits as well. Once a pregnant woman shrank away in terror as if a club foot were a contagion, a curse put on Mary by God. Although Mary believed she was strong enough to withstand the insults, she was fearful as to their effect on John.

They arrived in the porch and John saw the first shocked look in the eyes of the welcoming Elder. As they followed him to their pew, a small wave of silence washed away the chatter. The three of them knelt in prayer. On either side of her, one brother prayed for strength, the other for mercy. As for Mary, she asked nothing for herself. A passing thought for the baby perhaps, truly a curse until now, but her mind was full of the first kindness any man had shown her since she'd been born. With all her heart, Mary prayed for John. She remembered the mocking words of her seducer, the pity in the doctor's eyes. For the first time she had reason to thank God for the actions of another and she did so with all her soul.

The three of them sat facing the lectern, waiting for the word of the Lord. Round about the devout could hardly wait for the service to end so that they could tell one another, wasn't it a shame about poor Mr McKie?

Davie disobeyed and wrote to their parents before the wedding. As a result, Helen Shields travelled to Darlington. Alex had gone to her directly, with Davie's letter. Together they visited the Hamiltons who listened to the news but refused to believe it. Everyone agreed the marriage had to be prevented. The favoured diagnosis was that John must be ill. Drains, never a problem among the crofters, were known to be very unreliable in England.

The question of who was to put matters right was easy to solve. Alex couldn't possibly travel so far – he couldn't trust himself not to get lost in a strange land. Helen sighed. If anyone were to make John see sense, it would be herself, she knew. The Minister was prevailed upon to run the school for a few days. As she announced this, Helen saw with grim satisfaction how it dismayed the children.

Alex accompanied her to the ferry. She intended making the journey in easy stages, staying overnight in Glasgow. It meant she would only reach Darlington on the Friday before the wedding but it was the best she could do. As he helped stow her belongings, Alex handed her a parcel. For a dreadful moment she thought it was a crab but he opened the wrapping to show her the family Bible.

'This is our most precious book. In it are all the names; his grandfather who was killed for his beliefs, his great-grandfather and the rest. The date Jeannie and I were married, then when he and Davie were born. There is a continuity, a strength in that page of this book. If John reads it, he'll surely do what is right.'

As she put it into her Gladstone, it added more than simply its physical weight. 'It was with that Bible John used to teach his mother and me the English,' Alex told her. 'My family couldn't read or write. The Minister had to enter the names and dates: then they put their marks.'

'I'll take the greatest care of it,' Helen promised.

He waited in the soft mist until *The Pioneer* was out of sight. Helen stood watching him, the sound of the paddles making her dizzy, the damp seeping into her arthritic joints. Pain made her angry. What a fool's errand this was! What on earth had got into John?

Arriving in Darlington, she showed the address to the porter. 'Is this very far?'

'I'd take a cab if I was you, mum.'

In Coburg Street, the driver used the knocker vigorously. He'd caught sight of the tight mouth behind the veil. 'I'm glad it's not me that's in a spot of bother, whatever it is,' he thought, and stumped off as soon as he heard footsteps, to gather up the reins. Mary opened the door, shielding the parlour from cold air as usual. She gasped as she recognized the visitor. Helen's words dropped like particles of ice.

'I wish to speak to John McKie.' Mary stood aside without speaking and the school mistress entered the room.

John and Davie were at the table doing their paperwork. Bills, receipts and order books were in piles, samples and swatches of cloth from Leeds were spread over sofa and floor. Deep in the happy land of figures, John didn't immediately comprehend what was happening but Davie did. He leapt to his feet.

'Good evening, Mistress Shields!'

162

'Mistress . . . ?' John stared at her in bewilderment then saw the guilt in his brother's cheeks. 'Oh, Davie!'

'May I sit?' Davie hurried to clear away samples and Helen perched bolt upright on the sofa. 'I would like some tea,' she told him and Davie fled with Mary into the kitchen.

School mistress and pupil stared at each other. My goodness, he was older! He looked as if he hadn't slept for a week. Despite herself, Helen was disturbed. Where was all the youthful enthusiasm now? She felt her resolution to be hard fading as she faced this prematurely aged man, his eyes full of naked emotion. 'Please sit, John. There's no need to stand.' Still bemused, he rubbed his eyes as though he couldn't believe what he saw.

'I'm glad to see you,' he stammered finally. 'Are you well? And my parents, how are they?' As she inclined her head, the iridescent butterfly glistened in her hat. She lifted the veil. John was alarmed to see the familiar mouth trembling.

'Oh, John, what are you thinking of? This marriage to Mary Hamilton, it cannot – it must not take place.'

He was astonished. He stared at her, completely bewildered. What was she saying?

'I don't understand.'

Helen grew impatient. 'Of course you do. It's true, isn't it? What Davie wrote in his letter? That you intend marrying Mary Hamilton tomorrow?'

'Yes, it is.'

'But why, John? For Heavens' sake, why!'

'Mistress Shields, it was you that asked me to.'

'I? Don't be ridiculous!'

He quoted the words from memory, ' "Do your duty . . . Do what is right by Mary." ' Helen frowned.

'I'm well aware I wrote and asked for your help, John. You've been most kind in the past, assisting others to find work in England and I'm most grateful. All I meant, all I *intended* by that letter, was for you to find a suitable position for Mary, nothing more.' He leaned across the table, half hysterical.

'But what about the baby!'

'What – baby?'

John stared. In the silence, slowly, very slowly, he

163

understood. He laughed and when that disturbing sound was finished, neither of them spoke.

There was a tap at the door and Davie entered with two cups of tea. He put them on the table and left. Helen recovered first and roused herself.

'So she's pregnant,' she said at last.

'I thought you knew all about it . . . ' John's voice sounded as if it came from a long way off. 'I never even asked Mary if she'd told you. I just assumed you knew about it – because of that letter.' Helen shuddered, not simply from cold. She gulped the hot tea and tried to think sensibly.

'Well now . . . it's obvious what's to be done. Thank goodness I arrived in time.' She put the cup down and said carefully, 'As it's clearly not your child, you don't have to marry her. In fact, it's the last thing in the world you have to do.'

John looked at her sadly. 'Just because you didn't know of it, Mistress Shields, that baby isn't going to disappear.' This time Helen's mouth had recovered its normal grimness.

'Don't be stupid! It's not your responsibility. That silly girl must tell the father and he must marry her himself.' John's hands reached across the table in an effort to make her understand.

'But he won't! He knows all right. He got her turned out of her place when she told him. That's why Mary came to England. She'd no money, no "character" – she couldn't keep a place anyway, not once the baby begins to show. So what's to become of her, Mistress Shields? She and the bastard will end up in the workhouse, you and I know that perfectly well!'

Helen drew back, to retreat from his words. John stared. After all he'd gone through, this was her reaction. *She* was trying to dissuade him! It would be farcical if it wasn't so tragic. Only now was John's mind beginning to grasp the whole of it.

'It's no use, Mistress Shields,' he said wearily. 'Don't you understand? I've promised Mary I'll marry her. I intend to do so. She cannot be let down twice.'

Helen looked as if she would argue. John held up his hand. 'I will not tell you who the father is – Mary told me in confidence and I refuse to discuss it with anyone. I would appreciate it if you would say no more but drink your tea.'

164

Helen didn't give in that easily. It was a considerable time before she acknowledged the futility of further argument. John wouldn't change his mind, she could see that he wouldn't. 'If I do, what is there for Mary, tell me that?' was all he would say. And Helen couldn't produce an answer. She knew the girl couldn't return home. The Hamiltons wouldn't open their door to shame: John was right. It would mean the workhouse, degradation, she couldn't shy away from those facts, but what of John's sacrifice? Helen could have wept had she not been so angry!

'That stupid, wicked girl!' But he wouldn't even let her have that.

'I don't believe she was. I know her a little better now. Perhaps it was a sin but wasn't the man as guilty, too? And I don't find her stupid. She believed he loved her . . . ' Helen snorted. 'I think if I were a cripple,' John said quietly, 'I'd want to believe as she did.' The school teacher shut her eyes at such quixotism.

'You don't love her,' Helen said accusingly and added cruelly, 'You'll never love her. How can you go through life with that?' He started back as though she'd slapped him.

'That is my business!'

'Please, John, for my sake don't go through with this marriage!' He rose, white-faced.

'Mistress Shields, it was *because* of you. At first I believed I was doing so because I was in your debt: had I not failed you in not becoming a doctor? Well, now I'm going ahead because of Mary. There is no more to be said. But I tell you this, Mistress Shields, I have absolved myself of you! I owe you – nothing!' He'd really hurt her but it gave him no satisfaction. 'Please,' he begged, 'Let us begin again, as friends. Accept what I have to do. Do not tell my parents about the baby.' Helen shrugged helplessly.

'Everyone will know once it's born, John. People can count, you know.'

'We will tell everyone it's a seven-month child.' Helen Shields' eyes filled with tears.

'Then I will pray for both your sakes that it's not.' John wasn't going to worry about that. The hate that he'd been carrying for her dissolved but he couldn't cope with her tears.

Silently he held out his hand. Equally silently, Helen reached for it. 'You're a good man, John . . . stronger than any of us.'

There was a tap at the door. Davie called hesitantly, 'Supper's ready.'

'One moment,' John said hastily. He must give Mistress Shields time to recover. 'Would you like to go upstairs?' he whispered. 'There's a wash-stand and towels in the bedroom. You could wash your face.'

'No, thank you.' Helen produced a square of linen and blew into it vigorously. John ventured a tiny joke.

'Do they all have their handkerchieves still, up in Scotland? I don't think they've ever recovered from that at the Big House.'

(viii)

It was a strange meal. They squeezed round the kitchen table now covered with one of Davie's samples. He whipped off the label as Helen entered the room. Mr Nettles was introduced and sat opposite, awed by the formidable presence. Helen couldn't bring herself to speak to Mary but for John's sake she exerted herself and asked Mr Nettles questions he could expound on, about the manufacture of brass.

Mary waited on them, moving deftly between hob and table. She made sure Helen was served on the one china plate, that her tea was in the only matching cup and saucer. Supper was broth with dumplings. Mary was an excellent cook, Helen decided. She watched how the heavily built-up shoe dragged across the kitchen, how the weight emphasized Mary's limp. She found herself thinking if Mary had been an animal, any farmer would have let her die at birth. She sighed and scolded herself for such an unchristian thought. All the same, it was a wonder she was still pregnant the way her body twisted so each time she took a step. Would she manage to carry the child full term? Helen shivered and almost caught herself praying that it shouldn't happen; but then she remembered the child was the only reason for the sacrifice. No, it had to happen, please God. And for the first time Helen wondered who was responsible.

166

Davie was aching to know what had passed between them in the parlour. Was the wedding going ahead? He'd guessed why the school mistress had come. Neither he nor Mary discussed it but he felt guilty. Unable to face the prospect of a gloomy evening, he set himself the task of making them laugh. He told them respectable travellers' tales, of visits to fine houses peopled by eccentrics. Once John asked him about the trip to Leeds but Davie managed to change the subject. Helen noticed and wondered what mischief he'd been up to there. She sighed. They were still only boys and tomorrow, one of them was to be married. It was ludicrous! She looked at the watch on her fob. 'If I'm to find a hotel tonight,' she began. John immediately jumped up. He'd ask Mrs Beal. Some of her neighbours had rooms to let but Helen was firm. It had been a long journey. On her return she'd have to face Alex and Jeannie McKie. Tonight at least, she'd be pampered. Where, she asked them, could she find the most comfortable bed in Darlington? It would have to be in a temperance hotel, naturally, and suitable for a lady.

John and Davie accompanied her. In Coburg Street, Mr Nettles retired to his room and in a corner of the kitchen, Mary sewed the last pair of sheets. Her hand shook as she thought of what must have passed between John and Helen but as he'd put on his coat, John managed to whisper, 'Nothing has happened.' She tried not to show too much gratitude; she knew it embarrassed him.

In the bright lights of the foyer, Davie was surprised to see that Mistress Shields' hair was grey. He'd always remembered it as brown. Her back was still the same, ramrod straight. 'May I call for you tomorrow morning? The wedding isn't until one o'clock. I'd like you to see the town while you're here.'

'Certainly, Davie, but not before ten o'clock.' The two men raised their hats and Helen walked stiffly up the ornate staircase.

The chambermaid banked up the fire and Helen sat gazing at it. Behind her the bed looked inviting but sleep was far off. She was troubled. This tragedy for which she was partly responsible was going ahead. Although she'd come to prevent it, she couldn't. John had demanded she examine her conscience over Mary, and face the consequences for her and the child. Had she

167

the right to condemn the girl? It was a dilemma Helen Shields hadn't faced before. She'd been brought up on the simple premise that a woman who fell from grace deserved her fate; until now she'd never questioned it.

At school, Helen taught morality. She left instructions on matters temporal to the parents. Once during her girlhood, there had been discussion at the vicarage of a fallen woman who'd been returned to the parish by the district where she'd sought refuge. Helen recalled her father lamenting the burden of supporting the fruits of wickedness out of the rates. Helen wondered what had happened to such women. Once they were swallowed up inside the workhouse they were rarely heard of again. Despite the warmth of the room, she shivered.

There were other unpleasant facts to be faced. When Mary first asked for help, she'd found herself recoiling as she'd done when the girl attended school. But weren't the lame entitled to her compassion? She admitted to herself now that this same revulsion had made her write that letter, passing the problem on to John. She'd wanted to rid herself of it, speedily. Once Mary caught the train to England, Helen Shields knew she would be unlikely to see her again and that was the truth. Well, John had dealt with the problem. How could she now complain? It was too late for any recriminations; tomorrow John would do his duty as he saw it. Helen Shields must think herself lucky he'd offered her a hand in friendship. Had she not been responsible for ruining his life? 'We must hope he can make the best of it,' she murmured to the empty, lonely room and bent to unlace her boots.

The brothers returned to Coburg Street in silence. There were so many questions Davie wanted to ask but he knew better than to begin. He must wait until John was ready. He wondered if he'd finally learn the reason for the wedding. As nothing had been said over supper, he assumed it was still taking place. Whenever he'd tried to ask lately, John always gave the same reply. 'Afterwards. I'll explain afterwards.'

Davie wondered idly what arrangements had been made for after the ceremony. If John and Mary were to occupy the back bedroom, he presumed he himself would move back into their old room at Mrs Beal's. It was a pity. A chap could be much more comfortable when Mary was managing things. Davie

168

sighed and resolved to eat all his meals at home. He wasn't forsaking that.

Beside him, John felt utterly drained. He'd been worn down by the fate that had made a puppet of him. In Coburg Street he stopped, looking at the clear night sky full of stars. 'We're only specks in that universe, Davie. Have you ever considered that? Two atoms of dust that don't matter one little bit.'

Mary had on her cloak, ready to leave. She'd been weeping. Davie called 'goodnight' and hurried off up the stairs. John could deal with it, she was his problem. The betrothed pair were alone for the first time that day. He tried to comfort her.

'Never mind Mistress Shields, Mary. She came and said what she did for the best but it hasn't altered my purpose. It will be all right, you'll see. Now, no more tears, for my sake.' Mary wiped away the last ones and tied on her bonnet.

'May I tell you what I've arranged for tomorrow night?'

John blushed scarlet. So far they hadn't discussed this and the mere thought of it embarrassed him. 'Yes?' Weary though she was Mary sensed his mood and her reply was prosaic.

'I've borrowed the truckle bed from Mrs Beal. I shall sleep in the kitchen. During the day, the bed can be folded away in the scullery.' John was fiery red as he mumbled, 'What about the lodgers?'

'As I shall be the last to bed and the first to rise, what Mr Nettles thinks is of no concern provided he pays his rent on time. Besides, I doubt whether he will notice.' It had been a long day and she yearned to sleep. 'It will suffice for the present, John. Once the baby arrives . . . ' she shrugged, 'I daresay I shall think of some other arrangement.'

'I wondered,' he began, but he couldn't bring himself to finish the sentence. She'd no idea what he had in mind but the tiny phrase kindled the smallest of hopes. Would there ever come a time when he could bring himself to look on her kindly? It was as much as she dare believe.

'It's better if I'm downstairs,' she said simply, to ease the confusion between them, 'That way I shan't disturb any of you when I rise in the mornings.'

'Yes, of course.' Her practical approach reassured him. They walked the short distance to her lodging and John murmured, 'It was kind of Mrs Beal to make the loan.'

'I've done mending for her in return. We're not in her debt, John. She assumes we need the bed for Davie.' The conversation had taken a wrong turn again and he was glad of the darkness. They went in through the back yard, for Mrs Beal was still particular about her parlour carpet, and at the door, Mary held out her hand. John bent and kissed it. It was the first romantic gesture of his life.

'I will see you tomorrow, Mary,' he promised.

(ix)

The postman came early in Coburg Street. John answered the door in his shirt sleeves. The letter had been carefully copied out as though Alex had given great thought to the matter.

My dear son,

Yr. mother and I are greatly troubled. We have had no word from you since receiving Davie's letter.

I know you would do nothing to hurt yr. mother's feelings. She misses you both but does not complain. We know it is for the best that you and Davie have to live and work so far away.

Mistress Shields is making the journey at her own expense. She would not accept one penny towards the cost of the ticket. She is a sensible woman. I beg you listen to what she has to say.

The old cow lost her calf on Saturday and died herself in the morning. Alla does not remember a time when the gales were so bad.

Yr. loving father,

ALEXANDER MCKIE

Underneath Jeannie had written:

My love and prayers go with you both.

John tucked it in an inside pocket where the pain of it burned through to his skin.

By ten o'clock, Davie was in the hotel foyer, full of impatience.

170

'I would like to show you Darlington,' he told Helen when she arrived, 'It's a fine, prosperous town.' She was feeling much better. The chambermaid had trudged up and down with jugs of boiling water, pouring them into a tub in front of the bedroom fire. Helen had soaked her limbs back into a semblance of ease.

'Not too far,' she warned, 'Walking on pavements isn't the same as on the moors.'

They went at a sedate pace to give her time to admire the sights. Davie had a shopping list and made a few small purchases.

'It's not much for John,' he said regretfully, 'considering it's the happiest day of his life.' Helen didn't comment. He bought a few small bunches of flowers, determined to do his best. He'd asked his brother one last time when they woke this morning. John's reply was unequivocal. The wedding would take place. Now Davie was doing all he could to make it festive. 'There's just one more shop,' he coaxed, 'then we can go back to Coburg Street. You can manage a small step farther, can't you Mistress Shields?' She looked at him sharply. She hadn't missed the change of tone.

'If it's absolutely necessary?'

'Yes, it is. Indeed it is.'

They were at one end of Skinnergate. Helen had been admiring the portico of the Mechanics' Institute. Lifting her skirt to avoid the mud, she splashed across, following Davie into Armitage's.

Davie looked toward the butter counter: she was there, standing behind the slab, very trim in her brown overall. He beamed and it was as if the sun had come out. Energy and happiness emanated from him in a manner no one could miss. Helen Shields spotted it instantly, her nose rising like a pointer bitch. Where was the cause? She saw Charlotte and the corners of her mouth tucked in. Good Heavens, Davie was far too young!

Mrs Armitage sensed it too, sitting in her cage above the shop. Mr Collins had already intimated that one of the customers was enquiring after her treasure. Was it this red-headed giant of a fellow? Her bosom expanded with a fearful intake of breath. The row of buttons took the strain. Charlotte's demeanour was extremely correct. Her eyes tried to

171

stay frosty but they had to melt a little. 'We are glad to see you again,' she told Davie. 'May I be of assistance?'

If the wedding feast was an odd mixture, no one seemed to mind. There were several sorts of cheese, half a pound of ham and a quarter of best butter. Mrs Beal had offered to 'oblige' but was nonplussed to find there was no cake. Guests would have to make do with the ham instead. The parlour table had been decorated by Davie with flowers, ribbons and tissue paper. Helen Shields had to admit it all looked charming.

Mary had spent the morning giving John the only gift within her power, a shining home. After preparing everyone's breakfast, she got down to work. First the sash windows were tackled then the front step scrubbed and stoned. When Helen and Davie returned they were dazzled by the whiteness and the deep ruby red of polished lino inside the front door. They were also half choked by the smells of sugar-soap and wax. The horsehair sofa in the parlour had been rubbed till it gleamed so that Helen hesitated before daring to sit on it.

Upstairs Mary had washed the dingy dado on the landing, the pine bedroom doors with the bell-metal handles. Her fingers had been itching to give those a proper shine ever since she first arrived.

Mrs Beal found her with hair straggling over her shoulders and flushed with exertion, 'Miss Hamilton, pet,' she said reprovingly, 'It's high time you stopped all that and got yourself ready. There's a jug of hot water in your room and a piece of my good soap so run along.'

Davie met her at the foot of the stairs with two small offerings. 'For your dress and bonnet, Mary.' Impulsively, he stooped and kissed her gently on the cheek. It was more than John had done. If she remembered hearing Davie's harsh words to John that first evening, Mary gave no sign now but accepted all three gifts with heartfelt thanks.

She limped up the aisle on John's arm, the lace collar softening the neck of her bodice and the French silk violets sewn to the ribbons of her straw. She'd done what she could with her only gown; it had been cleaned and ironed that morning in Mrs Beal's kitchen.

John slipped the thin gold band on her finger, noticing how soda had roughened the skin. She works so hard, he thought absently and looked into her eyes. Love shone out, astonishing him. He'd never for an instant imagined Mary would care for him, not in that way.

Mr Wingford went briskly through the ceremony. He'd been as shocked as his congregation when he'd first seen Mary. One pitied the halt and the blind because it was meet and right so to do; one didn't necessarily marry them. He suggested to John a little awkwardly that perhaps he and Miss Hamilton should delay a while. It was embarrassing; a man's choice of mate was after all, his own concern. John had blushed and hinted at a long-standing arrangement between their families. Mr Wingford asked no further questions and John added guilt to his many problems.

The service was nearly at an end. Mr Wingford had cut several references to procreation. He assumed it unlikely Mary would bear children. He'd reasoned it out that John must be marrying her for the sake of her dowry.

As she heard them pronounced man and wife, Helen Shields emerged from her reverie. She'd taught John his alphabet, now she'd given him this double cross to bear; it was the saddest day of her life. As for Davie, he imagined how beautiful Charlotte would look, standing where Mary was, and his heart wept for his brother.

As for Mrs Beal, she was determined gaiety should prevail. To this end, knowing how abstemious the McKies were, she brought her own bottle of port. She and Mr Nettles indulged in a glass or two while they waited for the party to return. What an odd lot they were, she thought, as she passed round assorted cups and glasses, it was more like a funeral. A toast was quickly drunk and she retired to the scullery, to wash the same crockery before serving them tea. There was a knock at the front door and she went through to answer it. Mr Nettles had provided the happy pair with a unique wedding present. Having established that Mary's cooking was excellent, he'd persuaded his two friends to join him as lodgers.

If the two were surprised to see their prospective landlords wearing favours, they didn't show it. Their concern was to convince John of their respectability. Davie asked in a whisper if all was ready and the bride nodded. Within a few minutes, the business was completed.

173

'That's lucky, pet,' Mrs Beal confided. 'A houseful and all of 'em earning. I hope you'll always be so fortunate.'

As a married woman, Mary had been promoted in her eyes, to a lodging keeper of equal footing. Helen couldn't understand it; if those three were in the front bedroom, John and Mary in the back, where on earth was Davie going to live? She hadn't time to ask, she'd a train to catch. There was one more ceremony to perform. John entered the date in the Bible together with his name and Mary's. A cab was called. Bride, groom and Davie accompanied Helen to the station.

There were a few stilted exchanges on the platform before the train arrived, and promises of a visit to Scotland, 'when it can be managed.' The brothers climbed on board to stow her luggage and Helen turned to take her leave of Mary.

'I shall never forgive you for what you've done today,' she told her. Mary went red then white.

'I think you might have done the same, in my position.'

'I should never have found myself in that quandary,' replied Helen tartly. 'All that I have to say to you now is do your utmost for John McKie. He has wasted his life by marrying you. Try and make it up to him.'

Mary gave a small sob. 'I shall dedicate my life to him,' she whispered but Helen didn't hear; she climbed onto the train instead.

As Davie and John stood on the platform below her carriage window, Helen shouted above the steam, 'You may tell that young woman I enjoyed the ham!' John wondered what on earth she was talking about.

(x)

Back in her scullery, Mary set to with the mop to clean the floor and Davie was dispatched for three penn'orth of pease pudding. John settled to finish the paperwork the wedding had interrupted. Although it had been agreed with Mr Nettles and his friends to let their room on a bed, breakfast and supper basis, tonight Mary was excused. True, she had to prepare porridge for six and put the hay box by the bread oven for it to cook overnight before damping down the fire, but those were small tasks.

John came into the kitchen and put out the Bible ready for the Sabbath. While Mary dished up the pease pudding she said quietly, 'If you're agreeable I would prefer to attend evening service in future.' He and Davie understood her meaning. The fashionable crowd disported themselves in the morning. The evening was for those more interested in devotion than millinery.

'As you wish,' John told her. It would be a relief, certainly, not to have to endure those pitying looks, the well meant remarks as ladies asked how Miss Hamilton did in front of her, as though Mary were a deaf mute.

He and Davie completed their preparations for bed. Boots were coated with polish and left to dry overnight. Mary disappeared outside with the ashes and both men took turns at the sink. It was only when he was in shirt sleeves it occurred to Davie to ask where he was to sleep.

'Upstairs, as usual,' John said shortly. So *they* were moving in to Mrs Beal's! Fancy having to pay rent again, thought Davie worriedly, John wouldn't like that. There was no doubt about it, marriage was an expensive business. Thank goodness Mr Nettles had persuaded his friends to come. He padded upstairs with his candle.

He was immersed in a book when the door opened and John entered. Davie watched dumbfounded as his brother said his prayers and climbed into bed.

'What about Mary?' he asked stupidly. John lay back against the pillow and stared at the ceiling.

'She will be sleeping downstairs,' he answered dully. 'I will tell you everything now, Davie. I've married Mary to give a name and a home to the child she's carrying. Despite what has happened, I respect her and would ask you to do the same. It was the only solution. But please . . . don't ask any questions. I'm so tired!'

Davie turned each word over separately because together they didn't make sense. Mary? A baby? Slowly, he understood. He sat on the edge of his bed, wanting to reach out and comfort, but he daren't. What a terrible thing to have done. To have given your name to another man's bastard.

175

John's eyes were closed. Even by the soft light of a candle there were lines about his eyes and mouth Davie had never noticed before. As if he were conscious of the scrutiny, John murmured, 'It's up to you now, Davie. All the plans we made. All the hopes Father had. Up to you . . . ' and the weary bridegroom slept.

Davie had never been so lonely. He wanted to cry out, to destroy something – anything, would give a sense of relief. It wasn't fair! It was monstrous! There'd never ever been such a gulf dividing them. The gulf between a man who could still hope for a dream and one who has denied himself the chance. Davie was helpless. What could he do anyway, without John's guidance. John was the clever one.

'I'm only a trader,' he whispered, 'a fellow who chats to the lassies and sells them bits of stuff.' He'd never worried about the future, made plans; he'd left all that to John.

Without disturbing him, Davie padded across to the window. The room was suddenly a prison. He wanted to break the pane so that they could escape. Where to? John had responsibilities now. In his frustration he leant against the cold glass. He'd given up imagining he could see the hills that concealed London. That was all part of the abandoned dream. The reality was here now in Darlington – and he was cold. He shivered and hurried back into bed.

Faintly below he could hear Mary moving about. A baby! Whose was it, he wondered. He couldn't have acted like John, he didn't have the generosity or the strength. His feet were painfully cold. Davie pulled his overcoat on top of the blankets, tucking it well in. 'It's all very well,' he grumbled. 'All I want is to marry Charlotte Forrest.' The thought had crystallized into words for the first time. Charlotte . . . with the blue eyes. And despite himself, the impetuous lover slept.

It was another hour before the bride crept into her bed. All was tidy downstairs. Grates were raked out and fires laid. Three pans and the kettle stood on the warm hob full of water, ready for morning. Empty ewers were ranged alongside. She'd already done the bits of washing the three lodgers had put outside their room. This morning, as a spinster, it wouldn't have been proper to handle such garments. Now it was different; she was a respectable married woman. Flannel shirts and woollen combinations hung in a moist steaming row in front of the kitchen range. She would need to be up early to iron some of those shirts. They would all need a clean one to attend Chapel.

The small bed was tucked into a corner. Mary lay looking at the shadows made by the moonlight. On the high, narrow shelf that ran round three sides of the room above the picture rail, she'd stowed her possessions: the French silk violets, carefully unpicked from her straw hat, had to be kept for special occasions, as had the lace collar. It was too good for ordinary Sundays. She saw the shapes of the tissue-wrapped packages and below, distorted and grotesque, the shadow of her built-up boot: without her skirt to conceal it, the metal brace and straps looked like a medieval instrument of torture, but she needed them to support her weak leg.

She felt, as she always did, the shape of her deformity using her healthy toes. Only the outer edge of the club foot touched the ground, the rest curled inwards, gnarled and taut as a fist. Nothing would ever straighten it. The remedies that had been tried when she was a child made her feel sick even to think of them. Under the thin blankets she felt the weak leg muscles relax. Always there was an ache across her hips and spine. The only time she was free of it was in those first, blessed moments when she emerged from sleep.

She was so physically exhausted now she had to fight to stay awake to say her prayers. She begged the Almighty's pardon for not being on her knees before giving thanks once more for John. Then she closed her eyes, ready to open them again at five thirty next morning.

It was another month before she visited the doctor. The man was puzzled by some of the answers to his questions and sent a message asking John to visit. They faced each other aross the cluttered surgery desk. 'Mary was pregnant when we married,' John admitted quietly and the doctor sighed with relief.

'That was obvious from the dates,' he said brusquely, 'but you should hear some of the tales I'm expected to swallow.' There was a gentle tap and the nurse poked her head round the door.

'Come in, Hannah, come in. He's not ill – he's going to be a father.' She brought with her a frothing jug of beer and the doctor sighed, this time from pleasure. 'Marvellous sight. Means there's no one else waiting to see me. Have a glass?' John shook his head. The nurse left them again and the doctor swallowed thirstily.

'Got a busy night ahead,' he explained. 'Two souls on their way out of this world – one of them fighting every step of the way, poor fellow. Another scrap of humanity about to gladden her father's heart – unless it's a boy. He's got seven of those already. Now then . . . '

The doctor leaned across, addressing John seriously, 'this business of your wife's, it's going to be – let's say, it's not going to be straightforward. For obvious reasons.'

'I feared as much.'

'It may mean . . . surgery. I hope not, but the position of the womb – ' He halted abruptly, looking at John. 'You're not going to pass out on me, are you? If I tell you about it?'

'No.' It was ironic. If only it could have been he on the opposite side of the desk, fully qualified and caring for the sick.

'She's brave, your wife. Knows all about pain with that foot of hers. Now, this happy event is due to take place in July, right?'

'I – I understand so, yes.'

The doctor looked up in surprise at the hesitancy.

'Haven't you discussed it?' John flushed but made no reply and the doctor spoke involuntarily. 'Good Lord, it's not your child, is it?'

'That is my business!' John was scarcely audible. The doctor strove to recover himself.

'Yes, well . . . I think we can safely assume it will be July. Or thereabouts. Has she . . . have you any female relatives, anyone who can be with her?' John shook his head.

'There's my brother and I. And we have three lodgers who work in the foundry.' The doctor's mouth twitched.

'Well, maybe I'll arrange for a nurse to attend your wife, Mr McKie. Just in case the five of you need a bit of help. Now there are one or two general points . . . '

When John emerged into the spring night his head reeled. He hadn't given a thought to the practical aspects of what was to happen. There had been so many other matters to occupy his thoughts. Davie's trading had expanded so much – he'd got a gift for it, thank goodness – they'd spent hours worrying over whether to take on another assistant. Surgery! He came back to the present with a rush. He hadn't bargained for that. As he'd paid Dr Cullen his sixpence, he'd been warned that it could be expensive. Of course there was the free hospital . . . John shook his head. Mary deserved better than that.

The first thing he saw as he entered the parlour was Mary carrying two scuttles of coal. 'You must leave that for Davie and I,' he ordered. 'It's important you don't over-tax yourself from now on.' Mary smiled serenely.

'Don't worry, I can manage. The baby's doing fine. I hope the doctor told you so.'

It amazed John to realize how they had all drifted into a routine where Mary cooked, washed and ironed, cleaned the house and waited on them. Not that they didn't appreciate it, he said to himself. Young Nettles and his friends were forever praising her cooking – but how were they going to manage in the future?

Mrs Beal had supervised half the pregnancies in Coburg Street. She took on a new authority when John and Davie consulted her. A girl must be employed, to help Mary and to do the 'rough'. But where was she to sleep? A jobbing builder was called in. The house couldn't be changed permanently, for the brothers were still paying rent for it, but perhaps a system of partitions could be devised, John asked hopefully. After all, the rooms were very large. 'Enormous,' echoed Davie loyally. The builder sucked at his remaining teeth and suggested a solution. The dining table would go in the parlour and a cubby hole would be devised in the kitchen. When Mrs Beal came to tell them she'd found a girl, she was shocked. How could Mary bear the indignity of losing her parlour? Of having no room full of shining, polished objects, set aside for 'best'? But Mary smiled. She didn't mind and John was happy with the result. Every square foot of the house had been put to good use, and Ada's wages were only two shillings a week. They would hardly notice the expense.

It was after the workmen had finished and Davie was putting stock away on new shelving in their bedroom that the two of them realized they hadn't thought of anywhere for the baby.

'Don't worry,' Davie said cheerfully. 'Such a wee thing. It

won't need more than a corner or two for a long while yet.'

As July drew nearer John found himself thinking more and more about Mary's ordeal. Enquiries made by friends at church were a worry: always the pretence had to be maintained that nothing was expected before September. Mr Richardson asked politely whether Mary was 'at home' to visitors as his wife wished to call. John blushed and muttered she remained indisposed. Mary had met the Quaker household at the time of their marriage. After that there had been no further contact apart from letters. It was safe for Mary to reply to those. When Mrs Richardson learned about the baby, she sent gifts but Mary couldn't call to thank the lady, her bulk was too far advanced.

John discovered he cared very much about what was to happen. He lay awake worrying about surgery even though Mary seemed unruffled. She moved more slowly about the house and the strain on her weak leg showed in her face but all she ever said was, 'I'm well, thank you, John.' If fate had decreed that she of all women could conceive then she must be destined to have her child. It gave her the confidence to ignore Mrs Beal's gynaecological forebordings.

Another discovery surprised John, more important than the rest; the day arrived when he no longer spent time brooding about Mary's seducer. During the early weeks of their marriage, he avoided contact with his wife. She'd only to offer to help him on with his coat for John to feel revulsion. But such strong dislike had to fade in the force of Mary's sheer energy in caring for him and their home. There were so many little ways in which she contrived to make life pleasant that John found himself positively eager to return home in the evenings. Nor could he sustain a vendetta against a phantom. He'd never met her lover nor had Mary given a description. The subject was never spoken of between them. Without an image on which to concentrate, John's intense feelings against him began to appear futile.

He knew Mary to be utterly honest. Why should she lie therefore about so important a matter? The truth was that she'd been deceived like many another woman before her. Christ had pronounced Magdalene forgiven and if John hadn't the strength to do the same with Mary, at least he no longer shied away.

It surprised him to notice that Mary had particularly expressive eyes. Davie remarked on them and John remembered to look next time Mary spoke to him. Also, her pale complexion and dark hair were so neat as to be almost attractive – for he abhorred frizzled hair on a woman. He ceased to think of her as a cripple – her limp was so much a part of her – but as someone with a keen mind, ready to discuss any matter he chose to raise.

The day came when John realized he hadn't once thought of her seducer since rising that morning. He'd helped Mary with household tasks, their hands had touched and John hadn't moved away. So was it over? Would he still continue to fret about the baby girl – he was convinced by ancient beliefs that the fruits of sin had to be female – attributing disagreeable character traits to that unknown father? He decided he wouldn't. Besides, Dr Cullen had given him something else to worry over: the baby might not be healthy. Mary's deformity was one that could be inherited.

CHAPTER SIX

Married Life

Davie's courtship wasn't rapid. He knew from the first it would be a long-drawn-out campaign. Each time he entered the citadel it was apparent how well the treasure was guarded. He'd only to step over the threshold of Armitage's to be a marked man. If there was the slightest excuse – one other customer was all Mr Collins needed – to divert Davie from his objective, he was handed over to another assistant.

Davie had declared himself openly, that was the trouble. It was impossible for him to dissemble. He'd shown his feelings by beaming at Charlotte once too often.

She had other admirers, too. He watched jealously if he found her chatting to any of them. Male customers would become aware of a threatening presence; glancing round nervously, they'd find themselves confronted by a glowering giant. Charlotte was annoyed at such behaviour. It was bad for trade, apart from being undignified. But how to stop it? And did she really *want* to send Mr Davie McKie away? She enjoyed being the centre of attention, to be heiress apparent of the

Establishment, but her aunt's watchfulness and Mr Collins' vigilance could be irksome on occasion. It was all so – so unsettling! Did she but understand it, she was a bird flapping her wings, ready to fly the nest.

Davie took to leaving small gifts. Bunches of flowers, a poem copied from his favourite book. Finally, in open declaration, a morocco-bound volume of Burns. Charlotte behaved with the utmost correctness. She returned his gift, via the delivery boy, carefully wrapped and with a note. She had consulted her Aunt Armitage; Mr Davie McKie's gift was too generous. Although conscious of the great honour he did in bestowing it, she begged to be allowed to return it, with her best thanks.

It had to be admitted that Charlotte did so without much of a pang. She liked the *appearance* of the book, the shiny red leather with gold lettering, but she hadn't the same passion Davie had for poetry. When Charlotte visited the lending library, she remembered the hats rather than the contents of any book. Nevertheless, she recognized the gift for what it was: a token, a gesture and one that couldn't be ignored. Davie was ready to begin the siege in earnest. But first, he had to tell John.

(i)

Inside the crowded house in Coburg Street, it was understood that in the evenings the lodgers had the parlour to themselves. After the evening meal, John and Davie retreated to the partitioned kitchen with their paperwork. Davie chose an evening when John had no engagements: he wasn't sure how long it would take to screw up enough courage. He sat, unable to concentrate on his order book, fiddling with a pen.

'John, I want to get married. To Charlotte Forrest.'

Mary was the first to take in what he'd said. She gathered up Ada and the two of them retreated to the scullery. John blinked, keeping his finger on the place in the column of figures. Forrest . . . Forrest? Was she a member of the Dorcas Society? Marriage! 'She's Mrs Armitage's niece,' said Davie.

So that's why they'd been inundated with cheese recently! John stared at him. 'Have you spoken to her?'

183

'Not yet, I want to do it properly. Will you come with me, to ask permission of Mr and Mrs Armitage?' Davie leaned forward, eyes shining. 'She's a beautiful girl, John, and I think I'm in love with her.'

The word had no meaning for John so he never used it yet here was Davie, obviously brimming over with it. He took off his spectacles, the better to focus on him. 'Does she – does Miss Forrest – reciprocate your feelings?'

'I haven't presumed to ask! I wouldn't dare! Not yet, anyway. I don't think she's – indifferent.' Davie was scarlet and his fingers threatened to snap the pen in half. John replaced his spectacles.

'Where would you live?' he asked quietly. 'I doubt if you could bring her here even if we asked Mr Nettles to move out – '

'Oh, no. Miss Forrest couldn't live in Coburg Street, Mrs Armitage wouldn't permit it.' Davie hadn't given the matter a moment's thought before but so much was obvious.

'So where will you go?'

In an instant Davie was reduced from carefree lover to hapless younger brother. 'I don't know,' he admitted, 'I hadn't even considered.' He looked at John, full of hope. 'Can you think of a solution?' John took a pencil, drew a line under the column and closed his account book. It was no use trying to do any more with it tonight.

'Leave it with me. There may be a way but I'm not promising.'

'And you will come with me? To see Mr and Mrs Armitage?'

'You'd better do things properly: write and ask for an appointment. I warn you, Davie, what I have in mind – it could take time.' For a long-cherished idea was beginning to take shape.

'Oh, I don't care how long it takes,' said Davie airily, the red curls recovering their buoyancy. 'As long as Charlotte Forrest becomes my wife at the end of it.'

But this was June, with July only three weeks away, when there was another matter due of even greater concern. Perhaps it was as well, thought John when he remembered; it would permit Davie to discover whether he was in love or had been bowled over yet again by a pair of blue eyes.

Perhaps because he'd talked so much of September, John had come to believe himself that Mary wouldn't be confined before then. It was Davie who pointed out how fortunate it was that the foundry would be shut for the annual holiday in July. John nodded vaguely but didn't give it much thought. Whenever Mary visited the doctor, she never referred to her pregnancy except to assure him all was well. He supposed he would be told when other arrangements had to be made.

One evening early in July, Mr Nettles came home with important news. His 'intended's' parents had agreed to receive him: he was leaving for Sunderland the following morning and needed to make the best possible impression. The Adam's apple quivered with anxiety. Mary understood and washed and starched all his shirts. It meant working late into the night. Despite Ada's protests, she took her turn at the heavy iron mangle.

Whether it was that that caused her pains to start, she didn't discover. They began as Mary climbed into the small borrowed bed. She sat, gasping for breath. It was past midnight and she didn't want to disturb the household.

For a while, she suffered as silently as she could, gripping sheets, blankets, anything, as each wave overwhelmed her. At last she gave in and crawled across to rouse Ada. The girl woke to find her mistress clinging to the partition, covered in sweat.

'Fetch the doctor. Go quietly mind, we must try not to wake them.'

The busy man was attending another patient. Ada had to walk a further mile through rainy streets to find the house. She knocked. From an upper window, a voice enquired what was the matter. Ada replied and was told to wait. Presently the doctor joined her. They went in his trap back to Coburg Street. 'How long has she had her pains?' he asked brusquely, but Ada didn't know. 'I hope it's not too late to move her to hospital,' he grumbled. 'Now, you're to be a good girl and do as I tell you. Understand?' Ada nodded. As the eldest of six there wasn't much she didn't know about childbirth.

They went through the yard and entered by the scullery door.

Five minutes later, the doctor was clattering up the stairs and rapping on the bedroom door. 'It's your wife, Mr McKie. She's started.' John pulled on his trousers.

If the doctor had been surprised at the sleeping arrangements, he didn't comment. There was too much to do. Davie was shaken into consciousness and given sharp instructions. It was too late to move Mary to hospital but she must be got into a proper bed. The baby would be born here, in this room. John and Davie must vacate it immediately.

And Davie must run and ask the nurse to come straight round, then he must wake the lodgers and take them to Mrs Beal's. The apprentices weren't due to go on holiday for another couple of days but they must be got out of the house.

Davie rubbed the sleep from his eyes and staggered off into the night. Ada made up his bed with Mary's sheets and went back to iron one clean shirt for Mr Nettles. At least that way he could be persuaded to leave for Sunderland. She went back upstairs with the first jug of hot water then down once more to begin slicing bacon for their breakfasts. She wasn't excited; what was there to get excited about? One more mouth to feed, that was all. When Davie returned, incoherent, unbrushed hair standing on end, Ada put a cup of tea in his hand and stood his shaving mug on the kitchen table. 'There's plenty of time,' she told him, 'They've got the missus upstairs and the young chaps are down the road. Don't tek on.' She went upstairs with tea for the doctor.

Mary was in a deep chloroform coma when the doctor and nurse eased her baby into the summer morning. She never heard the boy's first cry nor the thankful curses as the doctor examined the tiny body and found it perfect. The nurse washed the child and wrapped it in a blanket. When Mary was attended to, still mercifully unconscious, they bandaged her from her hips to her knees in the approved manner of the time. Thus swathed she would remain immobile for a fortnight, as all mothers did.

As he examined her torn body before they bandaged her, the doctor said, 'She's going to be in agony after what I've had to do. Can you manage here, nurse? Or shall I ask for more help?' The woman looked round the small back bedroom, assessing what little income would be available. Not much, she decided.

'I'll train that girl downstairs,' she told him. 'She looked fairly clean.'

There was a knock and John came with coals and kindling, as instructed. Doctor and nurse were of the new school of thought: plenty of fresh air and warmth for the baby. So the dawn breeze crept under the sash and a fire blazed. The doctor patted John's shoulder. 'She'll pull through – I hope. But he's a fine child. You've no worries there, Mr McKie,' he said, and went downstairs for a wash.

The nurse took the scuttle from him. 'Would you like to see your son?' John was speechless and she smiled. It was always the same. She pointed at the drawer beside the bed. It was from the kitchen dresser. Mary had lined it in readiness with bits of flannel and sheeting. Inside lay a very small human being. John knelt. He didn't quite know what to do so he poked it very gently. There was a movement. The tiny rosebud mouth opened and yawned. John felt excitement welling up such as he'd never known before.

'A boy, is it?'

'It is, Mc McKie.'

'Well then, he is to be a doctor! What do you think of that?' She looked at him in disbelief. A doctor, indeed!

'I'd leave it a week or two, Mr McKie, before you set him up in practice.'

Downstairs the doctor was tucking into bacon and eggs. He'd sent Ada for a jug of porter and pointed to a chair with his fork. 'Sit down, Mr McKie. There are one or two things you and I need to discuss. Your wife up there, she's had a bad time. She should have been booked into the hospital – I can't think why you didn't arrange it. I could've done a Caesarian if we'd got her there in time. As it is, we must simply be thankful, but . . .' He waved the fork again. 'There are to be no more, d'you understand?' John was confused. 'Babies, Mr McKie. She couldn't stand having another, it would kill her.'

John stuttered in his effort to reassure him. Didn't the doctor remember the circumstances? The doctor did but he was also accustomed to human nature, to men with tears in their eyes as they made empty promises and to terrified women who, nine or ten months later, struggled exhausted to bring another unwanted child into the world. He was listening to a man who

187

assured him he'd no intention of touching his wife, but that was nonsense. He'd married her, hadn't he? The doctor swallowed a mouthful of bacon, 'I only hope Mrs McKie will get over this birth and not be an invalid,' he said with meaning. 'She'll need a great deal of help, to get up on that foot of hers again and start walking.'

'It's as bad as that?'

'She's not strong, Mr McKie. I had to use plenty of chloroform up there.' The sweet sickliness clung to his clothes and filled the room. John could taste it in his mouth.

'Mary will get better, won't she?'

'With time, and good nursing, I hope so.'

'She won't be bedridden? Anything like that?' The doctor wiped the fried bread round his plate and sat back replete.

'Mr McKie, up there we managed a bit of a miracle. You may not have realized it, but we did. I've told the nurse to stay on, by the way. You can manage her wages, can't you?' John nodded. 'Your wife's womb . . . ' he burped, 'with the way her body was twisted . . . ' he burped again, 'and out of that came a perfect male child. Be very thankful.'

'Oh, I am!'

Ada came in through the scullery. 'I had to knock them up and they weren't best pleased.' She pushed the jug of beer across the table. The doctor drank deeply.

'There's a good girl. Here's a penny for you. See you do everything the nurse tells you to.' He pulled on his coat. 'Good day to you, Mr McKie. I'll call again this evening.' He picked up his bag and John followed him through the yard to where the trap waited in the back lane. The doctor took in deep breaths of fresh summer air. 'Have you decided what to call him?'

'Who?'

'That small boy upstairs.' He looked John firmly in the eye, 'Your son, Mr McKie.' John blushed and nodded again, deliberately this time.

'My son. No, we've no name for him yet.'

'You can discuss it with your wife in a day or two, when I say she's well enough.' He clucked at the bay and flicked the reins.

Davie had taken refuge with the lodgers, at Mrs Beal's. When he finally summoned up courage to return, he found John sitting in the kitchen reading his Bible. Terribly afraid, Davie asked,

'Is it over?' The house was so silent! John smiled. How many weeks since Davie had seen him do that?

'It's a boy, Davie. A healthy wee boy – nothing wrong with him at all! Perfect, the doctor said. I'm choosing him a name.'

'A boy!' Somehow Davie had not imagined it before, Mary's bulk having substance. 'And everything's all right, you say?'

'I touched him and d'you know what – he opened his mouth!' John was suffused with happiness now, 'But he's so small, you'll never believe it.'

'What about Mary?'

'The doctor says she'll need nursing. It'll take time but she should recover.' He hugged Davie impulsively and seeing that happiness, so long absent from John, Davie beamed too.

'Oh, Davie, a boy. Think of it. To be a doctor!'

Realization made Davie shout. 'Why, of course! Why didn't I think of that!'

'Ssh! That nurse is a real terror. Would you like to see him?'

'I would!' Davie's whisper had the force of a gale.

'They went upstairs in stockinged feet. Timidly, they knocked. The nurse surveyed them coldly. 'Well?'

'It's the baby. This is my brother . . . Just a peep, nurse!'

'Only for a moment . . . and that's an order, Mr McKie. After that your wife must have absolute quiet.'

Davie went in on tip-toe, trying to ignore the sickly smell, not daring to look at the figure on the bed. Bursting with pride, John stood in the doorway, watching him. Davie held his breath and bent his huge frame over the tiny being. The child didn't move.

'Are you sure he's all right?' he whispered.

'Yes, praise be.' The nurse looked pointedly at the bed. Despite himself, Davie glanced and saw the shrunken face and slack mouth. He listened to the shallow breathing. Mary's eyes were shut, the skin beneath almost purple. Dear God! 'Will she live?' he asked fearfully. The nurse hurried him outside.

'Of course she will, they both will. Now be off the pair of you and send that girl up.'

So Ada trudged back upstairs as she was to do so many times

in the next few months, to collect the first of countless bundles
of washing the nurse had ready for her.

Downstairs Davie assured John that never had there been so
perfect a specimen of a male child. He hurried back to Mrs Beal
with the good news. John took out pen and paper. Why did he
feel so happy? As if he really was the father? He couldn't think
of a reason but he didn't try too hard. He was glad and that was
enough, glad that he had a son.

> Dear Father and Mother,
> I am happy to inform you that Mary was delivered of a boy
> this morning. He is a strong, healthy child, according to the
> doctor, and Mary is as well as can be expected. We have a
> nurse for her. The boy will be baptized Luke and is to be a
> doctor. Please give my respects to Mistress Shields and tell
> her the news.
> > Yr. loving son,
> > JOHN

It wasn't a brave letter. He hadn't written honestly or openly
since the wedding. He'd only mentioned once before that Mary
was expecting a child. It was a bare six and a half months – now
they'd all realize it wasn't his. He hoped and prayed they'd
accept Luke as he had done. Why did he not write to Helen,
separately? He'd lost all hatred for her long ago, but at the back
of his mind was the niggling thought that although he had a son,
he also had a wife and she was going to recover.

In the croft, Alex read the letter in silence then handed it to
Jeannie. When she'd finished it, she said softly, 'It's what I
thought . . . why he did, what he did.' Alex was tremendously
angry.

'You never spoke out – never told me! We could've
prevented it!'

'No. We didn't have the right –'

'Right! You and I have rights, Jeannie. The right not to have
a bastard brought into the family.'

'It's not a bastard, it's John's son. He's said so in the letter.
And the boy's name is Luke.' She felt sorry for her husband,
for his hurt pride. She knew what was going through his mind.
Alex had never let up his efforts; slowly but surely the savings
had increased, to send his grandchild to university. If Jeannie let

him, Alex would disclaim the boy, refuse his inheritance. 'Our son is a good, kind man, Alex. He would expect no less of you and neither do I.'

Davie was the first to receive a reply to his letter. In an old-fashioned, spidery hand, trembling here and there with emotion, Mr and Mrs Armitage granted Messrs Davie and John McKie permission to make an appointment for the following Tuesday at half past four o'clock, when Mrs Armitage would be pleased to give them tea.

Davie crowed with delight and tossed it across to John.

'She's agreed to see us! She must know why we're calling.'

'No doubt,' John said soberly, 'and it's time for me to start our plan moving.'

'What plan is that?'

'Wait and see.' It was such a huge undertaking, John wasn't sure he could manage it.

His discussions with Mr Richardson were detailed and serious. John was in the best possible position to know how well the Quaker was faring, how much trade had increased over the last two years, but he was nervous lest his employer think he was taking advantage of that knowledge. In front of his study fire, Mr Richardson sat and brooded. John waited patiently. 'It would be a risk, Mr McKie. You've no collateral to offer me.'

'No, sir. The sum I can pledge is as I've described it. It represents our total savings.' It was larger than Mr Richardson had expected. John McKie must be a very thrifty man, he thought.

'And your brother, Mr McKie . . . ?'

'He has a natural talent for such a venture,' John replied, 'I think it is his charm. He has proved an excellent trader and his time with Mr Gordon is nearly at an end.'

'And now he wants to get married. He's very young for that, surely?'

'Davie is twenty-three. It is young, I agree, but I think marriage would be the right step for him to take.' John was as serious as if he were discussing money. 'It's his charm, you see.

It has made the ladies more aware of him. I know my father was worried about it.'

'And has he met a suitable person? I ask, Mr McKie, because the success of your plan will depend on your wives as much as yourselves, I think.'

'Yes, Mr Richardson, I agree. But if Davie succeeds, I think it will prove an excellent choice. He is about to ask permission of Mr and Mrs Armitage . . . their niece, Miss Charlotte Forrest . . . they have no children of their own.'

'Armitages? In Skinnergate?'

'Yes.'

'Ah . . . ' And Mr Richardson understood. 'Then I think all I can say at this stage, Mr McKie, is come to me again once the young couple are . . . affianced.' John bowed and withdrew. He'd sown the seeds and he knew they'd fallen on fertile soil. If, as he supposed, his proposition appealed to Mr Richardson, then it was only a matter of time. And of Davie.

Did he pause to consider he was manipulating his brother's life? And that of the unknown Miss Forrest? John did not. Since his own had changed direction from the day he'd arrived in Darlington, slowly but inexorably he'd set his sights on the target: his own business. Davie wouldn't argue, Davie was happy with whatever John arranged, he had complete faith. It never occurred to John that Miss Forrest might wish to be consulted; he hadn't yet noticed Charlotte's chin. Nor Mary, but then she was only his wife. John had never asked her opinion except over household matters. And now his ambition included Luke. It gave John a purpose. He felt the same surge of gladness he'd felt the day the child was born. That evening when Davie finished penning his acceptance to Mrs Armitage, John even offered to go to the post with it.

The great day arrived. Charlotte had been banished for the afternoon, to sit with her uncle. She knew why although nothing was said. But her aunt was wearing her second-best dress of Florentine green silk and she'd never been seen in the shop in that before. So Charlotte read patiently from the *Northern Echo* because her aunt declared Mr Armitage preferred it, and Bertha toiled up and down breathlessly, with secret whispers. 'They're here . . . Mr Collins is showing them into the morning room.'

Mrs Armitage had waited in the cage where she could survey the shop. Her bosom had trembled as Mr Collins intimated that her visitors had arrived. She looked down on the two heads, the red curls not so far below and beside them, John's drab, mousy hair, receding a little already. Neither brother stirred. Davie had warned John what to expect. They waited, clutching their hats.

Mr Collins made a dignified return. The other assistants strained to hear. 'Mrs Armitage requests you will be so good as to follow me, gentlemen. She will attend you in a moment or two.'

The cloth was the same chenille as when Jane and her baby first sat there. Furniture still stood in formation, polished, dusted but never used. Davie fumbled with the fringe as Charlotte once had done. Neither he nor John spoke. They heard the swish of silk, the heavy footstep. Both rose. Mrs Armitage, palpitating, lace handkerchief at the ready, entered. Behind her, Bertha staggered in with a tray. Davie bowed low. 'Good afternoon, Mrs Armitage. May I introduce myself? I'm Davie McKie and this is my brother John.'

When Charlotte returned to her counter she was well aware what had transpired. She gave no sign. Her aunt was back in her cage and there were the usual customers in the shop but the atmosphere had changed. Other assistants sneaked glances. Charlotte sliced ham calmly. It would be after closing time, when she and her aunt were alone, that the subject would be discussed.

Bertha put down the cocoa, banked up the fire and departed. Mrs Armitage drew her niece to her, 'Oh my dear . . . My dear Charlotte. My little girl!' Charlotte submitted gracefully. When the spasm was over, she waited.

'Charlotte, I expect you are wondering why Mr McKie and Mr Davie McKie called on me this afternoon?' It was all part of the ritual: Charlotte waited to be told. Her aunt's next remark took her by surprise. 'I must confess to a small disappointment. Since receiving Mr Davie McKie's letter – and particularly as his brother accompanied him – I had hoped . . . I wondered – whether it would be Mr John McKie who requested permission to call on us. Mr McKie,' her aunt explained, 'has an excellent reputation in Darlington. He is personal assistant to Mr Richardson.'

'Yes, Aunt,' said Charlotte impatiently, 'but Mr John McKie is married.'

'Oh, is he?' Mrs Armitage's informant had been vague on this point. 'Does his wife receive? They are Presbyterian, I know, which is why we've never seen them at St Cuthbert's.'

'Mrs McKie is an invalid, I believe. She and Mr McKie have recently had a happy event. The baby's name is Luke.' Charlotte's researches had been more thorough.

'Oh, dear . . . ' Mrs Armitage's hopes had been dashed. 'But Charlotte, we know very little, my darling, about either of the gentlemen.'

'They are from Scotland, Aunt,' Mrs Armitage had nothing against that country but neither did it reassure her.

'If only there were someone to ask!' She clasped the lace handkerchief, 'Someone – reliable.'

'Perhaps Mrs Wingford?'

'She hardly ever comes into the Establishment herself, she always sends a maid nowadays . . . ' Mrs Armitage spoke absently. 'Two pound of best butter, five pound of sugar loaf and half of ratafias . . . Perhaps she has an "At home"? I could leave cards.' Charlotte had no wish to be discussed over biscuits or tea-cups.

'Why not ask my uncle?'

'Of course, my darling!' Charlotte knew this was the way the matter would finally be settled. Also, that her aunt had been waiting for her to suggest it. It was always so. Once, aware that her uncle couldn't speak, could only implore with his eyes above a mouth dribbling spittle, she'd been curious enough to wonder how he conveyed so much to her aunt. She'd listened at the door. Mrs Armitage had told her spouse of the latest problem. There was a short silence followed by, 'There, I knew you'd agree. I'm so glad we're of the same mind, Mr A!' Charlotte had been ashamed of eavesdropping. She'd gone back to the sitting room and when her aunt burst in saying, 'He agrees, he's told me I'm doing the right thing,' she'd managed to look pleased.

This time she waited impatiently. Her aunt was undecided, that was obvious. It would be foolish to deny this might produce an unfavourable result. And Charlotte now admitted to herself, she didn't want that. For days she'd been pondering. She was well aware any decision would be irrevocable. To accept Davie McKie as a follower would be to commit herself. To withdraw without good reason afterwards would mean gossip, censure and the loss of reputation. Charlotte was well schooled in the niceties of behaviour. And if she were to decline his advances now, that too would be known: nor would he try again.

There had been other young gentlemen, sprung on her like rabbits out of a hat, at *Conversaziones*, St Cuthbert's bazaar and suchlike. Among the tradesmen's sons of Darlington, Charlotte Forrest was considered a catch. Until now she'd declined every advance. This time it was different. To say she felt the same strong feelings for Davie as he did for her would be to put it too highly. Charlotte knew he adored her and she'd no objection to an admirer who felt like that. It wouldn't be proper for her thoughts to stray any further in his direction, not yet. She would admit of her affection by degrees, when pressed.

Sitting alone by the fire, Charlotte dreamed a little. Mr Davie McKie was a very fine figure of a man, very large. His beard and moustaches were like the Prince of Wales and whenever he came into the shop, always laughing, it was amazing the effect he had on the other assistants. They behaved like silly girls! Mr Collins had to be sharp with them sometimes. Charlotte had never simpered in her life. All the same . . . she had a very neat waist. And those arms round it might be . . .

The door burst open, spoiling her reverie. Her aunt stood there trembling. 'We have decided that Mr Davie McKie may call, my darling, if you wish him to do so.'

'Oh thank you, Aunt Armitage!'

'But we will not rush matters. There's no need to do that.' Had he been there to hear, John would have sighed with relief. He needed plenty of time for his plans.

So Davie called once a week, on Sunday evenings after church. For several weeks there was a total formality that froze the proceedings but Davie persevered. He brought his poetry books and read aloud. He charmed Mrs Armitage. It took a great deal of charm to melt that solid bosom but eventually the jet trembled with pleasure. Then came the evening when Mrs Armitage had a suggestion to make.

'Mr A and I wondered, as the weather is clement, whether Charlotte might care for a walk?'

195

There was frost and the smell of snow but Davie didn't hesitate, nor did Charlotte. She was far more certain of her feelings now. She chafed at the restrictions of the sitting room, with her aunt and Bertha in constant attendance.

They walked stiffly at first, like strangers, shy of intimacy. Alone for the first time, it was as though Mrs Armitage were still watching over them even after they'd turned into Bondgate. He offered his arm tentatively. The small hand crept out of the muff and tucked itself under his elbow. He shortened his stride so that Charlotte could slow down to a trot. Soon the weather worsened and snowflakes began falling. Everyone except the lovers hastened indoors. Davie opened his umbrella and they huddled beneath.

Conversation was so delicious, the admiration in Davie's eyes so delightful, it was only when her boots were soaked through that Charlotte realized how late it was. They hurried back to Skinnergate. Mrs Armitage waited in her bow window above the street.

'I thought it was you, Charlotte, so I sent Bertha down to open the door.' In front of aunt and maid, Davie made his farewells, raising a sodden hat and hurrying home on wings of love.

Mary was in the kitchen at Coburg Street. It was her first time downstairs since the baby's birth six months ago. She couldn't yet stand but sat, close to the fire, to superintend the supper, much to the relief of the apprentices. Ada still had much to learn about cookery.

There had been changes. The nurse had gone, Ada helped Mary with the baby and Emily Beal came in every day to do the housework. The doctor told John emphatically that mother and child must stay in the back bedroom if they were to improve, so Ada moved in with them. Down below, Davie squashed his huge frame into the little partitioned cubicle off the kitchen and John resumed the truckle bed. It was only temporary, he told Davie, until their plans came to fruition. Davie sighed but accepted it. John would explain everything eventually.

Tonight John held the baby in his arms and read aloud to it from *The Pilgrim's Progress*. Ada, as she took Luke off to bed, said she didn't think he would understand about the Valley of

Despond, not at six months. Her brother Tommy, who was the clever one, he hadn't said a word till he was over a year old.

'Luke understands, Ada,' John said confidently, 'You don't notice his eyes as I do when I read to him. And the sooner he has a good vocabulary, the better. He's to be a doctor, remember.' By the kitchen range, Mary smiled. A doctor – her little baby! It was incredible. She hoped she'd live to see it. When she moved these days, the pain in her weak leg was terrible.

The doctor still looked in on Mary after his rounds. The nurse had told him privately how she suffered. He called to administer opium to ease her through the worst, warning her of its dangers. John wasn't told, Mary was very firm about that. 'He has enough worries over business,' she said, so Dr Cullen held his tongue.

Eventually, knowing she had to try if she were ever to walk again, Mary took her first steps across the bedroom and told herself she could endure it. Today was the first time she'd come downstairs. She'd done so while John was at church, for she didn't want him to see her exhausted, sweaty state. Ada wiped her face and tidied her hair. When he returned, Mary was able to welcome him. It had been worth it, she told herself. She'd take plenty of medicine later, to make her sleep.

When Davie came home, flinging wet clothes all over the kitchen, he was in such ecstasies over the ravishing Miss Forrest he had them laughing, including Mary. He was indignant. How could they make fun of such a pearl among women? He flung his muffler onto a chair. Mary dodged the spray of rainwater, and slipped. As she fell, her scream was raw with pain.

Davie pushed the others aside and lifted her up. John was white, Ada tearful, so it was Davie that took charge, issuing terse orders. They rushed to fill hot water bottles, to take candles up to the bedroom. As tenderly as he could, Davie carried Mary upstairs and laid her on the bed. Ada told him she could manage the rest, the nurse had shown her how. Soberly and quietly, the brothers went down again.

As he put out the supper plates, Davie said, 'She doesn't improve, poor girl. What does the doctor say?'

'The same as before, that it'll take time. Last time I saw him he suggested we take on the nurse again, to care for Luke as well as Mary.' John sighed. 'It's true that we expect too much of Ada.' Davie knew it was the expense that worried him.

'But where would she sleep? Now Ada is in with Mary we couldn't fit the nurse in there as well. It would mean renting another room somewhere.' John came to a decision. He asked suddenly. 'Have you told Miss Forrest you want to marry her?'

'No!' Davie was astonished, 'She's the dearest, sweetest girl but these things take time, John – '

'But if you did ask her, d'you think she'd accept you?'

'Oh, yes . . . ' Davie remembered the pressure of the dainty hand, 'she feels the same way I do, I think. But how can I ask her? Mrs Armitage would never agree to Charlotte coming to live here.'

'Of course she wouldn't. It's time for us to make a move.' And for the first time since his own marriage, John wrote an honest letter to Alex.

I know you will understand why I could not write beforehand, due to the circumstances of my marriage. Please believe me when I say it has brought a measure of happiness I never thought possible. Luke gladdens my heart. He is my son as much as if he were of my flesh. I cannot condemn Mary, either. I beg neither you nor Mother will do so. What happened is past, now we pray for her recovery. She works so hard for Davie and me, but one of the reasons we must move away from here is so that she will not need to climb stairs. The doctor fears this taxes her too much. As for Miss Forrest, I know Davie has written about her. I believe it will be an excellent match. She is a steady, sensible young woman. When the time is right, I intend to discuss with her aunt the plans we have so that she will agree to the marriage taking place.

The property I have in mind . . .

His letter to Helen Shields was much more brief. If another pupil was prepared to make the journey south, a girl interested in nursing, John would be glad to make her acquaintance. She would spend six months being trained at their expense. After that, they would provide board, lodging and two and ninepence a week. Durability rather than good looks was essential, he hinted. She would have the responsibility of caring for Mary and Luke. Ada would resume the housework. Helen thought the arrangement satisfactory and Katriona was dispatched, to stay with Mrs Beal while she attended classes arranged for her by the doctor.

Slowly, very slowly, Mary returned to a semblance of health. She tried to give up the medicine, apart from the nightly dose to help her sleep. Towards the end of her training, when Katriona began to spend more and more time with them, Mary had periods of idleness. When all the household mending had been done, she embroidered. Soon there were bright cushions and antimacassars with drawn threadwork, and John had an unusual pair of slippers. It was when a tapestry appeared on the parlour wall that he decided enough was enough. Abraham slaying the lamb had so much red-wool blood, it almost put them off their food. That night John came home with a package. 'For Luke,' he said. Inside was a slate and some chalks. 'I thought you could start him on his letters.'

(iv)

Whenever Davie broached the subject of a wedding, Mrs Armitage backed away. 'There's no need to hurry,' was all she would say. It was Mr Collins who precipitated matters. One evening he requested an interview after closing. When the ritual of tea was complete, he began as delicately as he could, 'As Miss Forrest is shortly to be married, madam.' Mrs Armitage looked as if she would interrupt so he continued quickly. 'The wife and I were wondering about the, er – the Establishment?' Mrs Armitage looked blank. 'Whether you – and Mr Armitage – might be considering . . . retirement?' The bodice heaved tremendously. 'Not all at once, of course.'

'No indeed, Mr Collins. If ever.' The lady was flustered. The matter would have to be discussed, at length, with Mr A. Mr Collins inclined his head.

'There would be many details to talk over,' he agreed, 'Many, many details. But if you – and Mr Armitage – were ever to consider, putting in a manager, I should be . . . ' He'd rehearsed the next words carefully. 'It would be the pinnacle of

199

achievement for me to occupy such a position. Mrs Collins and I would deem it – a great honour.'

He'd said sufficient. The bell was rung and Bertha showed him downstairs. Mrs Armitage sat alone. Charlotte was in the bedroom, reading to her uncle. Retire? She'd never thought about it before but the idea appealed greatly. An end to the daily worry and strain! But where would they go? She and her spouse could not continue here, Mr and Mrs Collins would need the accommodation. Mrs Armitage clutched her breast at the thought of another woman sitting in front of 'her' fireside, or over there, in the bow window with its excellent view the length of Skinnergate. And what about Mr A? The burden of worrying about that exhausted her. When Charlotte returned, her aunt begged that she send for Mr Davie McKie. 'We must ask his advice, my darling. He will know what to do for the best.'

When Davie received the note, he showed it to John. Was this the end of the campaign, was the siege nearly over? He hurried round. After the first few sentences, he said deferentially, 'Mrs Armitage, might I suggest we consult my brother in this matter? He has an excellent head for business. I've never known him make an unwise decision.' So the boy from the shop was sent to where John, in a clean collar and tie, waited for the summons. Were all his plans coming to fruition?

He listened and when she had finished said, 'Mrs Armitage, I have considered, for some time, setting up in business in Darlington, in partnership with my brother. As I see it, he and Miss Forrest would be ideally suited to manage it. It would be an establishment of a superior nature, to appeal to a better class of customer such as those whom you serve, ma'am.' Mrs Armitage acknowledged his bow with her handkerchief. 'There is a sad lack of high-class businesses in Darlington . . . ' Mrs Armitage nodded in agreement. John ventured further, enthusiasm banishing his nervousness. As he described his plan, Davie was stunned by the extent of it and by this new side to John. He was flushed and excited as he talked of a shop that would embrace all that he and Davie had learned of household furnishing, a shop that would incorporate millinery, ladies' and gents' outfitting – 'It will, in short, be an emporium,' said John triumphantly.

He sank back. Would they laugh at him? The stout woman opposite with Charlotte beside her, they were the first to be told all the details. Did they find them far too bold? If Mrs Armitage dismissed them, would that be an end to Davie's hopes? But the lady nodded thoughtfully. She wanted to hear some of it again – why didn't Charlotte ring for refreshments? She would need to talk to Mr A of course – he had such an excellent head for business – but would Mr McKie be so kind as to go through it all slowly, so that she could explain it to him afterwards?

John couldn't remember when he'd felt so happy apart from the day Luke was born. He brought out his precious envelope and gave her a set of his notes, copied out for just such an occasion. Each prospective department in the emporium was described, the range of goods it would carry, the capital expenditure involved to provide those goods. He'd thought out carefully how each area should lead to the next so that a customer would be tempted to walk on. He described lines that Gordon's traders carried and pushed to the back of his mind any thought of confrontation with him. 'The horse trams are so reliable, and the trains. People are accustomed to travelling farther and farther. When I was a boy, a man went as far as he could walk in a day. Then the bicycle opened up the countryside to him. When the railways reached Scotland, people came to our peninsula who had only seen the place in the atlas. It was a wonderful experience . . . '

John was almost carried away. He came back to Darlington. 'I see no reason why customers will not travel regularly to buy hats, provided those hats are of a superior nature. And the department will be laid out in such a way that they will feel – comfortable. A lady will be able to sit and consider the hats. In fact . . . ' He was so relaxed it was like listening to Davie. 'I plan to sell hats that are as excellent in their way as is the ham in your establishment, ma'am.'

Mrs Armitage inclined her head in acceptance of the superior ham.

'I feel confident,' John went on, 'that Davie has already established enough goodwill among our customers that although many will come initially out of curiosity, they will return because they are satisfied! And . . . ' he'd been keeping this till last, 'for those who have to make long journeys, our

201

emporium will offer – refreshment. Where ladies can sit with their friends before making their purchases.'

This last idea appealed to Davie most of all. 'That's a wonderful thing, John. Ladies need time, they're always wanting a cup of tea before they decide. Thank – ' He'd been about to thank his Maker for a sound bladder but remembered in time, where he was, 'Somewhere – respectable – for them to meet – '

'At present most of them go to Hunter's cocoa palace – '

'But this will be inside the shop?'

'At the far end . . . ' John answered happily. 'They will have to walk past the goods to reach it – '

'Why don't we buy the tea for our shop here? At Armitage's!'

John was more cautious. 'If Mrs Armitage approves, Davie?' Mrs Armitage bowed graciously.

'Our salon . . . ' It was the first time John had used the word. 'Our salon within the emporium will require a most superior person, to impart the right atmosphere. A lady herself, whom our customers would take pleasure in meeting, who would make them feel – at home.' He looked at Mrs Armitage and saw the idea had taken root. 'It would be a managerial role, not too arduous . . . Both Davie and I would benefit from your years of experience, madam.' He rose to go, motioning Davie to follow suit. It didn't do to press matters too far on the first occasion.

Once outside, questions tumbled from Davie pell-mell. He didn't notice which direction they walked nor did he wait for answers. When John stopped and asked, 'What d'you think?' he saw they were at the junction of Blackwellgate and High Row, looking at a derelict building once used as a furniture warehouse.

'That?' Davie was startled.

'It'll need a bit of work,' John admitted, 'But there's plenty of room above and a yard with stabling at the back. I've had my eye on it for some time. We could all fit in.'

'Can we afford it?'

'If the Armitages are prepared to invest, I think we can. I've already written to Father . . . I know he thought of his savings for the next generation,' John chose his words carefully, 'to send our sons to university, but we would replace that money first,

202

when we made a profit, and pay Father interest.' Davie was bemused. It was all worked out. John was telling him of the Quakers, how much they would lend them. He'd been thinking ahead all the time while he, what had he been doing? Davie considered. He'd been meeting people, new customers. Now he'd tell them about the plan – whet their appetites. Maybe he wasn't so useless after all?

An emporium – that great barn of a place – full of people? Yes, he'd enjoy working there, working nearly as hard as John.

'Would you give up Coburg Street?'

'Certainly not!' John was shocked. 'With the lodgers, it's paying for itself. Never give up property, Davie. It's collateral. We're going to borrow against it. I'm offering Nettles the running of it when we move out.'

Their first lodger was about to embark on matrimony himself. So far he hadn't found anywhere suitable to live. 'D'you mean he and his wife could run the place?'

'And live there rent free, Davie.' It didn't occur to either of them that the bride might not view running a lodging house with the same keenness. Fortunately, when they were introduced the following evening, the sturdy young woman had already grasped the advantages. John contemplated her with satisfaction across the parlour table; she was built for work. Her 'best' blouse did not conceal her brawny arms. Beside her, Mr Nettles looked anaemic.

'I think we should consider four in the front bedroom, Mr McKie. My betrothed and I can be accommodated quite spaciously in the back. I'm sure I don't mind the cooking and washing provided we can agree terms.' Her beloved appeared bemused but John recognized a kindred spirit. The future Mrs Nettles wanted more than a rent-free dwelling, she wanted profit from laundry and food. John didn't mind; if she was prepared to work that hard, so much the better. Her intended said faintly, 'That will mean an awful lot of washing, Carrie,' but she argued vigorously: he could put up extra washing lines across the yard; they would have a girl to help.

'I believe you have one and she sleeps downstairs?'

'Ada is coming with us,' John said quickly. Ada was trained, she'd nearly learned to cook. Let this frail vessel find her own skivvy.

203

Ten minutes later the fianceé declared herself satisfied. She'd agreed to work a fourteen-hour day in return for free accommodation plus one third of the rents. Washing would be an 'extra' and the money would be her own. In return, she would of course enjoy the security of matrimony. The engaged pair issued an invitation to the wedding and departed.

(v)

If he thought moving nearer his goal would bring contentment, John was mistaken. Davie went to bed and dreamed of Charlotte: John lay awake hour after restless hour. Mary usually crept past to fetch water for washing. This morning she found him wide awake and dressed.

'What's the matter? Couldn't you sleep, John?' She pulled her shawl round her more closely.

'Here, let me help.' John moved to the range to pour water into her ewer. Under her shawl he could see her chemise and he'd never seen his wife in this state of undress before. 'I'll get out of your way.'

He sat at the kitchen table pretending to check his paperwork. Mary used the bellows to make the fire glow and took her hot water through to the scullery. It saved another climb up the stairs. John sat listening to the small intimate sounds. It distracted him to realize she always rose so early. He'd done so himself when he'd first started trading and had to reach outlying villages. But that was ages ago. Davie's assistant visited those now. Which reminded John, they would have to speak to Gordon. He knew the trader would not take kindly to the idea of a shop that competed directly with his business. John sighed.

Mary came back into the kitchen wearing her bodice with her apron pinned over her petticoat, her normal garb. When he saw she was making them tea he tried to help but he couldn't remember where the things were kept. He was ashamed. In her quiet way Mary had taken over running the household again and he hadn't noticed. She put a cup in front of him. 'What's troubling you?'

204

'You know we've decided to start in business for ourselves, Davie and I?'

'Yes, he told me last night. So that he can marry Miss Forrest. I think it's a fine idea, John. I'll help in any way I can.'

It didn't occur to him that she'd first heard of it from Davie nor that it affected her whole future, too. 'I'm worried as to whether we can manage, if I'm aiming too high.' The words were spoken; he felt better.

Mary watched him drink for a moment then asked, 'Have you discussed it with Mr Richardson?'

'In principle. I think he sees it as a good investment.'

'Why not tell him the details, as you did Mrs Armitage? Davie told me how it was when you spoke last night . . . ' Mary only wished she'd been there to hear. 'He said you'd planned everything, even as far as the teaspoons.' She didn't know what this signified but when she quoted Davie's words, it made John smile.

'I try to be thorough,' he admitted modestly.

'Then tell Mr Richardson. He's always advised you well before. And I'm sure you'll be welcome at the bank. There's this house to set against a loan. It will be a most profitable concern once Mrs Nettles moves in.'

He was dismayed when he remembered he hadn't consulted her about that either. He hadn't even asked Mary whether she agreed with the move. During their discussions with Nettles last night, Mary had been in the background, making them tea, mending the fire; he couldn't remember whether he'd even introduced her.

'You don't mind, do you, Mary? It is for Luke most of all, as well as ourselves. I want him to have the best. If we make a success of it, that might be possible.' She almost reached out to touch his hand, she was so pleased, then stopped herself.

'I know, John, and I'm thankful. Now, have a shave and I'll make breakfast. If you go to the warehouse early, you might be able to see Mr Williamson before you start.' He took the shaving mug, sobered by her calm acceptance. He must consult her in future, though. After all, she was his wife.

They were scarcely in Coburg Street during the next few weeks. Davie extended his round farther afield, always mentioning the future emporium to lady customers. After a day's work and an evening teaching at the Institute, John was closeted with members of the business community. Davie had to attend occasionally. It seemed to him they sat for hours while figures were discussed, percentages agreed and loans of a size that frightened him tossed casually in the air. How could they ever repay? How could John remain so unmoved? Alex had replied by return of post and sent every penny of his savings with a loving, kind letter, full of affection. He'd referred to Luke as 'your son' and John gave thanks with a full heart. It was his mother's doing, he felt sure.

From that sum, John took enough to purchase brand new suits. Davie was amazed; not even from Mr Fawcett?

'We must appear prosperous,' John explained. 'Our lady customers will notice and tell their husbands, who will consider investing with us. From now on we must always look our best. It is part of our new life.' Davie had no objection. He wore his new cap at a very jaunty angle when he walked out with Charlotte.

John increased their subscription to the Sunday plate. Casting bread on Presbyterian waters had, he found, brought favourable returns on the tide. It took nearly three months to secure the property but he got it on excellent terms.

When they stood inside for the first time Davie was utterly dismayed. What an overpowering smell of decay! But John was satisfied. He'd already received a report from the builder some weeks previously. This dour person, after describing how much rotten wood had collapsed when he kicked it, gave it as his opinion that 'most of it were basically sound, Mr McKie.' That same individual, Mr Clough, was due in half an hour to make estimates.

'Let's take a look upstairs,' John said eagerly.

The warren of rooms surprised him. So many and on such different levels. It was as if the previous occupant had divided space as each new need arose. 'Shall we put them back into a few large rooms?' Davie asked.

'I don't think so. We'll need many of them as they are and it would be an unnecessary expense.'

'Why so many?' John listed their requirements. 'There's you and Charlotte, that's a bedroom and sitting room plus a couple of extra rooms for your children – '

'Steady on, man! We're not wed yet.'

'There's Mary and Luke plus a room for Katriona and Ada. We might need a separate sitting room but I thought we could all share a dining room, what d'you think?'

Davie tried to imagine all these disparate persons sitting round one table. 'Who's going to do the cooking?'

'I've no idea. I'll ask Mary, she'll think of something.'

'What about Mr Armitage?'

'You say he's an invalid?'

'Oh, yes, completely bedridden. The three of them look after him day and night. And there's a nurse comes to attend to him.'

'Will Charlotte expect to have a servant?' Just as he accepted responsibility for an invalid, it went without saying, Charlotte Forrest would be in a higher social sphere than Mary.

'I don't think so. She and Mrs Armitage have Bertha, I don't think they'll want anyone else.'

'Good . . . ' So far there were no surprises. Davie was already reeling but John went on calmly, 'We'll need rooms for some of the assistants. Those who are apprenticed will definitely expect to live in. And we'll need plenty of good dry storage for the stock. Our lines won't be in boxes at the Temperance Hall!' Davie managed a faint smile. 'Perhaps we should think of using the stables for stock.'

'I'd forgotten we had those.'

'There are two across the yard at the back.' Davie hurried to find a window, to get away from the expensive list. He stared at the dingy smoke-stained brick building. Doors hung off their hinges and one or two panes were broken, but stables! Only gentlemen had those.

'How on earth can we afford all this?' John sighed. He'd gone through everything so carefully the previous night. Then he remembered Davie had always had a weakness over figures. He began all over again, very slowly.

'There's Coburg Street. We've stopped paying rent and have taken out a mortgage to buy it. The lodgers cover that and the bank is happy to advance a further loan with the house as security. Mr Richardson has lent one thousand pounds unsecured at two and a half percent. Two of his colleagues, you don't know them but they live out at Barnard Castle, they've given five hundred apiece on the same terms. As I explained, we'll use the rents to repay the house and the surplus to pay the interest – or rather a tiny part of it. We'll live on my income until the shop begins to pay, which will mean going extremely carefully but Mary understands that. She will help me with the running of things while you and Charlotte superintend the shop. I've discovered Mary has a talent for figures, by the way.'

'Oh, good.' Davie felt as if he was clutching at straws. So much money and all of it to be repaid!

'Mrs Armitage has agreed that Charlotte's dowry will be invested in stock – I must say, Davie, I think they have behaved very generously. She's paying all their expenses, and Bertha's wages. I only agreed to that for the first two years. After that I think we should review the situation, don't you? We mustn't take advantage of her kindness. I must congratulate you, old fellow. You couldn't have picked a better mother-in-law!' Privately John was less certain about Charlotte. He admired her beauty, but unlike Davie, had now noticed the strength of her chin.

'There's Father's money.'

'Yes . . . six hundred and thirty-eight pounds. I'd no idea he'd saved so much.'

'I think he's got out of the habit of spending any of it. We are going to pay *him* back, aren't we?'

'Oh, goodness yes!' John was shocked. 'I think we should put him top of the list, I hate to think he might be penniless – he'd never write and ask even if he needed it. He and mother aren't getting any younger. I've told them there's a place for them here if ever they need it.' Where, thought Davie?

John had heard something and was heading towards the stairs. 'Come on, I think that's Mr Clough. We shall have to talk to Gordon next week,' he called. 'I want to negotiate for your two assistants to come and work in the shop. They can stay on the road until we've enough business to justify it but I want to put the idea in his mind. It'll mean paying off their indentures but I'll go with guineas in my pocket. You know what the sight of gold does to Gordon – '

'But John,' Davie cried plaintively, feeling swamped, 'd'you think we'll ever manage to pay *any* of it?'

'We must, Davie. We've given our word. That's how it is in business.'

(vii)

It was a very quiet wedding. Frightened by the size of Mr Clough's estimates, Davie persuaded Charlotte that showiness was unnecessary and she agreed. Mrs Armitage was relieved, too. How to explain to the curious why her husband could not attend such an important event? Inhabiting an imaginary world where Mr A was always on the mend, she knew outsiders would ridicule if they learned the truth. It was better not to have one single guest than for that to happen.

There was a party for the assistants in the Establishment the night before. A cold collation had been prepared. When the blinds were drawn they tucked into it, then Mr Collins proposed a toast and the health of the happy couple was drunk in best port. Davie made a graceful reply. Very poetic, the assistants decided and one young lady wept because it was so romantic. They trooped out into the night and the wedding group retired upstairs.

'I think we should share this moment with Mr A,' declared his wife. Charlotte agreed nervously. Davie had met the grocer but John had not. She needn't have worried. John walked into the room and stood beside the bed.

'How d'you do, sir.' He spoke quietly. 'I've heard so much about you from your wife. May I take the opportunity of thanking you for your great kindness in our enterprise.'

The eyes stared past John to a limbo none of them could share. Spittle dribbled and Bertha wiped it away. The only 'good' hand moved just a little. 'He's so pleased, so very pleased to meet you,' said his spouse, satisfied.

She and John had discussed a few more details while the betrothed gazed at one another. During the weeks since he'd met her, John had come to understand Mrs Armitage's worth. With his sober nature, he wasn't a man to find others comic. If, occasionally, excitement appeared to be too much, if the bosom heaved in an extraordinary fashion and the lace handkerchief fluttered, then her suggestions over business matters were very helpful indeed.

It was Mrs Armitage who had discussed a role for Mary and had gone to Coburg Street to discuss it. She was, John recollected, the only person Mary had received, so self-effacing had his wife become. But Mrs Armitage encouraged her to talk. She'd explained the principles on which 'our Establishment' was run and suggested it be applied to the emporium.

Mr Collins visited Mary to go through the day-to-day management of running a shop. Mary had written it down and presented it as a finished thesis for John's approval. He'd been so proud, he asked her to copy it all out again so that he could have it at the warehouse, to show to Mr Richardson.

Last week Mrs Armitage had called at Coburg Street again and in the kitchen over Pekoe Tips – 'A new line, dear Mrs McKie, I would like your opinion of it' – Mary and she had polished the final details of how the emporium was to be governed.

The fact that Charlotte was not involved in all this was accepted from the beginning. She would be the public face, beside Davie. She would be 'so busy', it was natural that Mary would work behind the scenes to ensure everything ran smoothly.

And Mrs Armitage had insisted on one further matter: Mary must have new clothes. John hadn't realized his wife possessed only one decent gown. She'd gone through her pregnancy in an old darned skirt, letting it out progressively. She still wore that every morning, to do her housework, changing into her dress every evening. 'Mr McKie, your dear wife will be in a position of authority in your emporium. It behoves her to look the part, you know. The young assistants, they need to respect her – '

'Yes, I'd no idea . . . of course Mary must dress well!' John was embarrassed by what he felt was implied criticism but Mrs Armitage smoothed the path for him.

'Your dear wife – all her efforts were directed until now at economy. To further your savings for the emporium. But now, Mr McKie, now is the time to spend!'

And would it never end, he wondered? Each night he woke in a cold sweat over estimates that had been exceeded. But this evening he'd actually come to ask the Armitages to spend some more. He'd brought the plans of their living quarters and samples of wallpaper for approval. Mr Clough and his men were ready to begin work on the ground floor.

Mrs Armitage and Bertha crowed delightedly over the heavily flocked papers. 'Just the very thing! How clever of you to choose the colours Mr A finds so restful, Mr McKie.' Personally, John found them overpowering. He'd described the colours and style of the Armitages' sitting room and Mr Clough had imitated them. John's own efforts were directed at the salon. He refused to let anyone help him with that.

Mrs Armitage was examining the plans. 'Oh, look Bertha – a water closet. On the same floor, too!' Bertha was equally ecstatic. There would be no more stairs, no chamberpots, an end to all that drudgery. Basking in their delight, John described how each of the families would have their own closet. It was an expense, he admitted, but with so many souls under one roof, perhaps it was worth paying for.

'Oh, Mr McKie – it is!' Bertha left him in no doubt.

When he could drag their attention away from the best place for the sofa, John discussed the practical details of moving the grocer. A closed carriage had been hired; what else was needed?

'I have asked the doctor to attend, Mr McKie, although as you know I've very little faith in medical men. But he can at least assist Mr Collins and I. Bertha will be there too and a nurse from the hospital. It will all help install Mr A in his new home – with a water closet. Oh, wait till I tell him about that!' Her bosom heaved with joyful rapture.

It was time to leave. Davie was permitted a chaste kiss, watched by all of them. Mrs Armitage looked on emotionally. 'Poor dear Beatrice . . . and Jane,' she murmured. Davie went home on wings of love but John took a longer route, via the emporium. He wanted to check that Mr Clough was up to schedule. They'd already booked a series of advertisements in the *Northern Echo* and the *Darlington and Stockton Times*. But the weather that winter had been exceptionally severe, so building work had fallen behind. John shuddered at the thought that they might not be ready in time.

(viii)

The next morning was sharp and clear, with a north-east wind to make their eyes water. Holding onto their hats, John and Davie walked quickly. They were calling first at the jewellers before going to Skinnergate where a carriage was to take the wedding party to St Cuthbert's.

The ring and Davie's wedding gift of a locket were ready. Beside them was another small velvet box containing a charm. Inside a tiny gold envelope was a sliver of a letter. He showed John the message, 'To Charlotte from Davie' and tucked it back inside, pressing shut the tiny flap. The smallest possible ruby sealed the envelope.

'Just a wee surprise for her,' Davie explained. 'She knows about the locket but she won't be expecting this.' John sighed. There had been far too many of these wee surprises, in his opinion.

Inside the silent bedroom, Charlotte bent to kiss her uncle. 'I'm so sorry you can't come but Davie and I will only be away a few days. Goodbye for the present, dearest.' On the landing she pirouetted once more for the admiring Bertha and ran downstairs into the shop. The shock when she saw her beloved, standing in front of Charlotte's very own marble counter, was considerable. He'd ordered himself the full dress tartan of his clan: kilt, ruffled shirt and velvet jacket, plaid and tam o'shanter. On Davie's massive figure, the effect was impressive. Red hair and beard glistened in the sunlight. He stood, peacock proud, ready to claim her. The costume revealed more than his figure. For the first time Charlotte was able to see Davie's well shaped calves. They led to his thighs but she refused to allow her thoughts to reach any higher. Not yet. It would have been improper. She was stopped in her tracks by his magnificence but being Charlotte, she recovered. 'You look like the photographs of the Prince of Wales,' she told him. There was enthusiastic agreement from the lady assistants.

212

As for Charlotte herself, she wore the best that Mrs Armitage could provide. It was the spring of 1896; women thought they were emancipated, and indeed in some respects they were. Some even rode bicycles but to see Charlotte on that cold, bright morning it was difficult to imagine how. Her sleeves were very full, the gored skirt of stiff blue broadcloth and the waist as tightly corseted as could be. Above her belt, the blue silk blouse fell loose and full over her breasts, to be confined in a high boned collar. Grey kid shoes matched her gloves and the feathers in her hat echoed the sheen of the broadcloth. Charlotte, the epitome of Darlington fashion, glowed with love.

Looking at the two of them, so handsome, so bound up in each other, they scarcely noticed those around them, John couldn't help remembering Mary. Then he thought of Luke and his heart lifted. He offered his arm to Mrs Armitage. 'May I have the honour, ma'am?' There was a spontaneous cheer from the assistants and three hip hurrahs led by Mr Collins. The four went outside and took their places in the flower-bedecked carriage.

After the ceremony, the cake and champagne, there was one further rite on the way to the station. Charlotte laid her posy on Jane's grave and looked at the marble angel guarding her. 'She was very young,' Charlotte was disturbed as she realized. 'Only twenty, not much older than I am. She must have had a very hard life.' Her husband put his arm round her shoulders.

'My love, we must hurry. The train . . . '

Charlotte still thought of her mother as they sat, upright and formal, facing each other in the carriage. 'I wonder why she named me Charlotte. She never explained to Aunt Armitage.'

The honeymoon was to be spent at Saltburn, far superior to neighbouring Redcar, Charlotte assured Davie, and healthier, never a suggestion of typhoid. Battling their way through the scouring gale, up the hotel steps, Davie thought he understood why. It was a very superior hotel too. He was thankful he'd taken the precaution of writing beforehand, for the tariff. They could stay for three days, John had decided, not a minute longer.

If he'd been concerned that his wife might find the place overpowering, Davie needn't have worried. Almost as the ring was placed on her finger Charlotte assumed a mantle of respectability that rivalled her aunt's. That evening Davie waited in the lobby for Charlotte to join him. He saw other men's heads turn, and knew the reason was his wife. The hat had been replaced by tortoiseshell combs which gleamed in the heavy auburn chignon. Now the jacket of her 'tailor-made' was off, the blouse and tiny waist were revealed but it was her deportment, the way she carried her head so proudly, that made loungers straighten their backs and waiters hurry before her to open doors. Charlotte smiled charmingly at these courtesies before turning to her husband to ask, 'Shall we dine, Mr McKie?'

Her aunt hadn't prepared her very fully for matrimony. There had been guarded allusions during which the jet quivered and the handkerchief was frequently used. Charlotte decided that something warned against so often – and so alarmingly by the Church – must be delightful. She smoothed the leg o' mutton sleeves of her lawn nightgown and settled placidly to wait. Was Davie nervous? Of course he was. It is one thing to face such dignity across a dinner table, quite another to find it propped up against the pillows. Fortunately, as she saw him appear from the bathroom, Charlotte's *amour-propre* was shaken. Her husband had obviously divested himself of his kilt, and what was alarming was that underneath his dressing gown, he didn't appear to be wearing a night-shirt! To her surprise he began to shovel coal on the fire. 'I thought we could let it die down dear?' Deliberately misunderstanding, Davie called cheerfully,

'Don't worry, Charlotte. I shall put the fireguard back.' For what he had in mind, he didn't want the temperature to fall. He extinguished the lamp and approached the bed, the dressing gown hanging open. This time her thoughts didn't pause at Davie's thighs. By the firelight, Charlotte could see far more. What a giant of a man she'd married! He reached forward; there were ten pearl buttons fastening her nightgown, three yards of pink ribbon and six yards of lawn making up the gown itself. Inside was his wife. As he unfastened it and reached inside to caress her delicate skin, Davie crooned the most loving, tender words he knew, 'Behold, thou art fair, my love; Behold, thou art fair . . . '

And Charlotte? Thinking about it afterwards, she was disconcerted. That it should have been so enjoyable, but so improper. To be naked in bed with a man! And to think so many other people must have done the same. She was glad Davie couldn't see her face; it felt bright pink. Had Aunt and Uncle Armitage once behaved as she and Davie had done? Of course not! How ridiculous . . . and yet, and yet . . .

'I think we should keep our clothes on in future.'

'What? Didn't you enjoy it, Charlotte?'

'I'm sure it's not considered nice . . . behaving like that.'

'But my dearest girl!' He reached across again but found she'd retreated inside the voluminous lawn. 'Charlotte, please . . .'

'I enjoyed myself, Davie. I shall always be happy to do my duty, now that I know what that is. But I don't think we should behave like savages. Poor heathen creatures who don't wear clothes because the missionaries haven't explained to them. We know it's wicked to be naked, don't we?'

'Not in bed, dearest,' moaned the crestfallen lover.

Charlotte wouldn't be convinced, not in one night. The years of Victorian rectitude made a mighty mountain against which Davie would have to pit his strength. There was only a glimmer of hope, as his wife settled herself for sleep. 'I did enjoy myself,' she assured him, 'I didn't expect to but I did,' and with that her ardent husband had to be content.

He lay awake. Outside the sound of the sea reminded him of home. Would he and Charlotte ever be as entwined as his parents? Looking back it seemed to Davie they were truly one flesh, loving, giving, supporting each other. Would he be the rock on which Charlotte could lean? Probably not, he told himself ruefully, she was far more self-reliant, even with the waiters in the dining room tonight. No one would've guessed it was the first time Charlotte had been inside such a place.

He thought of John and Mary and their strange marriage. That it had never been consummated, Davie was certain. What would happen when they moved to the emporium? From the plans he knew that John's living quarters included three small bedrooms, one for Luke, an adjoining one for Katriona and the remaining one for Mary and John. Would they be able to continue their separate existence? Davie yawned. As he'd climbed aboard the train today, John had said, 'It's the beginning, Davie. Our new life. Today it really starts.' And tomorrow John was superintending the first removals to the new premises. He hoped it would keep fine. Two more nights, that was all he had in this splendid place with his wife. Two nights to convince Charlotte it wasn't wicked. He'd succeed. In the dark Davie chuckled to himself. He'd have to convert Charlotte to becoming a savage again. He'd begin first thing in the morning. Very gently he kissed the curls on her neck and fell asleep.

CHAPTER SEVEN

The Emporium

Charlotte hadn't set foot inside the emporium. It was all to be a surprise when they returned from Saltburn, Davie told her, a magical kingdom where she would reign as Queen.

John hadn't been there to hear the lyricism but he certainly thought it better Charlotte shouldn't see the extent of the wet rot. Some women made a fuss about such things. In his opinion, Miss Forrest might well turn out to be one of them. Instead, John preferred to discuss such matters with the sensible Mrs Armitage. He was relieved when that lady agreed her niece should be spared unnecessary worry.

There had been a fair amount of rot but Mr Clough declared it had been 'dealt with'. It wouldn't come back, he guaranteed, because he'd used enough preservative to sink a ship. John thought he might be right. In place of the musty smells the place reeked of chemicals and paint.

Under Mary's command, Mrs Beal had organized an army of women from Coburg Street to clean the place. Twopence an hour plus free cups of tea. John was scandalized. 'A penny an hour would've been sufficient!'

'Not if we're to be ready on time,' replied Mary firmly, 'They've agreed to work through the night, remember, we must allow extra for that.' He didn't argue further. After two days and a night it was finished; a huge, empty shop with a warren of rooms behind, divided into separate living quarters all bright and shining ready to house them.

The last act had been to remove the cladding that hid the exterior from curious townsfolk. Mr Clough's men levered away the wood and canvas and there it was revealed: John's dream come true.

At the station, Davie gave the address and the cabbie was scornful. 'I saw it this morning. I said to the wife, why would anyone want to go somewhere as big as that? You could get lost in a shop like that. She reckons folk'll just stop by it to get out of the rain.'

John had come to the same conclusion and had decided to exploit it. He and Mr Clough had devised an elegant colonnade along both sides of the busy corners, giving protection from the elements whilst encouraging passers-by with a tempting view inside the windows. As for the steep climb from the High Row, John had written the first of several letters to the authorities, suggesting a flight of steps would be preferable.

Leaning out of the cab for his first glimpse, Davie was overcome by its sheer size. John had had the emporium painted white – Davie hadn't expected that. It looked huge. 'My goodness, Charlotte, did you ever!' His wife saw and her commercial instincts approved. Above the colonnade, gold lettering against the white informed the world that 'McKIE BROTHERS' were Drapers and Milliners. Below, drawn blinds concealed the interior. John had decreed that these wouldn't be raised until the opening on Monday.

The cab stopped and Davie jumped Charlotte down, both hands encircling her waist. She enjoyed it even if it did endanger her poise. The bags were unloaded, the man paid and leaning on her husband's arm, Charlotte stepped inside her new home.

Noise overwhelmed her. Everywhere was in chaos. Looking round, amazed, Davie saw Mr Collins, borrowed from the Establishment for his expertise, roaring orders to a temporary workforce who rushed to do his bidding. There was a sense of purpose though. It was recognizably a shop in here with counters, shelving and display cabinets.

Stepping over the debris, Davie and Charlotte paused to marvel at the overhead cable from which were suspended tiny leather buckets. A pull on a handle and each of these could travel upwards to the cashier where the customer's money could be exchanged for a receipt – what a novelty!

At the back of the shop through an arch was a sign: *Salon de Thé*. More astonishment. Here all was pale blue, the delicate pastel walls garlanded with pink and white flowers. From the ceiling hung a crystal chandelier! Davie was stunned. He turned to find John watching him, grey-faced with fatigue and waiting for the verdict.

'Man, this is a poem!'

Tension fell away. John actually grinned. Pent up inside him was a yearning for beauty that he'd never been able to express until now but Davie hadn't finished. 'It's like the Palace of Versailles!' Neither of them had seen it except in photographs but that didn't matter. John's breast swelled. He found himself shaking Davie's hand in idiotic relief, saying over and over again, 'I'm glad you approve – it's cost a fortune!'

Mrs Armitage left her band of helpers to embrace her niece. 'My dear, how well you're looking! Marriage agrees with you.' Now it was Charlotte's turn to admire – china and glass, elegant gilt chairs and tables – in what was to be her aunt's domain. 'I shall only supervise, of course,' Mrs Armitage whispered. 'Mr John understands. It is Bertha who will wait at table.'

Upstairs, Mary waited apprehensively. She had done what she could to make the living quarters attractive but spending had been kept to a minimum. In the communal dining room, a huge table bought cheaply at auction was surrounded by twenty assorted chairs. Against one wall was an old-fashioned court cupboard of heavily carved oak, black with age. Above it, Mary had hung her tapestry of Abraham and the blood-spattered lamb.

She and Mrs Beal had cut and relaid the worn Turkish carpet. They'd hung alternate red and blue curtains for there hadn't been sufficient of one colour available in the market. Now the two of them waited for Charlotte. It was clearly understood that before matters could proceed, it was necessary for 'Mrs Davie' to approve.

Charlotte swept in, flushed and happy, assured, above all: beloved. She greeted her sister-in-law with concern. 'My dear Mary, such a lot of work!' and Mary smiled bravely. She'd been on her feet for the best part of fourteen hours and under the fine eyes were patches of fatigue but she waited for Charlotte's verdict.

'Saltburn was most beneficial,' said Charlotte as though in answer to a question. 'We can thoroughly recommend the hotel to you and Mr McKie. It is perfectly situated above the promenade.'

'But the dining room,' Mary asked tentatively, 'Is it to your liking?' Charlotte gave it a careless glance.

'What an extraordinary table. I'd no idea they came so large.'

'There will be many of us once the apprentices move in – '

'Yes, of course.' Charlotte wasn't particularly interested in shop assistants. 'I think you've managed very cleverly, Mary. In this light, one can hardly see that the carpet has been patched. Did I understand that our rooms are on this floor?' She was anxious not to engage Mary in conversation for her sister-in-law looked exhausted.

'Along the passage.' Mary led the way. 'Directly above those of your aunt and Mr Armitage. There is also a private staircase between them.'

'What an excellent idea. I shall be able to visit my aunt without passing through the shop – ah . . . ' Mary had thrown open the first door. She'd tried to make this apartment the most handsome of all but she was afraid that Charlotte might not like it.

Only two rooms had been furnished so far, a sitting room and one of the bedrooms. It was this they entered. A fire burned and gas on either side of the mantelpiece had been turned down low. Golden light flickered over Charlotte's own brass bedstead and quilted counterpane, over the ornate wardrobe with the bevelled mirror set in the door. By an armchair, a table covered in heavy velvet had all Charlotte's favourite ornaments set out. Mrs Armitage had chosen the wallpaper – heavy flock strewn with roses – and the brand new carpet echoed the same colours.

Charlotte sat and indicated that Mary should take the stool. She stared about in complete satisfaction. There was no taint of the auction here; all was richness. 'How splendid!' She reached across and kissed Mary impulsively, 'Thank you for making Davie and I such a pleasant home!' Mary almost wept with gratitude.

On the floor below, John and Davie were examining the Armitages' rooms. The grocer was to be moved in tomorrow. In his bedroom, a mirror had been cunningly hung, 'so that the old chap can get a glimpse of the shop,' John explained.

Adjoining the bedroom was the dressing room where Mrs Armitage would sleep, next to it was the parlour and beyond, Bertha's chamber. At the end of the passage was the first of the water closets. 'Polished elm seats with lids and the very latest movement,' said John proudly and Davie shook his head in wonder.

'A miracle. What on earth did Father and Mother say when you wrote and told them?'

John rubbed bleary eyes. 'D'you know, I think I forgot to tell them.'

'Let me do it. And Mistress Shields. She cannot deny we've made progress when we tell her of this!'

They wandered past storerooms, past the cubbyhole for the lady assistants to the last of the ground floor rooms, John's office-cum-study. In it were a rolltop desk, two chairs and an oilstove with a rag rug in front of it, covering the linoleum. Not a penny had been wasted in here. Nevertheless the room itself had been carefully chosen. It was next to the outside yard and travellers could enter and leave undisturbed.

Davie sat in the swivel chair, spinning this way and that while John, in a weary croak, explained that he'd persuaded Gordon to release the other two Highlanders from his employ. 'They join us here tomorrow. Gordon laughed as he took my money. He said, "Six months, that's all I give it." ' John stared at the wall, hollow-eyed. 'What if he's right?'

'Nonsense!' Davie was over-emphatic because he could sense how near despair John was. 'Of course we'll make a success of it. Tell me, where does that other door lead, out in the passage?'

'Nowhere. It's a lift that goes up to the kitchen. Come and see. Clough's fitted it out so that Mary can use it.'

It was a diversion they were glad of. Davie squeezed into the narrow space, and pulling the ropes, soared up and down like a

221

schoolboy. 'Time we were in bed,' he said eventually. 'Come on, old chap, you're out on your feet. Nothing that can't wait until tomorrow.' John followed him obediently. 'Your rooms are above Charlotte's and mine, I suppose?'

'Yes. Katriona and Ada are in the attics with the lady assistants.'

So John and Mary would be on their own, apart from Luke, thought Davie. Had his brother become reconciled to his marriage? Would he and Mary share a bedroom? Rejoicing in his own happiness, Davie dare not ask. He felt nothing but pity. All this effort and no joy except that which Luke's existence brought. Surely John could see how much Mary had done, for his sake? Wasn't he aware how much she cared for him?

In the shop, now empty of Mr Collins and the rest, moonlight flooded down. Davie marvelled at what had been wrought. Shelves waited for stock, sawdust covered the floor ready to be brushed away once the dust had settled. It was a bare stage, waiting for the players to arrive. Suddenly he was as nervous as John.

'Will it do, d'you think?' He'd lapsed into Gaelic.

'Aye. It'll mean hard work, though.' Davie wanted to stay but John thought only of the morrow and all that remained to be done. He wanted his bed.

'What's it for?' asked Davie. 'Is it for ourselves, or what?'

'It's for Luke and your sons when you have them. It's for our posterity. We'll send the boys to university, set them up as professional men.' John grew fierce with a last spurt of energy. 'Luke will stand beside any man's son. He'll never need to obey a summons to fight, to pay with his life as our grandfather did.'

'Those days are gone!'

'Not far enough for me. They still haunt my dreams. But what if we fail, Davie?' Moonlight shone blue-white on his naked fear. The sight of it brought a change to Davie's mood; he felt strong, confident, he would conquer the world!

'Go to bed,' he ordered gently. 'I'm here to help you now. Forget the ghosts. It'll all look different in the morning.'

222

Upstairs, John took a last look at Luke, as he always did. The boy slept in a separate chamber but John's room and Mary's had an adjoining door. This had been left ajar so that Mary could creep past in the mornings without disturbing him.

His bed had been turned down, his nightshirt wrapped round the 'pig' that warmed his bed and his dressing gown was over the chair. Everything for his material well-being, Mary had done. As he began to unlace his boots, he was aware of her, undressing in the room beyond. He stopped to listen. There was a tap; Mary stood in the doorway.

'Try to sleep, John. I know it's a worrying time but it's rest you need most of all.' He thought he'd never seen her look more tired.

'Mary . . . ' He moved toward her, hesitantly. She waited calmly, the shawl pulled round her shoulders. 'Mary, of all people, I've never thanked you for what you've done. You've worked harder than anyone.'

'You're my husband, John, and you've given Luke a name. Of course I want you to succeed.'

'It's not just that. It's – this.' He indicated his comfortable bedchamber, uncertain how to put it into words. 'All the little things. You're always thinking of new ways to please.' She gave a ghost of a smile at this.

'Ah, yes . . . Those things come from the heart, John. Goodnight.' She didn't wait to see his embarrassment. After a moment alone, John struggled into bed. For a minute or two he listened, trying to discern if she were asleep but the room beyond was dark and silent.

With her marriage, Charlotte transferred her religious allegiance. It hadn't been a difficult transition. In fact, it could be admitted, Mrs Davie McKie embraced her husband's faith. To be in 'trade' and to attend St Cuthbert's was to be one of 'them', not one of 'us'. And despite the excellence of Armitages' ham, it meant occupying an inferior pew. But the God of the Presbyterians favoured business. His name was heartily invoked over any new venture. To Him was the praise and the glory with financial details included, for any success. In St George's, profit was a wholesome word and to be a part of such a magnificent enterprise as the emporium was to be nodded to, smiled upon, to have one's hand fervently shaken by those who'd invested money. It was, in fact, to have arrived. And as Charlotte acknowledged privately, it meant a new congregation of ladies to admire her smart blue tailor-made with matching feather hat.

Davie too, beamed at the congregation. If he hadn't entirely succeeded in converting his wife to abandon heathen ways, he wasn't doing badly. As Charlotte was ushered into a most satisfactory seat on the centre aisle she felt a warm, hand-shaped pressure on her left buttock. She couldn't believe it! It burned through broadcloth, flannel and cotton petticoats, even her stays. She turned on Davie such a look that John, kneeling on the other side of her to pray, forgot what he was supposed to be doing and asked his Maker what on earth was the matter? Fortunately for all concerned, there was no reply, but Davie came to his senses. He already knew it didn't do to upset his bride. And today, it was essential to make a good impression. He quietened his thoughts, composed his features and sat calculating how many hours and minutes remained till bedtime.

It took longer than usual to leave because everyone wanted to congratulate them. As he shook each hand and introduced Charlotte, Davie didn't forget to murmur, 'And tomorrow – at our grand opening – we shall be most pleased . . . ' John didn't linger. He wanted to return to his new office and frighten himself, estimating how much compound interest had increased their debts in the last twenty-four hours and what might happen if they couldn't pay. Within half an hour he was nearly demented.

Mary guessed where he was. She sent Katriona down with Luke to distract him. 'Put the baby on Mr McKie's lap,' she told her, 'and leave the slate and chalk, it'll take his mind off things.' But as he watched Luke painstakingly scrawl squiggles, John still remembered how much they owed.

On the great day it rained, heavy, persistent rain that beat steadily on the roof of the colonnade. From inside, John saw gloomily that he'd been right. People did shelter underneath from the weather – but they were all looking the other way! Watching out for trams to take them to work. Would none turn round to glance inside?

'Light the gas,' Davie said suddenly.

'Why? It's not that dark?'

'But we must be a beacon, to seize their attention.'

He'd judged correctly, they turned like moths to the flame, but none of them entered. It was seven when they'd unlocked the doors; now it was ten minutes to eight. John was close to tears. He'd have to leave for the warehouse soon and they hadn't sold a thing! Slowly one of the doors was pushed open. At first Davie was frozen then he rushed across, 'May I assist you, madam?' He summoned the first lady apprentice, 'Over here if you please. Attend to our customer.'

The elderly woman blinked to be the centre of so much attention.

'I don't want much . . . ' But the assistant smiled her sweetest smile.

'Yes, madam?'

'Have you any calico? Unbleached? Only I need a new apron.'

In a breathless hush everyone watched as two and a half yards was measured out. In vain the assistant tried to tempt the customer to consider buttons and tapes as well. 'No, thank you. Waste not, want not. I'll cut them off my old pinny.' Her few pence soared skywards in the bucket. At least this made for conversation and the old biddy watched, fascinated, as Davie and the cashier sent leather buckets whizzing up and down the wires for her amusement. But all good things must end and she left them, the package wrapped in 'McKie Bros' paper tucked under her arm. Silence fell heavily into the empty shop.

John forced himself to go to work. Only sixpence farthing taken in nearly an hour – they could face ruin in six months! In the warehouse, Mr Richardson was waiting. 'Good day to you,

John McKie. How's business?' John's smile was that of a death's-head.

'Slowly, thank you. That's only to be expected of course.'

'A pity about the weather. I wish you good fortune.' As the Quaker left, John found himself holding the edge of his desk for support: his legs were buckling under him. Twice during the morning he sent the youngest clerk with an umbrella to take a quick look. On each occasion the lad reported there were 'plenty sheltering from the rain but only a few inside, sir'. John's remaining confidence oozed away. He sent word he would not be home for lunch. He felt too ill.

The Quaker didn't mind the rain. He stood at the opposite side of the busy junction and was impressed. From the first, he'd been certain John's idea was sound. He'd never have suggested it to his friends as an investment otherwise. McKie and his brother had transformed the place but people had to get used to the idea of such a large shop, they were accustomed to smaller establishments. In other words, it needed a push or two to get it started. He went home to discuss it with his wife.

Fortunately the rain had eased to a gentle dampness by the afternoon. Bystanders were able to see the first carriage pull up outside the colonnade. Much to his surprise the coachman had been ordered to lower the canopy but then Mr Richardson intended that his wife should be seen. She and two of her friends were gravely handed up the cobbled slope and entered the shop.

By another strange coincidence, or so it seemed to Davie, at that particular moment a photographer arrived with his apparatus. Mrs Richardson didn't appear a whit dismayed by his request but sat patiently, beside a display of millinery, until the magnesium flash exploded.

After that the three ladies insisted on examining every counter in the shop. Outside more and more people gathered, attracted by the white flares, for Davie, with a florin, had swiftly persuaded the photographer to fire again. The audience watched purchases being made and when these were concluded, the three ladies insisted on having a cup of tea. They complimented Mrs Armitage on its excellence before departing under the shelter of Davie's umbrella for their carriage. He shook Mrs Richardson's hand fervently, 'Many thanks. Many thanks indeed, ma'am.'

'How is Mrs John McKie. Is she at all better nowadays?'

'She is much stronger, ma'am. And Luke is doing splendidly.'

'I should enjoy meeting her again, and your wife too, Mr McKie, perhaps she would call? My At-homes are on Thursdays. If Mrs John McKie would prefer it, Wednesday next would suit me also.' Davie bowed in understanding. Mary would undoubtedly prefer to call privately, as much as Charlotte would enjoy being seen in public, he realized. He turned back to the shop and saw with delight a steady trickle of people entering ahead of him.

At the end of the first week the takings were very small. Ladies came, marvelled, made the occasional purchase, drank tea and departed. Even their former customers treated it as though it were a museum, not a shop. Goods stayed where they were, on the shelves. Only Mrs Armitage could show a profit as she handed over her takings from the salon on Friday. Supper was gloomy but over the economical mutton stew, Davie had his first brainwave: 'I've got it! Charlotte must wear the hats!' They looked at him in surprise. At the other end of the large table John asked, 'What d'you mean? Hats?'

'It's the Jubilee next June, remember.' Davie turned to Charlotte, 'On Sunday, try the purple one.'

Davie wore his kilt. John thought it vulgar but Davie insisted, 'We must draw attention to ourselves, not hide away.'

'There's such a thing as discretion.' On Sunday morning he followed them up the aisle, two paces to the rear. Charlotte led the way. It reminded John unhappily of the day he'd first brought Mary here. The quiet chatter subsided then rose up again but today it was excited. 'Dear Mrs McKie – did you see . . . !' He had to admit though, Charlotte was extremely elegant.

Charlotte wore a day dress, an item from her trousseau, of greeny-blue damask satin with a matching bolero jacket. The leg o' mutton sleeves were huge. He'd come down to breakfast to find Mary padding them still further with tissue paper so that the crisp width emphasized Charlotte's tiny waist. The seamstress too had been called in, to replace the revers and tight lower sleeves with a coloured velvet to match the hat. So many hours spent on one woman's apparel, thought John guiltily as he knelt to pray. Then he remembered the overdraft and knew God would forgive them.

227

For the hat was a pinnacle of achievement. On a straw base, purple feathers rose upward in a crescendo, culminating in a Prince-of-Wales triple of ostrich plumes. Under the straw at the back, a bunch of roses concealed the hat pins. Purple veiling secured the weight beneath Charlotte's chin and for once John was thankful that it was a prominent feature. All the same, he hoped she wouldn't lean too far forward in prayer.

Davie had been responsible for ordering the hat, from a supplier in Leeds. When he'd first seen it, John had protested. Conservative Darlington would never dream of buying anything so lavish. Now he wasn't so sure. From all sides he could hear the whispering . . . 'Mrs McKie's hat, dear. Over there . . . ' As for Charlotte, she put aside the white silk gloves and parasol and waited contentedly to hear the word of the Lord. He – and she – were the centre of attention.

On Monday morning the photograph of Mrs Richardson appeared in the newspaper. Over the marmalade, Davie gloated, for in the display behind her was the same purple feathered straw hat. 'There'll be no stopping them,' Davie prophesied. 'They'll be showing their husbands this and telling them they want the same. And to make it all respectable here's Mrs Richardson telling the world she shops at McKie Brothers.'

He was right. By evening they'd sold out of hats in every shade of purple. Davie telegraphed to Leeds for more. In the salon, Mrs Armitage and Bertha were run off their feet with the press of ladies. 'At one time, dear Mr McKie, there were *four* ladies waiting to be seated!'

Nor was Mrs Armitage spared when on Tuesday she went to Skinnergate to buy an additional two pounds of Darjeeling for the salon. Davie produced a bonnet exactly the same as that worn by Her Majesty. Mrs Armitage received it from him very solemnly indeed. 'Are you sure, Mr Davie, are you quite sure we're not being – improper.'

'Her Majesty would be flattered, ma'am, to see how well it suits you.'

As for Luke, Katriona was instructed to wheel him along Victoria Road and twice round South Park in the most delightful baby's cap in the emporium. Luke was too big for the perambulator but fortunately he was a biddable child, fond enough of his jolly uncle to want to please him. As a final

228

touch, Davie persuaded Katriona to pin new streamers to her cap. The fluttered like pennants in the breeze so that there wasn't a nurse in Victoria Road who hadn't described them – or the baby's garments – to her mistress by the end of the morning.

It was in fact the Jubilee that sealed their success. John grew quite anxious about the Queen's health when he heard what Davie had arranged. On the morning of June 20th, the blinds were raised to reveal to Darlington a tableau made familiar by all those photographs of Balmoral. Davie had obtained a lifesize model of Her Majesty. She stood on a heather-covered bank wearing, rather surprisingly, a crown and sceptre. At her feet knelt a much smaller replica of John Brown, identifiable by his kilt although John was unhappy about the tartan. Beside the Queen a rocking horse, devoid of rockers, deputized for a Highland pony. A rug carelessly draped over his flanks covered mouldering patches in his hide. He was attached to a dog-cart festooned in flowers. Behind the tableau on a painted backcloth supplied by the Theatre Royal scene staff, hundreds of subjects raised a silent cheer. And John heaved a sigh of relief that Her Majesty continued to reign over them, at least until they'd sold the last of the special Jubilee souvenirs.

Their window attracted plenty of comment. The *North Star* carried an editorial praising it. Crowds made a special journey to see it and many went inside. Mrs Armitage had to double her order for tea yet again, the shop assistants wore tartan ribbons and favours, and for the entire week banners above the counters announced that sprigs of heather 'plucked near Balmoral' would be given to every customer whose purchases exceeded five shillings. John shuddered when he saw the description. Davie grinned and told him to close his eyes to it. 'Most of our customers don't even know where Balmoral is. And anyway, some of it might have come from there.'

In his study on Friday however, John was able to add up cash with a glad heart. They'd never had a better week. They had a core of regular customers now, enough to justify the delivery boy's wages. They were all learning to live frugally on his ware-house salary. As well as paying off the interest in regular instalments, next week he could begin repaying the loan from their father.

Behind the scenes all was not going smoothly. Mrs Armitage was delighted with her new situation; she never tired of telling her customers in the salon how beneficial it had been for Mr A. Bertha too was enjoying life. Apart from assisting her mistress she also shared the cooking with Ada and Katriona. Between them the three women nursed the grocer and cared for Luke.

For Mary there had been many changes. Thanks to Mrs Armitage's tuition, running the stockroom wasn't difficult, nor supervising the young apprentices. Best of all, she could move more freely, thanks to Mr Nettles. On one of his routine visits to Coburg Street, the doctor had been accosted in the parlour. Stammering, the Adam's apple bobbing furiously, Mr Nettles claimed there might be a way of improving Mary's boot. A lightweight alloy from Germany was being tested, not brittle like so many others but durable. If the doctor would provide a design, Mr Nettles would see what he could do.

The heavy, bulbous shape was examined under the gas light. Mr Nettles made a sketch; the doctor re-worked it. When the prototype was brought to his surgery, he strapped it to his own own foot and staggered about, to test its strength. Finally a frame was produced that satisfied both of them. The cobbler fitted a soft leather slipper inside and the result was presented to Mary.

Delicacy prevented Mr Nettles being there to see it put on because Mary had to remove her stocking. The doctor cradled the club foot in his hands, examining thick grey scar tissue.

'When was this done?'

'When I was a child. A man in Fort William claimed he could reshape my foot. He cut into it deeply . . . ' Mary's voice faltered. 'There was a great deal of pain but despite his efforts, my foot remained the same.' The young doctor stared.

'D'you mean . . he didn't use an anaesthetic?'

'You must understand, that cost extra. And we'd no money to spare.'

'Butchery! He must have known it wouldn't do any good.'

'The point was, doctor, my father didn't know.'

'Come, try this on,' he said brusquely. 'I can't cure you but, thanks to Nettles, I think we can relieve the strain on that leg.'

She couldn't believe it – the lightness! The effortless way she could move, actually lifting her club foot off the floor instead of dragging it. Hearing the noise, Mr Nettles knocked impatiently.

'Come in, come in!' cried the doctor, 'Take a look at this young woman before she flies down Coburg Street!'

And without them noticing it, John too entered, wondering what all the laughter was about. Mary turned and saw him. Flushed, happy, she flung out her arms. 'Look, John, look! I can walk!' She moved the short distance between them, her arms still wide, her weak leg tapping on the linoleum. She didn't twist any more, the limp was negligible, she was so full of joy it filled the room.

The two inventors watched smugly, waiting for him to embrace her.

'I – don't understand.' John stood there woodenly, reddening at the lie. He knew perfectly well what they'd been planning – young Nettles had even brought samples of the alloy for him to examine. But a new emotion swept through him as he saw Mary with them: jealousy. That they had achieved so much and he not a part of it. For it wasn't simply Mary's body that had been eased: the doctor expressed the thoughts of all of them. 'It's taken years off you, Mrs McKie – I've never seen you looking so – so relaxed.' He'd almost said handsome but one had to take care, in front of a husband.

Miserable with his own awkwardness, John slipped upstairs to put away his coat. If only Davie had been here, he'd have found the right words. As it was, he hadn't even thanked the other two. John hurried back to the kitchen but Mary was alone. Worse still, she'd retreated into her shell.

'They've gone to celebrate,' she called over her shoulder as she stirred a pan on the hob. 'I think the doctor intends persuading Mr Nettles to help other cripples.' Had she used the word deliberately because of the way he'd behaved?

'I'm very pleased for your sake – ' he began, but Mary interrupted him.

'Your supper is ready, John. Would you like to sit up at table?' Nor would she allow him to refer to the successful boot again. Love, tender and strong though it be, needs encouragement if it is to flourish but John had none to give.

At the Emporium it was Charlotte who found her new role uncertain and it affected her temper. It was all very well for Davie to describe her as queen of the Emporium. Certainly the other women deferred to her and customers looked gratified whenever she chatted to them, just as they had in Skinnergate. But Charlotte lacked Mary's particular status, that of mother to Luke.

It irritated her to see everyone idolize the child. In his play-pen in a corner of the dining room, Luke played happily for hours, ready to smile at anyone who cooed at him, particularly the young apprentices. Davie had told Charlotte in the strictest confidence that John was not the child's father. With her upbringing Charlotte naturally assumed Mary was a widow. There were many sorrowing women throughout the country thanks to the Boers. Davie didn't enlighten her, he thought it wiser not to and he was most emphatic that neither Mary nor John wanted the subject discussed.

But for Charlotte it seemed that everything revolved around Mary's child. Katriona brought him down so that he and John could breakfast together. Each evening the boy would be pressed against the bars of his pen, waiting for 'dada'. Davie was nearly as bad. He made excuses during the day to go upstairs and see Luke, chuckling proudly over any new sign of progress. Even pregnancy didn't cure Charlotte's mood for she felt so uncomfortable. 'Indisposed' was the way Dr Cullen described it, and he lectured her about her corsets. For a young woman accustomed to pleasing herself, the experience was galling. Particularly as he was so unsympathetic about her nausea.

Mrs Armitage was very concerned about the coming event. It didn't matter that John and Davie assured her no expense would be spared to ensure the best possible medical care; in her experience that meant nothing. She poured out her worries to her spouse.

'Charlotte is so like poor Jane, my dear. But I do my best, I insist she drinks beef tea three times a day. Look how it does you good. I told Mr Collins only yesterday – he was enquiring of you as he always does – "Mr A is picking up remarkably." '
The vacant eyes watered, but such a small amount, it went unnoticed among the spittle.

When Charlotte decided she was too unsightly to appear in public, the first of the assistant traders gave up his books to join them. John called at the Temperance Hall to hand over the agreed sum. Mr Gordon had begun to notice how his own trade had fallen off. The amount of whisky he was drinking made it worse. He shouted that his customers were being deliberately enticed away but John shook his head.

'The womenfolk prefer to come into Darlington to shop for themselves. You knew this would happen once the horse trams were established, surely? They can meet their friends, there's a choice of merchandise – did you see another draper has opened premises, at the far end of Northgate?' This was scarcely consolation. Mr Gordon refilled his glass.

'All I know is, John McKie, that you are using the same suppliers. The people I introduced you to – and you're undercutting me!'

'I've been scrupulously fair, Mr Gordon. Where we have stocked the same lines, I've kept the price the same, even though I object to the mark-up. But you'll find we have a greater variety of goods, and we use many more suppliers. Davie still travels to Leeds but he's visiting Glasgow next week. We're expanding, Mr Gordon.'

It wasn't likely to assuage the trader's feelings, reminding him that he was behind the times, but John had a long memory. The price he'd had to pay all those years ago still rankled. Now the guineas to buy out Mr Hart's contract shone on the table between them. The sight of them prevented Gordon letting fly at him. Instead, he put down his glass. 'And what d'you suggest I do, John McKie? When you've finally taken away all my customers?' John managed a wintery smile.

'Why not invest in us? You'll find our terms are excellent. In fact, I doubt whether you'll find better in Darlington.' After that, it was time to leave.

Mr Hart was their first male assistant. He started in gents' gloves and hats and helping Mary with the stockroom. Anything of a female nature was deemed unsuitable for him to touch despite his previous experience with Mr Gordon. This was different, John told him, a different *class* of customer altogether. Mr Hart also fetched, carried, summoned cabs and was at everyone's beck and call. Only the errand boy was inferior in status.

Perhaps this, and an ambition to succeed that John had already spotted, stimulated Mr Hart into suggesting the first alteration to the shop. Supposing they had a proper gents' section? Not just a couple of counters, but equal in size to the ladies' departments.

It was Friday night when John collected the cash and doled out wages. He took off his spectacles and sat back in the swivel chair. Perhaps Mr Hart would like to explain? The young man cleared his throat. He had taken the liberty of measuring the space available. In his (humble) opinion, there was ample to divide the area in half in what was now haberdashery.

From an inside pocket, Mr Hart produced his plan and laid it on the blotter. Would Mr McKie be kind enough to examine it? John resumed his spectacles.

'Very good,' he announced after a moment or two. 'Well thought out, Mr Hart.' The young assistant glowed.

'That is what Mr Davie was good enough to say, and Mrs McKie. She hoped your reaction would be the same, sir.'

'Davie . . . ?'

'I discussed it first with him and Mrs McKie. I didn't want to waste your time, sir. Mr Davie suggested several improvements and it was your wife's idea to angle the shelving like that, so that full-length mirrors could be incorporated . . . ' But John was no longer listening. The emporium was his creation, his, not Davie's. He should have been consulted first. And why ask Mary? She'd not been trained for business. Mr Hart talked on, unaware.

'Yes, yes. Leave it with me. I'll have to consider, check the figures. It's not a matter we can rush into, it requires consideration.' Mr Hart was slightly disconcerted.

'Those figures have all been checked, sir, by Mr Clough. It's his estimate I've been describing. I'll leave it with you, shall I, Mr McKie?'

Within a week, John had overcome his hurt pride and gave

234

instructions for the work to proceed. He even managed to thank Mary. Did his mood show in his voice?

'I hope I did right, John? You've always said Mr Hart was to be encouraged. I thought it would be sensible for him to see Mr Clough?'

'Yes, indeed – '

'But you must tell me if you prefer me not to interfere?' He didn't reply.

(v)

Besides being private, Davie and Charlotte's quarters were also isolated from the shop. Alone each afternoon, obeying Dr Cullen's order to rest, Charlotte grew bored. Katriona was sent to keep her company but her interests were limited to Luke and the latest gossip concerning the actor, Mr Du Maurier. Charlotte disapproved of tittle-tattle. She said sternly, 'Ask Mrs McKie to come, please.'

It was a tête-a-tête Mary had been avoiding since Davie's wedding. No one was more conscious than Mary of the delicate balance between Charlotte and herself. Mary deferred in every possible way to Charlotte, but it didn't compensate and she knew it. Charlotte had been accustomed to being the centre of attention all her life, not second fiddle.

There was the equally awkward matter of Luke. Davie told Mary privately what Charlotte had assumed, about her widowhood, but Mary had no wish to sustain the lie. Neither could she risk Charlotte learning the truth. Until now she'd managed to avoid any intimacy which could lead to questioning about her background. When Mrs Armitage asked kindly whether Mary didn't miss her parents, she'd managed to stammer that marriage to John more than made up for it. Overhearing this, John blushed furiously, leaving Mrs Armitage with the impression that they were two very private people, shy of strangers.

Today there was no escaping Charlotte's request. Mary went reluctantly up to the first floor and along the passage to the bedroom. Downstairs, Katriona had been ordered to send word the minute Mary was needed elsewhere – and that the sooner such a summons came, the better.

235

'Hello, Charlotte, how are you today?' The fire was blazing, the lamp lit because Charlotte preferred it to gas. It was a warm and inviting room, conducive to idle chatter. Charlotte reclined on the chaise longue rather than her bed, with plenty of pillows to cushion her back.

'I'm so bored, Mary, and this is a frightfully silly book.'

'Shall I change it next time I go to the library?'

'Would you? Bertha fetched this one. She always forgets what I've asked her to find – I didn't want this at all.' The despised volume was flung aside.

'Would you like a cup of tea?' The spirit stove, primed and ready, stood on the hearth.

'What I'd like is for you to sit and talk to me. You can spare me a few minutes, surely?'

'Yes, of course, Charlotte!' Mary eased the armchair back a little, trying to forestall confidence.

'It's so warm by the fire,' she apologized, nervous that Charlotte would see through the stratagem.

'I can hardly see you over there . . . ' Mary took crochet work out of her apron pocket. 'It's too dark in that corner. Move closer to the lamp.' Lacking a further excuse, Mary obeyed. 'What's that you're making?'

'A little cap, Charlotte, for your baby.'

'I've a drawer full of caps. Everyone keeps giving me caps.'

'I'll make this a little larger, for when he's older,' Mary promised. She was allowed a few minutes peace while Charlotte speculated on whether indeed it would be a boy. Suddenly she stopped speaking, arched her back and groaned. Mary hurried to adjust the pillows. 'Is that better, dear?'

'Is it always like this? Did you feel poorly when you were carrying Luke?' They were on dangerous ground. Mary busied herself with the rug. 'Well?' Charlotte demanded.

'I was fortunate. I seldom felt unwell. When I did . . . ' Mary flushed slightly, 'It was usually my leg.'

'Davie says you're walking much better since Mr Nettles designed your new boot.' Charlotte sounded as if she were accusing her of self-pity.

'Oh yes, I am much better. I can't begin to describe how much easier – '

'It will help next time, won't it? Your leg won't trouble you as much?'

'Next time?' Mary looked at her stupidly.

'When you and John are expecting a happy event,' Charlotte answered patiently. Misunderstanding Mary's confusion, she went on, 'You must be thankful not to be having another baby just yet, while we're still so busy. I wish Davie and I could've avoided it a little longer . . . I'm frightened, Mary!' she wailed, 'so frightened. It killed my mother, you know, having me. Aunt Armitage had always told me I resemble her.' There were genuine tears and Mary tried to soothe them away.

'Dear Charlotte, you're so strong. And from what I've heard, your poor mother suffered dreadfully on that voyage. Seeing your father die like that – what she must've endured! Perhaps it's your father you take after? Mrs Armitage never knew him, did she?'

Charlotte blew her nose. 'I'd like that cup of tea now.'

'Yes, of course.' Mary hastened to light the wick. 'Try not to worry. Dr Cullen is kind and gentle, and the nurse. They will do all they can to ease the pain.'

'Was it very bad, having Luke?'

'No, dear. They gave me chloroform.'

'You will have another, Mary?' When Mary didn't turn round, Charlotte asked curiously, 'You are going to give John a baby, aren't you? He must want one of his own even though he dotes on Luke.'

'If God wills . . . ' Trapped, helpless, Mary faced her tormentor but Charlotte wanted more of an answer.

'Perhaps John would prefer a daughter?'

'I – don't know.' Mary prayed the water would boil to divert attention.

'Goodness, Mary, Davie and I are far more modern. We discussed how many babies we wanted before we were married.' Charlotte sat upright, the better to give advice. 'Of course, *he* wanted too many. Four, I think. I said two at the most – one if I find it troublesome.'

Boil, boil!

'What about you?' Charlotte demanded, 'Surely you want another, a sister for Luke?'

'The doctor told John . . . I wasn't strong enough . . . ' Mary

237

spoke very low but Charlotte heard.

'Goodness, how sad. How awful for John! That means he'll never have a son of his own?'

'Charlotte!' Mary was hurt, angry, 'Charlotte – John looks on Luke as his own, he always has!'

'Yes, I know . . . ' Charlotte retreated back against her pillow, 'I'm sorry if I offended you.'

'It doesn't matter. I'd rather not talk of it though, it distresses me.'

'Yes, of course.' Too late, the kettle began to hiss. Mary's hand shook as she measured out the tea leaves. Charlotte made an effort to change the subject.

'What was their house like, in Coburg Street? Davie couldn't take me there, unchaperoned. I expect Aunt Armitage would've permitted it if you and I had known each other then.'

'On my first visit, it was empty. They'd only managed to furnish one bedroom and the kitchen.'

'How uncomfortable!'

'And it was very dusty,' Mary managed to smile as she remembered. 'They'd been living as I imagine bachelors always do, without any women to look after them.'

'Didn't they have a servant?'

Mary smiled. 'I don't think they could afford it. John and Davie were very poor to begin with, you know. They saved every penny towards this place.' But Charlotte wasn't interested in poverty.

'It doesn't cost much to keep one maid, surely?'

'Whatever it cost, I doubt whether John would've thought it necessary, and once we were married I managed on my own. Emily Beal came to help whenever I needed it. It was a very modern house, Charlotte, gas light in parlour and kitchen, water piped to the scullery, not out in the yard. But it didn't have a single pair of curtains when I first saw it.'

'Really! How on earth did they manage?'

'I've no doubt they were very careful with the candle when they undressed,' said Mary, drily. Charlotte thought this very forward. She frowned as she accepted the cup of tea.

'I trust you had curtains at all the windows before you moved in?'

'Oh, yes. Mrs Beal and I were fortunate at the auction rooms.

238

Some of them have since been altered to fit the attics here.' But the servants' quarters were outside the realm of Charlotte's interest.

'I'm glad Davie and I came directly here after our honeymoon. I do prefer to live in the town. Victoria Road is quite genteel, of course, but I like to feel the bustle all around. Coburg Street . . . ' and she shrugged her elegant shoulders. 'My aunt never permits credit to overrun in that part of town.'

Mary offered a humble defence of Luke's birthplace: 'The parlour was handsome. Above and below the dado, the walls were a dark chestnut – and the fireplace was set across the corner of the room – '

'Nevertheless, it isn't a smart address,' said Charlotte and the subject was closed.

Later, Mrs Armitage shook her head over the sadness of it. Poor Mr McKie, such an excellent father. Perhaps God would relent and send him and Mary another little stranger?

But the Almighty was set on tormenting John at present. No sooner had John emerged from a discussion with Davie, his wife's praises ringing in his ears – 'She was the one who put Hart on the right track, John. You should've heard her, brimming over with ideas when he showed her his plan!' – than John was waylaid by Dr Cullen after one of his visits to Charlotte.

'Could I have a word, Mr McKie, if you're not too busy?' John led the way to his study.

'I hope nothing's wrong?' He indicated Charlotte above.

'Oh, no. Strong as an ox, that young lady, despite all that lacing she's been indulging in. No, it's your wife I wanted to speak about. I'm very pleased with the way she's improving.'

'Oh . . . ' John looked at him blankly.

'You must've noticed yourself, Mr McKie, how the change, the move here, has done her good. She's put on weight, she moves easily and she's a much better colour . . . ?' John was expressionless. Mary was a fixture in his life. She was there at breakfast, through the day she worked in the emporium, he at the warehouse. In the evening, she presided over the dining table. At night, she slept in the tiny dressing room adjoining the bedroom, and although she was there, she was separate.

'Very pleased with her . . . ' Dr Cullen repeated, nodding to

239

himself. 'She's stopped taking that medicine, clever girl. I hate giving that stuff but sometimes it's the only way, but she's wise enough to understand the risks.' He looked up and smiled. 'I'm very pleased to tell you, I don't think there's any longer too much risk. A baby?'

John still didn't speak. 'What I'm trying to explain is that you and Mrs McKie can go ahead, have a family.' He looked at him encouragingly. 'I'm sure young Luke needs company, don't you? A brother or sister – '

'Yes, yes, I understand!' John was on his feet, poking the stove vigorously.

'It must come as a bit of a shock, I realize, Mr McKie. After what I told you both before. I haven't yet spoken to your wife, by the way. I thought I'd tell you the good tidings first. But next time she visits me . . . I examined her last week. That's when I first noticed the improvement.'

'Thank you – very much.' John knew more was called for but couldn't bring himself to say it.

'I'll leave it to you to tell her, shall I?'

'Oh – yes. Thanks.' The doctor reached for his battered hat.

'Leave it a month or two more, I should. But she's getting stronger all the time. Must be all the hard work. Making a success of it, are you? Good, good . . . ' Dr Cullen accepted John's silence as shock but hadn't more time to spare. 'Don't bother to see me out, Mr McKie, I know the way.'

(vi)

With the addition of 'Select Items of Apparel for Gentlemen' John decided to expand the catering. A small alcove beyond the salon was to be opened up. There, smoking would be permitted. Mrs Armitage was agitated.

'It will be respectable,' he assured her, 'for our gentlemen customers, those whom we know. Strangers will not be encouraged.' She had an anxious consultation with her spouse.

'He is agreeable,' she reported back to John, 'provided Mr Davie keeps an eye on everything. Mr A does not wish me to be – exposed, to anything unsuitable.'

240

Davie replied gravely that he considered it a matter of honour to guarantee the safety of every lady in the emporium. In his absence on business at any time, Mr Hart would be his deputy. Mrs Armitage sighed. Compared to Davie, Mr Hart was such a spindly young man. John pointed out that there was also the messenger boy who, should any disaster occur, would run for the constable. Eventually a compromise was reached and a discreet brass bell placed within Mrs Armitage's reach. It was clearly understood that at the first sound of alarm, everyone in the emporium would rally to her aid. It was never used but Bertha saw to it that it remained well polished.

They continued to live frugally, on John's wage from the warehouse. Any profits were re-invested in stock after the interest on the loans was paid. In Coburg Street, after rents from the lodgers finally cleared the mortgage, John promptly re-borrowed the amount from the bank, to expand the shop. If Davie was nervous, he had complete faith in his brother. The small sum he was paid each week went mostly on gifts for Charlotte, which was all he wanted. The shop was flourishing, John was pleased and Charlotte was expecting their first child. Davie wrote lyrically to Scotland and radiated joy in his work. The lady customers were overwhelmed; they kept coming back. Shopping at McKies was 'such a pleasure', 'nothing was too much trouble.' 'Almost the same as visiting Armitage's,' one of them said. Davie thought this most felicitous and repeated it.

'Almost,' Mrs Armitage conceded when she heard. 'Mr Collins does his best, I am sure. But no one . . . ' She paused to give additional emphasis, 'no one has ever had the same – flair – as my dear Mr A.'

Fortunately for John, Mrs Armitage continued to pay Charlotte the same allowance she'd enjoyed previously. Davie could not have kept his wife in style on his meagre wage. John had once, half heartedly, suggested Charlotte should be paid out of the business but Mrs Armitage shook her head.

'Pray let me contribute, dear Mr McKie. Are you not providing a home for my dear husband and myself? And if anything should happen . . . ' She raised her eyes. 'I should depart knowing my dearest ones are cared for. What more could any woman want? I have what I need, let me give the rest to Charlotte.'

And give she did. Every corner of Charlotte's rooms was filled with muslin, lace and knitted items. John recalled Luke's beginnings, the drawer lined with flannel and the very few garments hung to dry each evening in front of the fire. Naturally, nothing but the best was good enough for Charlotte's layette, but he wondered if any baby needed quite so much.

By the time it was born, they had repaid the initial interest and were beginning to make inroads into the loans themselves. Alex protested at receiving money, if only a trickle at this stage. When he urged them to keep it, John told him sternly to put it in the bank against a rainy day. If he and Jeannie didn't want to join them in Darlington, there might come a time when the work of the croft was too much. Alex understood. It wasn't possible that any of his children or grandchildren would return. Some day, therefore, he would need to pay hired help to work the land. For he and Jeannie couldn't bring themselves to leave it; this was theirs, for which their forefathers had paid with blood. Thank God his children had made their escape, he thought ruefully, but he and Jeannie couldn't break away, the croft was too much a part of them. Besides, how could he leave a land of such beauty? So he wrote and thanked John for the money, promising he would put it by for when it was needed.

(vii)

John and Mary were in the habit of taking a last cup of tea before going up to their separate beds. Long ago John had discovered his wife was an excellent listener; he could talk of plans and she wouldn't interrupt. This evening he wanted to discuss the future, as usual. 'If we continue as we have been doing, the business will belong to us entirely by the time Luke goes to school. Maybe a year or two later if we use the money to reinvest instead, but near enough. It's quite an achievement, isn't it?'

Mary smiled. No reply was needed. They had done well; none could be singled out for praise for all had contributed equally.

242

John's eyes closed as he relaxed for a moment. She felt the familiar heartache to see the worry lines fade. He looked young again. She feasted her eyes because he wasn't conscious of her watching him. This half-dead unrequited love was always there to vex her, she couldn't rid herself of it.

She heard Ada calling for her and got up quietly so as not to disturb John. It had been one of Charlotte's fancies to have Mary beside her during her confinement. As the time approached and Charlotte admitted her fears, Mary had been able to soothe her. Now Charlotte demanded she be there to see her through the worst.

The pains had begun in the early hours that morning. Throughout the day, Mary had toiled back and forth to the bedroom, wringing out hot cloths that brought ease to Charlotte's belly, grasping her hands when the agony was severe. At tea-time, Dr Cullen had chased her away.

'This baby won't come for several hours – it's not a cooperative infant like Luke,' he'd said, and Mary had gone, grateful for the release. Now it sounded as though she were needed once more.

Another shout, and this time it was Davie. Footsteps thudded down the passage. The door burst open, startling them. He stood there sweating, beaming from ear to ear.

'What is it, what's the matter?' John was confused. Davie lunged at him, scooped him up in his arms and whirled him round and round.

'It's a boy, it's a boy!' he shouted and just as suddenly let go of him and raced away again, crying, 'I've got to get back to Charlotte – she wants you too, Mary!' His voice faded away, 'A lovely little boy!'

Mary was the first to recover. 'I'm glad it's over sooner than expected. And Davie has a son.'

'A son, yes . . . '

'I must go to Charlotte. And warn them in the kitchen. You know Dr Cullen, by now he'll have a terrible thirst for his porter.'

'Give her my congratulations . . . ' John still spoke absently and uttered the next words without thinking, 'I wish we had a son.' The moment they were out, blood pounded in his head. He looked at Mary imploringly, 'Pray, don't misunderstand,

Luke is our first-born. He will never be supplanted.' Confusion overcame him.

'But – you want a child!' whispered Mary. She felt so faint she clenched her fists so that the nails bit into her palms. 'Yet you don't love me.' There was a terrible pause. 'Do you?'

'I don't think I know what love is.' His honesty was even more painful and it got worse. 'I respect you, indeed, I like you – ' Mary couldn't stay in the same room with him after that. The torrent of love she cherished for him threatened to choke her and she stumbled away.

On his own, John clasped his head in his hands. what had he done! That careful half-life he and Mary had built up had been exposed in all its frailty. He'd been so clumsy – but it was true, he did want a son. He couldn't deny it, the feeling was too strong. He wasn't jealous of Davie but he yearned for his own flesh and blood to stand alongside Luke.

Mary's sobs echoed in his mind: How could he hurt her so! He found her at last in the sanctuary of Luke's bedroom. The boy was asleep so John kept his voice low. 'I apologize . . . what I suggested was impossible – without love. I didn't intend to insult you.'

The door closed behind him and Mary rocked with the pain of frustration: such a desire to give John a son – how could she bear it!

Emotion was too strong for either of them to attempt sleep. Like Mary, John had stifled feelings so often when they emerged, the force of them frightened him. In the face of Davie's joy, he couldn't pretend to be fulfilled. He loved Luke, the emporium was a dream come true but without love, life was meaningless.

(viii)

In her brass bed Charlotte was extremely glad it was over. She was exhausted. No one had warned her how bad it would be – and that stupid nurse, telling her how lucky she was it had happened so quickly. Even the doctor was surprised, shouting instructions, saying how she'd fooled them all, it'd been so fast.

Fast! She'd been in pain for hours! Her aunt and Bertha had been sympathetic – and Mary. Why hadn't she been here at the finish, instead of the humiliation of the nurse shouting at her rudely, ordering her about. Charlotte would be glad to be up and about, mistress of the emporium again. She had a son now, like Mary. She was on equal footing at last. Charlotte turned her head to see. The tiny face poked up out of its wrappings. Her aunt had gazed at it through a haze of tears, 'Oh Charlotte, what a lovely little boy!'

How could she say such a thing? The child was red and wrinkled and . . . Oh dear! Charlotte caught sight of the top of its head for the first time. He'd got bright red carroty hair, not like his father's but very, very common!

The door opened a crack. Charlotte shut her eyes, pretending to sleep. People kept coming in and out, no consideration. It was Davie. He stood, clutching John tightly by the arm.

'Can you see him? He's in the cradle beside Charlotte.' The nurse looked up from re-making the fire.

'Hush, Mr McKie, your wife is sleeping!'

'Just a peep, nurse, then we'll go away.' They sidled past. Standing beside the cradle, John thought there was no comparison with Luke. He'd been a beautiful baby. John recalled the thrill of that rosebud mouth yawning at him; it helped calm the turmoil now in his breast.

'Very nice,' he said. 'A very big baby. What are you going to call him?' From her pillows but without opening her eyes, Charlotte said quickly, 'Joseph Edward, after my father and Uncle Armitage.'

Davie looked apologetically at John. 'I hope Father won't be disappointed,' he murmured. 'He'll likely think you and Mary . . . will have another.' He forced the words out, unable to meet John's eye. They were breaking with tradition, having two boys and neither bearing their father's names of Alexander John.

In the embarrassed silence, Charlotte spoke again from her pillows. 'Joseph Edward. Please tell Aunt Armitage.'

Her aunt was extremely gratified. 'How kind! How thoughtful of Mr McKie and Mr Davie!' But the boy was never known as anything but 'Young Ted'.

When a sister arrived two years later, Charlotte was irritated by Mrs Armitage's assumption that this time the child would be named Adelaide.

'She will be baptized Jane after my mother. I shall never know why I was not as I cannot abide the name Charlotte.'

Thus the link with the pauper's grave was ended. Lotte's immortality finished with Charlotte. Yet if she'd not existed, would the villagers have been spurred on to leave? Charlotte might never have met her aunt nor enjoyed the comfort Mr A delighted in providing for her as she grew to womanhood. But for Lotte, Jane's daughter could have ended up like herself, married to a pitman, struggling all her life to avoid the curse of the workhouse.

As she nursed her daughter, Charlotte told her aunt that this baby was the last. Pregnancy was most unpleasant, she couldn't abide it, and there would be no chance therefore of another 'Adelaide'. Unless John and Mary could overcome their scruples, of course. Charlotte considered her sister-in-law looked healthy enough to try. She tried to ease the disappointment for Mrs Armitage.

'My children will call you great-aunt, as Luke does.' By mutual consent they glossed over the fact that she was their great-great-aunt. No lady likes to be reminded too emphatically of the passing of the years.

In 1899, when Jane was born, the McKies counted themselves among the lucky ones. For two years since young Ted's birth, smallpox had swept the area, so virulently that a floating hospital, the *Osprey*, had been moored offshore at Eston in an attempt to prevent the contagion spreading. It was pitifully inadequate, increasing the beds available to two hundred for the one and a half thousand victims.

In the emporium, trade that had increased with the Diamond Jubilee fell to almost nothing. Now, in early summer, Dr Cullen confirmed the official prognosis that the worst was past. They could begin trading again, even with suppliers in Middlesbrough, where the epidemic had been dreadful.

'I'd say it's safe to walk abroad, although God help us if the authorities don't do something about the sewers before next year. It only needs a bit of warm weather to bring the typhoid back again.' He sat gloomily over his empty glass and Mary came across to top it up. 'Thank you, my dear.' He watched her move, appraising her limp and pallor. 'You've been overdoing it, haven't you?' And when Mary shook her head, 'Oh yes, you have. I know why. It's that sister-in-law of yours, isn't it? Ignore her. She's as strong as a horse and you're not.'

'Pray, don't let Charlotte hear you compare her with that!' Mary raised her eyebrows in mock alarm. 'Not a horse, Dr Cullen. She would think that – '

'Improper?' The doctor grinned. 'Pretty little girl, your new niece. Got her mother's looks, not a carrot-top like young Ted.'

'Davie is ecstatic this time. He was glad enough to have a boy – but a girl!' Mary shrugged to show how glad he was. 'Every time he opens his mouth, it's to shout with joy. The nurse tries to quiet him but it's not in Davie's nature to be so.'

'No . . . ' Luke was sitting beside the doctor's chair and the man tousled his hair affectionately. 'Some of us are more peaceful, thank goodness. Still scribbling his letters, I see?'

'Yes. He's doing well – and he wants to please Papa, don't you, Luke?' The child looked up eagerly.

'Soon be going to school, eh Luke?'

'Oh, yes!' Doctor and mother laughed.

'No stopping him, is there?' Dr Cullen slipped easily into the topic that concerned him. 'And with this young man off your hands, now's the time for you and Mr McKie to consider having another, my dear. Why not join Mrs Davie in the nursery stakes? I promise to make it as painless as I can next time.'

To his dismay, Mary looked close to tears. 'Now, now, my dear. Haven't said anything to distress you, I hope. Not been trying too hard the two of you, been over-anxious, that sort of thing?'

Her expression this time stopped him in his tracks. To give them both time to recover he made another fuss of Luke before gathering up his belongings. As he reached the door, he said softly, 'Think about what I've said, Mrs McKie. I like my mothers young, it's better for the babies. But if there's something troubling you . . . come and talk it over.'

247

Outside in the passage, Ada waited with his hat. 'Don't bother to see me out, I know the way.'

'Babies are all very well once they've arrived – and there's a nurse to care for them,' said Charlotte, 'It's having them that's so undignified.' She was holding court. The baby slept, its cradle tucked into the shadows while Charlotte in her new peignoir sat with her feet up, Mrs Armitage and Katriona beside her and Mary beside the fire.

'You look so well on it, Charlotte. Doesn't she, Mrs McKie? Such a pity there are to be no more.'

'Oh, Aunt Armitage! You wouldn't have me with half a dozen clinging to my skirts like those poor women who live in Potter's Yard. Whenever the Dorcas Society visit, there always seem to be more children.'

'Perhaps, after the epidemic, it's as well there are,' said Mary quietly. 'So many families have lost one or two little ones.'

'Oh, Mary, don't!' Charlotte shivered, 'That's all over now.'

'I shall still insist more on carbolic being poured into the drains, whatever Dr Cullen says. I owe it to Mr A. Supposing he should catch an infection. It doesn't bear thinking of.'

'I shall be glad to be up and about again,' said Charlotte. 'I'm fortunate, I know, but staying in bed is the last thing I want to do now. I'd much rather be back in the shop beside Davie.'

Despite the drop in trade, the shop was prospering. But an ingrained terror of poverty, rooted in Charlotte since babyhood, acted as a spur. Two children were sufficient. They must work hard, the emporium would succeed, then the spectre of the workhouse would disappear for ever. It was extremely annoying therefore, having made such a public declaration, to discover there were to be three. What was more, the old Queen was responsible, or so Charlotte claimed.

It was the end of an era that had been slowly dying for years. The Jubilee had brought a brief revival, a celebration, but as long as any of them could remember, there had been this figurehead as part of their existence. Her influence had patterned their lives; her respectability had tightened their corsets, increased the layers of petticoats – in some cases it had stifled young women – but above all it had brought comfort to the middle classes. After her death chatter and speculation about the future were in much more excited tones in the Gentlemen's 'Smoking'. But first, there was the funeral.

Moved by the death of Queen Victoria though he was, John had to admit to Davie it couldn't have happened at a more fortuitous time, in January. Another month and they would have ordered the year's summer stock. As it was, McKie Brothers were first with a bulk order for crêpe. England was plunged into mourning and would remain so for at least six months. As the town's uncrowned leader of fashion, Charlotte wore the most impenetrable black of all.

Davie mounted an impressive tribute. In their main window stood a lifesize model of a soldier, dressed as a hero of Mafeking, head bowed. In front of him on a purple catafalque lay a very small crown full of shiny glass jewels. Outside in the bitter weather, women stood weeping over this display. They had lost someone as close as any member of their family, for the unpopularity the Queen had enjoyed a decade ago had faded with age. They'd thought she would reign over them for ever, that she was immortal. How was it possible she'd gone? The queue stretched past the colonnade, past each window full of photographs of her relatives including the lifelike portrait of the Prince of Wales which Davie had secretly purchased when Charlotte remarked on his own resemblance to the Royal Consort; hour after hour the queue continued to form as women gathered from every village in the county to buy their blacks.

No doubt Her Majesty would not have been amused by John's ecstasy on Friday night. Because they'd managed to get their crêpe on offer first, he explained to Davie, and at a half-penny a yard cheaper than anyone else in Darlington, they'd already sold out twice. He'd had to telegraph to Glasgow and Manchester, for their regular suppliers could no longer meet demand – and take a look at the figures!

He flung them across and Davie stared at them, columns and columns, all in black, not red, he noticed. What else did they mean? John tore off his spectacles and paced the room in his fever.

'We've done it, Davie! We've managed it at last!' It was obviously good news.

'Done, what?'

'Paid off the secured loans, paid off over half of what we owe Richardson – it's virtually ours now – the emporium! No one can take it away – we own more than our creditors do. Oh, man, it just needs plenty of women buying hats for the Coronation – '

'What about Father?'

'We paid him off first, surely you haven't forgotten? Maybe we can increase our allowance to him now, we can afford it, and persuade him to come on a visit? Supposing I send him a banknote to tempt him!'

Davie had never heard of such recklessness. He could scarcely believe it. So many years existing with only a tiny weekly allowance, just enough for baccy and a gift or two for Charlotte. Theirs had been a frugal way of life with nothing wasted, the only time they spent lavishly in the collection plate, and now this! John was saying there was money to spare – it was intoxicating. It was frightening!

'Go easy,' he urged, 'don't do anything foolish. We're not clear of debt entirely, you just said so.'

'But we will be. There's no doubt if we continue as we are – see here, I've plotted a graph so that you can check for yourself. All we have to do is continue at our present rate. And in ten months' time we can begin to invest money properly for the children's future. How about a dram?' he finished triumphantly. 'I think we deserve it!'

Thank goodness it was one of the bottles a commercial traveller had given them last Christmas. For one crazy moment Davie thought John had gone truly mad and spent money on liquor.

But nothing could spoil John's mood. His face, wreathed in smiles, was as happy as Davie had ever known it. It was as though a dam within him had burst, releasing years of tension. The worry, the sleepless nights, he confided it all for the first time, explaining to Davie how bad it had been. Davie was stunned.

'I can understand how you wanted to spare Charlotte and me but what about Mary – did you share any of it with her? Didn't she help?'

'I wanted to,' John admitted, 'but I didn't think it fair to worry her.'

250

'But she's your wife!' Davie sensed this was dangerous ground, but he pressed on. 'Mary's the one *we* depend on when you're at the warehouse. Mr Hart and I always consult her whenever there's a problem. She's got a good clear head when it comes to business, far better than mine. Besides . . . ' Davie splashed more whisky into the glasses to give himself courage, 'she adores you. You know that, don't you? I've watched her light up when she hears your footsteps at night. I wish Charlotte felt the same about me – not that I'm complaining,' he added hastily, 'I'm no great catch for a lovely woman like Charlotte. But the way Mary feels, like Mother does for Father . . . You're a lucky man, John.'

It was out in the open and the embarrassment was terrible. Eventually John said gruffly, 'You're exaggerating.'

'No, I'm not.' Neither could meet the other's eye, 'I've sometimes wondered if you realize how Mary feels. You were right to marry her and I was wrong to try and dissuade you, I confess it. It was the best day's work you ever did, bringing her into the family.' The turn in the conversation paralysed John's tongue but the whisky removed all normal restraint from Davie's. 'I hope, one day, you and she have another child. Not to displace Luke, he'll always have first place in your heart, I know he will. But to make your marriage complete. You deserve it, John . . . ' All he could see was the top of John's bowed head and the crimson tips of his ears.

Davie rushed to pour the rest of the whisky into their glasses. 'Come on, let's finish it, there's not much left. And fill your pipe, John. Tonight it's Christmas and my birthday rolled into one! I'm sorry if I spoke out of turn but don't hold it against me. We're fond of you, old chap!'

John struggled to regain control.

'You and I must not forget who is responsible . . . who started the ball rolling when Charlotte wore that hat. We must drink to the – instigator – of our good fortune . . . ' He was unsteady as he rose to offer the toast, 'Our great Queen . . . God bless her memory!'

John's mind was in turmoil but he was suffused with happiness and contentment. The stove burned low. Occasionally one of them remembered to put on more coal. He needed to talk, the pent-up feelings had still not subsided, but not about Mary.

Was she so in love with him as Davie insisted? He remembered the way she'd looked at him on their wedding day.

'Remember the time when young Hart started? How the lady assistants led him a dance?'

'He soon got the measure of them. He's an excellent chap to have around, John. And Mrs Armitage has come to depend on him, which is important. I think we should consider giving him a change of status, and a rise. How about making him under-manager of men's apparel? He's worked for our prosperity as much as anyone.'

Mary – loving him the same way their mother loved Alex, heart, mind, body and soul, as Davie had once described it. And Charlotte not caring for Davie as much? John struggled to keep hold of the present. 'How's the new cashier coming along?'

'Miss Bennett? She'll do. Not as quick but then she hasn't had much practice yet.'

Mary, caring for him in every way a wife should but he denying her the right. Could he pretend to love her? Could he change and look on her with new eyes? He wanted love as desperately as anyone, it was a great ache within him, especially tonight.

'Hey! We've forgotten something.'

'What?.

'We haven't told old Armitage . . . ' Davie waved John's graph of figures, 'We must tell him about this. Without him and Aunt Armitage, we'd never have got this far so soon. Remember all those things they gave us when we started? C'm on, let's go and tell him now. This is empty anyway.' The bottle missed the waste basket and rolled across the floor. 'Not a bad drop of whisky . . . ' Davie gave his judgement with care, 'In fac', a very good drop of whisky indeed.'

They were amazed to discover everyone had gone to bed. Was it really that late? Mrs Armitage assured them she didn't mind, her head had only touched the pillow, they hadn't really wakened her but perhaps they should lower their voices for the sake of the others? Oh, what splendid news! Of course they must tell Mr A, she wouldn't hear of them leaving it until the morning.

Davie sat beside the helpless wreck, tenderly cradling his

lifeless hands. 'It's marvellous,' he whispered, 'we practically own the whole of this now . . . ' The gesture threatened the table of medicine bottles but Mrs Armitage moved swiftly to save them.

'How pleased he is for both of you, you can see it in his eyes.' John tried to tell her he would repay her kindness, he would take over Bertha's wages, he would pay her for managing the salon; words poured out of John in his guilt over Mary. Not understanding but overwhelmed by such generosity, Mrs Armitage shushed him gently. Bending over her husband she appeared to be listening to the twisted mouth.

'He says he wants the three of us to take a glass of best port!' she cried.

Alas, grape and grain entwined. In Davie they released a glorious wave of joy. He roared a serenade as he made his way back to Charlotte. She was scandalized but only one thing would stop him, he told her. He had to celebrate: the world was a beautiful place and his wife the loveliest thing in it.

(x)

John went more quietly, turning Davie's words over and over. Of course his brother was drunk, they both were. He wished he hadn't drunk the port. Already he was feeling sick and thirsty. Clean, sparkling water from the spring near the croft, that was what he wanted. He made do with the water jug in the bedroom, trying not to make too much noise.

The dressing-room door was ajar. Mary left it like that so she didn't disturb him in the mornings. John listened. Was she asleep? He couldn't tell. His wife – loved him. Adored him, Davie said. Was he not entitled to that love? John pushed the door open still farther.

Moonlight spilled over her couch but the pillow was in shadow. He could see the darker shape of Mary's braids and her head against the linen.

'Is that you, John?' She wasn't surprised or startled but calm as always. 'Is anything the matter?' He was immediately tongue-tied. When he managed to speak it was disjointed, phrases about the shop, the loan, anything but his true purpose.

She listened and when he'd finished, searched and found his hand in the darkness. 'Why not come to bed, John. Here with me . . . '

It wasn't a satisfactory coupling in that narrow bed. There were loving arms on one side, and tenderness, but with John there was inexperience and confusion. He'd never felt a woman's naked body before; warmth and softness excited his inflamed mind. He found himself apologizing but out of control. He knew he must be hurting her yet he couldn't stop himself. He wanted to be kind. Her very gentleness made him feel worse and when it was over, the great wave of life force left him spent. He wept and his wife cradled the stricken head. 'There, there . . . don't be upset.'

'I wanted – I wanted . . . ' What had he wanted? To love her? He couldn't say that. 'I'm so sorry,' he repeated.

Mary continued to soothe him until he slept, exhausted. Under the eyes of the moon, tears rolled down her cheeks. It was better than nothing but it wasn't love. Yet there was a little comfort, even in her sorrow.

Unaccustomed to the small bed, John woke. Finding her awake too, he shyly kissed first her cheek then her breasts. When Mary's forgiving arms held him once more, he kissed her full on the mouth. 'I'm sorry I hurt you. I wanted it to be loving.'

'I know you did.'

'I didn't mean to force myself – '

'Hush! You're not to say that, you didn't hurt me.'

'You're so kind, Mary. May I stay with you tonight?'

It was a beginning. When she kissed him in return, she tried to withhold the passion she felt for fear of making John nervous, but it was she who urged him to make love again as moonlight faded into grey dawn and they could make out one another's features. She allowed her fingers to smooth away the worry from his face and stroked the lean body that clung to hers.

This time it was gentler and less urgent. When he felt himself inside her, John buried his head on Mary's shoulder, unable to meet her eager, loving eyes.

CHAPTER EIGHT

Changes

As her belly swelled, so Charlotte's temper worsened. She felt so foolish, she confided to her aunt, after telling everyone two children were sufficient. Mrs Armitage held her peace but her eyes glowed. Perhaps there would be a little Adelaide after all!

Mary said nothing. She continued to rise at five-thirty. On her way downstairs, she tapped lightly at Bertha's door. Up in the attic Katriona and Ada were already stirring.

Once the fires were lit and breakfast for fourteen had been prepared, cups of tea were taken to John, Davie and Charlotte. In the attics, lady apprentices were shivering as they pulled on their clothes. It had been a restless year so far, with agitation among some shop workers to have their hours reduced. John had followed Amos Hinton's lead: from henceforth the emporium would shut each night at ten PM, not eleven PM. Braver spirits in Middlesbrough demanded holidays as well but all the employers agreed this was too much. Three days were already set aside for this purpose: Good Friday, Christmas and May Day, with its celebrations and May queen – what more could anyone want?

Upstairs girls sighed as they donned their mourning. Not a breath of relief for six months and then only grey could be worn. Normally they wore black when on duty behind the counter: Mrs Davie McKie watched over that very strictly. But it was possible, with a knot of ribbon, a brooch, a bunch of artificial flowers, to transform a plain blouse. At present this was impossible, unthinkable – it would indicate a lack of respect! For fresh-faced, pretty young girls, 1901 was a very drab year indeed.

Privately, without telling anyone, Mary visited Dr Cullen. He was delighted. 'Just what I've been hoping would happen all along. How's Mr McKie taken the news? Cock-a-hoop, no doubt?'

'I haven't told him yet.'

'No? Wanted to be sure, I suppose.' Dr Cullen was surprised. With a second child most mothers didn't need prompting.

'John wants a son of his own. He loves Luke but that isn't sufficient – and I understand. It is his own boy that John needs, an extension of himself.'

Dr Cullen nodded in sympathy and squeezed her hand to reassure her. 'That's what I've felt all along. And if he wants *another* son,' he emphasized, 'then let's hope that's what he gets. Although I cannot see Mr McKie being disappointed if it turns out to be a girl, especially if she has her mother's fine eyes.' Mary smiled faintly. 'That's better. Now come on, out with it. What's troubling you?'

'The possibility of a deformity.'

'Ah!' He held onto her hand. 'Well, my dear, you're an intelligent young woman. We both know it *is* possible any child of yours *might* inherit Talipes but you're also sensible enough to know that medicine is improving by leaps and bounds. Miracles are possible with surgery nowadays. Anyway, for the present, let us assume all will be well. It certainly appears that way to me, so put it out of your mind. Tell Mr McKie and make him a happy man.'

She did so that evening. As she watched joy spread over John's face, she wished she could feel the same. Hadn't she prayed for this to happen? Above all things she wanted to give John a child, convinced that this would finally change his feelings toward her. Now that it had, why not share his elation? 'I'm tired,' Mary told herself. 'I'm not as young as when I had Luke.'

The genuine warmth of John's kiss banished other thoughts from her mind. She dared, for once, to embrace him passionately. 'Is it – all right, Mary?' he whispered thickly. 'Is it safe? Would it harm the baby if we . . . ?' and she laughed to be asked such a question by him. Maybe his feelings were changing already?

Later, sadly, she knew they were not. He was kind and considerate, but his concern was for his unborn son. Only when speaking of him did John's eyes suffuse with love.

He'd never been in such a ferment: a son! Blood and bone of his body. It wouldn't change his attitude to Luke – he said so repeatedly – but now Luke would have a brother as he'd had Davie. A companion to teach and guide. 'Maybe they'll both become doctors! One a physician, the other a surgeon, how about that?'

He was young again, life was coursing through his veins, he'd never felt more glad to be alive. Why was Mary so sad? 'Thank you, thank you for letting me love you.' He kissed the soft skin of her neck and missed the spasm of pain his words caused. 'There's nothing wrong, is there?' Normally Mary responded so eagerly.

'I fear I'm a little tired, John. It will pass.' Perhaps one day it would be different? She tried to shake off her mood but it stayed. Dr Cullen's words, intended to strengthen her commonsense, were swallowed up by superstition. Then there was that other fear she hadn't been able to mention. It came back to her now. A childhood memory of her father, drunk, her mother's screams and the forced coupling together with moans of protest, 'Don't put another bairn in me tonight, for God's sake! Weren't you full of drink the night I fell with *her* . . . '

That was it: the secret fear that when she and John first made love, he'd been drinking. Hadn't the baby sprung from that union? And John couldn't love a blemished child. Surely that was the reason he couldn't love *her*? In the dark, Mary's tired brain swam with desolate thoughts. Until the child was born, despite Dr Cullen's words, she would carry the superstitious dread.

(i)

As both pregnancies advanced that black-clad spring it was as though one diminished the other. Charlotte ripened as Mary withered. The close-knit family in the shop watched anxiously. Indeed, Mrs Armitage was heard to reprove Charlotte on one occasion when her niece grumbled about her state. 'How can you complain when you're so well? Think of Mary and hold your tongue, Charlotte! I'm sure we'd all be happier if she had half your strength.'

It was true and in many small ways they tried to help. Mary knew she was surrounded by kindness; she heard the whispers and she also knew John looked at her anxiously. If only she could bring herself to talk of her fear but wouldn't that turn him from her entirely? If he thought his son wouldn't be perfect?

Perhaps if John had been able to cradle her in his arms, tell her he loved her, Mary would have told him. John, with his whole being rooted in common-sense, could have talked her out of it. But after the excited night when he'd first heard the news, he suggested they return to separate beds, for the sake of the child.

One evening, after a visit by the two pregnant women to his surgery, Dr Cullen sent for John. He poured beer for them both and unburdened himself.

'I hate to say it, McKie, but that wife of yours isn't doing at all well. I'm blessed if I know why. She's not eating enough but when I bully her, she says it makes her sick if she tries to eat more. And she looks so worried. Constantly. Do you know the cause? She's not like Mrs Davie, she broods too much. In my opinion she's losing her strength. We've got to get to the bottom of it.'

In John the guilt was as deep-rooted as the longing in Mary's breast. What could he tell his old friend? Within the intimacy of the surgery, he blushed. Dr Cullen observed it but said nothing. Eventually, to break the silence, John mumbled that he had

258

been drunk when he forced himself on Mary. The doctor scoffed kindly.

'My godfathers, McKie, d'you think that's the first time that's happened? Half the human race – three-quarters of it maybe – arrived as a result of that. Thirty seconds, less, of liberated manhood and another female prayer that wasn't answered.' He went on more seriously, 'Whatever the manner of it, you and Mrs McKie wanted another child, didn't you?'

'Yes, but – ' John began painfully.

'Well?'

Having begun, John found the need to confess too great. He held nothing back, from the school mistress's fateful letter to his delight in Luke and his subsequent behaviour toward Mary. The relief was enormous and John could see his friend wasn't embarrassed. At the finish, Dr Cullen said simply, 'You've had a time of it, the pair of you. It can't have been easy. Coming back to the present, can I give you a bit of advice?'

John shrugged: why not?

'It's going to be a long haul. Mrs McKie may need to consult a specialist if she doesn't perk up soon. Let's see what a breath of sea air can do first, eh? Send her and Mrs Davie. It'll do 'em both good. Mrs D can keep an eye on your wife; she'll enjoy doing that.

'As for your personal life, give it time. Never mind about love – that's a luxury. When she has that new baby in her arms – your baby – she'll come round to being her calm, quiet self again. I've never known it fail. After that who knows? So go and tell her to forget her troubles and pack for a week at Redcar, eh?'

As John was leaving, Dr Cullen had a final thought: 'You don't think she is worrying about the baby being deformed? She did mention it once when she was here – not been listening to any old wives' tales, has she?'

'Who – Mary?' John was incredulous. 'She's the last person to behave foolishly.'

Everyone agreed Redcar would be the very thing. Mary wasn't allowed time to think. Full of happiness, Mrs Armitage told her she must go for John's sake. Charlotte assured her it was her duty to get well and Katriona murmured in Gaelic that it was time to think of herself for a while. Bertha and Ada could manage perfectly well on their own for a week or two.

So the hotel was booked. They were to travel on Monday and John would see them onto the train before going to the warehouse. On Sunday night, however, they were all to attend one of the newly instigated penny concerts at the Temperance Hall. All the fashionable world attended: it was therefore important for the owners of the emporium to be there, too.

On a spring evening after a day of sudden warmth that had left them feeling giddy, they retired to dress. Outside daffodils opened tight buds in cautious exploration and men unbuttoned their overcoats an inch or two while in her room Charlotte debated between a new straw or her winter felt.

Mary felt strangely detached. All day she'd rested while others did the packing for her holiday. She watched listlessly as Bertha layered tissue paper between each garment. Now they all gathered in the empty, shrouded shop, ready to leave for the concert. Mary descended the stair carefully. Below she could see Davie looking up at her.

'Are you all right, Mary? You're very pale.'

'Mama, Mama!' It was Luke behind her, wanting another caress before going to bed. Mary turned, letting go the banister, and he leapt into her arms. Davie did his best but he wasn't quick enough, none of them were. John heard the cry, paused long enough to glimpse the frozen tableau on the floor before reponding to Davie's urgent, 'Dr Cullen, man, quick as you like!'

He ran without coat or hat, not caring as Sunday evening worshippers turned to gape. The doctor, at his supper, didn't even pause to untie his napkin. As he knelt beside Mary, the square of white linen brushed her face. On the other side of her, Katriona whispered, 'She's begun to bleed.'

It took six hours before the foetus was finally expelled. Dr Cullen ordered a pot of strong tea and went down to the study in search of John. He sat alone, grey-faced. Dr Cullen said quietly, 'I'm very sorry, McKie. I did what I could . . . ' John's eyes were steady. 'The baby's dead. Try and put all thought of it aside just now. Concentrate on your wife instead. We were wrong about her.'

'In what way?' whispered John. Dr Cullen chose his next words carefully.

'It seems she was worried – that the baby might be deformed. When she was in pain, she cried out. Said it was better the baby should die, that you wouldn't love a child that wasn't perfect, just as you couldn't love her.' The agony in John's face was too much; the doctor looked away. 'I'm sorry. I thought I should tell you.'

'And was the child . . . ?'

'Perfect. In every way. Too small, of course. Didn't stand a chance. Mrs McKie refused to look at it. I tell you, I'm worried. She's almost hysterical – you must go to her, McKie.'

John pulled himself together. 'Yes, of course.'

'I think if she is to recover,' Dr Cullen added quietly, 'affection may prove a necessity after all.'

Mary lay in his bed. The door to the smaller chamber stood open; inside the hired nurse and Katriona murmured together. Mary's eyes glittered as John kissed her. 'Don't look . . . it's better you don't see it,' she whispered.

'Why not?'

'It's deformed, like me.'

He went into the dressing room. Katriona and the nurse regarded him warily. 'Give me the baby.' Katriona had wrapped it in a lacy shawl and John's hands felt clumsy. He took the bundle back into the bedroom and laid the tiny puppet beside its mother. 'We'll look at it together.' Very, very tenderly he lifted the delicate wool and saw his baby boy for the first time. 'Look at his arms, Mary . . . no bigger than my little finger. And the nails, how perfectly formed. See his feet? Neither of them are blemished.'

'I don't believe you!'

'See for yourself, dear. I'll hold him, shall I?'

Tears rolled down her cheeks as she cried, 'A son! You wanted a son so badly.'

'I need you more, Mary.' Laying the infant against her breast, he lifted the coverlet and gently kissed her weak leg. 'I'm ashamed you were unable to confide your fears. I might have been able to help.' She watched him replace the quilt, too full to speak. For a few moments they sat together, the infant lying between them in Mary's arms. As he saw her eyelids drop, John asked softly, 'Shall I take him so that you can sleep?'

'Will I see him again?'

'I think not, dear.' He held the boy so that she could touch the waxen face with her lips. When he stooped to tuck in the covers once more, she said simply, 'Come back to me soon, John.'

(ii)

In an age when many families expected to lose at least one of their brood, neighbours supposed Mr and Mrs McKie would have another child. Dr Cullen suggested it might be possible but that Mary needed time to recover first. It was John who was cautious for as she grew stronger, Mary was eager to try.

Partly out of guilt that he had failed when she needed him most, John couldn't bring himself to tell Mary of his dreams. In them, his tiny dead son had grown to manhood and was standing beside Luke. When the two smiled and advanced toward him, John would wake in tears, afraid of disturbing his wife. To think of supplanting that young man was impossible. John could reconcile Mary to their loss but not himself, nor could be bring himself to discuss it. In the end he told no one. He was always considerate and kind to Mary but the hopes that had been re-kindled faded away. Her husband lay beside her; she must learn to make that suffice and ignore the ache in her heart.

(iii)

In September, amid muted rejoicing, Charlotte had a healthy son. Matthew Alexander joined Jane and young Ted in the nursery and for the next two years the emporium continued to prosper despite increasing unemployment in the region. The steady tramp of labour from the land as men sought higher wages in the towns continued but trade was stagnant. Heads wagged at the Lit and Phil. It wasn't as though there hadn't been a war to stimulate business: the one in South Africa had dragged on long enough, but now survivors were returning, adding to the jobless and, what was worse, making them restless. What was to be done? No one had the answer to that.

Despite industrial gloom, life became undeniably gayer. It was as if, with the passing of the great Queen, the nation had been let out of school. The atmosphere, the mood of the people, reflected it and so did their clothes. Davie was the first to draw their attention to it, and unfortunately he chose as his illustration the new, more relaxed shape of ladies' corsetry.

'Mr McKie!' Charlotte was horrified. 'That is not a fit subject for the dining table.' Davie was abashed. He didn't argue but he managed to wink at John, sitting at the other end. One certainly had to be careful in Charlotte's hearing. Nevertheless, in the shop John wandered into 'Ladies' Costumes and Mantles' and looked at the lines of a row of tailor-mades. Davie was right. The tight, rigid confines were softening.

A sad though inevitable event marred their contentment as the Victoria era loosened its hold. Mrs Armitage broke the news one Friday evening after she and John had checked the weekly taking from the salon.

'I have some bad news, I fear.' John looked up. To his horror, tears were already coursing toward the heaving bosom.

'My dear Mrs Armitage!' Excusing himself, he hurried outside to tug the lift rope. It was a signal to Mary in the kitchen that he wanted tea. At such an unusual time he hoped she'd understand. She did: she also knew what the bad news might be.

Back in the study, Mrs Armitage explained. 'It is Mr A. I fear his time has almost come. Dr Cullen came this morning and confirmed it. As you know, generally I pay no attention to medical men but in this instance . . . ' she swallowed, 'he may be right. He is returning this evening to attend to my dear husband.'

As the first medical man Mrs Armitage trusted, the responsibility was a grave one, but Dr Cullen was aware of that. After a brief examination, he and she helped make the grocer comfortable before rejoining John. The doctor sat quietly for a moment or two before he said, 'I'd like to congratulate you, ma'am.' Mrs Armitage was confused. 'How long is it since Mr Armitage had his first seizure?'

She had to work it out. 'It must be – nearly seventeen years. Charlotte was only a little girl. Bertha had to go to the school that afternoon, to fetch her.'

Dr Cullen studied her quietly, seeing a stout, elderly body that a stranger might find comical. 'I know of no one who could have kept such a seriously ill patient alive and well as you have done, ma'am. It's a pity you didn't join the medical profession yourself.' He leaned forward and patted her hand. 'You're a remarkable woman, Mrs Armitage.'

Those familiar words spoken often but so long ago by Mr Armitage unleashed a storm of tears. The doctor waited until they'd ceased as though he'd all the time in the world. When she'd recovered a little he began making practical suggestions for easing the grocer's suffering, then took his leave.

John accompanied him into the yard. 'There's nothing I can do, McKie, as no doubt you realize. Don't hesitate to call me though, if the old lady wants it. How's young Luke?' They stood for another moment chatting then John returned to find Davie and Charlotte.

They were in the nursery. 'How much longer?' asked Charlotte when he told them the news.

'I don't think he'll linger. He's much weaker after this last attack, apparently.'

Charlotte hugged Matthew closely. 'Poor, dear Aunt Armitage. She'll be lost without him.'

They took it in turns to sit in the dying man's room. In the early hours one morning, when Davie was dozing, a faint sound was heard from the bed. After long years of silence the effect was uncanny. Mrs Armitage clung to the lifeless hand. 'My dearest, what is it?' she cried. Hopeless eyes looked at her. 'Please,' she begged, 'Help me raise him a little.'

Davie lifted him so that Mr Armitage could look once more towards his jewel, lovingly, longingly as his soul slipped quietly into eternity.

It was the most impressive funeral Darlington could remember. Mrs Armitage wasn't surprised. She always knew her husband was a great man. Hadn't customers told her so over the years when she'd passed on his latest opinion? Crowds lined the streets to admire the cortège. Customers from both shops waited patiently to offer consolation. Davie and John flanked the widow at the graveside. One by one, people filed past. The comment most frequently heard was, 'I never met him myself, of course, but talking to you, Mrs Armitage, I feel I've known him all my life.'

That night John decided on the first of the changes. They all needed a holiday. Apart from that, alterations had to be made both to the shop and to their living quarters. How much easier if they were all away during rebuilding, particularly the children.

Charlotte was delighted. 'Why don't we all go to Scotland? It's high time the children met their grandparents.'

John and Davie discussed it privately. They wanted to avoid any awkwardness for Mary. A compromise was reached. If Mrs Armitage would agree to a holiday in Harrogate Spa instead, Mary and Bertha could accompany her there, provided Mary was content.

Mrs Armitage embraced the idea fervently. She doted on the children, naturally, but a chance to get away from them for a while, oh my! Charlotte, however, was a little put out when she heard. She couldn't believe Mary wouldn't prefer to visit her own family after all these years. Davie deflected any curiosity. Sulphur baths would be beneficial; she mustn't forget that Mary had never fully recovered from her miscarriage.

Charlotte didn't waste more time speculating, there was too much to do. And Mary could go to Scotland another time? 'Perhaps,' replied Mary quietly.

The children were told. They would be travelling to another country to meet unknown relatives. Suddenly John found himself in the midst of chaos.

Every room had a clothes horse hung with freshly starched linen, the kitchen was stacked with jars of preserves and hampers filled the passage outside his study. 'What's it all for?' he demanded. Davie sighed. 'It's my fault. I told Charlotte there weren't any shops near the croft and she doesn't believe in taking chances.'

'But haven't you explained how small the place it? Where will all this stuff go?' Davie looked shamefaced.

'You know how difficult it is . . . arguing with Charlotte.'

(iv)

At the Lit and Phil, their holiday plans caused consternation. Was it true, one businessman demanded, that McKie Brothers intended giving all their shop assistants *paid* leave? Were they mad? At a time of high unemployment, when people were literally begging on the streets, why not pay the staff off? They'd be eager enough to be taken back on again when McKies re-opened and then they could be offered lower wages – wasn't that a better idea? There were far too many public holidays and street parties this summer, in honour of the Coronation, and that was a fact.

Another shopkeeper had a different argument. 'If you do it, McKie, they'll all want it – a fortnight's leave, I mean. If you close down your place we'll have to do the same eventually. What are you trying to do, ruin us?'

John was adamant. 'Most of our employees have worked as hard as we have, especially those who were with us from the beginning. If Davie and I have earned a holiday, so have they.'

(v)

Charlotte took particular pains with her appearance. She and the hairdresser devised a new coiffure. Davie was alarmed to see the familiar auburn curls swept up over a vast pad of false hair into a swathe on top of her head, the whole ornamented with a black velvet bow. 'Dearest, how will you manage in Scotland? It's an outdoor sort of life on a croft. Lots of fresh air – and wind!' She smiled indulgently; how foolish men were. Didn't he understand how important it was, as a daughter-in-law making her first appearance, to make a good impression? As for the children, they would be scoured to perfection.

On the morning of their departure, Davie found them, sitting in a row at the bottom of the stairs, tear-stained and subdued. They shone with soap. Their white petticoats and sailor suits crackled and the consequences should they be careless enough to sully either garments or themselves in any way were awful to contemplate. Katriona and Charlotte had combined their massive authority to terrifying effect.

'We have to be good,' Luke confided to his uncle, 'all the way to Scotland!'

266

In their bedroom, Davie viewed his wife with a sinking heart. The new hairstyle now had a fringe of crimped curls, a la Rèine. Her skirt was a tight band of pleats and above her shirt-waist, so fashionable that year, was a hat containing half an unfortunate bird. The entire outfit was in shades of grey and black, in deference to the memory of Mr Armitage, but Charlotte looked exquisite.

'Father and Mother . . . They are very *simple* people, dearest!'

Charlotte pulled on her glacé kid gloves. 'I haven't forgotten,' she replied crisply. 'That is why I haven't packed my new purple lace. Pass me my parasol, dear.'

In the hallway John looked at the mound of luggage in dismay. He was only going to be away a week; he had to return to supervise the various changes. Mary had packed him a change of linen in a carpet bag. She, Bertha and Mrs Armitage had a couple of small boxes between them but the mountain of necessities prepared by Charlotte and Katriona reached the level of the picture rail: cabin trunks, corded boxes, picnic hampers and, perched on top, a row of baskets full of food labelled 'This Way Up' in Charlotte's firm hand.

The solitary cabbie he'd sent for looked on in disbelief but, before he could speak, John said hastily, 'Go round to the Raby Hotel and ask two of your colleagues to come, quickly now.'

On the long pull up the station incline, John clutched Luke tightly. Sitting opposite, Davie nursed Jane on his knee. Did John remember his first arrival, he wondered, with the herring barrels and oat cakes? There was no time to reminisce, for young Ted was beating a tattoo on his toy drum: they'd arrived! They spilled onto the platform: a maelstrom of trunks, children, adults and hampers. John shrank from the confusion but Davie took charge, big, red-haired, shouting cheerfully at porters as he swung Matthew onto his shoulder to catch a first glimpse of the train.

The journey took two and a half days. They stayed one night in Glasgow and by then Charlotte was already too exhausted to do more than nibble a morsel of toast and sink into bed. Katriona was ordered to see to the children as their mother had one of her 'heads' coming on. Their room in the Caledonian Hotel helped soothe her. The bed was high, the sheets immaculate and the chambermaid, well tipped by Davie, filled the bath-tub and was attentive. It would do, Charlotte told her spouse faintly, it was sufficiently clean. Not the same standard as the Zetland at Saltburn but then that was a superior hotel.

John and Davie escaped, tramping Sauchiehall and Buchanan Streets, staring in elegant shop windows and telling each other McKie Brothers could put on just as good a display.

'All the same, Davie, if Charlotte wants a walk out after supper, why not take her to the Botanical Gardens in Byers Road? The fresh air there would be much more beneficial.' John had noticed the prices and recalled his sister-in-law's weakness for hats. And Byers Road hadn't a single shop likely to tempt her. 'Did I mention I'm thinking of breaking my journey here on the way home, to do a bit of business?'

'Good idea.' They were in Argyle Street, marvelling at the traffic: six motor vehicles, all within the space of ten minutes! It was all very well for Parliament to talk of a speed limit of twenty miles per hour, but in a place like this it could be suicidal! John brought his mind back to business. 'I thought I'd pay a visit to Arthur's, the wholesalers. Did you take a look at their catalogue?'

'Yes, I did. I thought it looked excellent.'

'Quality, Davie, and variety. We must move with the times and consider stocking some of their lines. We can't get that sort of range from Leeds any more, so . . . ' John shrugged. 'We must continue to offer our customers the best. They're accustomed to it, they deserve it. What is more . . . ' he never strayed far from the point, 'they can afford it.'

It occurred to Davie that if their new suppliers were in Glasgow, he could delegate any necessary journeys to Leeds to Mr Hart. Since his adventure he'd never felt entirely at ease going there. A glimpse of dark curls, a well rounded figure, could provoke memories. He wished he could confide in Charlotte but knew it would be most unwise.

The morning found them on the single-line railway that connected Glasgow with the new fishing port at Mallaig. Gone were the upholstered seats and brocade curtains, the elegant overhead racks and plentiful mirrors that Charlotte had so approved of the day before. Instead they sat on hard benches, all confined in one compartment, but outside some of the most glorious scenery in the world unfolded before them. Davie ached with the beauty of it – he was going home! He knew that John felt the same, he could see it in his eyes. The two of them grew younger with excitement at the thought of it. To say so aloud would have been disloyal to Darlington and to Charlotte but how Davie wished she could share his pleasure.

They were to disembark from the train at Fort William and take *The Pioneer* down Loch Linnhe, through the Sound of Mull to Loch Sunart, ending at Salen. A night's sleep had recharged the children's energy; young Ted was particularly impossible, Charlotte declared. His father took the hint. One advantage of this particular journey was that there were frequent stops to water the engine and for the relief of passengers. Luke and Ted were lifted down, urged to race to the engine and back, run and visit the guard, anything to use their limbs and lungs before re-embarking. Davie did his best but the frown lines on Charlotte's forehead deepened. If she'd had the slightest idea how big Scotland was, how far away from Darlington . . .

'Look, dearest, we're approaching Crianlarich – there's Ben More. Have you ever seen anything more magnificent?' Even the names were unfamiliar; she was an alien, Ruth in the land of Moab.

The throb of the paddle steamer soothed her and a picnic from one of their numerous baskets. Davie's prayers were answered; the water stayed calm throughout the journey. In the soft evening light they approached the jetty and the solitary figure that waited for them. John spotted him first and called to Davie. Instantly wife and children were forgotten as the two of them waved and shouted to their father until they were hoarse. Charlotte couldn't understand a word; they were using the Gaelic.

Ashore they contemplated Alla's donkey and cart. 'I didn't think you would be wanting her to walk,' Alex murmured to Davie, 'her not being used to it here in Scotland.' Without saying a word, John indicated the vast amount of baggage still being unloaded. Alex sucked his teeth in astonishment. 'My, my, have you brought everything with you from England?'

While he and Davie went in search of additional transport,

Charlotte waited wearily on a trunk, her elegance intact at the expense of her temper. In her arms, Matthew slept. Beside her on the grass, the starched white frock crumpled and stained, Jane was curled up like a puppy. Luke stood quietly as young Ted showed off, shouting to frighten the donkey. Why didn't Katriona stop him, Charlotte wondered irritably, but Katriona too was back among friends. She was chattering excitedly to a passerby, taking no notice of the children.

When he returned with a hay-waggon Alex was still too shy of his daughter-in-law to speak to her directly. Apart from a well rehearsed greeting in English he'd left the translating to Davie. Now he asked a question. 'Father would like to know if you'd prefer the donkey cart, which he scrubbed clean himself, or the waggon which he can't guarantee. He's pointed out that the waggon seat has a back to it, which you might prefer, and the cart has not.' Charlotte allowed herself to be helped aboard the waggon, mindful of her pleats. John spread blankets inside the donkey cart and lifted up the sleeping children. The luggage was loaded and they set off, the men leading the horse, Katriona driving the donkey and Luke and Ted racing to and fro with each new-found marvel.

Charlotte sat upright keeping a tight hand on her parasol. The lilt of voices annoyed her. What were they discussing now? She wished she could understand the odd word. From her vantage point she examined Alex McKie. Davie had often described the hard life up here but until now she hadn't comprehended the consequences. How old was he? She could see that he'd once been tall but muscle and sinew no longer held his frame upright. Beside Davie, Alex looked shrunken. She could see traces of both men in their father: John's anxious gaze, the way he had of tilting his head to catch every word, and Davie's laugh. Alex laughed now, the way Davie did, standing still, throwing his arms wide with enjoyment. Why couldn't they share the joke with her? Even Katriona was chuckling at it.

They travelled slowly, the waggon dipping over the rutted surface. Eyes closed, back not touching the grubby wooden seat, Charlotte slept.

She was in a daze when they arrived at the croft. The quickening pace down the slope shook her awake. It was nearly midnight but not quite dark so far north. She saw the outline of the house – it was so small! Why hadn't Davie said? A woman – his mother – was standing in the doorway holding a lamp, a dog was barking, hands were helping her down and the woman was folding her in an embrace, the smell of coarse wool and cold hairpins against her cheek. Davie was sweeping her up into his arms, saying, 'She's still asleep, Mother, I'll put her to bed. Are we to have the back room?'

'Yes.' Jeannie's nervousness increased the sibilance but she stuck to English in front of Charlotte. 'Katriona and your father and I will sleep at Alla's. The boys and wee Jane can have your old beds. We've put a cot for the bairn in with his mother. There's plenty of room for you all.' Hadn't she spent days tucking their possessions out of sight and cleaning the croft for their coming? It was as perfect as she could make it in Charlotte's honour. 'Can you manage on your own, son, or will I help?' she called softly.

But Davie always enjoyed removing Charlotte's corsets. 'Could you give Katriona a hand with the children?' he suggested instead.

Young Ted was overjoyed. To sleep in a hole in the wall with a door you could shut – what an adventure! He thumped Luke with delight, shouted his happiness at his grandmother. She, poor woman, tried to understand but he spoke too fast. Instead she contented herself with marvelling at his sturdiness as she unfastened each garment, showing Alex the quality. Not a patch on a single one of his things. And the wee girl with lace on her underclothes, did you ever!

'Would you like some fresh milk from the cow before you sleep?'

'We don't have milk, we always have cocoa.'

Cocoa? Jeannie looked at Katriona, baffled. 'You'll have milk tonight and thank your grandmama. You can miss brushing your teeth. Now get into bed this minute – and listen: one more peep out of you tonight, just one, and I'll tell Mama.'

Katriona had said the magic word. All three children vanished into the cupboard beds leaving a pile of small garments behind them. My, my . . . Jeannie tended the fire, leaving Katriona to smooth and fold. Four bonny children, so fit and strong looking, even the baby, but what on earth was 'cocoa'? She poured milk from the pitcher into three chipped mugs.

'Will they take porridge for their breakfasts?' she asked Katriona nervously.

'They will,' Katriona answered firmly. 'They've got some decent habits despite the fact they're English.'

Out in the byre Davie finished sweeping out the last of the dung and began spreading fresh straw. 'Are you sure you don't mind the beasts staying out, Father?'

'No, no. They'll come to no harm. The calf's big enough now.' Davie looked at the sky.

'I don't suppose it will rain but Charlotte's a bit fussy when it comes to luggage. Ready, John?' They grasped the first of the cabin trunks and staggered into the byre. Alex watched in admiration. His sons . . . John a proper businessman, with a waistcoat that matched his suit and a stiff collar like Mr McAlister. Davie's costume didn't please him quite so much. He lapsed into Gaelic once more.

'Why are you wearing the kilt? Like one of the English visitors?'

(vi)

It was unfortunate that Charlotte was woken by a goat. To be more precise, by young Ted leading a goat. He'd been up since daybreak, everything was so exciting here, and when he found this friendly animal he couldn't wait to show his mother. 'Look what I've found!' Too late he remembered that Papa had told him Mama wasn't to be disturbed. He tried to pacify her. 'His name's Billy goat.'

Less than a minute later a much quieter boy and a less curious goat were back in the garden. The goat recovered first. One evil, protuberant eye had seen the line of washing Katriona had pegged up. He sidled across.

As she struggled to dress Charlotte tried to come to grips with her situation. Lacking imagination, until now she'd accepted Davie's descriptions of his home without trying to picture it. No shops, he'd said, but he hadn't mentioned the lack of streets. Charlotte stooped to see out of the one tiny openings, hardly a window, because there wasn't glass, only netting. She supposed

272

they left it like this for the summer. There wasn't one single habitation in sight on this side, simply a well trodden path up the hill. She could hear whistling – Good Heavens! John, with his sleeves rolled up, carrying two buckets. Charlotte hoped the neighbours, wherever they were, wouldn't see him like that.

She turned back to the tiny room. A bed, a chair – not even comfortable – and a bit of curtaining across a corner. She peeped underneath. Stacked from floor to ceiling were all Jeannie's stores: wooden tubs of flour, oats and sugar, fishing tackle, winter clothes, sacks neatly folded, all of it put out of sight so as not to offend Charlotte.

And the room wasn't a room at all, it was a lean-to built onto the back of the croft. Alex had added heavy turves to the shingle roof for better protection. Generations of spiders nested in them unmolested. Charlotte watched as the largest she'd ever seen in her life descended a few inches then darted back up again. She opened her mouth to scream – but he'd disappeared. She couldn't spend another night with that bed resting against the wall!

Davie had always described this place so romantically. Fresh water from a spring up the hill. Well, she knew what that meant now. No wonder Mary and Katriona were always so enthusiastic about taps. Charlotte twisted her hair angrily into a chignon. It was all very well for Davie and John, they could bathe in the loch but what was she supposed to do? There was a knock and Katriona entered carrying a steaming jug and bowl. She put the bowl on the chair and emptied the jug into it. 'Good morning. We heard you moving about. Welcome to Scotland. Your breakfast's ready whenever you want it.'

Refreshed and in a better humour, Charlotte emerged to greet her parents-in-law properly. She was prepared this morning for the shock of Jeannie's appearance. Davie had always talked of her beauty, of the long dark hair his mother used to brush until it shone in the firelight. That the hair was now grey was to be expected but her mother-in-law had so few teeth! Those that were left were chipped and yellow and her cheeks were sunken. Alas, Charlotte didn't notice the fine dark eyes that gazed at her lovingly, merely the old-fashioned clothes. She was quite conversant with poor people. As a leading member of the Dorcas Society, she helped distribute warm garments every

273

Christmas and always contributed to sales of work, but to have one of the poor in one's own family! She would speak to Davie later. Something must be done. Meanwhile both Jeannie and Alex waited patiently beside the baskets and hampers. Katriona had explained that 'Mrs Davie' would superintend the unpacking.

Cords and straps were unfastened as Charlotte revealed cooked hams, game pies, jars of preserves and tins of tea. 'The very best from my aunt's Establishment,' she assured them. Alex and Jeannie looked on in wonder. This was better food than they had at the Big House, surely? But the contents of the final basket puzzled Jeannie. Embarrassed, she whispered to Katriona.

'What's the matter?' asked Charlotte.

'She is asking what those are.'

'Why, fruit cakes, of course. Two pound size. Four of our best Dundees. I always assumed they must come from Scotland?'

'Well if they do, Mrs McKie has never seen one before.'

'Tell them,' Charlotte spoke loudly for the benefit of her foreign relatives, 'that they're very good indeed. We will all have a slice with our tea this afternoon.' She was startled by the reply. Alex spoke the English slowly and carefully.

'My wife and I would be thanking you very much indeed. And where did Davie shoot the bird in your hat? Jeannie would like one herself.'

The week passed quickly in visiting and being visited. Charlotte was bewildered. There was no question of leaving cards; instead she had to stride across miles of moorland, her face and hair protected by scarves if they went anywhere near peat bogs because of the flies. Davie thrived on it. Charlotte did her best. She discarded all her petticoats in favour of an old flannel one, put on a serviceable skirt and folded her new pleats in tissue before putting them back in a trunk. After the first long walk over moorland, she soaked her feet in mustard and water and accepted Davie's offer of a spare pair of socks. She wouldn't give in, neither would she let him down. They had come this far to be seen: if friends and neighbours lived at the other end of the peninsula then so be it.

The most important visit was planned for Wednesday, to the

274

old school house. Katriona dressed the children with particular care, for she understood the significance of the occasion. Charlotte unpacked a new silk blouse. She ignored Davie's assurance that the school mistress would never notice. Helen Shields was a woman, wasn't she? From what Charlotte remembered of Helen's one visit to Armitage's, Miss Shields had a very keen eye indeed.

They borrowed the donkey cart, which the children would ride back in. Katriona was instructed to fill one of the baskets with cake and a ham. 'I remember you telling me how much Miss Shields enjoyed our ham at John's wedding.'

'Yes, dearest. And this is from Father.' He dropped the familiar sacking-wrapped parcel in the back of the cart. Young Ted whooped whenever the crab moved.

She waited in the open doorway, leaning slightly nowadays, grasping her stick firmly. This reunion, longed for so much and so often, had finally come to pass. Blushing with pride, Davie presented them. 'Mistress Shields, this is my wife, Charlotte. And this is young Ted, and Jane and finally, Matthew.' Helen shook hands gravely with each of them. Then she turned to the one she loved best of all.

'How d'you do, John. I'm very pleased to see you.' There was a slight tremor in her voice. He stood with one hand resting on the boy's shoulder beside him.

'May I introduce you to my son, Luke, Mistress Shields. He is to be a doctor.'

To Charlotte's surprise, she and Katriona were expected to get the tea and wash up. Miss Shields had more important business. Fortunately Katriona knew her way round. 'Those of us who weren't good at our lessons, Mrs Davie, we often had to help out, so that the school mistress could spend more time with the clever ones. She keeps her green soap in a jar under the sink here.'

Luke, young Ted and Jane were grouped round the teacher's desk in the schoolroom. Out of earshot, John and Davie murmured to each other. 'Man, it's so small! Did you remember it like this?'

'I did not. I always thought of it as a grand big room, too.'

The afternoon softened into dusk, the children went outside to play and the adults gathered round the parlour fireside.

Helen took the only comfortable chair and propped her stiff leg on a stool. 'Young Luke is a bright child. The brightest of the bunch,' she said quietly. Neither Charlotte nor Davie spoke. Alone with their thoughts, each acknowledged it to be true. Davie was humble enough to think it was because of John's teaching from Luke's earliest days. Charlotte told herself she was glad for Mary's sake.

'How is your wife?' asked Helen, as though reading Charlotte's thoughts.

'Mary has not been completely well since . . . since the death of our – other child. It too was a boy. I forget whether I told you at the time?'

'Your father came over specially, John. He grieved as we all did. We were all so thankful that you both have Luke to comfort you.' She looked at him steadily and John returned her gaze.

'He *is* a blessing, to Mary and myself. And we must hope that this visit to Harrogate Spa will help her. The doctor thinks it may.'

Helen said thoughtfully, 'That leg of hers, perhaps if she put less strain on it . . . Come outside a minute, I'd like to show you something.' She led the way past the vegetable patch to a garden shed that was new to them. The door stood open and inside was a small dog-cart. 'Why not get Mary one of these? I find it most useful. Young Hamilton loans me a donkey whenever I need to use it.'

'Wee Georgie? Mary's cousin?'

The mouth tightened in a familiar way. 'Wee Georgie's *son*, John. You are forgetting, both of you, that others have married besides yourselves.'

It was time to leave but they were reluctant to go. So much had been left unsaid. They wanted to tell her, to explain: even if they hadn't been to university they had worked. The emporium must represent something? But the words were not spoken. They seldom are until it is too late.

Helen led them back indoors to collect their belongings. She went through into the schoolroom, the stick tapping on the scrubbed boards. From the cupboard in the corner she produced a package. 'Send Luke to me.' The two other children stood in the doorway, curious to see what would happen. Jane

276

wrinkled her nose at the state of Ted's clothes. How typical he should fall into the loch. Wait till Mama saw, then he'd catch it!

'I'm giving you a present, Luke. How old are you now, seven?'

'I shall be eight next month.'

'Yes, of course. Well in that case, these will be useful to you straight away. It's never too soon to start.'

'May I open it?' She nodded.

Inside were five well used books, Greek and Latin dictionaries, a grammar in each language and *Caesar's Instructions to the Army*.

'Your father has his copies, I know. These are mine. We used to study them together. Now I pass mine on to you. Use them well.' Luke stroked one of the covers with a finger.

'I shall start a library with them.'

'A library! Well, well . . . ' She smiled. 'I must remember that.'

They loaded the cart and bade farewell but John lingered. There was so much he wanted to say but, being the people they were, he and Helen stayed silent. As he reached for her hand he said, 'Mary sends her best respects.'

'And mine to her.'

Another silence. He tried to remember what Mary had actually said. 'She wondered if there would be a chance of you coming to visit us? You'd be most welcome.'

'We'll see, we'll see . . . I find travelling difficult these days. Too much of an effort to leave my own fireside.' Still clasping his hand, Helen stared beyond him, into a limbo which troubled her. 'Last time we met it was your wedding day . . . '

John reddened, slightly afraid of what might be coming next.

'I was not as – charitable – as I should have been. I spoke very harshly to your wife, as I recall. It has bothered me since.'

'I'm sure Mary has forgotten it long ago,' he mumbled, anxious to avoid the pitfalls of emotion.

'I doubt she would,' Helen sighed. 'I know I wouldn't have done.'

'Our marriage . . . ' John began but scarcely knew how to continue, 'I do try . . . I think she is content. '

'You have done your duty,' she looked at him gravely. 'You've cared for Mary and Luke. I'm sure she is grateful.' But

277

John remembered Mary's longing glance; he'd not filled her needs, he couldn't pretend to himself that he had. To avoid further questioning, he made a feint of looking for his hat.

'I must be off. Catch up with the others.'

'You will remember my suggestion, about the dog-cart.'

'I will. Goodbye, Mistress Shields. I thank you for your kindess to Luke.'

She nodded, mouth tucked in firmly, head resolutely high, too full of tears now that the visit was ended.

(vii)

The day before John was due to leave had been earmarked for a picnic. The children, as a reward for tolerably good behaviour, had been promised a whole day on the beach. The morning held a promise of hot weather; a perfect choice of day, the adults told themselves, just what was ordered. To give them enough room to prepare food and pack the baskets, Luke, Ted and Jane were sent outside to play and Matthew's rug spread in the shade of a bush.

Suddenly shouts and galloping feet were heard. Alex flung the door wide. 'It's them from the Big House!' Davie looked quickly at John and swore. Surely the old custom had been stopped?

'Come on!' yelled Alex, 'the children!'

The three rushed outside. Charlotte went to follow but Jeannie held her arm. 'Let them be,' she begged, 'it doesn't do to interfere.' In her haste, she forgot to use English.

A dozen horsemen were riding over the croft, trampling neat rows of potatoes and turnips, smashing green shoots while their hounds encircled the calf, barking and snapping. Beyond, the cow mooed frantically. Alex stood in the midst of the mêlée, arms flailing at riders who eddied past, pushing and bumping him as though he didn't exist.

'We're shooting here in a day or two,' called a clipped voice, 'See that you keep your livestock penned up. Don't want to spoil the sport.'

'Get your horses off the crops!' roared Davie, beside himself

278

at the wanton destruction. John spotted Matthew beginning to crawl across the grass. A horseman less capable than the rest couldn't check his animal as it skittered towards the infant.

'Look out!' John screamed but Charlotte moved even faster. Every instinct of motherhood burned white-hot. Seizing a stick, she hit the horse across the nose with all her strength. As it reared, throwing its rider in front of her, she attacked him the same way, to clear a path to her baby. The frantic animal danced away, dragging its owner by the stirrup. Charlotte scooped up Matthew, clutching him passionately.

Everywhere was in uproar. Children screamed as horses pranced and lunged. Davie plunged into the fray, grabbing the nearest bridle. 'Get the children inside!' he yelled. Katriona seized Matthew from Charlotte and, tugging Jane by the hand, pushed Ted ahead of her into the croft. Left behind, terrified, Luke clung to John.

'Kindly explain your behaviour!' White with rage, Charlotte addressed the hapless rider, now disentangled and lying on the ground, surrounded by his friends. The words may have been ridiculous but the tone was not. Anger consumed her, shaking her body with its force. If she'd still been holding the stick, she could have killed the man. The power of her mood reached them and one or two backed away. The rider struggled to his feet, trying to ignore the pain from a dislocated shoulder. It was the first time there had been English people staying in one of these crofts.

'Don't follow you I'm sure, ma'am,' he sneered, attempting condescension.

'Then you must be as deficient in understanding as you are in manners.' The words were spat out. Other riders looked stunned. Her victim tried again.

'I would have you know, madam, we are standing on *my* father's land. These crofts are mere tenancies, rented out by courtesy of my father.'

'And by the law of Parliament, thanks to Gladstone!' Davie had recovered from the shock of watching Charlotte's attack but she hadn't finished yet.

'What other – courtesies – does your father extend to his tenants?' The words were like lumps of ice this time. 'You have completely destroyed a year's supply of food. You have allowed

279

your dogs to attack a cow and her calf. But for the grace of God, you all but murdered my son!' Her look scythed through them. One called out hastily, 'Come, Manners, let's get out of here. Mount up, man,' and hearing *that* name, John clasped Luke tightly.

Shamefacedly, one by one, riders began urging their horses off the croft and onto the path. Some tried to pass by Charlotte, including young Manners. 'For your behaviour here today, you and your friends deserve to be whipped,' she told him, 'And I shall not fail to inform your father so should I have the misfortune to meet him.'

Suddenly she saw Luke's face, full of terror now that horses were moving closer in their effort to get out of the gate. 'One moment! Stand still all of you, until I give the word.' Charlotte marched toward the boy. Horses and riders backed out of her way. 'Come dear, give me your hand.' She gently prised his grip away from John. 'Do not be afraid,' her voice was loud, 'these people are not gentlemen.'

Holding him close she walked through their ranks, forcing Manners to step aside for the boy that was his son. The incident froze for ever in the retina of John's mind. How was it none of the others noticed it? The boy had Mary's eyes but the rest of his face, and the dark wing of hair, were his father's entirely.

'You may now leave,' Charlotte announced, 'and never, never come back.'

Manners tried to have the last word. Once outside and remounted, he raised his whip using his one good shoulder. 'We'll return for the hunting, McKie, you can depend on it,' but the door to the croft was shut and his words fell on empty air.

(viii)

It was inevitable that the picnic should begin in subdued fashion but their tensions melted in the sunshine. Davie and Charlotte lay on rugs spread on the machair above high water mark. Below the three older children played the endless secret games of

280

childhood while John and Katriona went beachcombing. Matthew slept in the shade of his mother's parasol.

'Would you like to walk for a bit?' Davie was whittling a piece of driftwood. 'If we follow the stream bed up to the rocks, we might find you some jewels. There are supposed to be cairngorms and amethysts up there, though I have to admit neither John nor I found any when we were boys.' But it was no use trying to divert her.

'Was I right? To speak as I did this morning?'

Her husband grinned. 'You were magnificent! A queen among savages, Charlotte. I was proud of you.' He rolled onto his back and tipped his hat over his eyes. 'We could have done with you beside us at Culloden.'

'Don't be silly.' She spoke absently. 'If I had been there, I'd have been on the other side.' She stared unseeing at the sparkling water. 'I've never felt like that before. It – frightened me.'

Davie uncovered one eye. 'If *you* were frightened, dearest, think how they must've felt!'

'I had no idea such things were allowed to happen in Scotland. It was so absolutely wicked. Your poor father and mother . . . And it's such a perfect countryside.'

'Where every prospect pleases, eh?' Davie asked ironically.

'But it does!' She gestured passionately at the bay. 'It's so beautiful here. I don't know how you and John could bear to leave it. I admit I grumbled when we arrived, Davie, and I do think you and John could help your parents to a more comfortable home, but it's such a lovely place – '

'For sheep, Charlotte, not people.'

'I beg your pardon, dear?'

'To us it *is* paradise but with a canker at its heart. D'you see those houses on that hill over there?' She shaded her eyes. 'They're empty because of the sheep.'

'What have sheep got to do with it?'

He was saddened. 'My, there's not much you know about what the English did to Scotland, is there, Charlotte?'

The back stiffened immediately. 'My aunt required me to assist in the shop. There was no time for history lessons.'

He was penitent. 'I'm sorry, dear, I forgot. And it's old history, too. But this land has been ravaged, and it's my

281

country, Charlotte.' He ran a hand through his hair out of habit and the red curls sprang up. 'For more than a hundred and fifty years the Highlands have been emptied of their people, turned out of their crofts to make room for the landowners' sheep.'

'But where did all the people go?'

'To America, Australia . . . perdition, as far as the lairds were concerned. Or to England, which to some Highlanders is the same thing.'

The bitterness was something new and disturbed her. Charlotte tried to turn her attention to the wild flowers among the machair grasses, the silvery sheen of the sand. Too much anger had been unleashed today.

'You'll see the evidence in church tomorrow.' Davie sighed. 'How few young men are left. They can't stay because there's not enough land with a croft to make a decent living for a family. Yet look around, Charlotte, there's wonderful pasturage all over the peninsula. Years ago this land supported thousands; there were many small townships, but those three houses now . . . ' He pointed again. 'They're deserted, d'you see? No smoke from those chimneys any more and the roofs are falling in.'

'So they are. I hadn't noticed.'

'Well, that's where the Swordle crofters ended up. Three communities, prosperous ones, farming over three thousand acres between them. Fifty years ago, the laird ordered them to build new dwelling houses, fine big ones, to replace the homes they had then. We're talking about stone-built places with gables, the sort crofters weren't used to. Anyway, they did as they were bid, paying out nearly fifty pounds for each house, and what happened when they were finished?'

'Well? What?'

'Within two years those crofters were forced out of their brand new homes – for which they'd continued to pay rent – and given that land there,' he nodded across the bay. 'One acre per family. They didn't stand a chance.'

'Did none of them complain?'

'To whom? To the English?' She was silent. Davie flung pebbles at the water to relieve his feelings.

'In a way, they were lucky. Most survived long enough to

emigrate. Hundreds of others, especially in Sutherland, suffered far worse. Many had homes burned round their ears. Some were left to die in a ditch.'

'Not nowadays, surely?'

'In my grandfather's time. That's what made him a rebel.' Davie stood to throw his last pebble. 'Praise the Lord for William Ewart Gladstone, that's what I say. At least if we can never own our land, a father now has the right to pass his croft on to his son – if that son can make a living at it.' His bitterness subsided as quickly as it had arisen. He looked down to see his wife plucking at the rug in her distress. Tenderly, he bent and kissed her neck. 'That's why I was so proud of you today, dearest. You stuck up for us and bless my soul, you're English to the tips of your fingers.'

'What happened to your grandfather?'

'I'll tell you some other time. In his day though, when there was fighting, men had to obey the laird's summons whether they wanted to or not. The factors were sent, to round men up. Not many ever came back. And for all those uprisings, especially the Forty-five, the Highlands have been punished for ever and ever.' He rolled his eyes, to try and make a joke of it. 'You're married to a wandering Jew, Charlotte, condemned and cursed – '

'Oh, what nonsense! You're a Presbyterian.'

He laughed. 'I'll tell you what. Before we leave, I'll take you over and show you one factor who was beaten, in Kilchoan churchyard. MacColl. He evicted one old woman who cursed him with a terrible curse. Told him his soul would go down to everlasting perdition and naught but weeds would grow on his grave.'

'What happened?'

'It's covered with nettles and docken to this day,' said Davie happily. 'His family have tried everything they know to get grass to grow on it. It cheers my heart every time I see it. Just think of him, down there . . . ' He stirred the sand with his foot, 'Roasting away – ' ·

'Davie, don't!'

He gave an exaggerated sniff. 'Why, I think I can smell him, Charlotte. A fine piece of roast pork – '

'That's enough!' She scrambled up and began to shake out

the rug. 'And don't you dare tell the children, they'll be awake half the night.'

'No, my love.'

After a pause she asked thoughtfully, 'Those people from the Big House . . . are they the lairds in this area?'

'And loyal subjects of King George. They bought that house some years ago – I think they made their money in cotton in the South African war. They consider they're entitled to do what they did this morning although I thought the custom of riding over the crofts had been stopped.' He sighed, 'We must blame young Manners for that.'

Charlotte was outraged. 'But this is nineteen hundred and three! Such things must not be *allowed* to happen again. You must put a stop to it.'

'Me! How?'

But Charlotte had her reply ready.

'You must enter politics. Like Mr Gladstone –'

'He's dead!'

'Don't be flippant, Davie. I'm serious.'

(ix)

While Charlotte and Katriona repacked the picnic, the others went for a final swim. 'Mr John looks so much better, doesn't he?' Katriona sounded satisfied. 'Mrs McKie will be delighted at the change in him.' Charlotte agreed. John and Davie had shed years in the past few days. It was a shock when she realized that John was still only thirty-three. To her he'd almost seemed a different generation than Davie; always serious, hardly ever smiling unless he was with Luke, but now . . . He'd given up wearing pince-nez up here. There were no papers, no accounts to check. He'd been out walking before breakfast every morning. Charlotte felt slightly guilty when she thought about the makeshift bed John had occupied; it was cushions and blankets in front of the fire, but he'd assured her he didn't mind. No wonder he'd been first up every morning, though.

She shaded her eyes and gazed at them all, silhouetted against the rising moon: silver sand, a molten sea and small figures dancing from the sheer joy of living. A dim memory arose of Jane, such a shadowy presence now. Hadn't she once told Aunt Armitage that *her* baby had been born on a beach? Charlotte dismissed the thought as fanciful. What a stupid notion. Her poor, dear mother would never have been reduced to such straits, not even on lovely sands such as these.

'Come along, all of you,' she called. 'Time to go home.'

It was a long time before Charlotte slept that night. Beside her, Davie lowered his large frame cautiously onto the old feather bed, patted her buttocks amicably, and closed his eyes. But Charlotte was troubled. Her life until now had been spent in a comfortable backwater, she realized. She knew very little of what went on in the rest of the world. Of course she'd heard plenty of chatter in the shop of the recent war with those wretched Boer farmers, indeed one or two customers had sons in the Durham Light Infantry. Once or twice there had been extremely sad news but none of it had *affected* Charlotte. Now circumstances were different.

She looked at Davie. His grandfather had gone to fight in a war he didn't believe in as part of his rent for living in this shabby little cottage? And how many generations had already lived here? Why, they must have paid for it over and over again.

'Absolutely disgraceful,' she said aloud. Her husband stirred. Another thought disturbed her. Supposing *they* had lived in those terrible days and the factors had rounded up young Ted – that would have been unthinkable! She contemplated her sleeping husband. '*You* must make sure such a thing never happens again,' she told him but he didn't hear, which was just as well. Saddled with that responsibility, Davie wouldn't have slept at all. Satisfied that she'd made the right decision for both of them, Charlotte plumped her pillows and closed her eyes.

What followed was inevitable, given that the next day was the Sabbath and they were all to attend the kirk. The children were excused. Charlotte helped Katriona feed Matthew then watched as she and the three older children set off for a day on the hills.

Charlotte fastened Matthew's reins to the table leg. His grandmother sat contentedly beside him, shelling peas for ten hearty appetites. Charlotte pinned the garnet brooch Davie had given her to the neck of her new silk blouse and set off with the men to hear the word of God.

285

Alex and John walked ahead in their thick serge suits and wing collars. The sun was hot again; Charlotte adjusted her parasol. Davie was wearing a suit in a new light-weight cloth, a 'special line' the traveller from Leeds had urged him to try. She was glad she'd encouraged him. He was so handsome, she knew other Darlington ladies would imagine their husbands might look the same. Yes, the new worsted should sell quite well.

It was a comfort to be married to such a fine figure of a man. Not that they'd been able to enjoy conjugal bliss since coming to Scotland; Davie's size combined with the frail nature of the old feather bed prohibited it. Perhaps it was this that made concentration difficult. Once inside the church Charlotte closed her eyes in prayer but she was conscious of other eyes watching her. She rose from the cassock and settled herself in the pew. Directly opposite, staring at her, was the rider she'd unseated yesterday and beside him was a much older man, obviously his father. Charlotte flushed an angry red. Davie groaned inwardly. That those from the Big House should choose to come here today was what he'd dreaded most.

Equally unfortunate was the choice of text. An old man now, Mr McAlister didn't bother composing new sermons but rotated his favourite subjects instead. Today he'd chosen the Sermon on the Mount and as she heard humility extolled, Charlotte felt the same overwhelming surge of anger as yesterday.

Finally it was over. The congregation stretched numbed limbs. John and Davie followed Charlotte down the aisle and into the porch. Outside Mr Manners and his son stood waiting, watching for what Charlotte would do next. Without hesitating, she turned to the Minister and, raising her voice so that all could hear, said, 'There has been too much meekness here, Mr McAlister.'

'I beg your pardon!'

'And those in authority abuse their powers when they deliberately destroy other people's crops.'

'Madam – I – '

'You should have spoken against it, a man in your position. Who can people turn to if not their Minister and yet you have condoned this wicked, wicked practice. I shall not visit your church again.'

Behind her soft voices whispered excitedly as those who understood English translated for those who did not. Charlotte turned back to face the Manners, who still stood and stared. Smoothing on her glove so that she nearly split the leather she announced, 'There will be no more disturbance either to Mr McKie or to any other croft while I am here. Otherwise I shall be forced to write to the editor of *The Times*.' Her parasol snapped open like a gunshot and Charlotte swept past both of them.

Grinning foolishly, Davie shrugged at John. There was no stopping Charlotte in this mood and they knew it. 'Write a letter to *The Times*!' He swallowed his laughter and hurried after his wife. Why, she'd never read the paper in her life!

John distanced himself. He saw Davie offer his arm and Charlotte rest her hand upon it. Her head was at its highest angle. They walked off and John felt the eyes of the rest of the congregation burning holes in his back. He hurried away over the moor.

Alex went home a third way, with Alla for company. He hoped John would give Charlotte a talking-to; he knew Davie would not. For a woman to speak to a minister like that! It was unforgivable, even if it was the truth. Not a woman . . . !

'What is – *The Times*?' asked Alla.

They'd been walking for nearly an hour and had paused at the summit of a hill. Below they could see two small figures, arm in arm, walking along the path between the peat. Behind, a third figure was catching them up.

'It is an English newspaper,' Alex replied, 'and she is for writing them a letter if those at the Big House do any more damage.'

'Will it stop them, d'you think?'

Alex sucked his teeth as he considered.

'I've heard them say him at the Big House is wanting a knighthood from King Edward. He would not be wanting his name in the English newspapers until he has it.'

A slow smile spread across Alla's face.

'Maybe it *will* stop them then?'

'Aye, but she should not have spoken like that. After all, she's only Davie's wife.'

'My, but she puts me in mind of the old school mistress,

287

Alex. D'you not mind how she spoke to the Minister that time, when John could not go to the university?'

'Aye, aye – '

'You did not object then. Poor wee man, he's suffered at the hands of the English right enough.'

Alex refused to be mollified too quickly. He considered the pair below. 'It is a good thing for Davie his wife isn't as ugly as the school mistress.'

'She doesn't have hair on her lip,' Alla agreed. 'I'm thinking, Alex, it's time someone spoke out and said the truth of it.'

'But not an Englishwoman!'

'Maybe not, aye, maybe not.' ·

'I'm thankful Davie's children take after their father, all three of them.'

'Yes . . . ' Alla glanced at his friend before he said, 'I've heard Luke is a fine scholar.'

'He is.' Alex's face was expressionless.

'Mary Hamilton's son would that be?'

'Mary – and John's son. He is to be a doctor.'

'Is that so?'

'Mistress Shields has said he's the brightest of the bunch.'

'Aye? Then that's grand, Alex. I'm glad you've lived to see the day.'

(x)

Davie was to accompany John to the ferry and Alex went with them for the first five miles. At the crossroads, he held his son tightly by the hand as he bade him farewell for the second time in their lives. Davie walked on slowly, pretending not to notice.

'See that you remember us to Mary, mind.'

'I'll not forget, Father.'

'It was a noble thing you did, marrying her. Your mother convinced me of it but I hope you haven't suffered by it?'

John couldn't meet his father's eye so stared at his boots. 'She's a fine, good woman, and she works so hard for all of us. Luke is my son as much as he's hers.'

'Your mother and I have accepted that.'

288

John looked at the face, a replica of his own but so much older and worn with the privations of life.

'Thank you for telling me so, Father,' he whispered.

'See that he goes to the university as you should have done. There must be no mistakes this time. Your mother and I have saved more than half the money you and Davie have sent. It's all for the children, including young Ted.' Despite the solemn moment, John's lips twitched.

'He's a bit lively I grant you but he'll settle down once Davie sends him to school.' He glanced at the gap between him and Davie. 'Father, I must go or I'll miss the boat.'

Alex touched him lightly on the shoulder. 'Tell Mary we'll be teaching Luke to fish before we send him back to her.' He looked at the sky. 'Maybe tonight we'll give him his first lesson. It'll be dark enough I'm thinking.'

John hugged him and hurried away, averting his face. Never mind letters to *The Times*. There were other, quieter ways of settling scores with the Big House, and filling the larder at the same time.

Alex stood as motionless as the dog at his feet. Would he ever see John again? He couldn't expect him to make such a long journey often, not when there was business to attend to. A fine businessman, in England . . . Tears coursed down but still he didn't move.

Perhaps because they were conscious of him standing there, John and Davie didn't speak. Only when they'd reached the jetty, did Davie broach the topic.

'Charlotte suggested I should consider – politics. As a stranger, she was shocked by the way things are up here. I think that's why she reacted as strongly as she did . . . at the kirk.' He was apologizing obliquely for what had happened. John stared at the wild rhododendrons while he considered the idea.

'How d'you feel about it yourself?'

'I think something should be done. You and I have said so often enough in the past.'

'It's not simply because *she* suggested it?'

Davie reddened. 'Maybe so at first but not now.' He laughed self-consciously, 'I wish she could be the one, she's got the spirit for it.'

'Don't be ridiculous, Davie.'

'No, no. It was only a joke.' John's brow creased.

'If you do go in for it . . . it'll cost a great deal of money.' Davie hadn't considered the practical aspects for a moment. Inwardly, he sighed. It looked as if he'd no further choice anyway, not now Charlotte had made the decision and John was doing the sums. Somewhere above he heard a skylark and looked up eagerly. Not a care in the world and such sweetness!

CHAPTER NINE

Decisions

John opened the yard gate and went into the emporium the back way. He could hear hammering overhead but was too tired to face the problems Mr Clough undoubtedly had waiting for him. There was hammering going on outside too, and dust. In the High Row, gangs of labourers were digging up cobbles and installing cables for the new Darlington Corporation light railway. Electrical tram-cars! John shook his head. Nothing but change nowadays. But if they were to keep up with the times, as he'd declared they must, there was no ignoring it. Gas lighting had had its day, according to the last debate he'd attended, but those young bloods at the Lit and Phil who'd cried 'hurrah' at the result had no idea of the cost of the new luminosity.

John had attended the opening three years previously of the Power Station in Haughton Road. He'd even had a private word with the Borough's electrical engineer and laughed nervously when Mr Lunn produced his estimates. But he'd noticed how thick the crowds were, that first Christmas, in those shops which had the new light.

The library was the first public building to have it installed, then some streets in the centre of the town. Now there were dozens of lamps including a great arc light in Bull Wynd. No, there was no getting away from it, McKie Brothers were in danger of being left behind. The worry lines which Scotland had helped smooth away developed into familiar furrows. An electrical subcontractor had been brought in at vast expense from Newcastle. John examined the ornate brass switch by the study door. Dare he press the knob? Would he feel current running up his arm, crackling through his hair? He wouldn't meddle; the subcontractor could switch it on. The amount John was paying, the man could take the risk of blowing himself up instead.

On the desk was a pile of envelopes. John went through them rapidly and opened one from Mrs Armitage.

Dear Mr McKie,
Trusting this finds you in good health and thanking you for yr munificence in sending Bertha and I to Harrogate with yr dear wife.

Bertha and I have benefited from both the medicinal waters and the cream cakes! of which there are a magnificent selection here in Harrogate!!

Yr dear wife continues to improve. Bertha and I will return her to you in the best of health and spirits.

I do not exaggerate when I describe the hotel you have engaged for us as – LUXURIOUS! I know Mr A sees and appreciates as he watches over us from Above. I add his thanks to mine and remain,
Yrs most sincerely,
ADELAIDE ARMITAGE

The calming atmosphere of Mary's presence stole over John as he read her letter. She told him of the many little outings she and Bertha had devised for Mrs Armitage, how responsible Bertha was nowadays. She peopled the tea-rooms with vignettes to amuse them. Lastly she thanked him warmly for encouraging Luke to write to her. As he finished the last page, John found himself calculating the days to her return. It was the first time they'd been apart and he missed her.

He wondered if there was a chance of tea. He tugged twice on the lift rope. If there was anyone in the kitchen, they should understand, it was his usual signal to Mary. Ten minutes later there was a muffled crash as Mrs Beal pushed the study door open using her laden tray. John averted his eyes until the china was safe on the desk top before greeting her.

'Won't you join me for a cup of tea, Mrs Beal? I should like to hear all that's been happening?'

'Well, I can't stay long Mr John, what with the supper to get . . . ' But she managed a list of grievances against builder and electrician that lasted the best part of half an hour. John came to a decision.

'I think I shall be taking most of my meals out, Mrs Beal, until my wife returns. I don't want to add to your work in any way.'

'There is one thing, sir.' She didn't want him to escape, she'd been anxious for his return and clasped her tea-cup more tightly. 'It's about our Billy.'

'Billy?'

'My middle lad.'

'I don't think I've met him.'

'No, you haven't, nor Mr Davie. I'd sent him to his uncle's farm afore you came to me. He's a bit wanting, you know what I mean?'

John waited patiently.

'That's why his uncle took him on, you see, on the farm. He's good with animals, is Billy, always has been. Only Albert's wife died last year and he's married again, and *she* don't take to our Billy. Wants rid of him. And I was wondering . . . He's ever so strong, and willing . . . Whether he could come here. Just a bit wanting, that's all he is.'

She swallowed nervously. John sat and thought for a moment or two. It seemed quite natural that she should expect him to help, to take on this new responsibility. Hadn't Mrs Beal given him and Davie a roof, strangers in a foreign country? He suddenly remembered.

'I think there may be just the thing for Billy. How old is he?'

'Eleven. He's big for his age.'

'And you say he's good with animals?'

'Oh yes, like he understands them, you know.'

John nodded. 'You've solved a problem, Mrs Beal. I'm

293

going to purchase a dog-cart for Mary. We shall need someone to see to the pony.'

'Oh, Mr John!'

He relented and gave in to her pleas to stay for supper. There weren't many ways she could show her gratitude. Chewing his food, John re-read Mary's letter and the reference to Bertha. He agreed with his wife, Bertha had changed considerably. Working in the salon had given her a position in life and she filled it impressively. She it was who looked in on the 'Smoking' if the gentlemen's laughter had become too loud, her bulk and dignity had never failed yet. And it was time that Mrs Armitage had a rest. But they would have to be tactful. John knew how easily the lady became upset now that Mr A was no longer there. Her main topic of conversation, the lynchpin of her existence, had gone. Mr A's opinions could no longer be quoted and her own, of course, were of no consequence whatsoever.

But Mrs Armitage had discovered new horizons for herself in Harrogate. Among the widows taking the waters, one or two were from Darlington and some were actually customers of Armitage's.

'One has to be careful,' she told Mary, 'but one can understand a great deal from a customer's order, especially the tea she chooses. Mrs Ettersley was always discerning over tea.'

Mary watched contentedly the preparations for the outing. Mrs Ettersley was staying at the Old Swan and Mrs Armitage had been invited there to 'partake of a little something'. It had taken most of the afternoon to decide which new outfit was most suitable. Bertha had been extremely patient. For the umpteenth time Mary assured them both she would be quite happy on her own. Preening herself in her new grey wool trimmed with squirrel, Mrs Armitage sallied forth; laden with extra shawls, galoshes and an umbrella, Bertha followed.

Alone and feeling better than she had for years, Mary reached inside her reticule. She smoothed the creased sheets of paper tenderly and re-read the message: 'Dearest Mother . . . ' There was a knock and the maid entered with an extra scuttle of coal.

'Mrs Armitage's instructions, ma'am. She said you weren't to ignore the master's orders because you was on your own, please ma'am.' Mary smiled and the maid went about her task. The flames burned brightly, the maid withdrew and once again Mary stroked the paper. 'Dearest Mother . . .'

(i)

Up on the moor, Davie stretched indolently and looked at his wife's serious face. 'A penny for them?'

'I was considering which political party you should join.' He gave a yelp of laughter and she rounded on him.

'It's most important, Davie, I wish you'd give the matter proper thought.'

'I'm sure John would say I should join Keir Hardie.'

'Oh, nonsense!' There was such a thing as going too far.

'Well, what do you think?'

Charlotte frowned. 'I believe you should join the Liberals but I'm not sure. However, I don't think you should consult John –'

'No?' He stopped tickling her chin with a feathery grass, 'Why not?'

'Because it's England we're considering, not Scotland. They do things differently. And I'm sure if you'd had the right man in the proper party, all these wicked matters would've been dealt with years ago.'

'Yes, Charlotte.'

Helen Shields was startled. 'Member of Parliament? Whose idea was that?'

Davie looked uncomfortable. 'Charlotte's to begin with but I agree with it. So does John now. He's looking into the cost at any rate.'

Helen gave a rare smile. Was one of them to become a professional man at last?

'I hear Mr McAlister had a bad time of it last Sunday. Fancy having his sermon criticized! He's been preaching the same one for nearly twenty years, it must've come as a terrible shock to the man.'

Davie grinned. 'It wasn't just his sermon.'

295

'I heard that, too. In fact he's taken to his bed with a stomach upset if the gossip's to be believed, poor man.'

'Charlotte was magnificent. She must've terrified the Manners. Hunting's stopped entirely, all over the peninsula.'

'About time, too,' replied Helen firmly. 'Well, Davie, since you've asked me . . . '

'Yes?'

'Those at the Big House and Mr McAlister, they've supported the Tory party since the day they were born.'

'That's settled it then, it's the Liberals. Charlotte was right.'

(ii)

John wandered through the silent shop inspecting Mr Clough's alterations. Business was expanding, space had to be found for yet more new lines and Mr Hart had as usual made useful suggestions. Mr Clough had hurrumphed over the drawings but, John saw, most had been carried out and worked well. Hart was to be promoted to Manager, Menswear when they re-opened, another increase in wages. John couldn't stifle an automatic sigh but he mustn't complain.

He stepped cautiously over tools, spare timber and snaking cables on his way to the living quarters. Mrs Armitage's little suite had been re-arranged and newly decorated as a surprise. Bertha was to move into the grocer's former bedroom and Ada brought down from the attic dormitory and given hers. Mary had seen to it. John poked his head round doors and approved the re-arranged furniture. Nothing new of course, but all looked fresh and welcoming.

Upstairs, he considered the dining room. No amount of new paint could disguise the worn carpet but this was the communal room used by everyone, families and shop assistants. Now Davie was entering politics, he would need somewhere more private. A study of some sort with a small drawing room perhaps? The only rooms on this level were John's and Davie's but there was nothing spare because of the children. There wasn't an inch to spare among the attics either. They were planning to engage an additional lady apprentice next month, which would mean five young ladies plus Kationa sleeping up there unless they were lucky and found an applicant who lived in the town and didn't need accommodation.

By rights Katriona should have been offered Bertha's old room but that would have left the lady assistants unsupervised and that would never do. Charlotte and Mary were adamant. So Katriona had been consoled with new curtains and a rug in her tiny space under the eaves.

Where else could a prospective Member of Parliament entertain visitors? John would have to ask Mr Clough. And how did a man get started in politics anyway? John yawned. He'd have to look that up in the library. Nothing but expense whichever way he turned . . . he yawned again and before he'd finished unlacing his boots, John was asleep.

Mr Clough responded to the new challenge with the taciturnity of his calling. 'Happen I can build a couple more rooms, happen I can't.' He stomped off into the yard to gaze up at the building as if willing it to expand. John left him to it and went off on another matter.

He was nervous of ponies, he'd lost his childhood familiarity with animals. He stood in Mr Lowis's livery stables in High Northgate, staring at various hindquarters and swishing tails. 'I'll get a second opinion,' he told the ostler, and retreated. There was only the unknown Billy he could ask. Would he look a fool, going back to the stable with an eleven-year-old? It couldn't be helped, John couldn't think of anyone else.

Mrs Beal had arranged for Billy to be brought over next Monday, market day, and until then the matter could wait. Ordering a dog-cart proved much easier. John read an advertisement that same day in the *North Star*. He was dazzled by the fluency of the man selling the item: one elderly lady owner, used but once a week to take her to church, hardly any noticeable wear, nothing that a lick of paint wouldn't put right. John found himself halfway down the street before he realized how much money he'd parted with. The shock unsteadied him. He could have brought a new cart for that much, surely? He was about to go back when he stopped himself. Wasn't Mary worth it? It wasn't a happy thought but this was the very first present he'd given her. It was Davie who remembered birthdays and found something suitable for her at Christmas; John never thought of anything unprompted. He continued on down the street. He'd insist the man include all the necessary tackle as well. Soothed, he took himself off to the warehouse.

Mr Clough discovered him above the stables that evening. There were three rooms partitioned off up here, two for Mr Hart and his assistant, one for their elderly bespoke tailor. Fortunately there was still a further cubbyhole and John had sized up the space; it would take a bed and chair.

A plan was thrust in front of him, drawn on an old strip of wallpaper. 'I told the lads to get started right away. You'll be wanting it all finished by this time next week no doubt, as per usual.'

John examined the shapes between dirt and thumb prints and tried to imagine the result.

'I've done the best I can,' Clough told him. 'Thee and the wife and kiddie can move t'ground floor without much bother. That gives us thy rooms to play with.' John understood he was being shown an extension built out into the yard beyond his study.

'Yes, I see.'

'There's plenty of room,' the builder went on, 'and we've made a beginning upstairs on Mr Davie's new arrangements.'

John felt it had been far too expensive a day. Mrs Beal compounded it; she'd bought a piece of steak to tempt him, for supper. He would eat nothing but mutton from now on, he said sternly, at least until Mary was back.

Increased activity in the yard drove him out again. The place would remain in a turmoil for another two weeks thanks to the change of plan, and it would mean dawn to dusk, Mr Clough warned, a bit extra for some of the lads, he shouldn't wonder.

John made his way round to Crown Street. He would seek information concerning a parliamentary career in the reference library. If Davie was to succeed, John would need to guide him.

In Scotland and in Harrogate there was surprise at the brief notes advising them to stay away a little longer. Katriona was bidden to return as planned. John needed her to help with the assistants, for the emporium would open on time even though the family living quarters weren't ready. Davie was urged to

298

make use of the time in Glasgow and visit Arthur's. Mary was given a brief resumé of the new career in politics and informed that in future she and Luke would be living on the ground floor. The salon would remain closed until Mrs Armitage and Bertha returned.

Satisfied he'd made the best of things, John had a bed moved into the corner of the dining room, temporarily. It was the only room free from plaster and dust.

Mrs Beal grew nervous as Monday approached. Twice she chipped plates when washing up. She'd insisted on supplying the furniture for Billy's room. 'It's the least I can do, Mr John, and it'll make him feel comfy, seeing his old bits and pieces.' John was too busy now to worry about the new arrival. He and Mr Hart worked till midnight the Saturday and Sunday prior to re-opening, putting stock onto the new shelves, helped as usual by Mr Collins.

John described the wonders of Glasgow. Doing their best, the other two managed an approximation of Argyle Street shop windows then discovered new price tags had been forgotten in the upheaval. John was up at four AM to write them himself. In the dawn light his shadowy figure startled a constable pacing past the shop windows. 'I thought one of them dummies was on the move!' he whispered as John tried to comfort him. Incoherent with fatigue, John apologized.

At half past seven, the doors were opened and customers flooded in. John watched anxiously as assistants searched for goods in unfamiliar new surroundings. Placing Mr Hart in solemn charge, he tore himself away but once at the warehouse he was full of misgivings. It was the first time not one single member of the family had been at the precious emporium. John went hot and cold as he imagined each new disaster. Eventually he could stand it no longer and tipped the office boy threepence 'to nip round and have a look, Sowerby.'

By seven PM John was back behind his familiar desk in the study. The passage outside was narrower now, with a new door leading to the three unfinished rooms. A small group waited to see him. Mr Hart was admitted first with the day's takings and an optimistic report of customers' reactions to the changes. John began to breathe more easily. Then came Mr and Mrs Nettles with the rents, and a request that he consider purchasing another house in Coburg Street. 'I have only heard the sale whispered of as yet, Mr McKie, but it's worth considering I'm sure you'll agree. Being the end of the terrace and a slightly higher foundation, there is a commodious cellar which would be most beneficial on washday.'

John ordered more tea and settled to serious discussion. At the end of half an hour, terms were agreed. He would arrange a loan with Backhouses – the bank had become a branch of Barclays years ago but citizens clung to the former name. The Nettles would pay a peppercorn rent this time because it was understood that Mrs Nettles would make extra money taking in washing, and the couple also undertook to find someone suitable to take over the old house.

'You can rely on me, Mr McKie,' said Mrs Nettles firmly. 'After all these years, I know what you have in mind; a good worker and a church-goer, that's right, isn't it?' They rose to leave, profuse in their thanks. The proposed house had an additional bedroom as well as the cellar. John had no doubt it would be filled; whenever he saw Mrs Nettles she had a permanent bulge below her waistline.

He was stacking the cups on a tray, ready to begin his accounts, when there was another knock at the door. It opened a crack.

'Can I bring our Billy in now, Mr John?'

At first sight, John thought the boy had no neck then he realized it was the breadth of the shoulders and the length of the arms that made it appear so. Nothing was the right size in Billy Beal. His head was small and set too far back. He was forced to look up by tilting back on his heels. He stared at the world from pale blue eyes, guileless but frightened. His ape-like arms hung beside his skinny body and like most of the children from Coburg Street, rickets made him walk pigeon-toed.

He shivered as he stared at John. He knew he wasn't wanted on the farm any longer. The new woman shouted at him. His only comfort had been the animals. That morning his uncle had bundled his things in a sack and told him he was going back to his mother. Billy had hung round the market all day until she'd been able to collect him. Now she'd brought him in here, to meet this stranger.

He saw John's worried glance and felt his mother's grip on his arm. 'He's only a bit wanting,' she said, 'but he's ever so willing, aren't you, Billy?' Her son was too frightened to speak.

'Would he like some tea?' asked John automatically. Mrs Beal replied quickly.

'We'll be having our supper later, thank you, sir.' Table manners were not Billy's strong point.

John looked at the boy helplessly. He didn't know whether he was making a bad mistake. Certainly there would be no place for Billy in the shop. Either he could handle the dog-cart or he was no use at all.

John sat farther forward on his chair, trying to engage Billy's attention. 'I'm going to choose a pony tomorrow. Would you like to help me select the right one?' Billy's mouth moved slightly, trying out some of the words.

'He understands you, sir.' Mrs Beal sounded more confident than she felt, 'but he's not a great one for talking.' Suddenly Billy spoke. His tongue was too big for his mouth and he pushed the word through his teeth.

''Orses?' he asked urgently. He shambled across and grabbed John's hand. ''Orses?'

'That's right.' John was shaken by the fierce grip. 'A pony to pull a dog-cart for my wife. I want you to look after it, Billy.' The boy had returned to his mother.

''Orses, Ma,' he told her eagerly.

'That's right, Billy. In the morning.' She pulled the boy towards the door. 'I'll get your supper now, sir,' she said, 'then I'll take Billy across and show him where he's going to sleep, introduce him to the other gentlemen.'

That night John stood at the dining-room window and looked across the yard. He could see lights in some of the rooms above the stable but Billy's was dark. It seemed to John that there was a face pressed against the glass but he dismissed the notion. His eyes ached from checking accounts and he rubbed them tiredly. His temporary bed he moved nearer the fire, and lowered himself onto it. It was as uncomfortable as he remembered.

Across the yard Billy stared at the stars. He liked their sparkle, like bits of candleflame. He preferred the darkness; it hid him from cruel eyes. Clutching the square of blanket he used as a comforter, Billy Beal crooned himself gently to sleep.

John was ready at seven fifteen next morning. He wanted to finish the business of the cart and make his mind up about the boy before going to the warehouse. Billy was waiting in the kitchen. His mother had tidied him although the result wasn't noticeably different. Any jacket with sleeves long enough for his arms was bound to flap round the boy's knees.

He moved in a shambling run to keep up with John. They went through back streets rather than the main thoroughfare, for John had no wish to meet business colleagues at present.

The ostler was all bustle, shouting at stable lads grooming the horses. He told John to 'go right along inside, sir' and left him to his own devices. John followed Billy as he moved among the animals, rubbing their noses and flanks. As he spoke, he wondered uneasily if Billy understood a word.

'I want a quiet pony, to pull the cart. My wife isn't strong and if she is to handle the reins herself occasionally, it needs to be gentle, too.'

The ostler hurried over, confident of John's ignorance. He knew just the one for Mr McKie's good lady and began to lead it out of the stall.

John saw that Billy took no notice of the parading horse but stood patting a black pony, indifferent to the two men. In a pause during the enthusiastic sales talk, John asked, 'How much is the one the boy is holding?' It was five guineas less. Slightly reassured but with no real idea whether it was the right choice, John said firmly, 'I'll take it.'

He concluded the purchase of the dog-cart with brusque efficiency. The pony was harnessed and stood quietly between the shafts as the ostler had promised she would. The spare tackle was thrown in beside them and for the first time it occurred to John they had to drive the thing back to the Emporium. Could Billy cope?

'Home, please Billy,' he ordered.

The boy crooned and flicked the reins. They moved out of the yard and into the street. At once, Billy stopped.

'Ah doan't know . . . ' He looked at John full of fear, 'Ah doan't know . . . '

'Don't know what?'

'Where to go?' Full of relief, John pointed.

'Straight ahead.' The pony moved forward. If it was only directions, that shouldn't be a problem. Mary knew her way about well enough. The little vehicle bowled gently along. As they neared the noise of the roadworks, the pony's ears went back and John could sense her trembling. Billy jumped down and took her bridle. 'Walk beside her . . . ' he explained and kept the pony jogging along and in through the yard gate. John descended and raised his hat to Mrs Beal, who was watching anxiously from the kitchen window.

'I'll be off to the warehouse now,' he called. 'See you this evening at the usual time.' He replaced the hat with new confidence as he suddenly realized he was now a member of the carriage trade.

(iii)

The train from Harrogate was late and John's feet were wet. Shoes were the one item of apparel he couldn't bear to replace until they were completely worn out. Charlotte chided him about it but Davie told her privately not to bother. It haunted him too to put out boots for the tinkers while they still had wear left in them.

Tonight John shifted uncomfortably. What if Mary didn't take to the boy? Who else could handle the pony and cart? He looked back to where Billy stood beyond the barrier, stroking the black ears and whispering into them. Beneath the gaslight, the pony's coat gleamed. He had to admit the lad knew a thing or two about horses, much more than he did himself.

On the day of the purchase John had arrived home to find a harassed Mrs Beal with two farriers standing in her kitchen. Amid the comments and tears, John discovered that Billy had indeed proved 'willing' in his care for the pony. He had looked for foodstuffs and found none. He had therefore made his way back to the stables.

'And he stood there, Mr McKie, saying, "Food for the 'orse" till I could've clouted him.'

'Quite, quite . . . ' John was embarrassed, 'I fear I forgot to arrange matters myself.' Mrs Beal's sobs grew too loud and he said hurriedly, 'I'm sure these gentlemen could do with some tea, Mrs Beal.' She seized the kettle and he took the senior of the two to his study, to settle the pony's necessities. It was agreed that Billy should collect what was needed every week and the bill be sent monthly to John. 'But if you think he's over-ordering, you're to contact me immediately.'

'That's understood, Mr McKie.'

After they'd left John went to the stable. It was no longer forlorn and dark. Two stalls had been transformed. The pony stood contentedly in hers, munching away, sawdust and straw spread under her newly oiled hooves. On the beam, several nails had been hammered in and tackle hung in orderly loops. In the adjoining stall stood the dog-cart. A lamp, also acquired by Billy, shed soft light over a row of brushes and cloths. John wondered where he'd found those but thought it better not to ask. Billy obviously had a way of obtaining things. 'Wanting' he might be but it seemed to John the lad had wits enough. He saw the boy was smiling eagerly.

'You've done well, Billy.' The boy swayed. The pony was fed and warm but he'd something of importance to tell John. He pulled his lips tight over his teeth with the effort of forcing out the word.

'Blackie . . . ' he said hoarsely. John considered the name.

'I think we should wait and ask the children what they'd like to call her,' but Billy had shambled past him into the stall.

'Blackie, Blackie . . . ' he chanted softly. The rhythmic munching stopped and the pony turned her head. Despite many other suggestions when the families reassembled, the name was never changed.

Signals clanked above the platform and John stamped his feet. Tonight the damp seemed to penetrate his bones.

'Train's approaching now, Mr McKie.' John lifted his umbrella. The station master was a trustee of one of Mr Richardson's charities, John was another. Respected fellow citizens, each acknowledging the other's status.

Mrs Armitage's descent was regal, marred only by the height of the step and the shortness of her leg. She overwhelmed John with her boa, palma violets and enthusiasm. 'Dear, dear Mr McKie – what a splendid vacation! We've enjoyed ourselves so much and doesn't your dear wife look well?' The station master himself was offering Mary his arm. She stepped down carefully, her face coloured white and yellow by the gas jets, her smile radiant.

304

'I'm so glad to be home, John.' For a moment they almost kissed. It was a sliver of time when nothing moved then he bent clumsily over the proffered hand. He wasn't the man Davie was, for whom gallantry was as natural as breathing. Nor could he be uninhibited in a public place.

'You're looking much better, Mary.' She could see the apologetic look. She forced herself to say affectionately, 'Yes, indeed. We're all feeling the benefit of it,' so that he might not be embarrassed.

'Come, I've something to show you.' He tucked her hand under his arm, anxious to soften the hurt. They walked to the barrier where Billy stood close to the pony, fearful of this unknown woman. Would it be the same as at the farm? A kind face stared at the smart rig.

'I don't understand,' said Mary. John flushed, with pride this time.

'It's for you, to help you get about. And this is Billy, Mrs Beal's son, he'll drive you.' Mary held out her hand and found a piece of sticky sugar loaf pressed into her palm.

'Blackie . . . ' Billy urged, pulling the pony's bridle towards her. She smiled and offered the sugar to the soft black nose. Blackie crunched and submitted to having her ears fondled. She even stood patiently while Mrs Armitage and Bertha did the same. Both those ladies were a little startled at the sight of Billy but Mrs Armitage assured Bertha privately that Mr McKie must have had good reason for choosing such a handicapped boy.

Mary was handed into the cart with great ceremony and a rug tucked round her knees. 'Keep your umbrella handy,' said John gravely, 'those clouds look ominous to me.' There was a pause. Billy waited for instructions.

'Oh, the shop if you please Billy – and don't hurry on my account.' Mary was suddenly conscious of the steep slope and wet cobbles.

It took much longer to load Mrs Armitage into a cab because she wanted to help with various suggestions concerning the luggage. Eventually it was accomplished and once at the emporium, John left Bertha in charge while he made his way round to the stable. Blackie was already in her stall. Under the lamp, Mary sat on an upturned box, a slate in her hand. John

305

recognized it as an old one of Luke's. She had a piece of chalk and was writing the letters slowly for Billy.

'B . . . L . . . A . . . C . . . K . . . I . . . E. D'you understand, Billy?' He nodded, shaping the sounds with his tongue. Taking the slate, he climbed up between the stalls and hung it over Blackie's side.

'For the 'orse,' he told John shyly.

Later, when everyone had exhausted the topics of Harrogate and the alterations, John took Mary into his study for a quiet cup of tea. The smell of new plaster beyond the passage was oppressive. Mary declared she didn't mind. 'The sooner we can use the rooms, light fires in them, the quicker it will all dry out.'

'You don't object? I should have consulted you first,' John acknowledged belatedly.

'I don't mind, truly. You and Mr Clough have managed very well. I'm pleased it's because of Davie, though. Going into politics is a splendid idea. He has such charm, I'm sure he's just the person to persuade others what's best for them. After all, that's what politics is about, isn't it?' she finished drily. John was suddenly jealous.

'It was my agreeing to it that made it possible. It'll cost money, you know, and mean more work. We may have to – entertain people.'

'But Charlotte will enjoy doing that, you know she will. You are pleased, aren't you John?' she asked, surprised. 'Surely you're glad Davie has found a niche for himself? The emporium was always yours.'

He should have left it there but for some reason, Mary's approbation irritated him.

'It's all Charlotte's doing anyway. Davie would never have thought of it on his own.'

'Then she will be a great support, the very thing Davie will need most if he's to succeed. I'm glad he wants to speak out; there's been far too much apathy in the Highlands.' Her bland assumption almost caused him to spill out in temper.

'It'll be years before he can achieve anything. First he has to learn his trade. A man cannot simply become a Member of Parliament. Fortunately the library has a comprehensive selection of books on the subject.'

Mary lifted her eyebrows at the huge pile. It looked as if

306

Davie's leisure time would be full. And how typical of John to approach the matter like that.

She sensed his brittle mood although she couldn't account for it. To distract him, she took an envelope from her pocket. 'I've had another letter from Luke. It arrived yesterday morning just as we'd begun to pack. Would you like to read it?'

'Please!' He savoured the inscription on the envelope before opening it. 'He writes well doesn't he?'

'Very well, thanks to you.'

'No, no, he's a natural scholar, Mistress Shields confirmed it, did I tell you?' Mary nodded and waited patiently until he'd finished reading and re-reading.

'Not quite as neat as the one you helped with but a very nice letter, John.'

'There are two crossings out.'

'Ah well, doubtless Mistress Shields would've permitted that at his age.' That reminded him.

'She sent her love and gave a message to pass on to you.'

'Yes?'

'I was to say she'd felt troubled by the way she spoke to you last time we met. On our wedding day.' John looked at his wife curiously. 'I didn't know she'd been unkind, you never said?' Mary returned a steady gaze.

'It's all in the past, a long time ago. And she was upset.' Mary had never allowed him to know how deeply wounded she'd felt, nor would she now. 'When next I write, I will tell her I'd forgotten about it.'

But John was still uneasy, recalling the moment on the station platform. 'Mary – when we met today . . . ' She refused to help him but her gaze remained tranquil. 'I'm sorry . . . but I cannot love you. You know that, don't you?' There was a long pause this time.

'Yes, John, I've always known.'

'I am fond of you, deeply fond. And I've never wanted, never looked at anyone else.' He hurried on, stumbling over words, not daring to stop now he'd begun, 'You are dearer to me than anyone else in the world, and Luke of course.' He tried to find a morsel of comfort but couldn't and had to be honest. 'It was Mistress Shields who had the idea of the dog-cart,' he whispered.

Mary was glad of the dusk. There was no gaslight now the electricity had been installed and neither of them made a move to press the switch. She forced herself to speak in her normal low tone.

'I've always known how you felt, John. You've tried but you cannot love me. I must – accept that.' Was there a tremble? She took a deep breath. 'It's your loving care of Luke that fills my heart with gratitude . . . ' How could she admit her overpowering feelings? John would shy away out of guilt. She must do nothing that would provoke such a reaction. Briskly, she picked up the tea-tray. 'I'm most grateful too, for the dog-cart, even if it wasn't your idea.'

'How d'you find Billy? Does he give you confidence?'

'He handles Blackie beautifully, yes, I feel perfectly safe thank you, dear.' It was the only endearment she allowed herself and she used it sparingly. 'And now, if you'd open the door for me, I must see to the supper.' His hand remained on the handle. He was reluctant to end the conversation.

'You're sure you feel fit enough?'

'Oh yes, thanks to your generosity. The holiday was a complete tonic. I intend to prove it by returning to the kitchen. Poor Mrs Beal must be anxious to go back to her own.' This time he held the door wide.

As she edged past, he saw the tear stains for the first time. John was inexpressibly shocked; Mary never cried! He couldn't bring himself to speak and she slipped past, away to the lift. As at the station, the moment was gone before he'd managed a word to help. He shut the study door. The balance weights made their hollow reverberation in the passage outside.

'It's not my fault!' he whispered, 'I cannot love her,' but the empty rooms mocked his self-imposed loneliness.

CHAPTER TEN

A New Face

The autumn season of 1903 promised to be the busiest yet. It began with a surge of energy throughout the emporium. John didn't know what caused it but no one walked any more, they hurried, with scarcely time for a greeting. 'Morning, Mr McKie, can't stop sir, on my way to the stockroom.' From morning till night the place hummed with activity.

It began at breakfast. Fourteen sat round the dining table now, bought so cheaply because of its size years ago. Charlotte was at one end behind the coffee tray. Between her and Davie were Katriona and the children. Opposite, Mr Hart and his two assistants. At the far end, John had MacArthur the tailor beside him. An elderly Scot, MacArthur had gravitated to this position because of his silence, a quality John appreciated.

Mrs Armitage and Bertha remained in their rooms at this hour, preferring peace and quiet, but it meant that the lady assistants, smiling demurely across the table at the gentlemen, were relatively unsupervised. Katriona had her hands full. Charlotte, although eagle-eyed, couldn't oversee everything.

The result was inevitable; Mr Hart and Miss Bentley the cashier, had an 'understanding'.

John surveyed the happy pair gloomily. Doubtless the same thing might occur again, given such close proximity among his staff. He had another happier thought. Perhaps the future Mrs Hart would like to supervise the lettings in the new house in Coburg Street? It would mean the pair could live there rent-free and she would continue to earn her living, surely a bonus for any husband? Naturally it was inconceivable that she could go on working at the emporium. Married ladies were not permitted to work behind the counter, they had to retire. But this might be the perfect solution. Considerably cheered, John decided to put it to Hart on Friday evening.

On the other side of John, Luke saw his father smile; the day was improving already. It was the most important day of his life anyway for tonight they were to interview possible tutors. With Helen's gift, John told him the time had come to begin Latin and Greek! Full of joy, confident his father wasn't watching, Luke reversed his empty egg in its cup and slid it along in front of him. They played the game every week on boiled-egg day; John never failed to feign surprise when he sliced off the top.

In the kitchen, Mary presided over Ada and Emily Beal. Below she could hear the clank of the bucket as Billy scrubbed the floors. When he'd finished, he'd come up here to help his sister with the vast washing-up while Ada went below to sweep the carpets. It was a familiar routine now; the emporium was running on well-oiled wheels.

(i)

On her return from Scotland, Charlotte had been annoyed to discover Davie's parliamentary career couldn't proceed immediately. She herself had gone ahead, ordered new tea-gowns and increased her subscription to the collection plate. Visiting cards had already been distributed, telling friends and favoured customers she would be 'At home between two and four PM on Tuesdays and Thursdays'. Two afternoons, she told

Davie solemnly, that would be devoted solely to politics. He replied a little too quickly that he couldn't attend, he'd be too busy in the shop.

To be fair, Charlotte did her best. She entertained members of the town's Liberal Club and when a vacancy occurred on the town council later that year, Davie was elected unopposed. But Charlotte found it all too tame. Not for local politics had she purchased an ecru silk dress trimmed with matching lace and a heliotrope sash.

'You won't be able to help Scotland as a member of Darlington town council.'

'One step at a time, dearest. There's much to be learned here before I can think of London. And it depends if I prove myself worthy of such an honour.' Charlotte snorted.

'Don't leave it too long,' she warned, 'Mr Gladstone was already in Parliament at your age, he was Prime Minister by fifty-nine.'

'Charlotte, I've no ambition to be Prime Minister!'

'All the same, you could try a bit harder.'

It was perhaps unfortunate that at Davie's first council meeting the Boer War Memorial was discussed. Plans for one had been put forward in January, and now it was time to decide. When Davie reported back, John was outraged. He didn't begrudge one penny spent in furthering Davie's career, but a memorial to a war!

'It is for the Darlington dead,' Davie protested patiently.

'Much better they'd never gone to fight. And what about those who died on the other side, are you putting up a stone to them? They had fathers and mothers too, in Germany and Holland some of them, where Mr Richardson does business. Why should *we* fight over land in South Africa? Why not let them settle matters as they wish?'

Ignoring overtones of treason, Davie persisted, 'But there was a war, we did fight, and some men died. Surely there's no harm in commemorating them?'

'Will a cross help their womenfolk or feed their children? No, Davie, if there's money to be spent, let it be for the welfare of their families, not in glorifying war.'

Very wisely, Charlotte was not invited to take part in this argument. Much to her chagrin she was discouraged from taking part in any discussion of a political nature. It didn't take long for Davie to discover her views weren't necessarily Liberal so much as ambivalent. When he'd once suggested that members of his party might not agree with her, Charlotte demanded to know why not. 'My ideas are excellent.' To this there was no safe reply a husband could make.

Happily one of her opinions, outside party lines, coincided with a vote taken by the town council. It was on the form the memorial should have. Not a cross, but a representation of a soldier going into battle. The committee had been considering a design submitted by a stonemason from Leeds. When she saw the drawings of an infantryman clutching his rifle and storming a stoop, Charlotte approved. It was announced that the statue was to be erected on St Cuthbert's Green, the best Liberal decision, she told customers, the council had yet taken.

(ii)

That evening, the small group waiting to see John were not the usual commercial travellers; they were prim and correct, staring in front of them as though unaware of each other's existence. The last to arrive was different; he was younger and allowed himself to look disconcerted at the sight of the others. His self-confidence ebbed still further when he discovered he was the only one without an appointment. Mary told him he would have to wait till last.

After interviewing the first three, John said to her, 'Miss Harrison is about the best, I think. She's come with excellent recommendations.' He leafed through them on his desk. 'She put me in mind of Mistress Shields as soon as I saw her.'

'I felt the same,' Mary was less enthusiastic, 'I don't think she would be my first choice, however.'

'No?' John looked surprised.

'I didn't like her!' From his corner, Luke spoke up bravely, 'Please, Pa, she said she used the stick.'

'Quiet, Luke! I permitted you to remain so that I could introduce you to each of them, that is all. You are far too young to pass judgement.' Mary looked at her husband gravely,

312

'She did refer more than once to that cane, John. But before you decide, there's one other applicant. Here's his card.' John examined the pasteboard.

'Mr Frederick Crowther? No mention of any teaching experience?'

'He has a degree,' Mary pointed out, 'and he doesn't have an appointment because he only saw the advertisement this morning.'

'Show him in. And Luke, not a word. Understand?'

Frederick Crowther had come directly from an employment agency and this was his first interview. He shook hands gracefully, even though his own was trembling, and waited until Mary was seated before taking a chair. Catching sight of Luke, he gave a solemn wink. Observing it, John cleared his throat, peremptorily. 'Mr Crowther?'

'I beg your pardon sir, yes. As I explained to your wife, I was unable to apply in writing, as specified. Only heard you required a tutor today, in fact. I jotted down one or two particulars, the agency advised what you might wish to know. Hope this meets with your approval.' The sheet of paper was produced with something of a flourish but John received it far more soberly. Mr Crowther's small stock of courage continued to dwindle. He hunched a little in his chair. Behind the *curriculum vitae*, John noticed it. He remembered the old trader waiting in the Temperance Hall years ago. But this man was young, he shouldn't be downcast, he'd got his future in front of him. What was more, he was a gentleman, which disturbed John far more.

'I would like to ask, Mr Crowther, why you wish to apply for the post? It's not a full-time appointment, simply for five hours per week to teach my son Greek and Latin.'

'Yes, the agency explained that's all it was,' Mr Crowther sighed.

'Then may I repeat my question: why are you applying?' There was a wealth of meaning behind John's words. It implied that the excellent cut of Frederick Crowther's suit, the handmade boots and silk scarf did not belong to a part-time tutor. The young man reddened.

'I need to earn my living, Mr McKie, whatever way I can. You are correct, when you infer I haven't been brought up to it but sometimes, sir, a man has no choice. If after examining my credentials you conclude I am qualified, may I ask that I be considered?'

It was a dejected plea, as if he knew he faced defeat. From her position, Mary had a better view of him. She observed that although Mr Crowther wore excellent clothes, they showed signs of recent mud and wear and he'd forgotten to put on a clean shirt that morning. She also thought he looked hungry.

'We normally take tea about now, Mr Crowther,' she said abruptly, 'would you care for a cup?'

'Oh, yes, please!' He tried not to sound eager but he'd given himself away. Again John caught echoes, this time of himself. He re-read the sheet of paper. The young man turned to Luke.

'So you want to learn Latin and Greek, eh?'

'Yes, please!'

He laughed at the keenness. 'May I know your name? Mine is Frederick Crowther.'

'Luke McKie,' the boy answered shyly. They shook hands. 'I want to learn Latin so I can read this.' Luke thrust one of the new books at him.

'*Caesar's Instructions to the Army*, eh? Good old Caesar. I remember struggling with this at prep school. D'you know anything about Caesar? That he was an epileptic, for instance?'

Luke frowned. 'That must've been jolly difficult for his soldiers,' he said after a pause. 'You never know when a fit's about to start, do you?' Frederick Crowther looked startled.

'My son is to be a doctor,' said John coolly. Frederick's brow cleared.

'Oh, I see. Then you'll know all about fits, I expect. D'you think his aide thrust a spear shaft into his mouth, to stop him biting off his tongue?'

He'd gone too far.

'I think that is sufficient for the moment, Mr Crowther,' John warned. They sat in silence then John checked with him the names of referees and Mary returned with a tray. Even Luke observed how quickly Mr Crowther went through a plate of sandwiches.

'Our intention,' John explained, 'is that Luke be prepared for entrance examination to the grammar school. It is my hope that he'll be considered for one of the Chapman and Ward

314

scholarships since he's currently a pupil in a Darlington elementary school, which is one of the qualifications.'

Frederick Crowther nodded. He didn't know what John was talking about; he himself had been entered for Harrow the day he'd been born and had gone to Oxford because his father and grandfather had done. He'd never sat an entrance examination in his life. It occurred to him that this was an approximation of one, that if he wanted to earn a crust this week, he'd better apply himself.

'All that shouldn't be too difficult, sir, provided this young chap is willing. You are, aren't you, Luke? Keen to work?'

'Oh, yes!' What an odd question.

'You see, sir,' Frederick said cheerfully, 'halfway there already.'

But John wasn't to be charmed as easily as that. Within a few minutes, Mr Crowther was outside and on his way home, regretting his impetuosity. Sheltering from the rain inside the covered market, he cursed again. 'I'm a mean blighter, too,' he told himself, 'I could've saved a couple of those tit-bits for Cis.'

(iii)

John naturally intended to offer the post to Miss Harrison but for the first time Mary over-ruled him, supported by a silent Luke. She had an answer for each of John's arguments except Mr Crowther's lack of experience. 'He's still young, John. He told you himself he hasn't had to work until now.'

'And you expect me to engage an impecunious gentleman?'

Mary raised her eyebrows.

'I thought you wanted the best for Luke? Mr Crowther's academic background was better than the others, wasn't it? Won't you even consider giving him a trial?'

In the elegant suburb of Harrowgate Hill, the door to a large house swung open as Frederick mounted the steps. A girl asked eagerly, 'Well?' but he looked dejected.

'Sorry, Cis.'

'Oh, Frederick!'

315

Beyond her, he could see the familiar hall was empty of furniture. 'Good grief, have they stripped the place?'

She gave a sob of a laugh. 'Wait till you see the rest of it.' Cecilia Crowther followed her brother into the huge, empty living room, so shabby now that all their possessions had been removed. 'They've left us enough "to see us through to Friday" which was how the man put it.'

'Where?' Frederick was completely dazed by what had happened while he'd been out.

'In the kitchen. Come and see.' She led the way but whirled on him when he tried to offer the consolation. 'Don't be downheartedly, old love. Something will turn up, you'll see – '

'Never say that, Freddy! That was Father's catchword, and look where it's got us.' He caught the force of her anger.

'I'm sorry,' he repeated helplessly. In the kitchen all he could see was a table and two chairs. 'Is this all?'

'It's enough. At least we can sit to eat our meals.'

'Here? What's wrong with the dining room?' She stared.

'That's empty, remember?'

'Is it the same upstairs?'

'Of course. They've left us each a bed till Friday. I had to. plead with them to leave enough blankets.'

Frederick bounded up the staircase, needing to see for himself. She followed, the nervous energy that had sustained her giving way again to anger. 'It's all very well for you to come back and criticize. It's a pity you weren't here while it was going on. Now you tell me you didn't even get the job?'

Frederick was already inside his room. 'My clothes – they're all over the place!'

'No, they're not. I folded them and put them on the bed myself instead of the floor, and I hung your jackets over the chair.' She'd followed him into the room, and now she forced him to look at her. 'Don't complain. They're coming back to take that bed and chair on Friday. They'll be here at seven thirty sharp in the morning, he said. Freddy, we knew this was going to happen. Mr Marks warned us at the funeral. This is what it means to lose everything. Father owed his creditors thousands and even when everything's sold they won't get enough – '

'Creditors!' The weak young face, full of the same charm as

316

the one that had caused all this misery, repeated the word with the same contempt. Fury burst its dam in Cecilia Crowther. Without thinking she hit her brother across the mouth. In the silence they stared at each other.

'Creditors are entitled to their money, Frederick,' her voice was choked. 'Count yourself lucky you weren't here to watch our home being taken away. It was beastly.' She swallowed. 'Wherever he is, I hope our revered parent is suffering for it.'

'Cis!'

'Don't try and defend him, you'll make me even more angry. Everyone's been making excuses, even the Coroner. The balance of Father's mind wasn't disturbed, it was a cowardly act to do what he did and leave us in this mess. It was criminal to gamble away our trust money as well as his own fortune. I won't hear a good word spoken, there wasn't an atom of goodness in him – look at the pickle we're in!' She was shaking with emotion, 'You and I, brought up in idleness, not allowed to train for a career – '

'I know you wanted to go to the university,' he mumbled.

'Thank heaven *you* did, Freddy. You at least have the means to earn a living. I'm terrified when I think beyond next Friday . . . ' He moved away, unable to face her distress, and stood looking out of one of the windows.

'They might have left us curtains,' he said absently. 'Have you heard anything from Aunt Maud yet?'

'No. D'you think I'm looking forward to that?'

'A pity I didn't get the job. I think I could have coped.' He sighed. 'Teaching a kid Latin and Greek so he could go to grammar school, that's about my mark. Encouraging middle-class sprogs to aim higher.'

'Who's child was it?' Cecilia asked dully.

'One belonging to a McKie Brother. You know, where you buy your hats. The mother was nice.' He looked at his sister in alarm. She was crying. 'Here, steady on. It's not that bad, Cis.'

'I know it's silly . . . in the middle of all this . . . but I wonder if I'll ever own a nice hat again!'

Smitten with remorse, he put his arm round her, 'Chin up, old love. You will. Promise. I'll buy you one, somehow.'

Cecilia blew her nose and gave herself a shake. 'No time for brooding. We'd better sort our things. They've left us a tin trunk and a grip each. They took the leather stuff of course.'

'You mean – we should pack?' Frederick was still slow in accepting his plight.

'Yes. Any clothes you can manage without, put downstairs. I've asked Mr Fawcett to call tomorrow. He deals in second-hand suits.'

'My God!'

Later, when Cecilia was wrestling with the oven and bemoaning the fact she'd never learned how to cook, Frederick said hesitantly, 'There was another position advertised at McKies'.'

'Oh?'

'On the agency list. They're looking for a 'prentice lady counter assistant, accommodation and meals supplied.'

Flushed with heat and agitation, she replied, 'I'm a bit old to be apprenticed, Freddy. Look, d'you think you could manage without potatoes? They're still awfully hard.'

'Why not boil 'em a bit longer?' he suggested. 'It might soften 'em. I'm afraid I'm too peckish to do without. Did you have any lunch today?'

'I tried to make toast but I burnt it.'

'Poor Cis. I was given sandwiches at McKies'. Of course the tutoring job didn't include bed and board even if I hadn't flunked the interview.'

Cecilia prodded the potatoes despondently.

'We'll have to go back to Mr Marks. Ask if there isn't some money left to tide us over, until we both find a position.'

They sat under the wavering gas flame eating tough lamb and over-large potatoes that Cecilia hadn't known she should chop in pieces. The light shone on two heads, one dark and sleek, the other wavy, one determined face, one less so, as sister and brother tried to come to terms with a week that had begun with violence and threatened to end leaving them destitute.

(iv)

'I was strongly advised by our solicitor, Mr Mark, to go as governess to a suitable family. He does not approve of trade,

I'm afraid.' The voice was low, clear and decisive, a firmer echo of her brother's but again John was disturbed by the upper-class air, the apparent self-confidence, in Cecilia Crowther. 'It is my brother who is good with children,' she continued, 'I regret I have very little empathy with them.'

John gave a slight nod of acknowledgement. Despite misgivings he'd allowed Mary to prevail and Luke appeared to be enjoying lessons with young Crowther. John could not fault them, either. Whenever he questioned the boy, progress was apparent. Mary had suggested an evening meal in addition to the low fee they were paying; the tutor had accepted with alacrity. Now his sister was applying for the most menial position in the emporium, a woman of an age and class he would normally expect to find arranging dinner parties for her husband's guests. It was a mystery. Also, she was exceedingly handsome. This didn't occur to John because he didn't see it; nevertheless its effect was to make him more uneasy.

She'd brought a reference from the solicitor. John perused it again but it gave no clues. All it told him was that Miss Cecilia Crowther, recently orphaned, was the daughter of a gentleman and would be found trustworthy.

'Do I take it, Miss Crowther, that you have no employment at present?'

'Until my father's recent death, and the sale of our home that followed it, I have not needed to work, Mr McKie. I've been living on a temporary basis with an aunt at Barnard Castle. The arrangement suits neither of us; she resents having to offer me a roof and refers to the circumstance constantly. I wish to escape that humiliation.'

'The work here is arduous. I do not think you will find it any kind of escape, Miss Crowther, not after the life to which you've been accustomed.' John's quiet voice softened the severe words but she had to impress him if she was to succeed and Cecilia was desperate.

'I need to earn my living and provide a home for myself, hence I wish most earnestly to apply for the position you are advertising. I am prepared to work hard, to submit to those in authority with a good grace – my aunt is trying to break my spirit, Mr McKie. I will scrub floors rather than let that happen!' Her lip was quivering but John still needed to know more.

'Does your brother . . . can he not provide for you?'

'Frederick is staying temporarily with an old school friend but he too will have to find proper lodging when he can afford it. He's looking for additional employment of course but we've discovered there is a slump in Darlington at present. The agency could offer little choice.'

'And your father – was unable to leave you a sufficiency?' John asked at last. She stared at him; was there one person in Darlington who didn't know? Obviously Freddy had managed to avoid telling. Cecilia decided to make a clean breast of it.

'My father gambled away our inheritance after he'd spent his own in the same manner. He left debts totalling twenty-eight thousand pounds. Everything has had to be sold, including my mother's jewels, which had been left to me. My brother and I were allowed fifty pounds each by the creditors, out of pity at the way my father ended his life . . . ' As John still looked blank she took a deep breath. 'My father went out to High Force and blew his brains out with a shotgun. It was in the newspapers.'

'Good Heavens!' That Crowther! John experienced a mixture of emotions including anger that young Crowther hadn't already told him. 'Some tea, perhaps?' It was banal but it meant he could leave the study to tug at the rope and John needed a few moments to recover. He'd ask Mary to stay when she brought the tray; this young woman was too disturbing altogether. Nor had she wept, when describing her father's terrible end. John expected that of any woman. His attitude toward her hardened very slightly.

'Do I take it, Miss Crowther, you have no other resources than your fifty pounds?' She inclined her head.

'Had Frederick or I had the slightest notion how bad things were . . . I fear our family has an ability for spending money, not saving it Mr McKie.'

'I trust you do not inherit the trait, Miss Crowther.' She flushed scarlet. John said quickly, 'I'm sorry, that was extremely rude. What I wished to ascertain was whether you have the means to support yourself other than your small amount of capital? You must keep that intact as long as you can.'

Cecilia bit her lip in an effort to stay calm and answer such intimate questions from a stranger. Frederick had been so casual in his description of John, she hadn't expected anything so rigorous.

'My aunt treats me as a guest, I have no expenses while I remain with her although, as I've indicated, I must leave as soon as I can.' He pondered. Miss Crowther was so much older – twenty-five, was it? Certainly not what he'd had in mind. And yet . . . Thinking ahead as usual, he knew he would eventually need the equal of Mr Hart, in Ladies' Apparel. Charlotte was in the shop less and less nowadays because of Davie's career. In John's opinion, the emporium deserved nothing other than wholehearted commitment; perhaps, if this woman took to the work, it would prove advantageous in the long run?

'We cannot offer you accommodation here,' he said suddenly, coming to one decision.

'But . . . Your advertisement stated quite clearly . . . !' She was agitated, it was the only reason she'd applied.

'Pray hear me out, Miss Crowther. It's true we accommodate employees and I believe we're the only firm in Darlington to do so. My brother and I decided right at the beginning that we could not expect young men and women to travel home late at night alone, at a time when horse trams were infrequent. And we wanted to be able to employ suitable applicants from further afield. We also supply two cooked meals a day because we would not expect anyone to work long hours without proper sustenance. But neither the meals nor the accommodation are of a luxury nature, Miss Crowther. We are a shop, not a hotel. Our lady assistants who require to live in do so in a dormitory. You, I fancy, have never shared a bedroom?'

Miss Crowther's cheeks were very bright indeed. She hadn't considered this aspect. How would she manage, could she bear it? John was speaking again.

'What I propose, if you are agreeable, is a room in one of our houses in Coburg Street. My brother and I own property there and let out rooms. The houses are properly managed; you would be chaperoned, it would be a respectable situation although, I fear, in much more modest circumstances than . . . ' He looked at her former address, 'Harrowgate Hill.'

'Those days are gone,' she whispered.

'Quite. Well, Miss Crowther, I am prepared to offer you the

321

position as I have described it, at a wage of fifteen shillings per week during your apprenticeship. The rent for a room in Coburg Street will be four and sixpence plus an extra shilling for washing linen. For meals here, we deduct two and sixpence, a nominal amount as I'm sure you'll agree.

'After six months, provided you have proved yourself suitable, there will be an increment of two shillings, then sixpence annually until your wages reach the maximum of eighteen shillings and sixpence, which is sixpence higher than any comparable establishment. When you have considered the matter, perhaps you would be good enough to communicate your decision? Ah, here's my wife with some tea.'

Cecilia Crowther responded mechanically to the introduction, peeling off a glove that had cost two guineas to accept the cup from Mary. Kitchen ware, she noted automatically, not what she was accustomed to. Eight shillings a week to live on? How would she survive on that? Clothes, for instance. She would have to wear black in the shop, well she'd plenty of that, thank goodness, but a holland overall – could she purchase one for eight shillings? Cecilia had no idea what such garments cost.

She drank the tea thankfully; she hadn't had such a strong cup for days. She and Freddy had had to eke out supplies and her aunt was so mean the beverage was almost colourless. Cecilia examined Mary as she spoke of some private business to John. How strange Mr McKie should marry such a plain woman.

There was a tap at the door; Katriona had brought Luke to bid his father goodnight. John excused himself. Miss Crowther sipped her tea. Goodness, how the man lit up at the sight of his son! And what a vivid, attractive child, so unlike either parent.

She considered: what age would John McKie be? His was one of those faces it was difficult to judge, grave and impassive throughout the interview, those serious grey-brown eyes never wavering. His suit was old-fashioned, not nearly as elegant as Freddy's, but then her brother was a bit of a masher! Cecilia smiled fondly. More than one of her friends had attempted to ensnare him last season, before . . .

She forced herself back to the present. Mary was asking if she'd like more tea and Cecilia accepted despite an inclination to refuse. Such strong liquid trickling through her might give courage when it came to facing her aunt tonight. She could imagine the derision when she revealed her plans, for she had decided she would accept. Cecilia had no other option. Mary was speaking to her now, explaining the daily routine. Up at six AM!

'Miss Crowther would be living at Coburg Street,' John interrupted.

'Oh, I see.' Mary turned back to her. 'Then it will be five-thirty if you are to be here in time, Miss Crowther.'

Cecilia's brain accepted the information but was numbed by it. Five-thirty! Even at her aunt's, the maid only lit her bedroom fire at seven o'clock, never a minute earlier. As she listened, she revised her opinion of Mary. Mrs McKie wasn't plain when she spoke, the eyes were too intelligent. They watched her calmly, noting the fashionable dress, the autocratic manner, above all the beauty of face and figure. 'Is there anything you would like to ask us?'

'No thank you, Mrs McKie.' Cecilia rose. At the other side of the study, John was engrossed with Luke and the nursemaid, whose Scots accent was difficult for Cecilia to understand. Mary called,

'John, dear, Miss Crowther is leaving.'

'I beg your pardon.' Immediately the father changed back into a businessman. 'You will contact us when you have considered the matter?'

'I already have, Mr McKie. I wish to accept.' He nodded, understanding the need for immediacy.

'One moment . . . ' He reached into the desk and they all heard the clink of coins. John folded a piece of paper round them on which he'd scribbled something. Taking the money, Cecilia felt the first of many humiliations; this wasn't like being given a dress allowance.

'That is a loan, Miss Crowther, so you needn't draw on your capital. I will speak to Mrs Beal – her address is written there. She will accommodate you until your regular room is available. And we will expect you here on Monday by seven. Lady apprentices begin half an hour before the other assistants.

He saw her off the premises the back way, another new experience, he guessed, and returned to the study. Luke and Katriona had vanished; Mary was collecting the cups.

'Miss Crowther is to be engaged then?' There was no inkling of feeling in her voice but John found himself answering defensively. 'She needs to earn her living just as her brother does.'

'Yes, I assumed it was the same family. I read the account of the case in the newspapers.'

'You didn't tell me?'

Mary shrugged. 'Luke is enjoying his lessons, there seemed no point. I do not necessarily blame children for the sins of their fathers.' Piqued that she should assume he might, John said quickly, 'I had a valid reason for engaging Miss Crowther, not as a counterhand but a possible replacement should Charlotte wish to devote more time to Davie's affairs.'

'Ah yes, of course. Forgive me. It's simply that Miss Crowther appeared, well . . . too superior in manner to adapt. May I make a suggestion?'

'By all means?'

'Considering the furore caused by her father's death and her own change of circumstance, could she not commence training in the stockroom? She would then be invisible to any acquaintance visiting out of curiosity. No doubt their interest will soon flag but it might enable Miss Crowther to settle to her new life more easily.'

The suggestion was sensible. John agreed and held open the door. 'Did anything else strike you about her?'

'She's the most attractive woman I've ever seen.'

'Is she really? I hadn't noticed.' No more he had, Mary saw with relief.

'All the same,' she said drily, 'I don't think Charlotte will miss seeing it. You'd better warn Davie.'

(v)

Cecilia Crowther sat very still. Realization of what she'd done bore down so heavily she felt she couldn't breathe. She knew this part of Darlington existed, with its rows of terraced houses, but she'd never been here before, never set foot inside. Now she was to live here.

From her narrow window she could look down on the yard,

324

at the coal store and privy, the ashpit shared with the next house forming a link in a chain that continued to the end of the terrace in either direction. She could see a tin bath hanging from the back wall: who on earth used that? Then she remembered, the 'gentleman' lodgers. Cecilia herself would have to find a public wash-house.

Beyond the wall was the alley up which, Mrs Beal told her proudly, scavengers came at least once every week to clear the night soil. Horse droppings from their carts still littered the cobbles, each mound buzzing with flies. The sight made her feel sick. Cecilia moved back to the one small chair and stayed there.

Downstairs she'd already made a bad impression. Mrs Beal had done all she could to make this special lodger welcome but Cecilia's reaction was almost rude. First there had been her shock, when stepping directly into the parlour, of finding herself face to face with fellow guests who were foundrymen!' She didn't notice they were all wearing collars in her honour; she could scarcely bring herself to shake hands and welcoming smiles became sullen.

Mrs Beal, grim-faced, led her through the dining room-cum-scullery. As they paused by the slopstone sink and tap, Cecilia knew she was supposed to admire it but didn't understand why. 'Not everyone in Darlington's got one of those!' What, for Heaven's sake?

'What's that?' She pointed to where brick pillars supported a cauldron.

'That's the set-pot, of course, where me and Emily do the washing. There's only half of Coburg Street has them, 'an all. Washing's extra, did Mr McKie explain?'

'Yes . . . ' Evidence was everywhere with shirts, socks and underwear spread out to dry. Cecilia followed her landlady into the yard. The walls were lime-washed. Against a wall a few geraniums struggled towards the sun. Mrs Beal regarded them lovingly. 'I like a bit of a garden.' She flung open the door of the privy with smug satisfaction. 'You won't find a cleaner one in Coburg Street.'

Back up the whitened step – 'Some only does the front, I do both' – into the scullery and up the narrow staircase. Cecilia had time to note mattresses under the table. Mrs Beal had told her she and Emily slept 'out the back', was this what that meant?

Four foundrymen shared the front bedroom – four! Mrs Beal saw the look and her lips compressed. 'They're only in together of a Sunday night. Rest of the week they're on shift – and they always takes their boots off afore coming up so you won't be disturbed.' She slammed the door, leaving Cecilia alone.

Stuck-up? Hoity-toity? Cecilia knew she deserved their censure. She moved over to the window. How close the houses were, back to back, and the stench of those privies! How could Mr McKie expect her to live here?

Freddy had turned traitor when she'd told him of her decision, persuaded to by Aunt Maud. Cecilia must go as a governess, they insisted, not demean herself by working in a shop. Why, standing behind a counter, she might be seen by one of their friends!

Cecilia retaliated; she was the daughter of a man who'd stooped to fraud and killed himself rather than face the consequences, what justification was there in that for family pride? Echoes of the fierce argument came back to her now as she sat shaking in the dingy room. Then she heard another sound, real not imagined this time, of a violin. The performer was struggling but Cecilia recognized the piece: Schubert. How often she'd accompanied it in former days!

Emptying her grip onto the bed, she searched among the pile of music. Still moving quickly for fear of losing her nerve, she ran downstairs and into the parlour.

The foundrymen were in déshabillé now. They'd made the effort earlier but they'd been spurned. Collars were off, jackets slung over chairs and waistcoats unbuttoned. It was Sunday evening, theirs to enjoy. Pipe smoke, forbidden in here every other day, rose in a cloud.

They stared at her. Cecilia's heart was beating fast. She smiled nervously, 'Pray forgive me for interrupting. I couldn't help hearing. As there's a piano, I wondered . . . ?' Sheet music was held out in propitiation. The violinist spoke.

'D'you play then?'

'Yes.'

She removed the embroidered cover, the glass dome with its wax flowers beneath, and lifted the lid. Cecilia sat, and adjusted the height of the stool, on a piano untuned since the day it had been installed ten years previously, began 'Rosamunde'.

326

They didn't let her off lightly for their feelings had been injured. It was suppertime before they let her rise and even so the thanks were stilted. Cecilia Crowther learned not for the first time that slights weren't easily forgiven. It was a valuable lesson for the days that followed.

If she'd mused about possible difficulties, she'd no conception of how bad these might be. As soon as they discovered she was 'different', the other assistants treated her like a leper. Cecilia gritted her teeth: she wouldn't complain, whatever they did, she would stick it out. She did all the worst tasks, the meticulous, boring checking in the stockroom before moving to Dispatch, making up brown-paper parcels until her hands were raw, and more besides. She made a point of being first each morning and was usually among the last to finish. She thought her feet would never cease swelling but she kept on smiling as first Mrs Beal, then the newly wed Mrs Hart, provided hot mustard baths.

By the time she moved to the second house, Cecilia was much wiser. She made a deliberate effort this time to be friendly. If her new landlady had been in awe of her at first this changed when the woman recognized Cecilia's loneliness. Gone were all her former friends from Harrowgate Hill. Mary's assumption had been correct; they came, they whispered to each other and pitied, then they left, seldom to return. Cecilia tried to make the best of it but she had no one to turn to, no shoulder to lean on. In short, she was starved of female company.

Perhaps Charlotte could have befriended her had Miss Crowther not been so beautiful. For his part, Davie behaved extremely carefully. Mary treated her with the same friendly formality she extended to everyone in the emporium. It was correct but it lacked warmth and when, after six months, Freddy left to try his luck in London, financed by Aunt Maud, Cecilia was completely alone. Luke was sorry to see Freddy go and apprehensive when the formidable Miss Harrison was engaged instead. John issued strict instructions forbidding the use of the cane, however, and lessons proceeded amicably.

But Mrs Hart responded to Cecilia's approach. The two reached out across their disparate backgrounds and found more similarities than differences between them. It was Mrs Hart who gave her the strength to go on during the worst days. Then, at the end of three months, came the incident that was to prove a turning point.

A 'first-hand' in Ladies' Mantles, Miss Attewood, was due to meet her future mother-in-law. It wouldn't be an easy encounter. Cedric, her intended, was a catch: he was sole heir to his grandfather's coach-building business, and his mother declared Cedric could have done better than be snared by a shop girl. Miss Attewood needed, therefore, to make a very good impression indeed.

It was Cecilia who suggested diffidently how Miss Attewood's jacket might be made more fashionable, if Mr Hart could be persuaded to give them the off-cuts from his window display. Tackling Mr Hart was child's play for Miss Attewood. Cecilia took the bunches of braid, selected colours skilfully and tacked them in place for the other woman's approval. Lo and behold – a tame garment took on a dashing Cossack-like air. Seeing the intention, the millinery assistant fashioned a Shako, and Miss Attewood was transformed. It only needed the loan of Cecilia's remaining pair of smart boots – handed over with scarcely a murmur – to complete the outfit.

Seeing Cedric's excited reaction, several other young ladies recalled impending social events in their lives and for days, Miss Crowther sewed on frogging and epaulettes till she was heartily sick of it. But it brought rewards as Mrs Hart prophesied it would: Cecilia Crowther was no longer an outsider, she was accepted.

Not long afterwards, requesting a formal interview in the shop, Miss Crowther asked Mr Hart if he'd ever considered a one-colour window? Cecilia didn't approach him in Coburg Street where he was simply her landlord but àfter hours instead when juniors were permitted to speak to their superiors on such matters; she was learning the niceties of behaviour now. Mr Hart admitted he hadn't considered such a proposal nor, in his frank opinion, would it work.

A few days later he was surprised to find a watercolour illustration on the breakfast table. Mrs Hart put bacon and eggs in front of him. 'It's most unusual, Alfred. I don't think I've ever seen a window like it before. Very elegant.'

'What am I supposed to do with it?'

'Show Mr McKie, of course.'

328

He waited until the Friday night discussion. Both men stared at it. 'She did it without you asking her to?'

'Yes, sir, I'd no idea. She brought her paintbox as well as her music, you see.' Mr Hart was well aware he had the prize among Coburg Street lodgers. 'And books, Mr McKie. Miss Crowther has a tin box full of books. I haven't yet had time to put up a shelf for them so she keeps them under the bed. Lends them to my wife, too – '

'This – design,' – as usual, John kept to the point – 'Miss Crowther didn't ask for payment?'

'No, sir. And I certainly didn't offer any inducement. Told her it wouldn't work, as a matter of fact. Perhaps Miss Crowther took that as a challenge. She wants to get on in business, I think. And she has flair, Mr McKie. We've all noticed that.'

John pondered and this time Mr Hart stayed silent. He'd learned to on Fridays in here. John had never wasted anything, in Mr Hart's experience. What would he do with this burgeoning talent?

'If you're agreeable, Mr Hart, I think we might consider – for a trial period only – asking Miss Crowther to work as your assistant on window displays. Is it possible for us to execute this entirely from stock?' John certainly wasn't prepared to go to additional expense, not yet.

'Yes, we can.' Mr Hart was enthusiastic. 'That's why I consider Miss Crowther has been not only skilful but astute. She has selected items from all over the store in that same shade of azure, even linking the lady's slipper to the gentleman's cravat – '

'I take it you are agreeable then?' Mr Hart nodded. 'There cannot as yet, be any increase in remuneration. Not until Miss Crowther proves herself.' But after seven months John took the unprecedented step of asking his assisting display artiste whether she would consider becoming a trainee buyer.

(vi)

It was difficult for Charlotte. Although she recognized that she was no longer giving the emporium her full attention, neverthe-

329

less her opinion in matters of fashion had always been the decisive one. Indeed, until now it had been the only one. John and Davie knew better than to order direct from the suppliers without consulting Charlotte. John knew it was essential she did not feel supplanted in any way now. He dropped a delicate hint; Miss Crowther understood.

For several months, the 'trainee' asked Mrs Davie's advice on everything: French fashion trends, a preference for alpaca for spring coats, even prevailing Darlington taste. Cecilia never made a decision without having it confirmed first. John waited until Charlotte pronounced herself entirely satisfied before sanctioning the appointment. He even arranged it so that confirmation came from Charlotte herself, announcing to customers in the salon how delighted they all were with Miss Crowther's progress and what a reliable person had been chosen to work alongside Mr Hart.

But what of Mary, watching from the shadows? How long, she wondered, before John became aware of Miss Crowther's personal charms? Seeing the way the young woman had so swiftly woven herself into the fabric of their lives did nothing to alleviate Mary's foreboding. Her marriage had reached a static point following the death of their child. John continued to seek comfort from her, never love, and as time passed without any change in his attitude, Mary felt her own life shrivel. She tried to tell herself his love for Luke was compensation enough but she'd grown to know that was delusion.

It was Charlotte who guessed it at and told Davie. They were preparing for bed and he was engaged in the pleasurable task of helping her off with her corsets. Edwardian England had changed the shape of its women, he reflected. Cut free from restraints, waists were nevertheless pulled in tighter than ever, stomachs flattened – but *derrières* were allowed to protrude. After three children, Charlotte's needed no further encouragement nor did her bosom. Indeed it was one of her small consolations, following Miss Crowther's rise, to note how much more superior her own figure was, far better suited to the fashion.

Charlotte undid the two long suspenders attached to the front of her corset whilst Davie untied the silk shoulder ribbons. 'Miss Crowther will be spending more time with John now?'

'I should think she will, yes dearest.' He kissed the creamy-pink skin. 'What makes you say that?'

'She will be unchaperoned.'

He was puzzled. 'She always has been, Charlotte. But then Miss Crowther is a respectable, mature person, she must be at least twenty-five or six.'

'She is still a most attractive woman,' said Charlotte.

'But – what has that to do with it?' Davie was genuinely bewildered. 'You're not suggesting John . . . ? John is married to Mary!'

Charlotte raised both arms so that he could slip the nightdress over her head.

'Yes, he is. But he and Mary are not as you and I are, Davie. You must've noticed?' For a brief moment Davie had a vision of that night in Leeds, the dark ringlets and huge eyes. He blinked: the vision disappeared immediately.

'I'm sure you're wrong, dear. John would never do anything to – to hurt Mary's feelings.' He had to be careful, 'And remember how he dotes on Luke – the trouble he's gone to, to find a replacement for young Crowther. He even visits Miss Harrison during the lessons and helps with the homework – he's a true family man.'

Charlotte nodded in agreement, rubbing her waist where the whalebones had dug into it.

'I'm not denying any of that, nor am I suggesting anything will happen. I merely point out the danger, Davie. Miss Crowther is very handsome. You may not have noticed the reaction of some of our gentlemen customers, but I have. I've not been able to glean much about her personal affairs. There was a caller, I believe, but he disappeared at the time of her father's death because of the scandal. According to Mrs Hart, no one visits her now. Therefore Miss Crowther is unattached.'

'Now I realize, dearest, that this situation won't affect you in the slightest,' Charlotte knew Davie's affection was far stronger than her own. Being unimaginative, she didn't notice how it hurt him to be reminded of it. 'I know it won't,' she repeated, 'but it may disturb John. He's never cared for Mary the way she does for him. He never brings her flowers, for instance.'

This week Davie had surpassed himself and the bouquet on the dressing table glowed with colour. Charlotte pressed her

331

nose into it. 'I don't remember John ever giving Mary a single bloom.'

'He's not that sort of a chap.' Distressed by any criticism of his brother, Davie ran his hand through his curls. 'He buys Luke plenty, twice as many books as I give young Ted.'

'Ted hasn't the same application as Luke. In fact, Davie, I think you should have a word with his headmaster.' John was dismissed from her mind; her son's lack of progress was more important.

332

CHAPTER ELEVEN

Developments

The day the South African Memorial was due to be unveiled promised to be too hot. By breakfast this was already apparent. From his end of the dining table, John observed, 'At least the weather is fine enough for your hat, Charlotte.'

'I must say I'm thankful, Mr McKie.' Charlotte was always formal in front of the assistants. 'It would have been serious if it had rained.'

Young ladies and gentlemen smiled politely. The hat was well known, it had been the most important topic for weeks.

'No doubt Field Marshal Roberts will be glad, too.' Davie grinned. 'I believe his has even more feathers in it than yours.'

'Oh, mine has no feathers! They are not "in" this season.'

Charlotte turned her attention to Miss Attewood. She hadn't married but although she had been disappointed in love, for his mother had engineered Cedric's removal from Darlington, time had brought her some consolation. Miss Attewood was now the emporium's Senior Hand, but as far as Charlotte was concerned this did not bestow permission to transgress rules.

333

'More coffee, Miss Attewood? I thought I'd already poured a second cup?' The Senior Hand blushed, the cup was withdrawn. Two cups and no more was what was allowed for each person sitting at the table.

John looked at his watch and one or two began to rise; it was the signal that work was due to begin. Voices could be heard in the shop below as those who lived out were admitted. The older children were excused from the table and Katriona scooped up Matthew to be cleaned for a second time that morning. 'I am most displeased, Matthew.' His mother was unsympathetic. 'You are quite big enough to manage a cup and saucer.'

Assistants chattered quietly as they went downstairs. Dust covers were removed and given to Billy to put away, blinds were raised and, on the dot of seven thirty, Mr Hart gave the signal for the doors to be unlocked.

At the window upstairs, John watched the August sun shine on new finery; the town was already filling with spectators. Beneath the window one of the new electric tram-cars went past. Beside him Davie asked, 'Have you noticed how much cleaner the High Row is now the horse-trams have been withdrawn? There's scarcely any smell, even on a scorcher like today.' John nodded at one of the roadsweepers standing idly at the corner.

'No doubt he'll soon be looking for work, with all the rest of the unemployed. And your colleagues in the council chamber calling for another war, to solve the problem.' The memorial was still a sore topic between them. 'Has Miss Crowther left for Glasgow?' he asked abruptly.

'She went yesterday evening.' Davie was a little curious. Charlotte's warning about Cecilia's charms had been made ages ago but Davie often remembered it when talking to John. 'Her appointment with the sales manager at Arthur's was for this morning, I believe.'

'I'd forgotten. If she hadn't already left, I was going to suggest taking her place. One of us will have to go to Scotland. This came today. I didn't want you to see it until we were alone.' The letter John held out was in Alex's writing. 'Mother doesn't seem any better. I think one of us should visit, to reassure ourselves. I wondered about taking Luke with me, for a brief holiday. What d'you think?'

Davie handed back the letter. 'I agree. One of us should go.'

'You're too busy, what with this affair and your selection board.'

'True,' Davie admitted. After all this time he was to be interviewed as a parliamentary candidate at last! 'Can you spare a few days?'

'Yes. I'll call at Arthur's on the way.' John couldn't bring himself to rely on a woman entirely. 'I'd like to see what sort of impression Miss Crowther's making on them.'

'I must be off.' Davie picked up the tickets from the top of the sideboard. ' "Admission to the Freedom of the Borough of Darlington, Field Marshal the Right Honourable Earl Roberts",' he read out proudly, ' "And the ceremony of unveiling the South African War Memorial on Saturday Fifth August nineteen hundred and five at two o'clock and afterwards at St Cuthbert's Green".'

'All in the name of glorifying war, at half a crown each with children not even half price!' John was severe. 'And why have you got to get there so early?'

'I told you, as a member of the seating committee –'

'So you did. I'd forgotten that too – it's this business over Mother. Is that why you're dressed up like an Englishman, because you're on the seating committee?' Davie was resplendent in his kilt.

'No . . . ' he said abashed. 'It's because Charlotte told me I have excellent calves! Besides, she wants me suitably dressed to accompany that damned hat!'

'Calves! At her age!' John looked so shocked Davie laughed aloud.

'Come on. A woman's got a right to tell her man he's good-looking once in a while. Don't forget we're closing early because of the ceremony.' Still laughing and shaking his head, Davie ran downstairs and out into the street. John looked down at the red curls towering above the crowd.

So many people in Darlington knew him now because of his council work, Davie could hardly walk along the pavement without being stopped to have his hand shaken. John watched jealously. No one had ever admired his legs; they were as good as Davie's even if they were a bit shorter but no one had commented, not even Miss Crowther. 'Now why on earth should I think that?' he whispered, startled. He strove to recover

335

from the pounding in his chest but something else alarmed him.
'I'm going to be late at the warehouse!'

Red tunics and brass glittered. Luke gazed fascinated at the
sweat on a soldier's face. Drops trickled onto the man's eyelids,
splashing his cheeks as he blinked involuntarily. It was his only
movement. Luke followed the course of each drop downwards
as they plopped onto the brilliant red chest. He licked the sweat
round his own mouth and the taste lingered. How much salt did
a man have inside him? He would ask Dr Cullen at their next
question and answer session. Luke loved these lessons best of
all.

Ten last month, Luke was on course for his career. He'd
passed for the grammar school a year early and was waiting to
hear whether he'd been awarded a scholarship. Father had
already asked what he'd like as a reward if he had. Perhaps a
new fountain pen? There was a splendid one in Bowser's
window in Prebend Row – could he take Father past it casually,
next time they went for a walk?

Young Ted grabbed him by the shoulder. He was almost the
same height now, broad and sturdy, his carroty hair in wild
spikes with excitement. 'Look at the band!'

More brass glittered, fierce reflections dazzled them, then the
sound: thump . . . thump . . . thump, the drum was like a heart-
beat. Horses swishing angry tails came in a ragged line, irritated
by flies and the slow pace of the march. They sweated too, Luke
saw, great ripples of lather shimmering across their flanks.
Behind the Durham Light Infantry, the Darlington Volunteers –
Hurrah! These were the men who'd been out there – and had
returned. Suddenly the great man was opposite their stand.
Cheers from well bred throats lost all sense of restraint, lace
handkerchieves waved in abandon. The crowd went hysterical
at the sight of the man who'd led their sons into battle, and seen
them die.

The famous warrior bowed slightly, touching the brim of his
hat to the stand. A much smaller man than they'd expected, a

puppet astride his charger. Charlotte inclined her head in reply, equally cautious. Poise had to be maintained and the hat was extremely large. Young Ted was jumping up and down in ecstasy now, 'Look, Papa, look! The band!' He knocked askew the straw boater on the head of the man in front and leapt in the air shouting, 'Hurrah!' This was wonderful, he wanted to be a soldier!

There were speeches, long and scarcely heard. The ribbon was pulled, the memorial revealed. A bronze rifle gleamed dull gold against the massive grey bulk of St Cuthbert's, sightless eyes stared blindly at the enemy as the soldier stood forever poised in his headlong rush. More cheers and sobs. A woman near the front collapsed. Charlotte learned the following day that the aunt of Trooper Ianson had found the likeness so great, she'd imagined her nephew had returned. 'What a comfort it must be,' customers told each other, 'she can imagine she's looking at him each time she walks past. And his name's on the plinth too, you know.'

They stood for hours, Davie among the honoured ones escorting the great man. It gave Charlotte particular satisfaction to watch him on official duties. There was no one else to compare with that handsome figure. Her head went higher on the proud neck.

At last they were out of the sun and refreshments were offered, chicken and wine. Davie shook his head. 'I'm not feeling too grand . . . the heat, Charlotte. Here, Ted, Luke – you have my share.' He was pale and Charlotte made a mental note to put a dose of senna to soak overnight. It was her universal remedy and the very threat of it cured most ills.

(ii)

John handed Davie the telegram as soon as he walked through the door. Children eddied round them excitedly. 'From Mistress Shields?' said Davie, surprised.

'It must be serious,' John replied quietly. 'I've a bag packed. I was only waiting till you got back.'

'What is it? What's the matter?' Charlotte was defending her skirt from Ted's attack.

'Mother is ill, dearest. Mistress Shields bids one of us go up straight away.'

'I suggested to Davie this morning that I go, Charlotte. We didn't know then how serious it was.'

'Does she say that it is?'

'No,' John answered simply, 'but why else would she go to the expense of a telegram?'

Billy had the dog-cart outside the door. John stopped to kiss Luke. 'Look after your mother while I'm gone.' The boy looked solemn and reached for Mary's hand. 'I will write as soon as I can, Davie, to let you know how matters stand.'

'As soon as possible, John.'

They crowded into the doorway to see him go. In the excitement, Charlotte forgot all about the senna.

(iii)

Two letters and another telegram arrived the same day one week later. Davie had just finished reading the second letter when Bertha came in.

'I've told the boy to wait, sir.' Charlotte watched Davie's face.

'In a minute or two, Bertha, thank you.' She asked more gently, 'Will you go up for the funeral, dear?'

'Yes, I must.'

'Shall I accompany you?'

'No thank you, Charlotte. Stay with the children. I'll take the night train. Would you arrange for Billy to take me to the station?' He hurried out and up to their room. In privacy he looked again at the brief message: 'Mother died today. Funeral Monday. Please come. John.'

(iv)

A sea fret rolled in, smoothing indentations in the ground, filling the newly dug grave. John and Davie, Alex and Alla

338

faced each other, holding the ends of the cords. Gaelic was the only sound in the stillness. Occasionally Davie had to make an effort to understand; English was his first language now.

How little they had known their mother, he and John. She was their entire world once but since leaving the croft, apart from that one brief holiday, they'd had no contact. Alex had always written the letters. Since they left, her life had been spent in the shadow of her man, caring for him as once she'd devoted herself to them. How much she'd cared had been revealed to Davie yesterday evening.

'She knew what was to happen ever since we visited the specialist in Fort William,' Alex told him. Davie looked at John for confirmation.

'The visit was made last May, apparently.'

'But why didn't you tell us?' Davie demanded.

'Your mother wouldn't let me. She said it might interfere with your business and as there was nothing to be done – '

'We could have visited one last time!' They'd been speaking softly in the croft, as if they might disturb the deep sleep of the figure in the coffin. Alex's eyes filled with tears.

'I wanted for you both to do that, to see her again, but Jeannie wouldn't have it. She was in great pain. I couldn't disobey her wish, Davie.'

'Leave it!' John whispered urgently. Turning to his father he said gently, 'Why not show Davie what she's done for all of us?' Alex led the way through to the bedroom. They followed, guilt making them eager to escape death's presence.

'These parcels are for the bairns at Christmas.'

'Christmas!' The house was cold enough now he thought; the fire had been put out as soon as Jeannie died and would not be re-lit until after the funeral; but to consider festivities at this time seemed like sacrilege. Alex explained gently.

'After we'd visited the specialist your mother said it would be a shame to waste the journey so we bought these gifts for the young ones.' Never thinking to spend money on herself, thought Davie savagely. He and John took the packages, wordless at the sight of each careful inscription in the writing John had taught her years ago.

'Your mother set great store by her mementoes.' Alex was

rummaging in a box, 'See here. These are John's letters in eighteen ninety-eight.' They stared at each thick bundle.

'Did she keep every one we ever wrote?'

'Oh yes,' Alex smiled, 'You don't think your mother would part with anything that reminded her of you, do you? Look at this.' Inside a fishing creel were the first two pairs of boots, now so old the leather was crumbling.

'What will you do with all this?'

'Keep it,' Alex said, surprised. 'It'll bring Jeannie back, looking at things the way she used to.'

There was a tap at the outside door. 'That will be the first of them,' he nodded. 'They will all be here by morning.'

Throughout the night neighbours and friends arrived to sit in vigil until the small room overflowed and newcomers had to wait their turn.

As each one stared at the smooth white face and murmured, 'Aye, she's at peace now. No more pain,' Davie thought his heart would burst. What agony she must have suffered, and they hadn't known.

It was dawn, grey and cold, when Alla stirred. He looked at Alex who said tiredly, 'Aye. It's time, right enough.' A final lingering look before he let them fit the lid and hammer in the nails. Friends lifted the coffin onto the waiting donkey cart and began the slow procession up the track.

Last night John had wondered if it might rain. 'I hope not,' Davie replied, 'that churchyard is a drear place even on a fine day.' But the soft mist still lingered as they lowered Jeannie into her grave. Alex sighed. He hadn't spoken since they left the croft.

'Poor lassie. She always felt the cold so.'

(v)

They tried to persuade him to come back with them but Alex was adamant. 'No, no. I cannot live in a town at my time of life. It was all bustle when we visited the man in Fort William. Two motor cars passed each other while we stood and watched! I've no doubt Darlington is worse. No, I'll stay where I belong.'

'But how will you manage, Father?'

He smiled sadly. 'The way I've been doing ever since your mother took to her bed, John. There's friends all around me here, you know. Wee Georgie's daughter comes up with oatcakes twice a week. Everyone has a bit fish to spare for Alla and me when the catch is good.'

Davie managed a grin. 'Does that mean the fishing has been better, Father?'

'Well now, it has . . . There's a new ghillie at the Big House, d'you see. A very important sort of a man, from Berwick.' And Alex paused to shake his head that anything good could come out of the lowlands. 'What would a man from Berwick know about the hills? Or the way the deer run? Nothing, I tell you. Oh, there's been good eating since he came. On the crofts we're all very grateful to Mr Manners for appointing him.'

(vi)

They couldn't dissuade him but he walked back with them as far as the ferry. They stopped at the school house to shake hands with Helen. John had something he wanted to show her: Luke's first Latin exercise book. He'd managed to interest Jeannie in it before she'd died. The poor woman had stroked the page tenderly, 'He's a grand scholar, then, John?'

Mistress Shields was more critical. 'Tell the boy to revise his verbs. Conjugation must rest on a firm foundation.'

'He is only ten.'

That was a silly excuse.

'So were you when we reached this stage. Tell Luke to stick at it – he must if he wants to go to university.'

'Yes, Mistress Shields.' Alex put the crab in the sink. They hadn't spoken. Helen was unable to meet his eye.

'*Tempus fugit*, Mr McKie . . . I will call next time I'm passing.'

'That is kind of you.' Davie hugged her and hurried outside.

They watched their father until the boat had rounded the curve of the loch. Rhododendrons still bloomed in some crevices. Scents of myrtle, birch and spruce made the air rich following the rain. As the gap between them widened, the old man still stood though he did not see them for tears.

'I fear he's said goodbye for ever.'

'Oh, Davie, surely not?' The last few days had taken their toll. John gripped the rail and stared back anxiously. 'Father's strong and fit. Look how he can still handle the beasts.'

'That's not the point – how often are *we* likely to come back? What with the emporium and the children?'

'We'll come for holidays!'

'I doubt it,' sighed Davie. 'Charlotte's already decided on Seaton Carew or West Hartlepool this summer. She claims she cannot face the long journey.'

'Mary's not likely to come,' John admitted, 'her life up here was so unhappy. But that doesn't mean that you and I can't manage it.' The truth depressed him. 'We must try, we must make the effort.'

'Yes . . . I wish I could believe it but somehow I don't think we will. And it's all so beautiful up here.'

'Is it?' John looked about in surprise. He hadn't considered the landscape. Beauty for him was the salon or a window dressed to perfection by Mr Hart. Up here there was only nature, after all.

During the journey he grew more restless. Added to guilt over Jeannie – why hadn't she let Alex write, surely she'd wanted to see both of them one more time? – was another harsher reality.

'We've failed haven't we, you and I?'

'What?' Davie had been trying to immerse his sorrow in a book of poetry. 'What did you say?'

'They had such high hopes of us. Look at the sacrifice they made.'

'But surely?' Davie was bewildered, 'We've achieved something. What about the emporium?' He had a sudden flicker of anxiety. 'All's well, isn't it John? I know I'm lazy. I leave the business side entirely to you nowadays – '

'No, no. Everything's fine. You can see the figures any time you like.'

'Thanks, but I'd rather leave it to you. If it's not the business, and it certainly can't be Luke, he's doing so well, what is troubling you?'

Why not ask about Mary, thought John irritably, why assume because Davie and Charlotte were happy, the rest of the world was equally contented.

'We haven't done enough,' he replied. It was too vague, too lame.

'D'you want us to move to bigger premises? We're bursting at the seams where we are. Maybe we should open another branch? Or has the time finally come to consider London?'

That dream of long ago. Davie was half inclined to think it would remain a dream. Certainly *he* was happy to stay where he was. Even to consider such a step would destroy their peace, apart from any financial risk. 'If you think it has come, I'm willing to try,' he offered bravely.

'No, it's not that.' Davie tried to conceal his relief.

'What, then?' Did he sound too cheerful? John didn't appear to notice. He stood, hands in pockets, brooding at the distant mountains as if seeking an answer there.

'D'you think you'll be chosen as parliamentary candidate this time?' he asked at last. So that was it. It was Davie's fault after all.

'I doubt it, and I fear Charlotte is of the same opinion. She scolds me,' he sighed. 'She says I don't try hard enough.'

'I didn't accuse you of that.'

'No, John, but I think it's at the back of your mind. In some ways it's true. I don't – put myself about enough. Among people who matter. But you see, there's always so much going on in Darlington.' Davie shrugged deprecatingly. 'I never ask to be seconded to all those committees but I always seem to be. I think,' he said ingenuously, 'it's because I can see both sides of a question. I never find I get heated like some of them. If there's an argument, well – you know what happens. I bring 'em back for a cup of tea and a chat, to smooth things over. And Charlotte's always there,' his eyes lit up. 'Some of my fellow councillors, they'd feel cheated if I sent them back home without a glimpse of my lovely girl. All the same,' and Davie shook his head in despair at such behaviour, 'it's not the way for an ambitious man. And that's what the Liberals will be seeking.'

John continued to stare out of the window. There was no

343

doubt about Davie's popularity. As for ambition? That also was true. Davie hardly knew the meaning of the word. His brother had begun examining his pocket book.

'See here. Tomorrow for instance. There's a meeting of the park sub-committee. They want to build a tea-house of some sort. Then there's the visit of the Chinese Delegation and I'm on the welcoming party. Now that Darlington's to be a County Borough . . . I never have a moment to myself. Look, John.' Davie flicked through the pages, 'No wonder Charlotte complains I don't see enough of the children – '

'But do you want to become an MP?' John toppled the protective house of cards Davie had fashioned for himself. 'Ever?'

Stripped of everything but a sense of guilt, Davie admitted, 'No. I don't think I do. I'm sorry, John, after the hopes you had for me.' Held up for examination, tea-houses and visiting delegations weren't the stuff of government. Had he achieved nothing after all, since leaving the croft? Suddenly Davie experienced the same lassitude he'd felt at the Memorial ceremony. 'I'm not the man to do it, John, that's the truth. Charlotte would have been the better choice for politics, had it been possible.'

John frowned. He'd never found that idea amusing. 'In answer to your question, Mistress Shields doesn't think we've gone very far,' he said. 'You could see it in her eyes. And she asked, as we were leaving, what else you and I intended to do with our lives.'

So that was the nub of it. It didn't matter that Jeannie had died valuing them both so highly, what mattered was the school mistress's esteem.

'Hers isn't the only opinion,' Davie ventured.

'We're in danger of lowering our standards,' John warned. 'Can't you see it? We're sitting back, complacent. It's a failing when a man thinks he's reached a plateau in his life. I've seen it happen.'

I have reached it, Davie wanted to protest, I'm content. I've three healthy children, a wife I adore, what more do I need? He remained silent, humbled by John's stern appraisal. He didn't understand that although John had Luke, he also had Mary. But this time, John wasn't thinking about her: this time, for some odd reason, he was dreaming about Miss Crowther.

Billy was at the station. Taller now and in a jacket fashioned by old MacArthur to conceal his over-long arms, he could speak more fluently too, thanks to Mary's coaching.

'We've got too much luggage, Billy,' Davie told him. 'We called at the wholesalers in Glasgow. You take the baskets in the cart, and Mr John and I will find a cab.'

'Right, Mr Davie. There's tea ready and waiting for you.' It was a heavy load. John looked at Blackie doubtfully.

'Are you sure she can manage? I didn't realize we'd collected so much.' Billy grinned.

''Er needs to get a bit of fat off 'er, don't you worry, sir.' They waited to see him go before calling a hansom. At the foot of the incline their driver pulled up sharply. Davie opened the trap. 'Anything amiss?'

'A motor car, sir. Always gives the mare a fright.' Davie settled back.

'Perhaps we should consider selling the pony and investing in one of those.'

'What on earth for? Ponies are more reliable. You seldom see one of those broken down in the street. You mustn't get carried away by each new idea, Davie. A pity you weren't at the debate the Lit and Phil had on the subject, it would've amused you.'

It was late before John had worked through the papers on his desk and dealt with the last of the problems. He took off his pince-nez and rubbed the sore spot on his nose. There was a tap at the door and Luke stood there, pink from his bath, ready for bed. Mary was with him, carrying the usual tray. John held out his arms and the boy rushed into them. He'd soon be too grown up for that, John thought, burying his face in the dark hair. 'I've missed you, Luke.'

'So've I, Dada. Was Grandfather very sad?'

'Yes. We all were . . . ' John recovered himself. 'Luke, there's something you and I have to discuss. Mistress Shields

345

found some mistakes in your Latin. You're to learn your verbs more thoroughly. When she told me of it, I was disappointed.'

The boy flushed crimson. 'I'm sorry!'

'There is still time so don't worry too much. But you must be more sure of them before you can progress.' Seeing Luke's emotion, John felt near to tears himself. 'You still want to be a doctor, don't you?'

'Oh, yes!' It was a shout, not a whisper this time. 'I'm going to Newcastle University. Dr Cullen says it's the best in the world. He went there.'

'I must have a word with Dr Cullen – '

'And then I'm going to study some more and be a surgeon, to make Mama's foot better. We've discussed it, you see.'

'Well, you concentrate on your Latin otherwise you won't become anything.'

'Yes, Dada.' He got down from John's lap, kissed him and hugged Mary fiercely. As the door closed behind him she said, 'You've upset him.'

'I know, I know.'

'There weren't so many mistakes, were there?'

'No, but – '

'Then don't be too hard on him.' She put his empty cup back on the tray. 'He'll get to university, never fear. He's set his heart on it.'

'What's all this about Newcastle? I want him to go to Oxford.'

'You'd better stay in one evening when he and Dr Cullen are discussing it. Luke would like you to be there but you're so often working late, or at the Institute.' There was a slight edge to Mary's voice. 'I know you take pride in him but sometimes I feel you've distanced yourself. You see us as objects, to be assessed, and judged.'

Immediately John withdrew into his shell. 'I want Luke to do well,' he said mechanically. Mary picked up the tray.

'I hear from Davie that your father intends staying on the croft. I think he's wise to do so. It would be a completely different world for him here, no cattle or land for him to tend – '

'It was not my intention he should work,' John interrupted coldly. 'I wanted him to have comfort in his age.'

346

'But what would he do in Darlington?' Mary persisted. 'He's still very active, Davie says, as restless as you sometimes.'

'I? Restless?'

'Yes, John,' she replied calmly. 'I often wonder if you'll ever be at peace. Now, when you are ready, we have a rabbit pie for your supper.'

(viii)

In their bedroom on the first floor, Davie closed the door and came eagerly to Charlotte, 'My dear love . . . ' Her arms tightened round him almost as passionately.

'I've missed you, Davie.' Shutting that door meant complete privacy. Respectability, demeanour, a stately attitude toward their customers, Charlotte shed them all. In here she inhabited a different world known only to herself and Davie; not even the children were permitted trespass. Oh, the luxury of gazing into Davie's eyes now, seeing how much he cared! 'My dearest, what a weary time you've had.'

'No, no.' He pushed it aside, he wanted her too much to remember unhappiness. 'It's all in the past now.'

Closing her eyes, Charlotte leaned against the strong body, letting go of her senses. Davie watched her avidly, never taking his eyes from her face. 'My beautiful girl!'

With her matronly figure he no longer referred to her as his 'little savage'. Secretly, Charlotte was glad. Somehow that phrase had always made her uncomfortable. One had a certain minimum dignity to maintain, however abandoned one became in bed.

Davie undid each of his wife's garments tenderly as he helped her undress. There was no need to hurry, he could savour each moment. He was full of joy by the time his wife revealed herself. And Charlotte basked in his love, revelling in its intensity until she felt consumed.

'Oh love, oh Charlotte . . . Thank you!'

'Dearest . . . '

When it was over and he lay exhausted against her breast, she stroked the dark red curls. 'I feel so safe now you're home,

347

Davie.' What matter the other twenty-five occupants slumbering in the emporium, he was the only one that mattered. Still holding him she remembered one disappointment he'd had to face on his return. 'It was unfair of the Liberals. How could you have stayed to attend the selection board? I protested of course but they'd already chosen a candidate.'

Davie chuckled and the movement tickled her soft skin. 'How like you to think of Liberals at a time like this!'

Charlotte was offended. 'I was only concerned that you would be disheartened.'

'Not really. I partly expected it.' He looked sad. She didn't want to harp on failure; to divert him, she said charmingly, 'Thank you for my beautiful flowers.' There were so many they overflowed her dressing table into the empty hearth. Davie smiled eagerly,

'I wanted to please you.'

'I'm astonished John allowed you to take a cab via Kent and Brydon's,' she was mock-solemn. Davie grinned.

'He was very put out but I'd had enough of his scolding by then. When he began to lecture I made some excuse and went back inside the shop. Told them I'd forgotten to order a *second* bouquet of two dozen red roses –'

'Oh, Davie – not more!'

'Not for you, for Mary. I've arranged to have them delivered here tomorrow with a note: "From an unknown admirer".'

'Oh, my!'

'And left instructions for the account to be sent to John.'

'Davie!' But Charlotte laughed as heartily as he did. 'He'll be so angry – and I shan't be able to keep a straight face!'

'Oh, you must. For Mary's sake.'

'You know, I don't think he's bought her a single bloom in his life,' she said, meditatively.

'He's not such a bad chap,' Davie was defensive. 'And he worries on our behalf constantly.'

They lay silent for a moment or two before she asked, 'Was it very distressing up at the croft?'

'Father was brave but he's lost one half of himself.'

'Davie, hold me tight!' Blot out all thought of death, keep me from the terrors of the night.

348

'My love!'

She hugged him close and feeling his tears mingle with her own remembered that other time when Aunt Armitage had had to console her. As Davie described Jeannie's pallid lips, Charlotte thought of her own mother lying in the dark earth beneath the angel.

They made love a second time, Davie's skin feverish against her own. When he rolled over to his side of the bed she asked, 'Are you ill?'

'No. It's more than tiredness though. Something John said troubles me.'

'What is that?'

'He thinks that we haven't – achieved enough.'

Charlotte leaned on her elbow. 'In what way?' she asked, 'Because you weren't chosen by the Liberals?'

'Not entirely – '

'That's nothing to do with John,' she interrupted vigorously.

'Charlotte, I may decide I prefer to exist as a small fish in a provincial pond, not try for Parliament again.'

'Nonsense.' His wife was adamant, 'There's always a next time, when you're feeling more energetic. The journey to Scotland, twice in so short a time, has been debilitating, that's all. You need an iron tonic, Davie. I'll see you get one.'

'Yes, Charlotte.'

(ix)

In the morning Davie's joke backfired. The roses arrived at breakfast. Mary read the message and handed the bouquet back to Ada. 'These have been incorrectly addressed. Take them downstairs and give them to Miss Crowther when she arrives, please.'

At his end of the table, Davie dared not glance at Charlotte nor did either of them say a word until they were outside the dining room. Only then did she manage to hiss, 'You must go round to the shop immediately and pay for them. How dreadful if Mary discovered the bill had been sent to John!'

349

Davie went to the door obediently but stopped. 'Don't you find it odd that Mary should refuse the roses? And I wonder what made her think of Miss Crowther?' Charlotte didn't reply. After he'd gone, she shook her head and said to no one in particular, 'Oh dear, oh dear . . .'

CHAPTER TWELVE

A Changing World

Alone in her parlour, Helen Shields re-read John's Christmas letter of 1906. She had been right in her first impression. After telling of everyone's progress there were far too many references to this unknown Crowther person. Helen skipped ahead, counting them under her breath. Four! Why should he imagine she'd be interested in the doings of a shop girl? She wanted to hear more about Mary. 'Hrmmph!'

Luke was doing well; it was to be expected, but Davie worried that young Ted might not pass the examination to the grammar school – that shocked her. If she'd had the teaching of him, Ted would pass. Helen's lips tightened. It was probably discipline or rather the lack of it. Some boys needed it more than others. 'Takes after his mother,' Helen announced disapprovingly.

Jane was having dancing lessons? Ah well, she was Davie's little girl – poetry, dancing, it was all one. And Matthew about to start school – how old would he be, five or six? John's references to him were very brief.

Then followed paragraphs concerning the shop and Helen

tapped the letter impatiently. What did it matter if twenty-seven were employed there now? She wanted to hear more of the family.

Davie failed again to be selected? That was twice he'd been disappointed. She raised her eyebrows. Now that there'd been a Socialist landslide Helen thought Davie's time had come. He might call himself a Liberal but he was more Keir Hardie's man than Campbell Bannerman's. She heartily agreed with the next sentence though: the pensions for everyone promised by this Government would be a Godsend. 'We'll see the end of the poor house yet.'

Another reference to Cecilia Crowther! Helen broke off to pummel the fire with a poker. How old was John now, thirty-six? Old enough to know better! And he and Davie had been elected Members of Session at the church! She sat back and stared into the flames. He'd no financial worries any more so why wasn't he thinking of spreading his wings as Davie was trying to do? Why stay and moon over this Crowther woman, even if he had promoted her to manageress in Ladies' Mantles?

John had enclosed a sales catalogue and Helen glanced at it. The gaudy drawing on the cover must, she presumed, be the emporium. Above it a legend in red declared:

McKIE BROTHERS' ANNUAL SALE WILL ASTON-ISH YOU! LADIES – Can you afford *not* to attend? UNREPEATABLE OFFER! EACH DAY, SIX FREE SHIRTS WILL BE GIVEN TO THE FIRST THREE CUSTOMERS PURCHASING A TWENTY-FIVE SHILLING THREE-PIECE SUIT!!

Shopkeepers! Full of distaste Helen pushed catalogue and letter into a drawer.

(i)

Cecilia Crowther spent her Christmas with Freddie. He'd warned her his lodgings weren't up to much but she was still shocked by the two dismal rooms in North Kensington. They were far less comfortable than her own, nor was there a fire. Cecilia immediately set about improving the situation.

'Gosh, Cis – are you sure you can afford all this?' Freddie was amazed at the amount of food on the table and the scuttleful of coals.

'Of course I can. I'm on a proper salary now. I've even got savings!'

She pulled a face. 'Must be the first time anyone's had spare cash in our family, don't you think?'

'By Jove!' Freddie gave a mock cheer. 'All the same, you won't have any left if you carry on like this.'

'I'll manage. What about you?'

'Oh, I do this and that, you know,' he replied evasively. 'Mostly clerking in the city, but it don't pay much. When funds are really low, I address envelopes as well – '

'Freddie, you can't carry on like that!'

'Hang on a minute,' he protested. 'I've got prospects. Very sound ones. You're going to meet her tonight.'

Cecilia was alert. 'Her?'

'My lady friend, Ethel. She's going to make an honest man of me, so be nice to her. And Cis, don't patronize, there's a pal.'

When Ethel Lever arrived, Cecilia understood why he'd said that. Sturdy, sallow-faced, traces of her ancestry apparent, she would not have been received at Harrowgate Hill. Freddie introduced them awkwardly. Ethel and Cecilia eyed each other.

'Eth, this is my clever sister I'm always prattling about,' Freddie said desperately. 'Risen like a shooting star amid the bonnets and muffs, she has, dear girl. And she's supplied this banquet. So sit you down while I put the kettle on.'

'What about the meeting tonight?' Ethel's accent had a London twang and Cecilia thought it common.

'Oh, dash it!' Freddie cried in dismay, 'I forgot all about that. All right, all right.' He put up a hand to ward off any protests, 'I said we'd go, and we will. We can eat when we get back.' He turned to Cecilia. 'Come with us?'

'What meeting is it?'

'The Women's Social and Political Union.' Ethel looked at her steadily, 'It's at Caxton Hall at seven PM. We have to keep the speakers' names secret, for obvious reasons, but we've been

353

promised great things tonight.' The sallow face was animated now.

Cecilia tried to hide her displeasure. Freddie said nervously, 'You ought go once, Cis. Find out what it's all about.'

'I know what it's about, I read it in the newspapers! Unfeminine women, behaving raucously.' She looked at Freddie coldly. 'Are you involved?'

'Sort of. Only on suffrance because I'm a chap. I support Ethel, try and do my bit.' He looked to his lady friend for help.

'Well?' Ethel asked. 'Are we going?'

'Yes, we are. Wait a tick, old girl, while I fetch my things.'

'Don't forget the banner!' she called as he disappeared into the bedroom. Left on their own, neither woman spoke. Ethel stretched out her hands to the blaze.

'This is a luxury,' she said at last. 'I can't remember Freddie having a fire before and it does get fearfully cold, being an attic. It'll be different once we're married . . . ' She waited but Cecilia didn't comment. 'I get a decent screw. Between us, we'll manage.'

After a pause, Cecilia forced herself to ask, 'Won't you have to leave your employment, if you do marry?'

'I shan't tell them, never fear,' Ethel replied cheerfully. 'They'll turn a blind eye as long as it suits them. I'm a typewriting assistant. I work in the Strand.' Looking at Cecilia she said deliberately, 'You work in a shop, don't you?'

'As manageress,' Cecilia said quickly.

'Lucky you.' Ethel was cool. 'And you had to work your way up, Freddie said. But you got there quickly. I expect being good looking helped.' Cecilia was furious at the impertinence.

'I had to work, as you rightly assume. The position wasn't handed to me on a plate, you know.'

'No . . . ' Ethel wasn't ruffled. 'But if you had been plain . . . A friend of mine, her dad left her in a pickle. She had to go as a "lady maid". Know what that means? Means no one talks to you at all. You're too good for them below stairs and the mistress despises you. Girls who think they're superior can end up like that. You chose right. Poor old Freddie . . . I wish he was tough like you.' For a brief moment, Cecilia could see how much Ethel cared. 'Silly coot – he's useless, you know,' the girl

354

went on fondly. 'Can't keep a job down, never sticks at anything unless I'm there to bully him.'

She paused as if inviting Cecilia to comment but there was nothing to say. Every word was true and, for the first time, Cecilia admitted it to herself.

'He'll be all right once we're married,' Ethel said firmly. 'I shan't let us starve. So don't you try and put him off the idea, there's a good woman. And get your hat and come with us. It's time you found out what life's really all about.'

Freddie came back carrying the piece of cloth as though it were his most precious possession.

'Here you are, Eth. Guarded it with my life, I have.' She shook out the folds. 'VOTES FOR WOMEN' blazed out against the purple, green and white. Cecilia shrank from it instinctively.

'Come on,' Ethel insisted quietly. 'I dare you to.'

(ii)

They came in small groups, hurrying, purposeful. Once inside the hall they added to the noise, deafening waves of female voices like flocks of starlings, circling, returning, ever increasing in volume. Cecilia Crowther had never experienced anything like it before. She clutched the leaflet that had been thrust into her hand. Stunned by the size of the assembly at first, she recovered and began to read. On the cover the same vivid message, 'VOTES FOR WOMEN' and overleaf, the Suffragette alphabet:

> A stands for ASQUITH who sought the back door!
> B for the BANNER he cowered before . . .

Well, she thought, if he came here tonight there'd be plenty for him to cower about. Banners were everywhere, draped across balcony and platform, pinned up as curtains at the windows. She suddenly heard a snatch of conversation and spoke for the first time since they'd entered the hall. 'There are ladies here, too!'

It was Ethel's turn to sneer had she wanted but instead she

355

said evenly, 'Yes, there are all sorts tonight. Most of them work for their living like you and I but there are plenty of "ladies". Some even bring their personal maids so that they can hear the message. We're sisters under the skin – and we're all disenfranchised: that's a powerful bond.'

Freddie listened nervously. As Ethel's betrothed he did as he was bidden and was tolerated but he was afraid of what Cecilia's reaction might be. It was nearly two years since he'd last seen her and there were many changes. His sister had a harder edge and far more confidence. This wasn't a woman who was afraid of the future any longer, she faced it boldly. When she'd caught sight of *him* on the station platform and then when she'd seen his lodging, Freddie had recognized from the look in her eyes that Cecilia saw him as a failure. She almost appeared to pity him. He'd worn his best shirt but that hadn't helped. Both the cuffs were frayed. He could no longer afford a proper laundry and his landlady's method with dirt was brutal.

In the hall, the starling chatter ceased abruptly. A tall woman wearing the WPSU sash mounted the platform and began to address them. Freddie knew what to expect but it was all new to Cecilia. Speakers, mainly women, came and went and with each, the level of optimism in the audience rose. Anything, everything would be possible once they had the vote! All they had to do was persist. What changes they could force through Parliament then. Cecilia found herself thinking of their father. If only she'd had control of her and Freddie's affairs, what a different destiny theirs might have been. She might have prevented the disaster – she knew now she had a much better head for business than ever her father had. The speakers tonight were right – at present women were simply chattels under the law, like bits of furniture. Marriage only made it worse – after that a woman had no control. Her husband, however imcompetent he turned out to be, had complete charge over everything. It was iniquitous!

Suppose she had married? Cecilia had a brief flash of memory, of the handsome face and tall figure that had vanished as soon as the first whiff of scandal was known. Thank Heavens she'd been spared! She could honestly say now that her life was her own. She wasn't trapped in the middle-class prison of being some man's property. Excitement began to infect and possess her, and Cecilia applauded as fiercely as those on either side.

There was a great wave of noise, a shout; she didn't understand but Ethel did. The girl rose to her feet cheering and the rest of the audience did the same. Cecilia got up to see the cause. The woman being helped onto the platform was middle-aged, slender and elegant with dark eyes that penetrated the far reaches of Caxton Hall. A lorgnette dangling from a ribbon round her neck glittered under the lights. She raised both arms. The cheering peaked then subsided as the audience sat expectant in the presence of their leader.

Suddenly Cecilia was exhausted. Today had been never-ending, spent on trains, on provisioning Freddie with scarcely more than an occasional cup of tea to sustain her. Heat and emotion stifled her. Through increasing faintness she heard the quiet, compelling voice: 'Nothing has even been got out of the British Parliament without something approaching a revolution . . . I have heard Mr Gladstone himself say so.' But Cecilia heard no more.

She let them half carry her out of the hall into a cab. She was still in a daze as Freddie and Ethel dragged her up the dingy stairs to the two attic rooms. She watched as Ethel cut up bread and butter and forced her to eat. The fire had gone out, the room felt clammy and Cecilia shivered.

'See to the grate, Freddie,' Ethel was sharp. 'Don't pile on coal like that, it'll never catch. Clear it all out and start again. Here – let me.' She stopped chafing Cecilia's hands and said impatiently, 'You're as helpless as a baby sometimes.'

'I had a scout to see to it at Oxford, that's why.' Freddie was petulant at being shamed in front of his sister. 'I wasn't *trained*, you know,' he protested, half jocular. Ethel looked up at him.

'No more was I. I had to learn the hard way. Now come here beside me and I'll show you.' He knelt obediently.

Watching, almost resenting the way her brother was being diminished, Cecilia had to admit the girl was right. Out of his environment, Freddie was helpless, and he'd never return to that other life. If he were to survive, he'd need Ethel to support him.

She examined her own situation. That world of hers, snug

357

and secure as she'd fashioned it in Darlington, would never be the same, not after tonight. During those initial months she'd thought occasionally of a future in London. Perhaps in one of those Regent Street stores where she'd once had an account! First she had to win promotion and as each step was taken, she'd had too much to do to cope with the present than worry about the future. Now she forced herself to consider it.

Cecilia knew John McKie had a soft spot for her. Men had reacted that way throughout her life. What did it matter as long as she proved herself capable – and Mr Hart was her judge in that. His opinion was more important to her, he couldn't be swayed by a pretty face.

What was vital, was to move to London, she decided. After what she'd witnessed tonight, there could be no turning back. Even if there were a branch of the WPSU in Darlington, that would not suffice. Cecilia wanted to be at the heart of things. Equally important was the need to earn a living.

She spoke to Freddie, now holding a newspaper to make the fire draw. 'How would it be, once you're married, if I came to live with you – to share the rent?' Ethel looked startled. 'It won't be for some time yet,' Cecilia assured her. 'I need more buying experience. At least two seasons as manageress before I could apply for a position in London . . . ' Her confidence faltered because Ethel didn't offer encouragement. 'Only if it suits you to have me as a lodger?'

'Good Lord!' Freddie was aghast. The thought of two strong women living with him, governing his life, hit him like a physical blow.

'Look out – it's burning!' Ethel grabbed the paper and smothered the flames in the hearthrug. The taste of smoke was in their mouths and black smuts fluttered everywhere. Cecilia roused herself to fling open a window. When it was over, Ethel said shakily, 'It might work. It'll need two anyway, to stop Freddie burning the place down. Suppose we give it a try?'

And the Jewess from Whitechapel shook hands with the lady from Harrowgate Hill.

It had become tradition for Davie and John to spend the evening of New Year together in John's study. What had often in the past been a rush to finish the annual bookkeeping now became a leisurely proceeding. A firm of accountants prepared the audit. Although John regretted the expense he had to admit he preferred it.

During the evening a steady trickle of people visited them. Tenants from Coburg Street and from the new house they'd bought in adjoining Brunswick Street. Mr Clough came with a bottle of whisky. His rebuilding had gone as far as it could; rooms sprouted on the roof of the emporium and jutted out into the yard. Not for the first time he begged them to 'find something with a bit more space', and as usual they nodded and smiled. Privately they rejected the idea. Wasn't it only a matter of time before they moved to London?

'Perhaps we should set a date for it this year?' Davie suggested. John stared a his glass of port. The last visitor had gone and the bottle stood on the table between them. This too, was part of the ritual, in memory of Mr Armitage. Davie struggled to make his cigar draw. It had been one of Charlotte's gifts.

'That probably came from the back shelf of Stiggin's,' John told him. 'They get sold off at Christmas.' Davie agreed and flung it reluctantly onto the stove. The scent of stale Havana filled the room. 'What d'you say? Should we make plans?' he asked.

John refilled their glasses. He could neither bring himself to agree nor disagree because nowadays his whole being centred round the thought of Cecilia Crowther. It had been slow growing, first a preoccupation, then an obsession. It filled his day from the moment he opened his eyes until he slept. He flattered himself he'd managed to conceal his feelings then, like a schoolboy, told himself it didn't matter if he hadn't. He lost his puritanical ideals; they melted in the warmth of Miss Crowther's presence. In church he detached himself from any thought of personal condemnation; those strictures didn't apply to John McKie any more, they couldn't possibly do so.

Yet where could it lead? He indulged in fantasies, convincing himself that the status quo could continue, the object of his devotion playing an ever increasing role in the emporium until she became – his equal? Helpmate? Standing by his side – No! At that point, fantasy failed him: that place had already been filled.

Tonight John forced himself back to the present and considered Davie's question. Inertia had replaced that previous surge of energy and the fault was his own. The business had expanded as far as it could on their present site. Everyone was waiting for him to make a decision but he couldn't bring himself to do it. He wanted matters to continue. To disturb them in any way was to risk shattering the dream in which he preferred to dwell.

'I don't know,' he said eventually. 'What do you think?'

'Me?' Davie opened half an eye. His province was running the day-to-day business, not deciding their future, 'Why, I'll go along with whatever you say. But I don't know what's for the best. I've enough to cope with over the boys just now,' he sighed.

'Yes . . . ' John had hoped to avoid that topic tonight. He tried to divert Davie.

'Now that Ted has been accepted for the grammar school . . . ' It was over-stating the matter: Ted's exam result had been poor but Charlotte had used her influence with a customer, the head-master's wife. 'D'you think Ted will want to go on to university?' asked John.

'Of course.' Davie was beginning to lose his comfortable glow. 'Luke may be the clever one but my sons aren't completely stupid – '

'I never said they were!'

'No, I know.'

'It's just . . . ' Their uncle spoke cautiously. 'Ted continues to speak of going for a soldier. I hope he understands that in our family that would be unthinkable?'

'He will. When he's told old enough, I'll impress it on him.' Davie sounded more confident than he felt. 'I thought, once he's got a bit of learning stuffed into him, when he finds school is no bad thing, I'd put it to Ted that we'll need him working

360

here one day. Encourage him to study commerce, something like that.'

'Ye-es . . . ' John sounded even more doubtful. Port loosened his tongue. He raised the taboo subject, 'And – Matthew?'

'I've no idea,' Davie answered shortly and pushed his glass across. John refilled it and asked no more questions.

It was Mrs Armitage who'd broken the news about Matthew. Bertha had come straight to her, indignation making her angry. 'It's the tips, madam, left under the saucers. It's too bad, really it is. Those girls have earned the money – and none of them are liars. I know them well enough to say that.'

The jet quivered. The hand that clutched at it was mottled now. Thin white hair, carefully dressed, was covered in a lace cap. Mrs Armitage inclined her head toward Bertha. She was slightly deaf and anxiety increased it. 'Are you quite, quite sure?'

'Yes, madam.'

'And it's happened twice before?'

'Yes.' Bertha raised her voice. 'Today I saw him do it with my own eyes. I wanted to be sure before I came to you. As I said to my girls, I'll not believe it until I do. He's such a lovely little boy.'

Charlotte refused to believe it. Her indignation was greater than Bertha's. 'There must be some mistake!'

'I don't see how there can be, Charlotte. He has been seen stealing on three separate occasions.'

'But why? Oh, he doesn't know it's stealing! Not at his age. He's only a little boy,' she pleaded. Mrs Armitage looked to Heaven for an answer but none came. 'We will get to the bottom of this immediately,' and Charlotte rang the bell.

As the two of them waited Mrs Armitage said quietly, 'I fear he has been spoilt, being the youngest.'

'Not by me, Aunt. I've never spoilt any of my children.'

'No, dear, you've been stricter than most mothers. I was thinking of the shop assistants, Ada, Emily Beal, people like that. Matthew has always been a favourite with them, he's so attractive.'

'I shall give orders to everyone that in future Matthew is not to be singled out in any way. I trust you will see that this is adhered to, Aunt, in the salon at least.'

'Yes, Charlotte.' Her niece could be extremely forbidding when she chose.

The door opened. Matthew and Katriona stood there. When she saw Charlotte's face, Katriona withdrew. The boy walked steadily across to his mother. He was the fairest of her children, blond and angelic, and Charlotte felt the familiar leap of her heart at the sight of him. To counteract this she called out sharply, 'Stand where you are, Matthew,' thus distancing herself. In truth she was far more nervous than the boy. The idea that he could have been wicked made her shake. 'Matthew, I want you to listen to what Aunt Armitage has to say. It is a very sorry tale indeed.'

The old lady began, pausing many times to give him an opportunity to explain but Matthew remained silent. At the finish he smiled charmingly at his mother and said simply, 'I took the money because I wanted it.'

At Charlotte's insistence the cane was administered. It pained Davie far more than Matthew and Davie protested. 'Father never touched John or I. If we'd been bad he used to talk about it, with Mother there, so that we understood how wrong we'd been.'

'Did either you or John ever steal?' asked Charlotte grimly.

'Well – no . . . '

'Exactly.'

Davie still couldn't accept that Matthew had sinned. 'Why take money? He doesn't need it. He must've thought of it as a toy. Like taking marbles.'

'That would still be stealing, Davie. Matthew has broken the seventh commandment.'

'The eighth I think, dearest.'

'Whichever it is, he's broken it and must be punished.'

When it was over Davie said, 'You've made your mother very unhappy.' Matthew didn't believe him. He was angry. Why couldn't he keep the money? 'Finders keepers', Ada always said. He'd wheedle her later. Mama had said there wouldn't be any supper but he could always get round Ada or Emily. Emily once gave him a slice of chicken when he said he was hungry – she was a softie.

Maybe Mama would come up to see him later, to tuck him up. He liked her smell and her silk blouse as she leaned over him, all silvery. But Charlotte didn't visit her son. Just thinking of what he'd done made her so ashamed in front of the girls in the shop.

(iv)

In the study a spurt of gas flared among the coal. Davie sipped his port to take the taste of Matthew away. 'There is time, John. My boy will change, I'm sure of it. And it's much better a fault like that emerges now rather than later, so that it can be corrected.' It was an appeal and John nodded gravely in support. The thought of a grown thief in the family was intolerable.

'You're right, though,' John returned reluctantly to their main preoccupation. 'We should think about the future. It won't be so long before Luke begins at university.'

'Good Heavens, I suppose that's true. How long d'you reckon?'

John leaned back happily. 'According to his form master, he could be ready by nineteen twelve or thereabouts.'

'As soon as that!'

John slipped back into his daydream: Luke in cap and gown beside him, Miss Crowther marvelling, admiring. Luke would be the equal of her brother then, the one she was visiting in London just now.

'Who would have thought it possible, John? All those years ago.'

'Mistress Shields. And Father.' John was curt, he didn't like his dreams being interrupted.

'It seems we've almost got there. Have you Father's Christmas letter there? I wouldn't mind hearing it again.'

John adjusted the pince-nez. As he moved nearer the light Davie saw how his hair was receding. Instinctively he reached up to touch his own. Wiry coarseness reassured him. There was a little grey, Charlotte had pointed it out, but apart from that he was as fit as ever he was. Dear, lovely Charlotte! Davie stretched out sturdy limbs in luxurious anticipation. Apart from the occasional feeling of faintness which Charlotte insisted was indigestion, he felt as vigorous as ever. He didn't argue with her

363

about the faintness. In fact, he never argued with Charlotte. Long ago he'd decided that was futile.

'My dear sons,' John began. Davie's thoughts began to wander. 1912. It really wasn't that far off. He and John should start planning. They'd let matters drift this last twelve months. Now was the time for new resolutions, after all. There was always so much to be done. Another committee . . . and the church . . . they were talking of building a new hall . . . John must decide about the emporium . . . that would be best, to leave it to him . . .'

John took the glass from the slack hand. Davie always had such a busy time at Christmas, organizing the children's parties, taking them to the pantomime. John joined in but he knew who the youngsters preferred when it came to fun and games, even Luke. He couldn't blame them. He hadn't the same sparkle. John examined Davie's face in repose. Without the animation, his brother looked sad. John wondered why. There were more lines too compared to last year; Davie looked older while he – why, he felt young! He took out his watch and clicked it open. Almost midnight. Better let Davie sleep. The New Year, and Miss Crowther due back the day after tomorrow. John lifted his glass in a silent toast.

(v)

When Miss Crowther returned to Coburg Street she was a different woman. Mrs Hart mentioned it but her husband had already noticed. Mrs Hart had disturbing proof of the possible cause. She put his liver and bacon on the table in front of him. 'Miss Crowther's going to ask if *that* can go up at the emporium.' She indicated the tightly rolled paper on the dresser, 'In the cubicle the lady counterhands use.'

'What is it?' Mr Hart was partial to liver and his knife and fork were poised.

'I'd better let her show it to you herself. It is her business, after all.'

'Right.' Mr Hart put a sizeable chunk in his mouth and began to chew.

'It's a poster. "Votes for Women".'

'Oh, my lord!' His mouth was too full and he chewed a moment longer. 'Mr John won't like that, he won't like it one little bit.' Mrs Hart watched her beloved masticate. Alfred had lovely table manners, that was what had first attracted her, sitting across the table in the emporium dining room.

'Perhaps it's no bad thing, him being put off,' she hinted.

'What, lovey?'

'Mr McKie. If he gets upset. I don't suppose Mrs McKie will cry her eyes out over it?' Like so many connected with the emporium, she considered the fortunes of the McKies as important as her own. And as part of that interdependent web, Mrs Hart considered it her duty to be acquainted with gossip. 'I can't see Mrs McKie being upset if Miss Crowther stepped out of line, can you?'

Mr Hart gave his wife one of his aloof, masterful looks. 'As long as Mr John doesn't think *we* have been encouraging Miss Crowther in any – militancy.'

Mrs Hart was startled. 'I should hope not! He asked us to rent her a room in the first place. Mind you, I don't want to lose her. Miss Crowther's a good lodger. She's been led astray, I expect, mixing with the wrong sort of people in London. You know, Alfred, I still say it's no sort of job for a woman, gadding about the way she does.'

'Never forget, lovey, Mr McKie appointed her to that position because he thought her suitable,' Mr Hart reproved, 'and whatever his feelings, I've never known him confused when it comes to business. Be fair, Grace. Miss Crowther has proved herself very capable.' Alfred Hart was not a man to begrudge another's success, particularly as he now had window-dressing back under his own control. 'You never complain when I go "gadding" to Leeds.'

'Ah, but you're a man,' his wife pointed out, 'which makes it normal. It's not natural for a woman to go travelling alone, whatever Mr McKie thinks. Oh – Alfred!'

'What?'

'You don't suppose Mr McKie believes in votes for women, like Keir Hardie does?' For Mrs Hart, all Scots were revolutionaries at heart.

She needn't have worried. John was extremely firm and the

365

poster became a three-day wonder at the emporium. That Miss Crowther should have been so bold! So foolish! It was tempting providence to be so provocative, even if Mr McKie was smitten. Why, she might lose her place! All agreed it would bring a change in Mrs McKie's situation and watched avidly for signs.

Charlotte declared privately how relieved she was the wool had been torn from John's eyes. 'Although I must confess, Davie, I dare not speak to Mary on the subject. She can be very – withdrawn about her personal affairs. One cannot interfere.'

'You may have been mistaken?' Davie said hopefully.

'John's been infatuated since the day Miss Crowther first came here,' Charlotte said heavily. 'I don't think he was aware of it himself at first but lately he's been spooning over her quite dreadfully.'

'Poor old chap,' Davie sighed. 'I wish he and Mary were as happy as we are.' His wife didn't look very happy, in fact she was frowning.

'I trust,' she said, 'this fuss will soon die down and we can forget all about it.'

So the poster was banished and went up instead over Miss Crowther's bed. It disturbed Mrs Hart to see it there but she was a little too awed by Cecilia to take it down.

As for Mary, she hid her scars and presented a calm face to the world. If John had resumed his old habit of sleeping alone, no one knew of it but herself. She continued as usual to rise every morning at five thirty and began by superintending Ada and Emily Beal in the kitchen, then went to the stockroom to watch over the apprentice checking stores before returning to give the daily cleaning women their tasks.

When breakfast was over, Mary and Mrs Beal submitted the day's menus to Charlotte for approval before Mary and Billy set out with Blackie to do the shopping. Once a week Mrs Armitage travelled with them, to collect coffee and tea from Mr Collins for the salon.

By the time Mary returned, the living quarters would be polished and aired, the steps to the yard scoured and rugs hung on the line for beating. No one but Mary was permitted to enter John's study. She cleaned that room herself three times a week and whatever her feelings concerning Miss Crowther, it didn't alter the custom.

366

After lunch there was a pattern for each weekday. On Mondays, the laundrywoman and her daughter collected the washing. On Tuesdays bedlinen was returned for Emily and Ada to iron and on Wednesdays, clean clothes were delivered to be sorted, mended and put away. On Thursdays food was prepared for a week and Billy ferried huge meat and fish pies to and from a bakers in Tubwell Row where they were cooked. By Thursday evening the shop was full of entrancing smells and the children hung about the kitchen for the weekly treat of gingerbread fresh from the oven. On Friday afternoons, for two blessed hours, the women had nothing to do but please themselves. On Fridays, therefore, Mary paid her visits.

These began with Mrs Richardson and other Quaker ladies whose charitable causes Mary helped support. Then she travelled farther afield to see any employee who was ill, any dependant who'd been bereaved or wife who'd been confined. John always had the name of someone who deserved a visit.

With this routine of toil the emporium and all who worked there were fed, housed and their wants catered for. It was Mary's way of repaying the debt to John for giving Luke a name. She'd undertaken it when she was full of hope; that hope was fading.

(vi)

In another important way, Cecilia Crowther's visit to London had impact. There was no doubt her sense of style, given full reign since she'd been appointed assistant manageress, was impressive. Her clothes were McKie Bros' advertisement and were of the best. As her role expanded, so Charlotte's diminished, in particular as Darlington's leader of fashion. She found it hard to accept this. If a customer asked for 'a skirt like the one Miss Crowther wore last Tuesday', Charlotte felt slighted. Unwilling to discuss the matter with Davie, she sought out her aunt. 'I'm not old!'

'Of course you're not, my darling.'

'Mrs Outhwaite had the impertinence to speak as though she and I were contemporaries. She must be over fifty – I'm twenty-

367

nine! The same age as Miss Crowther but for six months yet she is treated as a young woman!'

'You are married, Charlotte, and Miss Crowther is single, that is quite different. And you have children. Once a woman has those jewels, she is elevated to that most beautiful state – she is a Mother!' Age made Mrs Armitage sentimental but these words didn't mollify Charlotte in her present mood. Being the mother of Matthew wasn't something she wanted to be reminded of at present.

'You make it sound as if it were only the children who matter.'

'Oh Charlotte, what nonsense! But you wouldn't want to be thought flighty, would you?'

'Certainly not.'

'Then you must accept the noble dignity being a mother confers,' Mrs Armitage reproved.

'Davie and I are still young!' Charlotte wasn't ready to hand on the torch. She felt trapped. 'If only he'd tried harder and been elected, we might have moved away from here, to a house in London,' she cried wildly. Mrs Armitage was shrewd enough to guess what Charlotte wanted was the glory of being an MP's wife. Nevertheless she'd heard the outburst too often and was fond enough of Davie not to let it fester.

'Charlotte, what you need is a proper holiday. You and Davie have had no time to yourselves lately, no privacy. Perhaps you should consider a week or two away from the children for a change?'

(vii)

Freddie was commenting on a letter from Cecilia. 'Seems like this chap McKie took a scunner to that poster all right. Told Cis he accepted in principle that women householders over thirty should be enfranchised – '

'Thirty!' Ethel nearly let the toast burn in her indignation.

'But that he was against the Suffragettes ever since their violence brought down Keir Hardie.'

368

His lady love shrugged. 'No one took the slightest notice until we were militant.'

Freddie skimmed through the rest of the letter. 'She hopes you haven't been injured in the rioting . . . says she's fed up waiting in a queue in the Ladies' Reading Room for the London editions to arrive with the details. The other Mr McKie has been boring her with his efforts at politics, telling her how the Darlington Town Council debated the re-siting of a municipal drinking fountain! Poor old Cis!'

'It sounds to me . . . ' Ethel removed herself and the pile of toast from the hearth rug, 'as though your sister's getting restless. D'you think she might be considering an earlier move to London?'

'Maybe,' Freddie agreed, 'She certainly sounds bored with McKie's. Let's hope she can find a position down here.'

'If she does – and moves in to help with the rent – shouldn't we think about setting a date?'

'I say!'

(viii)

Mrs Armitage's suggestion took root and grew into a sturdy plant. Davie couldn't ignore it: he and Charlotte were going to have a holiday. That much he accepted, but it was one of their customers who told him their destination.

'Biarritz – how wonderful!' Mrs Carstairs trilled on seeing him, 'How I envy you?'

'Biarritz?'

'Oh, dear – I've spoiled your wife's little secret, haven't I?' The elderly face simpered at him. 'Don't let her know it was me, will you?'

Davie tackled Charlotte as soon as they were alone.

'My mind is made up, Davie – '

'But what about the expense!'

She rounded on him fiercely, 'Why shouldn't we have an expensive holiday? You and I have only had three days alone in the whole of our lives – in Saltburn. On our honeymoon.'

He clutched at the straw. 'We could go back to the Zetland,'

369

he pleaded. 'You've always said how much you enjoyed it there.' But there was another reason it had to be Biarritz.

'Miss Crowther visits Paris whenever she likes – '

'My love, she's been there twice. And those are business trips.'

'Hrmmph! Mr Hart makes his business trips to Leeds.'

'Miss Crowther also visits Glasgow – '

'Davie, I want sea air and . . . ' Charlotte searched for the word, 'I want a little excitement! Biarritz is highly spoken of.' That could not be denied; ever since the King had visited, the name had been on everyone's lips. The resort was the most desirable, the most beneficial spot on earth for a lady of fashion. Davie fought back valiantly.

'We could go back to Scotland. You found the sea air there very healthy.'

But not the journey nor the cramped conditions on the croft, Charlotte told him curtly. Besides, John and Luke were going there. 'And Ted can accompany them,' his mother announced.

'Ted? Isn't he to come on holiday with us?'

'Certainly not, none of the children are. You and I will be by ourselves. We deserve it,' she said firmly. It was settled, Davie could see that it was; it was a waste of time to argue.

After a certain amount of hesitation, he spoke to Mary privately. Since the business of the poster, Davie had become observant. He was now convinced John was obsessed with Miss Crowther – but how to break the spell? There was no reason to dismiss such an excellent manageress. Davie felt increasingly guilty that his brother should behave so stupidly, but helpless too. He daren't speak to John, that would have taken too much courage. Davie simply prayed that John would eventually come to his senses. Fortunately Miss Crowther appeared unaware of his devotion.

Davie wanted to help Mary but wasn't sure how to approach her. Like Charlotte, he found her defences impenetrable. 'You probably know that Charlotte and I are to holiday in Biarritz,' he began. 'Everyone does except me – and I was only told yesterday. By Mrs Carstairs, of all people!' He pulled a face and Mary gave him the ghost of a smile. 'Who am I to argue,' Davie shrugged, 'when Charlotte tells me it'll do us good? A couple of weeks in France is what we need, apparently.'

'I'm sure Charlotte is right.' Mary was wary; why was Davie telling her this? He sensed her mood and said abruptly, 'Will you come with us? I know you'd planned to go to Harrogate as usual but you need a change as much as the rest of us, Mary.'

He'd gone about it the wrong way; Mary was fiery red.

'I prefer less fashionable resorts,' she replied. 'Was this Charlotte's idea?'

'No, mine. I do have them occasionally, you know.'

'Davie, I'm sorry!' He was smarting but as usual with him it didn't last. 'Come, do consider the notion a little longer,' he pleaded. 'I'm sure Charlotte would like you to come as much as I would. We know you won't be going to Scotland with John. Bertha is quite capable of looking after Mrs Armitage, so why not consider France? I'd like fine to have two lovely girls, one for each arm!' His infectious laugh touched her and when he gave her a gentle hug, she didn't stiffen. 'Please,' Davie begged. But Mary thought she caught a glimmer of pity in his eye and replied formally, 'I shall be better suited at Harrogate, thank you, Davie.'

(ix)

Helen Shields was extremely glad John was coming to Scotland. She'd written to him with a hint of reproach.

> Your father has not been well of late. He consented to visit the doctor but refused to discuss it afterwards. I know he finds the work on the croft an increasing burden. If you or Davie could spare the time to come and help, I know he would welcome it. For several summers now his neighbours have helped but this embarrasses him as he can no longer return their kindness.
>
> Anno Domini affects both of us the same way. When I first thought of retirement, I pictured all the things I would do, the walks across the moors, expeditions to Fort William and so forth. Reality is different. A half-hour walk with frequent rests, as far as the pier, is quite sufficient.

371

However, I must not complain. I enjoy good health and a wealth of visitors. I trust you will be one of their number soon.'

Helen Shields had retired to a cottage less than fifty yards from the school house. It had a stone-flagged floor and a lean-to kitchen with a pump outside the back door. Tiny windows in the thick stone walls gave a view across the loch to the pier. From her bedroom Helen could glimpse the school yard and watch new generations at play.

If the stone floor was damp in winter and made her bones ache, so be it. What was the use of trying to escape to a warmer climate in England? Two of her sisters were dead and she'd lost touch with Sophie – why, she probably wouldn't recognize her across a street, whereas here she knew everyone. In summer, former pupils returned like swallows, knocking shyly at her door to present wives or husbands, and children. As she washed tea things for the third time one Sunday afternoon, Helen paused to calculate exactly how many visitors had called that year. The result surprised her. 'It's like being an ancient monument,' she told herself with grim humour. 'I must be "worthy of a detour"!' The severe mouth softened ever so slightly. 'There's certainly no point in returning to England. This is where I belong.'

Now the most important visitor of all was due. It would have been perfection if Davie had come too but Helen understood why he couldn't. At Charlotte's age, she would have preferred a trip to Biarritz than to Scotland.

The shape in the distance resolved itself into the ferry coming up the loch. Helen sighed with satisfaction. Time to put the scones in the oven.

As it moved, ripples fanned out from the paddles across the silky water. Father and son stood gazing towards the jetty. Ted was below in the engine room. John hoped he'd use up some of his energy down there, it had been a tiring journey so far.

'Will we visit Mistress Shields before going to the croft, Father?' Luke had dropped all trace of childishness. 'Dada' had disappeared from his vocabulary the day he'd begun at grammar school.

'Oh, yes. We go near enough past her front door, it wouldn't do to ignore it. Besides, I told your grandfather not to expect us till nightfall.'

'She might give us tea.'

'Indeed she might,' John answered drily. Luke blushed.

'It's all this fresh air, it tastes different, not smoky like Darlington. It makes a chap hungry. Ted will be ravenous,' he added disingenuously.

Helen watched as the boat was tied up and the luggage handed over the side, then saw the figures disembarking. They sorted themselves into groups. Those going to the hotel climbed into the smart trap and bowled away. What a lot of summer visitors nowadays! Helen shook her head as she always did then returned her attention to the three figures loading baggage onto the cart, supplied by wee Georgie, no doubt. Increased excitement made her pulse quicken. At last! They walked up the pier and disappeared from sight behind the trees. She moved from the window to her one comfortable chair. On no account must they think she'd been expecting them to call.

A quiet tap came at the door.

'Come in.'

'Are you there, Mistress Shields?' They hovered on the threshold.

'Come in, do. Why John, this is a surprise! How nice to see you again.'

'We've just arrived. Did you get my letter?'

'Yes, yes.' She gave no hint of having watched and waited but went through the slow formality of greetings, each moment savoured, nothing rushed. It had been so long. Now her 'first-born' was before her – he'd got a few grey hairs! John had taken off his hat and Helen had put on her spectacles. She recovered and sent young Ted outside double quick to mend the pump (the handle had come off but he'd find a hammer among the tools). After he'd mended it, he could fill all the buckets. The school mistress was used to making snap judgements about lively boys. She always had a few tasks lined up, to get them out of her way. Besides, she wanted to take Luke through his paces.

He'd grown and matured. 'You're twelve, that's right isn't it? And how is your library progressing?' She'd set him off. Luke talked and talked, following her about as she made the tea, telling her about the books he'd bought with his Christmas and birthday money, the ones that Dr Cullen had managed to get him second-hand. Instinctively he watched as Mistress Shields leaned on her stick. The fingers that clutched the handle were bent. Arthritis. Once it was established in a person, it spread to all parts of the body, he remembered. He broke off from telling her his plans for Newcastle University. 'I'm planning to do research eventually. Into surgery or pain relief, I haven't decided. The medicines we have now are not good enough and some people grow dependent upon them.'

'Come, Luke, that's simply repeating what Dr Cullen has told you.' John was anxious the boy shouldn't over-reach himself.

They were interrupted by a banging on the kitchen window. Ted had not only mended the pump, he'd caused it to over-flow, swamping the yard. 'Outside and give him a hand,' Helen said quickly. 'See that you don't destroy my sweet peas.' She wasn't really concerned but she wanted a few minutes alone with John, too.

'How's Mary?'

'Very well. She's in Harrogate with Mrs Armitage.' Helen nodded and added boiling water to the pot.

'And how's the business world of Darlington?' She drew him out about the emporium and the warehouse, about investments in foreign shipyards, of wealthy customers for whom McKie Bros imported leather and lace, furs and beautiful clothes from Paris before asking, 'And your lady buyer, is she proving herself capable?'

John was suddenly tongue-tied. To ease his embarrassment, Helen went to the window to tell the boys tea was ready but they must wash their hands first. 'You wrote and told me of all the responsibility you were proposing to give to that young woman,' she said.

'Miss Crowther.'

'Crowther, yes.' Helen put the milk jug on the table. 'Has she proved worthy of your trust?'

'She's . . . she's an excellent manageress,' John stammered, 'Excellent. In every way.' Oh bother! thought Helen.

There was no more time for intimate discussion on this visit. Helen had her hands full fuelling the boys and guarding her china against Ted's enthusiasm. Eventually she said, 'You must be off. Donald has been very patient, waiting out there, but you will come back?' To Luke, 'I want to hear more about your plans, too.'

'We'll definitely be back,' Luke was keen. 'We're making a proper visit this summer.'

'Good.' There would be another opportunity. Helen Shields watched them as far as the first bend in the road. When they next came, she'd make an opportunity to talk to John again. She must be careful not to scold or interfere, she would be gentle. Even if it was foreign to her nature she'd manage it somehow, for Mary's sake. She owed it to her.

(x)

Beside Alex, the old sheepdog lay inert, soaking up the last warmth from the sun. They didn't often walk as far as this and the dog hoped they'd soon return. He could smell damp air and wanted to be back in the comfort of the croft. His master turned a blind eye to him in the corner nowadays although both of them knew his rightful place was outside in the barn. His master moved slowly these days, at the same pace as the dog. The dog didn't think of it in terms of age but of a tightening of the boundaries of his world. Neither of them went out at night any more; neither of them wanted to.

The dog heard them first. He could no longer see but he could hear. He sat, head cocked. Alex reached down and patted him.

'Aye, it's them. They're here at last.'

They began work on the croft the next morning. Any feeling of embarrassment at the way neighbours had cared for Alex quickly evaporated when John saw the list of tasks. His father admitted to saving them for him. 'I knew you wouldn't want me to be asking anyone else. Why not make a start with the roof?' It took two days to strip and replace broken shingles. Alex brought his chair outside to sit and admire and call out encouragement when they flagged. After that it was time to do the hay-making.

John's back had never ached so much. His pince-nez were left in the house, it was easier to work without them, and whole

375

days were spent in hazy focus, wielding a scythe as the boys stacked and baled. John kept telling himself it would soon be finished but when it was, other jobs were waiting. 'The old fence. It might get me through the winter but then again, it might not.'

'No?'

'It's the beasts, you see. In the spring they made that hole.'

'We'll start tomorrow.'

'Aye. While the weather holds.'

It held for three more weeks. Never had John offered up so many prayers for rain. Just for a day or so, to give his muscles a rest. He held the stakes steady as Luke and Ted pounded enthusiastically. Beside them, Alex split more wood. 'You're doing a good job, John. I'd no idea so much of it had gone rotten.' It took three days to cover the whole boundary but Alex's admiration was wholehearted. 'You're good boys, all three of you. It's a grand fence now. The beasts'll not be getting through that in a hurry.'

'Is that the lot, Father? You're all set for the winter now?' John tried not to sound too hearty. Alex nodded gently.

'Apart from the peat, aye.'

'The peat?'

'I've none cut, and I've used nearly all that I had.'

Tomorrow?'

Alex looked at the sky gratefully. 'I've never known it hold as long as it has.'

The respite came eventually. They would have a ceilidh, Alex told them, for all those neighbours they hadn't been able to visit yet, and so John and Alex could thank them for what they'd done in the past. 'I don't know if our supplies will be sufficient,' John said worriedly. Mary and Charlotte had packed quantities of food but it was amazing how little was left.

'I've sent word to wee Georgie Hamilton,' Alex assured him, 'he'll arrange everything.'

The day before was devoted to housework. Alex produced scrubbing brushes, soap and cakes of wax. 'It would be an idea if we tidied the place up a bit.'

'Whatever you say, Father.' At least, thought John tiredly, it keeps Ted out of mischief.

From his sunny patch in they yard, the old dog watched rugs, curtains and furniture brought out for cleaning. Luke and Ted worked as hard as John did, all of them tanned from days in the sun and filthy besides. At mid-day, Donald and his sister arrived, sent by their mother to 'help out a bit'. John thankfully resumed a supervisory role and by seven in the evening he was satisfied. Even Mary couldn't have managed better. Alex joined in the admiration before asking politely, 'Have the three of you time for a bit of a wash?' They stripped and stood in the yard, dousing themselves with icy water from the spring. 'At least it numbs the pain between my shoulder blades,' John told himself.

They arrived in small groups from all over the peninsula to visit their neighbour. The piper came last, fortified on the way with a dram or two. The wailing chanter filled the air and in the yard they settled to listen to it. Inside the croft, peat was piled high and women dealt with the pans. The northern summer sky hovered between dusk and daylight, to match the high, thin sound.

It began slowly, and hour after hour the piper played while the whisky circulated. The women brought out bowls of hough and oatcakes. Children ran in and out with plates of meat and bread and John's body ached for its bed. The bracing effect of cold water had long since worn off, but the party was just beginning.

There was a 'Whoop' – it was a signal. All at once, several of them formed a ring. Lamps were brought out and dancing began, fast, nimble, excited. No one thought of tiredness or the dull grind waiting tomorrow, they simply danced. Even Alex managed a reel. Overhead twilight changed from grey to blue and began imperceptibly to lighten. John joined in for a dance or two and then sank down to rest. Luke sat beside him.

'Did you and Uncle Davie do this often?'

'Not often, just sometimes. When there was something to celebrate.'

'The sun's coming up, look.'

'So it is . . . ' Looking round the yard he could make out the flushed faces more clearly. 'I never remember so many people coming before. It's a great honour, Luke, so many wanting to meet you and Ted.'

'Grandfather's enjoying himself.'

Alex began calling for quiet and beside him a girl began to sing. The melody was high, plaintive, reminding them of sorrows, then as she finished, a man began a marching song they could all join in. One by one they brought forth old tunes until the sun appeared clearly above the hills. The piper stopped and there was a moment of absolute stillness as everyone stared at it.

Luke felt panic grip him. They were a primitive people, reaching out for light, dependent on the sun's warmth for life. 'I'm one of them,' he thought for no reason at all, 'I belong with this tribe.' Just as suddenly, the feeling left him. He saw his father's weary face, eyes closed, turned to accept the sun's benison. Still a little frightened, Luke was back inside his schoolboy self. He reached out and clutched John's hand.

(xi)

In a third-class hotel in Biarritz, Davie lay beside Charlotte and wished they could be anywhere but where they were. The holiday was a disaster. To a certain extent, it was Charlotte's fault. Davie had tried to warn her what sort of holiday it would be but she had firm ideas of her own. It was impossible for her to imagine what Davie tried to describe. When he spoke of a 'quiet' hotel in the old town, Charlotte continued to picture shining white luxury on the promenade.

On their arrival at the station, anticipation had reached a high peak. Charlotte climbed into the cab with all the stateliness of visiting royalty. Here she was at last in Europe's most glittering resort, her pale blue travelling costume the most elegant McKie Bros could provide.

But they'd driven past the fashionable quarter into narrower streets. Davie murmured his warning yet again. Charlotte didn't understand and was puzzled. The buildings in this area were much shabbier with fastened shutters; was there a smarter part close by? The cab stopped beside stone steps leading to a forbidding wooden door, centuries old. Davie's heart sank still further. Money that would have purchased a comfortable room at the Zetland certainly didn't go far here.

Nor had the travel agent's hesitant words fully prepared him for this. He looked anxiously at his wife.

She peered out. They were in an alleyway with buildings so close women could call to each other from the upper floors. With no understanding of French, Charlotte thought their cries sounded more like shrieks, which made her apprehensive. The cabbie opened the door and Charlotte stepped out. Her foot touched something soft and unpleasant. There were rotting vegetables in the gutter! She was disgusted. Darlington was never as dirty as this.

In the shadowy reception, the proprietress waited, tall and gaunt. A mole on her upper lip sprouted two thick black hairs. Davie, struggling with the language and their baggage, tried not to stare. The cabbie had disappeared; in this area of town none of them lingered, the tips weren't worth it.

Madam indicated the lift. Davie asked, haltingly, that refreshments be sent up to their room.

By the time the tray arrived, Charlotte had already decided that the glasses would need to be re-washed. She'd stripped back the bedlinen to examine the mattress. She needed to satisfy herself was all hygienic enough before they unpacked, she told Davie.

He'd made the mistake of opening the shutters to admit the sunshine but closed the window as soon as the smell reached them. Alas, the light also revealed the dingy walls. Davie didn't look at Charlotte this time, he knew what her reaction would be.

As the sullen garçon was despatched with the glasses, Davie changed their order from mineral water to wine. It wasn't an extravagance, it was necessity.

He waited. Charlotte gave her verdict on the chamber, and Davie sent for a maid to sweep the floor and clean the bath. He looked up the word for fly-paper and promised they would buy half a dozen; all the time he kept refilling Charlotte's tumbler.

'This is a very, very poor sort of place, Mr McKie. Not what I am accustomed to.'

Poor Davie. He knew the signs. The greater the stress the more formal Charlotte became. But eventually the grape began to do its work and patience had a small reward. Charlotte agreed that their hotel was the least important aspect of their holiday. They were in Biarritz, after all. The sea was within walking distance, just. The sights and the fashionable panoply of European society were out there, waiting to be gazed at. They weren't likely to meet anyone they knew so what did it matter if they stayed here? Finally Davie produced his strongest argument. 'Think of the cost, dearest. We can stay for two whole weeks at this place, three if you wish.' Fatigue made him reckless. 'We couldn't have afforded three *days* had we gone to a hotel on the promenade.'

'But we can afford to have tea in one?'

'Of course! Maybe even dinner . . . ' He would need to study the menu closely first. 'Won't you take off your hat? I'll put away our things.'

She would take a little rest, Charlotte announced, she felt unaccountably sleepy. Afterwards she would tell Davie what she'd decided. When she awoke he'd already reconnoitred the area and purchased so many fly-papers the bathroom was festooned with them. If she'd recovered from the journey, he was ready to lead her down to the beach, to take tea at one of the desirable establishments. Charlotte allowed herself to be persuaded.

It was a sobering experience. Last year's Leghorn, retrimmed to match the pale blue costume, looked simply dowdy in the brilliant throng; even the costume felt old-fashioned. Walking at Davie's side Charlotte realized she was out-classed. She who'd led fashion in Darlington was a bystander. Her step lost its elasticity. Crowds jostled her. None of the glittering ones walked, she saw. Beautiful women sat in carriages, landaus or motor cars. The babel of voices was unintelligible: French, German, Italian. Sound and laughter overlapped. They sat in a fragile bubble that was their own exclusive world, one Charlotte could never enter.

Around these women, like butterflies, men hovered. Men whose suits were perfection, men for whom money was incidental. They shone more fiercely, glared arrogantly at those who were not like themselves. Their world of privilege needed to be defended vigilantly.

Charlotte knew herself to be a shopkeeper. Even the emporium dwindled when viewed from the bird's-eye pinnacle of Biarritz. How pleasant Saltburn was in retrospect. It flashed on her inner eye, wholesome and inviting. With acquaintances to bow to and envy in women's eyes at whatever Mrs Davie McKie was wearing. 'I have decided that this town is unhealthy,' she told Davie, 'from the – odour – I would say the drains are unreliable.'

An immediate return was unthinkable. The children, Jane and Matthew, had been dispatched with Katriona to join the Richardson family at Seaton Deleval. It would be awkward to return before they did. All the same, Charlotte insisted they leave by an earlier train. Self-respect demanded that much.

Davie bowed his head in acquiescence and to compensate for her disappointment swept his wife up the steps and into the smartest hotel in Biarritz for afternoon tea. It was the worst idea of all. Relegated to an insignificant table, Charlotte had ample opportunity to view the golden ones at close quarters. She compared their elegance, paint and jewellery with her own provincial style. It was total defeat. She, who'd come prepared to be one of them, to be admired, hadn't even been noticed.

They caused a sensation once. On their last evening Davie wore his kilt for their final stroll along the promenade. The stunned silence of Madam in reception was followed by a much livelier reaction out of doors. Crowds stopped and pointed, some of them even cheered. Charlotte was scarlet. 'Davie!' Indignation swamped formality on this occasion. 'Davie, they're laughing at you!' But he didn't care, he laughed and waved back.

'Never mind, Charlotte. They're probably jealous. They can see what I've got but imagine what spindly legs those little froggies have under their trousers!'

Charlotte wondered about breaking their journey in London but Davie preferred to go straight home. He didn't feel well enough for more sight-seeing. Alone in a shop still closed for the holidays, he allowed Charlotte to dose him with senna. It made her happy and it didn't do him any harm. The children were due to return from Seaton Deleval in a couple of days and that made him feel much better.

It was peaceful in the emporium, though they weren't entirely alone. Billy had remained to clean floors and attend to Blackie. Holidays didn't suit Billy. He needed a routine to guide him through the day. His mother came each morning to prepare his meals and supervise the other women from Coburg Street, for John had decreed the entire store be spring-cleaned while staff were away.

Charlotte went to the kitchen to get supper ready. It was such an empty room without the bustle of Mary, Ada and Katriona. A quiet meal for Davie and herself, nothing but good plain food to restore them. Mrs Beal had left a meat pie and a large basin containing spotted dick. Charlotte was cheerful as she set the tray. Would gruel be better for Davie? He'd complained of feeling bilious during the journey. No, she decided. Spotted dick was his favourite, especially with custard sauce. She was waiting for the milk to heat up when the doorbell rang. It was strange to walk through the deserted shop, her footsteps sounded so loud. A messenger boy waited on the step, round hat at a jaunty angle. Should he wait? Charlotte opened the envelope.

Davie heard the cry from the living room and flung aside the rug. 'Dearest, what is it, what's happened?' Charlotte had rushed back inside and was clutching the newel post as he ran downstairs.

'It's Matthew, we must go there immediately!'

He seized the telegram. The word 'diptheria' stood out from all the rest.

'Yes, we must!'

(xii)

They'd hung sheets over the walls and door and sprayed them with carbolic. Matthew saw them through a feverish haze, white veils moving in the draught. A spirit-lamp hissed sulphurously beside the bed. The noise hurt his ears, everything hurt so much, and why couldn't he breathe?

They'd taken away the carpets and furniture, covering the floor instead with newspapers soaked in disinfectant. The only other thing was a basin for him to spit into but Matthew had long since ceased to spit or shiver as the fever took a firmer grip. Now they brought in a kitchen table. A strange nurse in a loose gown and mask supervised Katriona as she scrubbed it. She

382

urged her in whispers to be more thorough. The scrubbing rasped Matthew's body like a saw. Each new breath rattled in his throat.

Outside on the landing the doctor spoke quickly. 'I want your consent to operate. There isn't much time.'

'Of course.' Charlotte gripped her umbrella. 'Davie, would you go downstairs and stay with Jane.' The doctor grasped her intention.

'Oh, Mrs McKie, please don't think of coming in here!' He was appalled. The last thing he wanted was the mother watching him. 'It will be an unpleasant sight.' He couldn't bring himself to be more specific; the father looked near to a faint.

'I intend to be with my son. What must I do to prepare?' He reversed his decision and capitulated because there wasn't time for arguments. Within five minutes Charlotte's sleeves were rolled up and her arms scrubbed, and she had on an apron and a kerchief doused in the carbolic mixture.

'The child was too ill to be moved.' The doctor paused, waiting for some reaction. Had this woman understood the implication? Would she lose her nerve? Charlotte simply nodded and followed steadily into the sick room. What he'd told her meant that Matthew was near to death.

The table was ready. Beside it, spread out on a white cloth, were the doctor's surgical instruments. In a jar of stronger carbolic, the tube he would use had been left to soak. The doctor saw it all and approved. A sensible nurse this, one who'd worked with him before. He didn't have to tell her how serious the situation was. She looked at Charlotte and her eyebrows rose. 'Mrs McKie insists on remaining with her son,' the doctor answered brusquely. To Charlotte he said, 'On that side of the table if you please. Do not attempt to speak or hinder us in any way, is that understood?'

'Yes.'

'Are we ready, nurse?'

'Yes, sir.' She lifted Matthew gently and laid him on the table. The doctor swore softly when he saw part of the torso was in shadow. Using fresh rags from a pile he adjusted the angle of the lamp then tossed the rags onto the fire. It was difficult to keep things sterile in here.

Katriona took up the first of her bandages to bind Matthew

383

to the table but she was too gentle. 'Tighter, tighter,' he urged, 'we can't afford to have him thrashing about.' The nurse cut through the nightshirt to expose the skinny chest. Charlotte's heart was in her mouth.

'Mrs McKie, you do understand what I'm about to do? Your boy has the laryngeal form of infection which means his trachea is clogged with mucous. I have to insert a tube here – ' he pointed to the windpipe at the base of the neck – 'to enable air to reach his lungs. If I don't he will choke to death.'

The nurse handed him the bottle of chloroform and a pad.

'Take a deep breath, Mark – '

'Matthew. My son's name is Matthew.' If he was going to die, at least let him not feel alienated.

'Breathe in, boy, that's the way.' The small chest gave a spasm and the body shifted a little.

'Pull those bandages tighter!'

Katriona's fingers trembled but she managed it.

'Now, hold that head in position, nurse.'

Charlotte couldn't even touch Matthew's hand. She'd had some idea that holding it might give him comfort. From where she stood all she could see was the arch of his neck as steel glinted under the light. Suddenly, blood spurted. Hands moved quickly but the blood continued to flow.

Fumes made Charlotte dizzy. She concentrated on remaining upright. Matthew might need her yet. The doctor was working as swiftly as he could – why did he curse so? Was Matthew dead? There was a movement and Katriona spoke, 'His feet – one of his feet has broken free.'

'Hold him steady, woman! I don't want to give any more chloroform. One more minute, that's all I need. Clean the wound, nurse, can't see what I'm doing.'

Poor little chap, he thought, skin like red-hot paper. Touch and go, this one.

'Right, that's better.'

Was it over? Charlotte was motionless as wax. The doctor had an ear to Matthew's chest, a finger on the fluttering pulse in his neck. 'Will he live?' she asked. What did it matter if she spoke now? 'Will he live?' she repeated.

In a room downstairs, Davie waited. Jane sat beside him, holding him tightly. 'Will they tell us soon, Dada?'

384

'Yes, Jane. Not much longer now.'

'They will make Matthew better, won't they?'

'If they can. They will do their best.'

The door opened and the doctor stood there. 'It's over, Mr McKie.'

(xiii)

In Scotland, John handed the letter to his father. 'D'you think I should return sooner, despite what Davie says?' Alex considered slowly.

'No, I don't think so. You would only arrive a day or two earlier and the worst is over.'

'What is it? What's happened?' asked Luke.

'Your cousin Matthew has had a narrow escape. Diptheria.'

'Gosh! I wish I'd seen him.'

'Luke! Don't be so morbid.'

'I might have seen what they did to him, Father. Dr Cullen says never miss an opportunity.'

'What about Davie's suggestion,' asked John, 'that Matthew come here to convalesce? I imagine they intend Katriona should travel with him.'

Alex was obviously troubled.

'He's a wee lad to stay with an old man, even with his nurse. Perhaps he could go to the Hamiltons? They've a brood. A couple more wouldn't be noticed.'

'Matthew wouldn't like that, Grandpapa. He always wants to be the centre of attention.'

Alex didn't like the sound of that.

'Does he indeed? Well, he'll have to learn to do what we think best.' But in the end they decided to leave any decision until John had spoken to Davie.

(xiv)

There was a last visit to the school mistress. John took Luke but left young Ted to work off his considerable energy stacking peat at the croft.

John went down to the ferry to check their departure time the following day, leaving Luke to arrive first at the cottage. Helen had already decided how to keep him occupied while she talked to John: her patch of garden needed digging over and her back was too stiff for the work. Indeed, as long as anyone could remember, the school mistress had been too stiff for gardening but visitors didn't mind, and neither did Luke.

She sat outside on a bench, reading aloud to him. When she turned over two pages by mistake, to her surprise he came out with the next line then laughed at the expression on her face.

'You've forgotten Uncle Davie's passion. He's always reading poetry to us.'

'Yes, of course.' Helen smiled to herself. Hadn't she introduced Davie to it? 'Has he any new favourites?'

'He doesn't like Tennyson much, or Kipling. He usually finishes with one of Shakespeare's sonnets, especially if he thinks Aunt Charlotte's listening.' Luke grinned. 'He thinks we don't notice but we do. And these days we're always having to learn poems for concerts, to raise money for the new church hall.'

'Ah, yes, Davie did write to me of it.' Luke stopped and leaned on his fork.

'Shall I tell you a secret, Miss Shields? Uncle Davie decided to use human frailty to advantage to boost those funds.'

'Good gracious me!'

'He collected quotations for a book to be published – you know the sort of thing – everyone's favourite verse or motto, the whole congregation contributed. Then he announced that he was having *two* editions of the book printed, one in paperback, the other in gold-tooled leather.'

'My, my!'

'But he then put it about, to customers in the shop, that the leather edition was a "limited circulation", available to "selected" persons . . . of a "superior" nature.'

Helen joined in the laughter.

'It worked, though,' Luke told her triumphantly. 'Uncle Davie even got the Minister to make an announcement from the pulpit. Those who wanted the leather-bound book were invited to put their names on a list in the vestry and', Luke imitated the Minister's unctuous tones, ' "to partake of a little refreshment". Of course they queued up after the service. No one wanted to be left out.'

'That was very naughty of Davie!'

'Oh, I don't know. The list's been over-subscribed three times. They've had to re-order. I still can't understand it myself, though. The leather one costs sixpence and the paper one threepence but the contents are exactly the same.'

'You and I are not gullible, Luke. Tell your uncle he can put me down for the threepenny one. I don't care if I'm thought "superior" or not. Ah, here's your father.'

Her poetry book was put aside for the pleasure of looking at them. How much healthier they both were. Helen paused to enjoy the two sunburnt faces, remembering how they had looked that first afternoon. She watched as John added his weight to the fork and the pair of them tried to shift an old tree root.

Luke was going to be taller than John. Dark hair, a vivid face, only his eyes were a reflection of Mary's grey-brown ones. Helen seldom thought about the boy's natural father but today it was obvious to her that it wasn't John. The root lifted suddenly and John came to join her.

Conversation drifted to Davie.

'He keeps trying to be selected,' John told her, 'but I don't think we'll ever see him in Parliament.'

'Why not? He's a good man.'

'When was that ever a necessary qualification?' he asked.

'John, you're too young to be so cynical.'

'Aye, Mistress Shields.' It was good-humoured if rueful. They sat in companionable silence as Luke went over the ground again with a hoe. Helen summoned up her courage.

'Talking of your youth, which is still apparent to me if not to you . . . ' John waited, slightly apprehensive. 'This lady manageress you've engaged, this Miss Crowther. There's been far too much of her in your letters this past year.' He didn't move but stared into the far distance, blood pounding. Eventually Helen said, 'You are still married to Mary, John, and that young man is your son – '

'Luke is not my son.'

'What!' Her cry was so sharp Luke stopped hoeing and looked up.

'Did you call, Miss Shields?'

'No, no. Carry on.' She stared at John. He returned a level

387

gaze. This time he asked evenly, 'Do you intend to direct my life a second time?' Helen flinched. It was several minutes before she recovered. Finally she blew her nose and tucked the handkerchief away in her pocket.

'Mary wrote to me, you know, after the birth of your – second child.' Helen kept her tone brisk. 'I'd sent a note. I hadn't expected her to reply. I've kept the letter but I won't show it to you just yet. Someday perhaps. It was of you, not the dead infant. Mary's sole concern was how the loss would affect you. Love shone out of that letter. Whatever your regard for her, her feelings for you are strong. You would do well not to forget that.'

'She loved me once. I think it died along with our child.'

'You may think that it did, perhaps you want to believe that it did because of this young woman, but I cannot accept Mary has changed so much.' John gazed steadily at the loch.

'I was wrong to deny Luke,' he admitted, 'I've never done so before. Even though he isn't mine, I've loved him and he has been open and affectionate with me, but I cannot care for Mary in that way.'

'No one can force you to,' Helen replied sadly, 'but you've come so far together. Even if you cannot pretend, don't hurt her, John. Don't be led astray by this Miss Crowther. What can you gain by it? Only misery in the end.'

Luke was almost at the end of his digging. Helen hurried to finish. 'Don't lose sight of his future,' she urged. His achievement will be your reward. Don't fail Luke, he depends on you.'

'Achievement doesn't fulfil a man's desires,' John told her roughly, 'I need more than a vicarious experience to satisfy that.' There was a slight pause before Helen Shields answered, 'I'm sorry that it has to be that way for you. I'm aware it must be inadequate. Sometimes, John, we all have to make do with second-best.'

They visited Helen once more on their way to the ferry. John had assumed his business persona with his suit. Perhaps he wanted to distance himself from her? Helen Shields wondered about it as she poured their tea. 'I haven't told you the gossip here since your last visit. Did you know there had been changes at the Big House?

'Oh yes?' John helped himself to sugar.

'Old Mr Manners died, you know. The elder son wanted to spread his wings so he has gone to Canada, which is a pity. The younger boy has taken over the estate and he's far too wild in my opinion.'

As he stirred his tea John reflected on Luke's occasional touch of arrogance. Even if the physical differences between him and the boy grew more apparent, at least he could be thankful Luke had inherited more of his mother's temperament than his father's.

'Look at that!' Helen was pointing through the open door. Two carts were passing each other but the driver's hadn't stopped to chat. They'd hailed each other and driven on. 'Nothing but hustle and bustle up here nowadays.'

John couldn't bring himself to smile at the exaggeration. Life was changing, increasing in tempo. Somehow this holiday felt like the end of a chapter. He put down his empty cup and reached for his hat, anxious to be gone.

'We must be off. Goodbye and – thank you. For your advice. As always, I know it was well meant.'

When the door closed behind them, the air felt colder. She had done her best, pray God he didn't hate her for it.

As they walked away Luke turned to give a cheery wave. It wasn't much but it sustained her.

(xv)

Charlotte and Davie were together in the quiet room. Matthew was asleep. Davie sat as he so often did, one hand resting on Matthew's arm, for reassurance. 'He is improving, isn't he, dearest?'

'Yes, he's much better. If there are no complications we can take him home at the end of the week.'

'And you haven't changed your mind? You'd rather he stayed with us?'

'Yes. I want to nurse him back to health myself. Perhaps I neglected him in the past, Davie? The other two had more of my time but the emporium had grown by the time Matthew was

389

born. I shall try and make it up to him.' Both knew she wasn't referring simply to Matthew's well-being.

'I'm sure that's all in the past, dearest.' It was comfortable to think any sin might have been sweated away with the fever.

'Maybe next summer, when Matthew's strong again, we can take him back to Scotland?' Charlotte suggested.

'Not to Biarritz?' Davie smiled.

'Certainly not.' The phrase was familiar and firm. It added to his reassurance. He watched placidly as Charlotte finished one row of knitting and changed needles.

'What a great many people there were there,' she sighed, 'in Biarritz. And all of them – so rich!'

'I fear Darlington is very small beer, Charlotte.'

'It is quite sufficient for me.'

'I'm glad to hear it. Of course we will be moving to London one day, when John decides the time is right.' He didn't want her to feel trapped again.

'I suppose so.' She didn't sound eager. 'I'm beginning to wonder if Darlington isn't the place for us after all.'

'Charlotte!' Davie could scarcely believe his ears.

'I know, Davie, I've always been the one anxious to move. But since Biarritz and Matthew's illness – '

'He's getting better, my love, he's improving every day,' Davie said earnestly. 'We're still young. Why shouldn't we move on? The world is ours to explore. Wait till I'm selected next time, then you'll see things differently.'

'Perhaps.' Charlotte was pensive, the knitting slack in her lap. 'I was thinking how strange that we all ended up here: you and John, my mother, returning from the other side of the world – '

'We must have ambition. You wouldn't have us stagnate?' She was sounding far too middle-aged.

'Perhaps,' she said again.

'A man has to reach out for the moon, Charlotte, or climb to see what's beyond the hill.'

I must try harder, he thought, I'm in a rut. Nothing but the emporium and the council chamber. He was thinking of ways to cajole her out of her mood when Charlotte gave a gasp.

'Look at the time, Davie! You'll be late for the fund-raising committee.'

CHAPTER THIRTEEN

Resolutions

It was autumn and pouring with rain, great droplets that bounced up from the London pavements, soaking Freddie's trousers. Under his sodden umbrella he looked remarkably cheerful for a man in such a state. Ethel hurried across from her office doorway, full of apologies.

'I'm sorry. They asked me to work late. Have you been here long?' The umbrella was large enough to conceal her fierce kiss and she clung to him, shivering.

'Marvellous news, Eth. Cis has an interview arranged in London next month.' Hugging his arm, she read, ' " . . . with a Mr Gordon Selfridge who is recruiting. His store is due to open next year." '

'Keep our fingers crossed, eh?' Freddie said happily. 'If Cis is offered a position – '

'And moves in to help with the rent – '

'We can afford to get married!'

'Oh, Freddie!' Passers-by averted their eyes from such a display of affection, but Ethel and Freddie never even noticed.

Cecilia hugged the secret to herself. She too was waiting, for a curtain to rise on yet another fund-raising concert. She hadn't particularly wanted to come this evening but buying a ticket was the best way to please the McKies, and it might not be too long before she would need a good reference.

The hall was heavy with middle-class respectability, emphasized by the rich, dark wooden panelling. Ahead of her, the McKies sat in a row, Charlotte at one end, wearing a very subdued hat. It was common knowledge in the emporium that Mrs Davie didn't approve of Jane's dancing lessons. She'd only agreed to please her husband and certainly wouldn't dress up simply to come and see Jane perform. Beyond her, Davie cuddled Matthew. It was the boy's first outing since his illness; he was a pale, sly-looking child in Cecilia's opinion. She much preferred Ted.

Luke and John were at the other end of the row, still brown from their holiday. Cecilia found it incredible that John should return to the shop with calloused hands, for all the world as if he'd been working as a labourer. Surely if one had been needed on his father's property, John had only to employ someone? Such behaviour was nothing but Scots parsimony, Cecilia decided.

As though he sensed her thoughts, John turned and looked at her. It irritated her: Mr McKie was given to doing that far too often nowadays. It made the other assistants giggle and undermined Cecilia's authority – thank goodness Mrs McKie didn't appear to have noticed. Never mind; it wouldn't be for much longer, she thought.

In their row, Charlotte declared in a whisper she was thankful there were so few people worth knowing here tonight. This wasn't the sort of event at which she wanted to be recognized. Beside her, Matthew looked half asleep. Charlotte wondered, as she so often did, what he was thinking.

John fidgeted again. Davie leaned across to murmur, 'It only lasts a couple of hours. We should be away by half past nine.' Overhead, lights began to fade.

'Is our Jane on at the beginning?'

'No, Ted, not until the third item. Be patient.'

The good and the not-so-good lolloped across the stage in a country dance. Parents smiled fondly. Friends kept polite expressions in place. John glanced surreptitiously at his watch: five minutes gone. He closed his eyes and thought about the conversation with the bank manager that afternoon.

'You ought to decide soon, Mr McKie, whether to expand into another shop.'

'We may move to London. My brother and I need more time to think it over.' The bank manager had sighed: this client used to be so go-ahead.

'It can't wait for ever, Mc McKie.'

Applause died down a second time and Davie shifted a little. Jane's solo was next. The curtain rose.

Slim arms were raised as the sylph drifted forward. John found himself thinking of butterflies above the heather, then as she moved more urgently, of gulls whirling in the spring as they followed the plough.

The music slowed and the figure became gentle muslin drapery floating gracefully. John recalled Davie's voice in the schoolroom years ago. 'Poetry, Mistress Shields!' Here was the same passion translated into dance.

It was over and the applause startled him. This was no polite clapping of gloved hands but complete enthusiasm. Davie beamed and John couldn't help the surprise in his voice as he told him, 'She's not bad, Davie, not bad at all.'

Over coffee and biscuits afterwards, Charlotte accepted the compliments; yes, lessons had been an excellent idea, Jane's deportment was much improved. But she ridiculed Miss Crowther's suggestion. Professional teaching in London? What nonsense! Jane would be joining her mother in the emporium as soon as her schooling was over. She could count herself lucky she hadn't had to begin work at seven years of age as her mother had. As usual, Davie didn't argue.

On the way home, Jane's small hand snuggled into his pocket beside his own. 'Did you like it, Dada?'

'Very much, my darling.'

'Maybe Mama will change her mind one day?'

'Maybe. We'll have to wait for the right moment to ask her.'

He looked across at his wife. How beautiful she looked tonight, he thought fondly, with the tortoiseshell combs in her hair beneath the veiling. Were they the same he'd lifted out that first night in Saltburn? She still let him brush the thick curls – he looked on it as a special treat – but wasn't as encouraging in other matters as she used to be.

She was tired, he told himself. Nursing Matthew hadn't been easy. Davie didn't know the real reason, for Charlotte hadn't told him. It concerned Matthew but she and Mrs Armitage were keeping it to themselves as long as they could; the boy had begun stealing again. Not only tips from the saucers; this week he'd slipped into the cashier's cage and taken money from her till. Whenever she thought of it Charlotte felt cold. She certainly couldn't bring herself to respond to Davie's embraces.

(ii)

On Christmas morning young Ted woke, caught his breath and then exhaled in a guilty rush. His stocking was there! The past year's record was definitely not without blemish. Anxiously he looked across at Matthew's bedstead and sighed with relief to see the bulging stocking tied with red ribbon that hung from the frame. Neither Ted nor Jane had expected Matthew to be included but Mother must have relented. Father had obviously persuaded her too. Ted had no doubt as to what had happened.

Slowly he laid out the familiar shapes on his counterpane, all of them wrapped in silver paper and tied with more ribbon: the orange, apple, a bag of nuts, a new penny, sixpence and an unfamiliar shape. He unwrapped it – a new shilling, gosh! Ted was astonished. This was riches. Best of all, hidden in the toe where he knew it would be, the pink sugar mouse with a chocolate tail. He salivated as he remembered the taste. Every year as they sat round the tree after Christmas dinner he would lick away at that tail. He laid the mouse beside the other treasures and padded across the cold linoleum. 'Wake up, Matthew. It's all right, you've got a stocking after all.'

Matthew was instantly awake. There was no halfway stage with him, no slipping in and out in a warm doziness but eyes open, alert. 'How much?' he asked. Ted did a quick calculation.

'One and sevenpence.'

'That's rotten. They should've given us half a guinea.'

His brother was stunned.

'Don't be stupid! Half a guinea? What d'you want as much as that for? You can get masses of bull's eyes for one and sevenpence.'

'Swop my sugar mouse for your money?'

Ted was on his guard. 'All my money?'

'Yes.'

'Nothing doing.' But the saliva increased, making him swallow. 'I might consider it for – a penny.' Mice cost tuppence, they both knew that. Matthew plunged his hand into the stocking and pulled out the silver package.

'You can have it for sixpence. That's my final offer,' Matthew tempted.

'Oh, all right.' Ted padded back to find the sixpence. What was money beside two pink sugar mice? He could eat one straight away and save the other for later. It was wiser to do that anyway, there might be trouble if mother found out he had two. Ted jumped back into bed and pulled the blankets round him. His feet were icy cold. Very carefully he peeled back the paper so that the tiny pink ears were revealed. He'd start at the head with this one. Across the room Matthew got out of bed and went to the door.

'Where are you off to?'

'To see Jane.'

'She won't give you her money. You haven't got any more swops.'

'Yes, I have. I'll sell her my bag of nuts.'

He was unlucky. Jane understood the value of coins; they meant new shoes for dancing, extra pennies to add to her savings. She would have to study in London eventually, her teacher told her so. And Miss Crowther. 'All the best teachers, the most famous dancers, they live in London, Jane. I'll take you with me one day and we'll go to the theatre together.' Miss Crowther was an absolute brick. Ever since the concert she'd been on Father's side, saying that Jane simply must go to London. She hadn't said so to Mama because Miss Crowther was very careful not to upset Mama, but she had said she would do what she could to help.

Jane woke to find Matthew untying her stocking. In a flash she'd scrambled to the end of the bed.

'Leave it, it's mine!' She grabbed at it but Matthew still hung on.

'You don't need all the money. Swop you the shilling for my bag of nuts – '

'I don't want your nuts!' Jane was nearly in tears. 'Let go, you rotten thief!'

'Don't you call me that!'

'Thief, thief!' she shrieked. 'You steal money from the shop. Everyone knows except Uncle John. Let go my stocking or I'll tell him!'

Matthew hit her hard across the face and pummelled the stocking out of frustration. He ran back to his own room, slamming the door behind him. Under the bedclothes Jane clutched the shards of her pink sugar mouse and wept.

(iii)

After Christmas dinner, while the women cleared the table, Davie built up an enormous fire in the dining room. The big table was pushed a little to one side to make more space and John wandered off to the shop to enjoy a few moments of peace. The rest of the day would be given over to games with the children. Davie enjoyed it but he didn't. Already he could hear laughter and music upstairs. Katriona was trying out her pianola. 'Second-hand, John, but very reasonable and she deserves a nice present,' Davie had persuaded. John sighed; it was ridiculous how generous Davie was. He sniffed the odours down here: clean sawdust and polish, cloth and leather and the chill dampness that seeped up when the heating was turned off. One or two lights were always left switched on. They added to the desolate emptiness but they also shone on the empty till drawers. It was Mr Hart's suggestion, that and never leaving a single coin overnight. John was slightly puzzled but Davie had backed Mr Hart. Leaving money about was leaving temptation so John acquiesced. Each evening, the tills were emptied into a satchel and Mr Hart took the money to the bank's nightsafe on his way home. Privately, Charlotte was extremely relieved.

John stood enjoying his kingdom: sheeted counters and shelves of merchandise, bargains ready for the annual sale and posters, thick with exclamation marks, ready to be put in the window. In a box were the labels they'd had printed this year: *Special Bargain – As Advertised!* Davie had taken a whole page in every newspaper. It wasn't excessive, he told John, they had quite a few items they needed to shift this winter. Miss Crowther's mistaken line of bicycling skirts, for instance. John looked at the rail and shook his head with a smile. His favourite had certainly over-estimated there. They were so short, too. He'd been as shocked as Charlotte when he'd seen them. True, the young ladies of Darlington were eager to purchase, but their mothers were not – and it was those mothers who held the purse strings.

Charlotte had taken inordinate pleasure in explaining to Miss Crowther that although not unfashionable, Darlington followed rather than led in matters of skirt length, that customers here were ladylike, not modern women. Miss Crowther bowed and held her tongue. Nor for much longer, she told herself.

Lately John had heard one or two disquieting rumours about his lady manageress. She had been seen walking along the banks of the Skerne accompanied by a gentleman; that same person had also stood beside her in St Cuthbert's and shared a hymn book. John cursed the unknown person heartily and asked Mr Hart if he thought it could be Miss Crowther's brother? Mr Hart was adamant that it was not; the person had been several years older than Miss Crowther, a gentleman farmer from West Auckland, it was said. The rumours reached Charlotte. She gave it as her opinion that no woman whose thirtieth birthday was in sight would turn down security if it were offered. None of them spoke to Miss Crowther on the subject because it wouldn't have been proper. She knew of the speculation and smiled to herself. She wasn't interested in the gentleman farmer except as a companion but let everyone think what they liked. She was due to meet Mr Selfridge in ten days' time.

In his study, away from the festivities, John made an astonishing resolution: the time had come to declare himself to

Miss Crowther. She was due to go on a buying expedition soon, to London. He would make some excuse to accompany her! The suddenness of the idea left him gasping. Then he had another. Miss Crowther always stayed at a club for professional women as was proper, but this time – and John trembled at the audacity of it – he would book a hotel room. He would tell her when they arrived in London. As to what would happen afterwards . . . and Mary? John brushed all other thoughts from his mind. He had the right, he told himself feverishly, to a little happiness.

(iv)

Upstairs, Davie watched happily as Charlotte unwrapped his gifts: a necklace of amethysts with a matching bracelets, kid gloves finer than any in the emporium and a dozen pairs of silk stockings.

'Oh, Mr Davie!' Mrs Armitage had unwrapped her present and discovered she'd been given kid gloves, too. She kissed him like an excited girl. 'Oh, how kind! They're exquisite! I shall keep them for "best" and I shall wear them . . . ' She hesitated for she rarely ventured far nowadays, 'I shall keep them to wear in the spring.' She blew another kiss and put the gloves beside John's gift: bedsocks.

The children unwrapped Jeannie's parcels solemnly. Dear Grandmama. The sizes were too small, as they always were. She never remembered how much they grew. But Matthew would be able to wear the jerseys intended for Ted and Luke. As for Jane, she hung the locket round her neck. 'I shall wear it on special occasions,' she whispered to Davie, 'because she was always kind and gentle.'

Davie sighed. How good Christmases had been on the croft. The quietness and peace beside the loch, the Bible-reading and the long walk to the kirk and back in the darkness. Sometimes there was meat for Christmas, sometimes only herring, but it never seemed to matter when they were children. Nor had his stocking ever felt full. It must be over-indulgence that left him feeling so unwell now. All the same, Charlotte had noticed and to placate her, he'd agreed to visit Cullen once the holiday was over.

Below, they heard the doorbell ring. Ted dashed to the window. 'It's them! I can see the lanterns!'

'Quickly then, run and tell Uncle John. He won't want to miss the carol-singing. Jane, you can turn the music for Katriona.' Forcing himself to forget his aches and pains, Davie prepared to receive the choir.

Later when the visitors had gone and the children were scorching themselves trying to roast chestnuts on a shovel, Davie asked, 'A penny for them, John?'

To his surprise, John blushed.

'Oh, I don't know,' he muttered, 'I think I was remembering how it was when we were their age.'

Davie was delighted. 'So was I, earlier. It was different, I'll say that.'

'It was better,' John insisted.

'No, not for some of us,' Mary spoke from the shadows, 'I can only remember the poverty.'

'Poverty?' Young Ted was curious.

'There were no presents at Christmas,' his father explained.

'None at all? Not even a sugar mouse?'

'There wasn't any money, Ted. And the Minister preached against it, too. Presents were considered a waste of money. I don't think your uncle or I ever missed them.'

'We didn't,' John agreed, 'and I can remember when I received my first gift. It wasn't for Christmas or my birthday, it was when I began at school. Those boots. D'you remember when you got yours?'

Ted rolled on the floor, yelling with laughter and waving his legs in the air. 'Father got boots as a present!' Charlotte reached out and clipped him hard across the ear.

'Be silent at once! And be thankful we don't have to make a gift of yours.' He was startled but, like his father, knew better than to argue.

From beside Mary, Luke tried to smoothe things over. 'I've been wondering about Grandfather. I wonder what he's doing today and whether we left enough peat cut to last through the winter. He told me when it gets really cold he lets the old dog cuddle up beside him to keep him warm.' Luke glanced at

399

Mary. 'I dare say he catches a few fleas, does Grandfather, but it's better than a cold, don't you think?'

This time Mary smiled. 'I should think he's toasting himself in front of the fire, wondering about you. And don't worry, he won't be lonely. We sent a card to the Hamiltons and some money so that they could buy him a grand dinner.'

Did we? thought John.

They were all smiling now, talking about the croft, then Katriona began to sing. She sat near the fire, staring into the flames. It wasn't written music but a much older sound, mouth music, telling of good times and bad, of the warriors in times past, of loved ones forced to leave the land. Sometimes it was harsh, sometimes sweet. When she had finished, no one spoke. Davie was grateful for the candlelight to conceal his tears.

Jane was the first to stir. She went and kissed Katriona timidly and John called out in the Gaelic, 'I thank you for that. It was from the heart.'

Charlotte stood up briskly, not having understood a word. 'Five more minutes then bed,' she announced and rang for Bertha to help with Mrs Armitage.

CHAPTER FOURTEEN

Upheaval

Looking back on the first few days of the New Year, Charlotte was to think of it afterwards as a period of peace, although at the time it scarcely seemed so.

First, there was the Grand Concert. In late November, when the Members of Session had shaken their heads over the short-fall in the building fund, Davie had suggested it. This time it wouldn't be a small affair but a full-blown evening's entertainment.

As it was his idea, he'd taken responsibility for it and thrown himself heart and soul into the project, making one of the rare mistakes of his life. He'd advertised in the local newspapers that any parents of talented children who might wish them to appear in the Grand Concert should present themselves for consideration at McKie Bros. On the appointed day the queue stretched away beyond the shop, through the colonnade and up Black-wellgate. Little boys in sailor suits vied with each other to torment sisters in pinafores and vast hats. Inside the emporium it was chaotic. Counter assistants chased children away from precarious displays. Babies began crying, toddlers refused to be hushed and Mrs Armitage decided it was a morning to retreat upstairs.

Mr Hart, whose best qualities were revealed in a crisis, sent the errand boy to buy five pounds of assorted gob-stoppers, at the double. 'The chewiest variety you can find, Finlay, but nothing chocolate-coated.' When the glass jars arrived, he set Billy Beal to patrol the queue. Any rosebud mouth that showed signs of opening was to be stoppered up and the teeth cemented together until Mr Davie had a chance to sort out the mess.

What a loss to political life Davie was, thought Mr Hart, making judgements Solomon would have envied, for faced with the choice of reducing the number of applicants without losing their mothers as customers, Davie had invented a brand-new choir. All those children not chosen to perform individual items were invited to join it. He whisked Katriona out of the kitchen and sat her at the pianola. Children were taken up to the dining room in batches to 'test their voices'. Fond parents were overwhelmed by the praise Mr Davie showered on them. His vigorous applause dispelled the fractiousness each felt at the sight of so many others. Mothers were eager to assure dear Mr Davie that Hettie or Eric, Maud or Alice, would be enchanted to sing, particularly when he described the special hymn he was in the throes of composing for the occasion.

By early afternoon it was over. Davie was worn out. He lay on the settee in their sitting room and Charlotte sent Ada to fetch the whisky from John's study. Her dearest had performed a miracle but it had taken it out of him.

'You'd better bring a pen and paper as well, Charlotte. I have to make a start on that confounded hymn!' Perhaps it was the spirits, maybe it was his natural exuberance returning, but the masterpiece grew to an enormous length. At the next meeting of the Grand Concert sub-committee it was presented with a flourish for their approval. In the opinion of many members, the newly appointed Minister earned his laurels over it. He saw the problem and dealt with it, tactfully.

'This is a fine piece of work if I may say so, Mr McKie. Very fine indeed.'

Davie gave a deprecating laugh. 'Kind of you to say so, Minister.'

The Minister looked round the table; others hastened to agree with him. Loudly.

'Of course it is unusual in its form. The chorus, for example. A four-verse chorus?'

'It's a new idea,' Davie was exceedingly proud. 'My own, in fact.'

'Indeed? Very, very unusual.'

'Those children,' Davie explained, 'that new choir we've just formed, I thought they deserved as splendid a hymn as I could compose.'

'And you have, Mr McKie, you have indeed. A song of praise to the Lord, fourteen verses long . . . '

Davie detected a flicker of doubt in the Minister's voice. 'Back in Scotland, in the kirk, we used to sing hymns longer even than that.'

'We did indeed, Mr McKie, in the good old days . . . ' Again he looked round the table for support. When he judged the flood of reminiscences had gone on long enough, he asked, 'Do you not consider that nowadays, our congregation tends to prefer something a little – shorter? About six verses, say?'

It took half an hour to reduce the masterpiece to a manageable size but the author was satisfied. At the Minister's prompting, the organist agreed that such a work should have its own score, also specially composed for the occasion. 'We will announce to the newspapers that the first performance of this joint work will be given at the Theatre Royal,' the Minister concluded.

For Davie had produced one very ambitious idea indeed. If this was a Grand Concert, one the whole world should attend, well, the world of Darlington and the north-east, it required a fitting setting, an auditorium large enough. What did the committee think of a proper theatre with an orchestra? The committee were delighted. Most of them had children enrolled in Davie McKie's new choir, and it was just the sort of news to please their wives.

'There's a vacant date in January. The manager of the Theatre Royal will not charge for the use of his theatre provided we acknowledge his kindness in our programmes.'

'Indeed?'

'Yes, Minister. And I thought we could ask some of the

403

bonniest young women in the congregation to sell those programmes for as much as they'll fetch.'

The all-male committee nodded sagaciously. Davie had, however, learned from his experience. 'Might I suggest two of our senior members select those young women?'

'Very right and proper, Mr McKie. All those in favour?'

Surprisingly for a group of Scotsmen, there wasn't a single dissenting voice.

(i)

When Davie told him, John observed sourly that he'd got the whole town sewn up. Children would be on stage, and it followed that their parents would fill the auditorium. Now nubile ladies would be selling programmes, attracting all the eager young men.

'Which leaves me with nothing to do except buy a ticket and I'm sure Mary will see to that.'

Davie shook his head. How John had changed these last few months. Once they'd been very close. Physical promixity was still there of course, but he could no longer claim to know John's mind on any matter. Plans for the future had been shelved; it was as though life itself was suspended, waiting for John to rejoin the family. That moment couldn't come soon enough. More and more the burden of running the emporium was being left to him – and Davie was always so tired.

He gave himself an impatient shake. This was no time for self-pity, there was too much to be done.

(ii)

Jane sought out Miss Crowther with a request: could she design a costume? Jane was to dance another solo. Cecilia smiled.

'Is it to be a nymph, like last time?'

'Oh no, a bird costume. I'm dancing a bird that's just been

404

born. It's the morning of his first day and he's learning to fly, exploring a magic river.'

'Goodness, how exciting. What sort of a bird is it? A king-fisher?'

Jane considered. 'More silvery blue. Not a real bird, a fairy-tale one. And shiny so it'll catch the light.'

'I'll do my best.'

(iii)

In Coburg Street, Mrs Hart observed, 'I don't think Miss Crowther will be with us much longer.' Mr Hart lowered his newspaper.

'Has she found rooms elsewhere?'

'No, but she's been writing to London quite a lot recently. I think she's after another position – and she wants to join in with those Suffragettes.'

'It's no business of ours what she does,' warned Mr Hart.

'No, but it'll make a difference to Mr McKie if she goes, won't it?'

Mr Hart pondered silently. He was as worried as his wife at John's infatuation. Like the rest of the emporium, he prayed it would soon be over.

Mrs Hart tried another tack. 'Did you tell Mr McKie about Miss Crowther refusing Mr Townsend?' Mr Townsend was the gentleman farmer from West Auckland, who was no longer escorting Miss Crowther.

'Yes, I did. He seemed quite pleased about it.'

'He'd no business to be!' Grace Hart was self-righteous. 'Him being a married man.'

Her husband was more tolerant.

'Human nature is very frail,' he observed. 'Sooner or later a weakness is exposed in most of us. Who are we to criticize, lovey? All we know for certain is that Mr McKie greatly admires Miss Crowther. Fortunately, being a lady, she appears unaware of the fact.' It wasn't a reply calculated to bring out the best in Mrs Hart.

'Hrmmph!' she snorted and returned to her other theme.

405

'I don't see why she turned Mr Townsend down, not at her age. You'd think she'd be glad of a husband with a bit of property. I know plenty round here who would.'

'You must remember, lovey,' Alfred Hart reproached his wife mildly, 'that Miss Crowther is not interested in matrimony as many women are because of her political views. She would not find it easy to love, honour and obey a man either, not after holding such a responsible position in the emporium. And for a lady solely interested in furthering her career, it isn't surprising if her thoughts turn to London.'

'Will you say anything about it to Mr McKie?'

'Definitely not!' Sufficient unto the day . . . it would be bad enough when it happened.

(iv)

The two elderly gentlemen who'd been given the task of choosing the fairest of the fair had a collective wisdom Davie lacked. Their first act was to beg Mrs Davie McKie for an appointment. Charlotte behaved extremely graciously and gave them china tea. Much to her surprise she wasn't invited to sell programmes but asked instead whether she'd play her part in the scheme by chairing a ladies' sub-committee.

'You see, dear madam, we believe the feminine touch is missing from our enterprise.

'It needs inspiration, an eye for detail, a woman's hand at the helm.' All spoken enthusiastically but kept deliberately vague.

'Above all,' said his partner, 'it needs Mrs Davie McKie.'

Charlotte overcame her disappointment once she grasped the importance of this new position. She would sit at the right hand of the guest of honour, the Mayor, during the concert. She would preside over the entire proceedings from a seat on the stage – and the programme sellers would be under her control.

Charlotte permitted herself a few dignified moments of consideration before accepting. The elderly gentlemen beamed and withdrew. Tomorrow they could begin the pleasurable fatigue of selecting a dozen of the most attractive ladies in the congregation.

Less than a week before the concert, two events happened

406

with consequences for everyone. The first concerned Davie. At long last he made an appointment to see Dr Cullen. He went at a time of day when his absence from the shop wouldn't be noticed.

The constant diet of porter had left its mark on Dr Cullen. He was as round as a barrel and his head perched on top of his very short neck like a cottage loaf.

After examining Davie he was unusually quiet and made a great play of finding pen and paper among the muddle on his desk. 'How soon could you arrange a visit to London, McKie?' Davie paused in buttoning up his shirt.

'Not until after the Grand Concert. Why?'

'There's someone I'd like you to see. I want him to take a look at you.'

'What on earth for?' Davie was puzzled rather than worried.

'Because I'd like a second opinion.' Still surprised, Davie said, 'Charlotte's been giving me an iron tonic.'

'Yes. I'm sure Mrs McKie has been right on many previous occasions . . .'

Davie finished the sentence for him. 'But not this time?'

'To be honest, I don't know. That's why I'd like another opinion. The man I want you to see isn't a quack, he's someone I trained with in Newcastle, but he's developed a very superior manner to match the furniture in his rooms in Harley Street.'

Davie managed a grin. 'It'll be one salesman trying to impress another then, won't it?' More uncertainly he asked, 'I take it, he is good? This friend of yours?'

'The best I know of,' Dr Cullen said simply. He could see the import of his words had reached Davie. He dreaded what might be coming next.

'I should have heeded Luke,' Davie announced unexpectedly. 'He's been urging for months that I should visit you. But you see I've felt so well in between. It's nothing serious is it? I'm as strong as ever I was?'

'How is Luke? Still studying hard I hope. I haven't seen him lately.'

Davie noticed the lack of an answer to his question.

'He's well,' he said briefly.

'This concert,' Dr Cullen had found his pen now, 'It's on January seventh, isn't it? My wife's already bought tickets.

Suppose we ask for an appointment three days after that? It would give you time to get your breath back. These fund-raising affairs involve such a lot of work. You've undertaken the lion's share as usual, no doubt?'

'People ask. I don't like to let them down.'

'Nevertheless, McKie, I'd rather you didn't overtax yourself. Let the young people give a hand instead. I'll write to Berwick and let you know when he can see you.'

'Charlotte mustn't be told,' said Davie suddenly.

'That goes without saying. I hope you can think of a convincing excuse for the visit to London? We don't want to arouse her suspicions unnecessarily.'

'I'll think of something. Our manageress, Miss Crowther, I think she's due down there then. I'll find a reason to accompany her.'

'Excellent.'

Davie rose and picked up his hat. 'This friend of yours – Berwick, did you say? In what does he specialize?'

Dr Cullen didn't look up from the paper. 'I'd rather you didn't concern yourself about that, McKie. I've been wrong before. No doubt I will be again. I'll be in touch about the appointment.' And with that, Davie had to be content.

He desperately wanted to tell Charlotte, to feel her arms surround and comfort him, but it wasn't fair to worry her. After all, it was nothing, Dr Cullen had said as much. He simply wanted to be sure. The iron tonic was running low. He'd buy another bottle to please Charlotte, he knew what faith she had in it.

He tramped through sleet, the cold numbing his mind as well as his body. It was serious, it must be serious. He recalled the series of questions Dr Cullen had asked. How surprised they'd both been when Davie calculated the first time he'd felt weak was as long ago as the day in 1905 when the South African War memorial had been unveiled.

The attacks these days were more frequent. His great strength was slowly ebbing away. Once, he told the doctor, he'd found himself, weak as a kitten, sitting in the passage beside the lift. Mary had discovered him and had fetched Billy and Mr Hart. It needed the three of them to get him upstairs, via the lift, to his room. He hadn't told Charlotte of course, no need to worry her, besides after an hour or two he'd felt perfectly well. As he did now, in fact.

Dr Cullen had looked at him across the desk and asked, 'If that's so, McKie, why after all this time are you visiting me today?'

'Because of the pain!' It had finally come out. Davie felt tension slipping away out of relief at being able to talk about it. He had kept the knowledge to himself as long as he possibly could, but now . . . 'Sometimes, it's as though my back has red-hot pokers through it!'

There had been no further questions, just a gentle probing. The fingers found the pain quickly enough and something else: an area where Davie couldn't even feel the finger tips.

In the pharmacy the chemist asked Mr Davie McKie for the third time whether he could be of assistance. Davie recollected where he was with a start. He pointed to the familiar bottle. It was taken down, wrapped and paid for. 'Is this stuff any use? Any use at all?' he demanded.

'Mr McKie!' Loss of faith would undermine the chemist's profits, 'My customers have been taking it for years – '

'No matter. Let me have it.' Davie thrust the package into his pocket and went out without waiting for his change. The chemist put the coins carefully to one side. What strange behaviour!

Davie had to talk to someone. Charlotte couldn't be upset, it would have to be John. John would know what to say, how to calm the irrational fear. It couldn't be that serious! He was in the prime of life, he'd the strength of three men, on good days.

John wasn't in his study, he'd been called back to the warehouse. Mr Hart was vague. He'd had an urgent message, but he wasn't sure what it was about. Yes, Mrs McKie and Mrs Davie were both out. He thought Mrs Armitage might be in the salon.

Davie slipped on his genial mask before stepping out from Gentlemen's Tailoring into the ladies' departments. On all sides, customers greeted him. It took more than ten minutes to reach the salon and an equally slow passage to Mrs Armitage. There was so much excitement about the Grand Concert, everyone reverberated with it; only two more days . . . And afterwards, thought Davie, I'm making my first visit to London – to see Mr Berwick.

Mrs Armitage quivered with pleasure. The sight of his bright smile made her feel better, she told him. This morning she'd had just the teeniest twinge of rheumatism but he could take her mind off it if only he'd sit and have a cup of tea. Listening to her chatter without hearing a word, Davie wondered how old she was. He did a swift calculation. She must be seventy or thereabouts. What wouldn't he give for the expectation of achieving three score and ten!

No, Mrs Armitage wasn't quite sure where Charlotte could be found. She would be sure to tell her Davie wanted to see her. Was there any message? But Charlotte mustn't be told! He'd agreed with the doctor, there was no reason to alarm his wife, the man had been wrong before.

'No message . . . ' Davie continued to smile at customers crowding round the gilt tables. Suddenly the whole place stifled him. He could feel tears hot behind his eyelids. 'It's so warm . . . must have a little fresh air!' Outside the cold wind had people hurrying home, heads bent. No one stopped to speak to him now. Davie had never felt lonelier in his life.

He was in the study when John returned. It was dark: the shadowy figure gave John a fright. 'Why didn't you switch on the light?'

'I'm sorry. I didn't notice how late it was.' John chafed his hands to warm them before going back outside to tug at the lift rope.

'It's been a shocking day and I'm ready for my tea,' he called, 'there's been a problem at one of the Middlesbrough docks – men refusing to unload. It's taken all this time to sort it out.' He returned to the study. 'Were you waiting to see me?'

'Not really.' How could he add to John's problems? What was there to say anyway? It was all a mistake, it had to be!

'You're looking a bit seedy,' John sounded critical rather than concerned. 'The sooner this concert is over, the better. It's taking too much out of you.'

'I don't think I'll bother with tea, thanks.'

'Oh, sit down. The emporium can manage without us for five minutes.' At this slight hint of sympathy Davie almost succumbed to the temptation to tell John. He was bracing himself to do so when Mary arrived with the tray.

'There you are,' she said in surprise, 'Charlotte's back. She's been asking for you.'

(v)

It wasn't in Charlotte's nature to dread, her lack of imagination precluded it, but she had learned to be apprehensive where Matthew was concerned. She and Mrs Armitage had congratulated themselves on the improvement. Since the boy had begun at school and was no longer in the emporium during the day, tips remained in salon saucers. The letter from Matthew's headmaster therefore, came as a blow. As usual, Charlotte confided in her aunt rather than Davie.

'He requires us to visit the school this afternoon, Aunt, but Davie has been so busy lately and he's not been really well since the holiday in Biarritz. I blame the French for many things including Davie's loss of appetite. I'm astonished the King continues to visit the country.'

Mrs Armitage clutched her shrunken bosom as she always did when upset. 'Are you sure it's wise to go alone, Charlotte? Why not take Katriona with you? She could wait outside until the interview was finished.'

'No, I must go by myself.' She took the envelope out of her pocket. 'This is the letter. From the tone, I think the fewer who know of it, the better.'

'Oh, dear!' Mrs Armitage had to use a magnifying glass. 'It's very short,' she said after finishing it.

'But not encouraging.'

Charlotte wore a thick veil and went through the churchyard rather than the main street. In the Headmaster's study she refused refreshment. She'd no wish to prolong matters.

'You understand, Mrs McKie, we have tried reasoning with Matthew. There have been other occasions and he's been punished. I didn't trouble you at the time because I believed we could deal with the problem ourselves. I regret to say we appear to have failed.'

'He has been chastised, of course.'

411

'But it does not alter his attitude. Far from being penitent, on each occasion he's been beside himself with rage. The point is, Mrs McKie, we cannot allow a thief to dwell among us. What if the contagion were to spread? With any other boy I would have contacted his parents earlier, but out of respect for you and Mr McKie, I allowed Matthew one more chance. To no avail.'

The Headmaster walked irritably to the window. He prided himself in being able to mould boys into embryo clean, healthy Englishmen. This was his first serious failure. 'You'd think with the example of his brother and cousin who both did so well at this school . . . How is Ted now he's at grammar school?'

'Not as successful as Luke.' This always rankled with Charlotte.

'We're not all academically gifted, Mrs McKie. Young Ted has many fine qualities. He will become a popular leader like his father, I've no doubt, given time.'

'So far his only aptitude appears to be boxing.'

The Headmaster hid a smile at the sight of Charlotte's grim face.

'Well, well . . . ' He returned to the disagreeable task confronting them. 'I'm afraid Matthew will have to leave this school.'

'Leave! Altogether?'

'I have no alternative. I cannot conceal from you any longer, Matthew is not only a thief, he's a bully as well.'

'But he's only a little boy!' Behind the veil, Charlotte was scarlet. Her grip on her umbrella was painful. 'I refuse to believe he's so wicked!'

'He tried to take money from another boy. When that child refused, Matthew twisted his arm. It was so swollen, the doctor had to attend to it. Matthew has been confined in a storeroom since the incident, away from the other children. I would like you to take him with you this afternoon.' He waited for a reaction but Charlotte couldn't speak.

'Believe me when I say how sorry I am, Mrs McKie. My first thought was to cane your boy in front of the school. Some would use the birch very severely but I do not believe it a universal remedy. In Matthew's case, it has been tried before.'

Charlotte disagreed violently. She was so angry she wanted to whip Matthew herself! The Headmaster was speaking again. 'If

412

you take him away now, it may prevent gossip spreading too far.'

'Yes, indeed,' she whispered. The whole of Darlington would know that her son was a thief. It was appalling!

The Headmaster sighed. 'None of us thought it possible, the first time it happened. Matthew's such an attractive child.' Charlotte remembered privately those other occasions in the store. She and Aunt Armitage had gone to such lengths to conceal Matthew's wicked stealing from John. Now he would be branded a bully and a thief.

'What can we do?' she pleaded.

The Headmaster retreated behind his desk. 'Matthew can be cured, Mrs McKie. It's simply a question of finding the right setting in which he can improve. To become the fine boy you and Mr McKie would expect him to be.' It was bluff and hearty and he didn't entirely believe in what he was saying but he had to give this mother hope. 'I have a list of suitable schools, here.' It was ready in his desk drawer.

'I think you should consider sending him away from home. Unlike the other two boys, Matthew needs a – a bracing environment, not surrounded by the comforts of home. He needs closer supervision, too – ' The Headmaster checked himself. It was beginning to sound as though he were inviting comparison with a prison cell.

Charlotte tucked the list away without looking at it. 'Mr McKie and I will discuss the matter.'

'Of course.'

'Is Matthew ready?'

'I'll send for him.'

Left on her own, Charlotte's head throbbed. What would everyone say? John, Mary, the counter hands! It was awful to contemplate. They'd criticize, they might even pity her for having a thief as a son! They mustn't get to hear about it, that was the answer. She would insist on it. When the Headmaster returned, she'd recovered a certain composure.

'I'll do what I can, Mrs McKie,' he replied. 'I cannot prevent boys gossiping among themselves. You can rely on my discretion of course, and that of my staff. More than that I cannot promise.'

The door opened and Matthew stood there. 'Mr Carrick says

I'm to leave. Not come here any more.' His eyes glowed like a cat's. When he smiled there was such sweetness in it.

'Get your cap and bid Mr Carrick goodbye. You are a disgrace to all of us.' Her voice trembled. She inclined her head and the Headmaster bowed in return, holding open the door. Matthew followed his mother, smiling slyly behind her back. He smoothed the pockets of his jacket and mouthed silently at Mr Carrick.

'You silly old goat.'

During the short walk home Charlotte didn't see anyone. She concentrated on keeping back the tears. Her feet kept time with the words 'I will not cry.' The umbrella tapping the paving stones had a different message for Matthew: 'Finders Keepers . . . '

They entered through the yard. 'Go to your room and stay there.'

'Yes, Mama.'

She still wanted to hit him, shake him – anything! She clutched the banister and watched him go upstairs. In the kitchen, she called sharply, 'Mrs Beal – where's Billy?'

'I'm here, M'm.'

'Go upstairs, Billy. Turn the key in Matthew's door and don't let anyone in or out, understand?' He nodded, frowning with concentration. 'You are to stay there until Mr Davie or I come.' Charlotte was breathing deeply now, trying to stop herself shaking.

Mary gestured impulsively, 'My dear Charlotte, is there anything – ?'

'Would you tell my aunt I wish to see her? I shall be in my parlour.'

'Yes, of course.'

And in the fastness of the parlour it was Mrs Armitage who wept, stroking her niece's hand as though she were a little girl again. 'Poor, poor Charlotte – and think what it will mean to dear Davie!'

'He cannot be told. Think how busy he is with the concert.'

'Oh, my dear, I don't see how you can avoid it. Suppose he were to discover through an outsider?' For Mrs Armitage had a far better grasp than her niece of how far the news might have travelled already. 'Would you like me to tell him?'

'No, no.' Charlotte felt herself begin to tremble again but she would not give way. She bit her lip hard. 'When he arrives, would you ask him to come and see me?'

'Yes, dear.'

(vi)

After Davie left the study, Mary said, 'Something terrible has happened to Matthew. He's been expelled from school. Mr Carrick sent for Charlotte this afternoon and she had to bring Matthew home. Davie doesn't know yet but that's why Charlotte wants to see him. She's worried about telling him.'

'I'm not surprised!'

'Will you help?'

John looked at her in surprise. 'What on earth can I do?'

'Davie will be very distressed. Afterwards, if he could come and discuss it with you?'

'Of course.' John was curt. 'He'll want to anyway.'

Mary looked at him steadily. 'I don't think he will. Davie has his pride as do you. You would not want to speak of it had it been Luke, not Matthew.'

'Don't be foolish! Luke would never do anything to merit expulsion!' Really, he found it difficult to converse with her when she said stupid things like that.

'I don't see why we should consider him differently,' Mary persisted. 'Ted and Jane have the same father and mother as Matthew. We would never expect them to behave badly. Luke does not come from the same stock.' John flushed. Was she deliberately throwing that in his face, and if so, why? The letter confirming the two hotel rooms was in his wallet close to his breast, two hotel rooms with a communicating door!

'Perhaps Matthew is a bad seed?'

'Please, don't say so, not to Davie. We could be wrong. Let us pray to Heaven we are. And Davie must not know what you feel. He will need all your strength.' She left him and he thought what an odd remark that was. One thing he'd secretly envied was Davie's physique. Not that he wanted to be as tall as that but a little more brawn would have been welcome.

He felt he couldn't wait for Davie in the study so went back into the shop. It was nearly closing time and the bustle soothed him. Looking round it seemed as though they'd never been busier. In Gentlemen's Tailoring Mr Hart now had three assistants plus a boy for messages. MacArthur in his alcove beside the counter had an alteration hand. There were fiddly tasks that the old man couldn't quite manage these days. John was aware of it. The young assistant had strict instructions not to refer to the failing eye-sight lest MacArthur feel uncomfortable. 'Just give him all the help he needs.'

In Ladies' Mantles one of Miss Crowther's new consignments of hats had arrived from Paris. Customers were gathered round, oo-ing and ah-ing over them. Some of the hats were enormous this season, he noticed. He hoped they'd sell. The amount Miss Crowther had spent in French milliners last autumn staggered him.

The boy who held open the door rushed in and out, summoning cabs as ladies finally tore themselves away. On his jacket, gold-embroidered letters twinkled their message: 'McKie Bros'. That had been Davie's idea. Free advertising whenever the boy ran down the street. It had all been going so well. They were still forging ahead, ever more prosperous. Now this had to happen. It wouldn't be long before Matthew's removal from school was universal knowledge.

A couple of ladies passed him on their way out. 'We'll see you at the Grand Concert, Mr McKie!'

Oh Lord, there was that, too! John shrank from the thought. How dreadful that Matthew should bring disgrace on them now – and how dare Mary suggest Luke might be tainted!

(vii)

As he entered their parlour Davie paused as he often did for the sheer joy of looking at Charlotte. She was so beautiful, this dear wife of his, but as he gazed he realized with a shock she was angry.

'What's the matter – have you spoken to Dr Cullen?' It was out before he could prevent it. Charlotte frowned slightly.

416

'No, why? Is there any reason?'

'None. I just wondered . . . no reason at all,' he floundered. He must be careful not to alarm her!

'It's Matthew,' she said flatly. As she told him, Davie felt an incredible lassitude steal over him; his limbs were heavy, his neck could no longer support his head. He sank into a chair, completely overcome. Unlike Charlotte, tears streamed down his face. The sight of them frightened her. Why such utter despair?

'Please, Davie, don't give way. There must be a solution. Matthew is only a little boy.'

He roused himself at last. 'May I see the list?' She took the envelope out of her reticule. 'Carrick is right, I think,' Davie blew his nose and wiped his eyes. 'Matthew must go away as soon as it can be arranged.' He forced himself out of the chair.

'Where are you going?'

'To see Carrick. He's given us a choice, but I'd like his advice as to which of these schools he considers most suitable. If I write to them directly, we can arrange matters by the end of next week.' He was feverish to do everything while he still had the energy.

'Shall I come with you?'

His voice was muffled as he reached down to fasten the buttons of his coat. 'No thank you, dearest. I'd like to be alone.' He picked up his hat and umbrella. 'We'll see Matthew together when I return. Tell Mary not to wait supper for me.'

On her own, Charlotte clenched her fists. He shouldn't have gone, she needed him. She wanted the strength of Davie's arms round her, sharing the burden. If his sorrow was great, so was her need of him. 'Davie!' The word burst out in an agonized sob. She grasped a chair for support. Never before had she felt so desolate.

Moments later, despite her despair, she remembered Billy Beal. He couldn't remain on duty all night, she must see to it. It meant leaving the safety of this room, to be exposed to the keen eyes of the shop assistants.

Charlotte's chin went up. She'd have to brave them sooner or later, better get it over. She splashed cold water on her face and used a discreet touch of papier-poudre. Before leaving the chamber she steadied herself by staring hard in the mirror and taking deep breaths. When she judged herself calm enough, she opened the door.

As a test, she walked deliberately through the fast-emptying shop. The news had spread, she could sense it. In the kitchen she found Katriona. Billy Beal must be allowed time for his supper then mount guard again. Katriona agreed and together they went to tell him.

Back in the dining room, throughout an awkward meal, Mary was an unexpected source of strength. So often retiring from any conversation she forced herself to support Charlotte, whatever the topic. Suffering had given Mary a sharp insight; she felt Charlotte's pain and tried to share it. As soon as she decently could Charlotte rose and left the room. She paused as the door closed behind her, listening to the silence. In the room everyone waited for her footsteps. For a few seconds nothing happened, then the sussuration of her skirts moved away down the passage. Mary looked round the table. In her opinion it was better to acknowledge what had happened than pretend; there had been too much pretence. 'You all know of today's sad event,' she said quietly. The silence became more profound. At his end, John stared aghast. What was she about to say – it was madness to refer to it! 'I would ask that you all remember Mr and Mrs McKie in your prayers tonight,' Mary continued. 'We all need forgiveness, not only Matthew. But let us pray for him most of all.' And with that she too left the room.

John waited for Davie in his study. He couldn't sit still. Mary's words confused him. What did she know? Had someone spoken to her? He'd done nothing. Why should he need forgiveness? But he'd missed taking the sacrament for the first time since coming to Darlington, the day after he'd written to the London hotel. He paced up and down, humiliated by imagined accusations, refusing to face the consequences. Where in Heaven's name had Davie got to? The door opened and there he was. John jerked his mind back to the present and the problem of Matthew. 'Would you like some tea?'

'Have you got anything stronger?'

'I think so.' He found the bottle and held it up to the light. Enough for two drinks, perhaps.

Upstairs, Charlotte was cold. She had a hot stone pig, plenty of blankets and an eiderdown but her thoughts chilled her. She listened to the night sounds, Blackie coughing in her stable, a distant train. Davie surely wouldn't be much longer? She pushed the pig across to his side of the bed. He would be exhausted and there was so much to do tomorrow for the concert.

Matthew had been a much quieter baby than the other two. The nurse had given a dire warning. 'The last one gets too much attention, Mrs McKie. Spoil him and you're done for.' So Charlotte had taken heed, treating Matthew with a tight strictness that didn't allow for soft words or loving arms. It suited her to be strict. She'd never have admitted it but Charlotte didn't like babies; they were a duty but worse, they distracted Davie's attention away from herself. She'd been too young to remember Jane's tenderness. Now for the first time she began to be uneasy. Had the nurse been wrong? Had she herself been too harsh? Most terrible of all, was what had happened in any way her fault? Charlotte's conscience so rarely troubled her she found it unnerving – oh, where was Davie?

Downstairs the whisky remained untouched. John knew he should offer comfort. All he said, lamely, was, 'Maybe the new school will help?' and Davie answered dully that it might. When eventually Davie rose, John tried not to show his relief. At the door Davie said, 'I've let Charlotte down, John. I've given her a rotten son.' To this John couldn't find an answer.

Charlotte heard him climbing the stairs. Outside he didn't pause but continued to Matthew's room. Pulling on a wrapper, she hurried after him. Billy Beal had long since gone to bed. The key was in the lock. Davie turned it and went inside.

Charlotte stood in the doorway as he stared at the sleeping boy. 'D'you remember the night he was conceived, how happy we were? It was the night we finally owned this place.'

'Come to bed, dearest.'

'I want him to know how it was between us, how he was made out of our love!'

'Another time, Davie.'

She took him in her arms and led him back to their bed. She made him understand for the first time in their marriage how much she needed him. That night her passion matched Davie's own. Out of their sorrow, love welled up, each wanting to give

419

and fulfil the other's deepest need. It swept away Davie's pain.
He couldn't possibly tell her of the visit to London, not tonight.
When it was finished and they lay exhausted, still tightly
wrapped in each other's arms, he kissed her and whispered, 'Oh
my sweetest, my bonniest girl!'

CHAPTER FIFTEEN

The Concert

Young Ted was subdued. Pride at having a notorious brother soon wore off. Apart from the upheaval Matthew had caused, the concert hung like a threatening cloud.

'It's beastly unfair!' He and Luke were on their way to the theatre for the umpteenth time that morning, carrying packages. 'Matthew's done the wickedest thing there's ever been and he hasn't even had the cane.'

'Mother says it wouldn't do any good. He's a thief and has to be cured,' Luke explained.

'You don't cure thieves. You crucify them on either side of Jesus, it says so in the Bible.'

Luke waited until they'd negotiated the crossing. 'Crucifying people doesn't cure them.'

'It might.' Ted wasn't feeling particularly friendly this morning. 'Matthew doesn't even have to *go* tonight, he's had all the luck.'

'I don't think it's being lucky having to go away to school.'

'Bet he enjoys it.' Ted kicked a stone disconsolately. 'Bet he gets round them there the same way he gets round Ada and Emily Beal. Mother thinks he's only having bread and butter but they're sneaking up with bits of cake. And he doesn't have to sing in the beastly choir tonight in a stupid, silly collar!' Mothers had been delighted at Davie's suggestion their offspring wear ruffs.

'Never mind,' Luke consoled him, 'this time tomorrow it'll all be over.'

Mary tried to concentrate on that thought, too. It was a bitter, rainy morning. She and Billy had been out since seven, visiting large houses on the outskirts of Darlington, collecting flowers. The Quaker community had done their best for her: gardeners handed over hot-house plants with scarcely a protest. Davie had thoughtfully included their names as well as those of their employers, in the concert programme. It meant that Mary was given some very fine blooms indeed.

Tickets had sold out. Newspapers confirmed that the Grand Concert was the social event of the season.

That evening members of Charlotte's committee gathered in the emporium before the concert to put on their gold sashes of office. They basked in Davie's admiration. He fell back as though dazzled. 'A bouquet of exquisite roses!' His arms were wide enough to embrace all of them. 'Mrs Watkins, you will turn heads tonight. Your husband will be a jealous man! May I?' Mrs Watkins was seventy-five but after an extravagance like that she floated on Davie's arm to where the carriages waited.

(i)

In the theatre the orchestra was tuning up. Around her, anticipatory chatter was excited but Mary didn't hear. The seat beside her was empty. She no longer thought about the concert; she'd done what she could to make it successful and behind the curtains, the banks of flowers were opulent, but what concerned her now was her own predicament.

Tonight she'd finally admitted to herself John wasn't 'coming to his senses', ever. It was Mrs Armitage's phrase, offered tactfully months ago and although Mary had pretended to be deaf, she'd hugged the words, wanting them to be true. All she had to do was be patient. But it hadn't happened. John hadn't shared her bed for over a year. She'd endured this pretence of a marriage long enough. She would leave him and he would be free to marry Cecilia Crowther.

But – where to go? Despite the heat, Mary shivered. Mary was a woman with no property of her own. Every week she paid the housekeeping bills, every Friday, rendered an account and handed any change back to John. Her clothes came from stock. Over the years John had given her money, but much of this Mary spent on presents for others. Since Christmas, very little remained. And what could she do to support herself and Luke?

(ii)

Behind the curtains, Charlotte took her seat in the place of honour. She wore cream lace that curved to her Gibson-girl figure with a startling closeness, breaking out from her hips in a train of cream taffeta flounces. The dress was cut so low it had elicited an anxious squeak from Mrs Armitage and a much deeper growl from Davie. It was obviously an affront to respectability so now a few pale camellias from Davie's bouquet nestled where they could provide a morsel of protection against the pearly pink of Charlotte's bosom.

The gold sash of office matched the jewellery round her neck and in her hair. In his harassed state the young Minister broke off from worrying about the seating plan to enjoy the sight. With her regal walk, Mrs Davie McKie reminded him of a swan on a stately progress down a river. Then dignitaries crowded on stage and he had his hands full once more.

The speeches were long, the prayers were short. The Minister knew the audience didn't want to be kept waiting. Promising to announce the sum raised in the interval, he stood aside for the Mayor to head the procession off-stage.

The first half went very well indeed. In her box, Charlotte enjoyed her ice. Relatives in the audience meant that every precocious child had been warmly applauded. Davie's hymn had been very popular. After it, the concert had been suspended while photographs were taken. Now Ted and Davie were up here beside her.

The interval bell rang and people began returning to their seats. Many had called at her box to offer congratulations, one or two of the gentlemen being particularly civil as to her appearance. Altogether, Charlotte was in an extremely benign state of mind as she prepared to enjoy the rest of the evening.

The Minister appeared in front of the curtain. Not only had they reached their target, they had surpassed it. (Gasps.) The Elders and Members of Session had decided therefore, that a new organ be installed in the church (applause) and the remainder – of over a hundred pounds! (renewed gasps) be sent to the Missionary Society. There were shouts of approval as well as applause at this; converting the heathen was the most popular of all Good Works. The Minister left the stage and the audience settled itself once more.

Charlotte had taken a polite interest when Miss Crowther tried to describe Jane's costume. She was sure Miss Crowther would devise something suitable and she hoped Jane had shown proper gratitude. In the programme the item was listed simply as 'Solo: Miss Jane McKie.'

Would it be another shepherdess's dance, Charlotte wondered? The Sunday School infants had performed one already in the first half; pretty little girls in mob cabs, all extremely disorganized. Shepherdesses were a suitable subject for a dance, provided they appeared without their sheep of course. Nothing prepared Charlotte for what was to follow.

The curtain rose: apart from one pool of light the stage was dark. At a chord, a quicksilver figure jumped into the light, startling the audience. Charlotte was horrified. Jane was dressed as some sort of bird, shimmery blue and silver material covering her body and limbs, glistening, transparent wings attached to her arms, but there was no skirt. Not a single layer of tulle hid her legs!

She stood poised, head alert, arms raised; an embryo from the egg, a dragonfly from a chrysalis, every new-born thing that had ever emerged into a dawn. Light increased to daybreak, music surged and the bird began to dance. Jane soared and flew

424

about the stage. The audience watched, completely still. No one coughed, parents didn't have to shush their children; everyone was spellbound.

Only Charlotte misunderstood. The first gasp was all she noticed. It stayed with her, evidence of Jane's shamelessness. To appear in public like that! To dance so that it disturbed one's emotions. Charlotte was utterly dismayed. A white-clad nymph was one thing. This wasn't even decent, it was pagan!

It was also fleeting. Within five minutes it was over. A final crescendo, the bird appeared poised in flight, arms, face and body in ecstatic worship of the sun then, with a leap, it vanished.

There was a moment of complete silence before the applause began. Up in the lighting gallery the electrician wiped away the sweat. The follow-spot was heavy but she'd been adamant as to what she wanted, this girl. In the orchestra pit, musicians relaxed. They'd been taken through their paces by the dancing teacher, demonstrating each change of tempo with her metronome during this morning's rehearsal. But it had been worth it; this young girl was good.

The audience thought so too. A torrent of sound filled the theatre. Not polite applause but hands beating in a frenzy so that gloves split across the palm, men and women standing to cheer. The Mayor was on his feet beside Charlotte. 'Bravo!' She was bewildered. On stage footlights were faded up as the manager held back the velvet for Jane to come forward and take a bow. Why on earth hadn't she put on a wrap, thought Charlotte?

The girl stood, clenched hands the only sign of nervousness, and curtsied. Applause increased then one woman threw her bouquet onto the stage. More flowers followed as men tore carnations from their buttonholes. The Mayor picked up his wife's garland and without even asking, flung it at Jane. More accurate than the rest, it fell at her feet. Laying it gracefully against her breast she swept a deep curtsey toward her mother's box. The audience applause reached a peak. Fancy behaving like an actress, thought Charlotte in disgust.

On stage Jane raised a hand in a final acknowledgement before turning to the Manager and requesting him to, 'Kindly pick up the rest of my flowers, please,' and walking off. There was a ripple of laughter as they settled in their seats. The Mayor sank back with a sigh, 'My word, Mrs McKie, how proud you must be of your daughter!'

Only then did Charlotte realize she hadn't clapped but then she hadn't wanted to.

CHAPTER SIXTEEN

Aftermath

It was a couple of days before Jane fully understood what was happening. It had been so exciting at the concert, with everyone telling her how wonderful she was – everyone except Charlotte. Aunt Armitage tried to explain. 'Your mother would have preferred that you had worn a skirt, Jane, as a shepherdess.'

'But I was a bird, Aunt!'

'Well, yes, but if you'd been a bird, in a skirt, it would have been so much better.'

Then suddenly all attention turned away from her and centred on Matthew. The event of the season, all three brilliant hours of it, was over. It was difficult to accept after all that rehearsal.

'They've raised enough money, that's why,' Luke told her, 'but you were splendid, Jane, so don't be sad.'

'But I want to go to London, to be a proper dancer!'

'I shouldn't tell your mother so just yet. Wait until Matthew's in his new school.'

Matthew, always Matthew. And Miss Crowther no longer

had time for encouraging chats, she seemed preoccupied. In fact all the adults had withdrawn into their separate private worlds. Jane felt completely deflated.

(i)

Davie had decided to tell Charlotte the truth as far as he dared. 'Cullen wants me to see a colleague of his in London, about these bilious attacks.'

'That's an excellent idea, Davie. When do you go?'

'Tomorrow. I should be back by evening.' But when a letter confirming the appointment arrived later that day, the time stipulated was four thirty PM.

'Why not stay the night, dearest?' Charlotte suggested. 'Rather than travel back on a late train.'

'Perhaps I will, if you don't object. D'you realize Charlotte, this will be my first visit there? I wanted us to go together – and explore what's on the other side of that hill!' She smiled at his enthusiasm. Still the eager young man she'd first married.

'Why don't we go together later in the spring?'

Oh, I do hope we can, he thought, near to tears. Recovering himself he went to find John. Miss Crowther was with him in the study and it looked to Davie as if they'd been having words. 'Sorry to interrupt, John. I came to tell you I have to be in London tomorrow, to see a friend of Cullens. I may stay overnight.'

'Oh, d'you need a room?' Miss Crowther spoke so quickly, Davie blinked. 'What I meant to ask was, Mr McKie, have you had time to book a hotel room?'

'No, I haven't, not yet. In fact, Miss Crowther, I was coming to seek your advice. Where should I stay in the great wen? Take pity on an unsophisticated Scot, ma'am, and give me the name of a hotel?' She joined dutifully in his laughter but she sounded strained.

'I think you are the answer to a problem, sir. Your brother too has to travel to London tomorrow, apparently – '

'Have you, John? You never told me?'

Miss Crowther pressed on, ignoring Davie's surprise.

428

'Not realizing I always stay at my club, Mr McKie has booked two rooms at the Berners Hotel assuming I would use one of them. Now you can have it.'

'That's – splendid.' Davie looked uncertainly from one to the other. 'Some business to do with the warehouse, is it, John? Fancy all of us being in London together. I'd better go and warn Hart.'

As he left, Davie thought again how odd it was John hadn't mentioned his journey before. He hoped whatever the problem was it wasn't serious – John had looked terrible.

The study door closed behind Davie. Miss Crowther said icily, 'If there was nothing further you wished to see me about?'

'Shall you leave – on an early train?' John asked, for the sake of something to say. He'd been stripped of all dignity.

'As early as possible. I have an extremely full day ahead of me.' Including an interview with Mr Gordon Selfridge. Once outside the study, her temper under control again, Miss Crowther said to herself, 'Well, well, well . . . ' Two rooms at Berners Hotel! Despite her anger, she almost laughed. A shopkeeper propositioning her! Whatever her circumstances, Cecilia Crowther still considered herself of the class into which she'd been born – it was ridiculous! It was also extremely delicate and inconvenient. She'd no wish to offend anyone at a time when she might be giving her notice and would need a good reference. She snapped open her fob watch; four more hours till closing time. The stockroom would be empty, she could tuck herself discreetly away in there and no-one would know. It was extremely unnerving, therefore, when Mary McKie arrived unexpectedly with two cups of tea.

'As you hadn't been up to the dining room this afternoon.' A ritual Miss Crowther should have observed. She tried to cover her embarrassment.

'That's very kind, Mrs McKie.'

How much did the woman know, or guess? Cecilia decided to tackle the situation head-on.

'I learned this afternoon that both Mr McKie and his brother will be in London tomorrow.'

'Yes, I learned so too.' Though Mary spoke quietly, Cecilia thought she caught an edginess in the voice. How fast news travelled in this hot-house!

'It is fortunate that they will be company for each other tomorrow night.' Cecilia wanted to be clearly understood. 'Tomorrow evening I shall be attending a WSPU meeting with my future sister-in-law.'

'I've no wish to discuss your private affairs, Miss Crowther.' Mary's colour was high. Dear God, what a mess, thought Cecilia, dismayed. First Charlotte furious about Jane's costume, now this – she'd be lucky to get any sort of 'character' at all!

'Thank you very much for the tea, it was most refreshing. I shall be returning the day after tomorrow at the earliest opportunity. I'm not sure what arrangements the gentlemen have made.' That spelled it out, whatever Mary did or didn't want to hear. 'Would you excuse me? I need to speak to Mr Hart.'

'Of course.'

Miss Crowther needn't have been so effusive about the tea, she hadn't touched it. Mary went back to the kitchen with her tray. She hadn't wanted to do it, doing so made her feel cheap. but she had to gauge Miss Crowther's feelings. After all these months, patient months of humiliation, Mary's self-control had snapped.

At supper Davie asked, 'Shall we travel together tomorrow, John?' When there was no reply, Davie filled in the silence by joking with Ted. 'What shall I bring you back – gold? The streets of London are paved with it, you know.'

'I don't want any, Father. You'd better ask Matthew. He likes it.' Which in the circumstances, didn't help.

(ii)

Back in her lodgings, Miss Crowther continued to be angry. She couldn't have been mistaken in John's intention, could she? No, of course not! He'd behaved so oddly, calling her into the study, stumbling over phrases about London, waving his letter. 'Two rooms, you see, perfectly proper arrangements,' he'd said, but his face belied the words. Anyway, Mrs McKie's arrival with that tea settled matters. She obviously believed the worst!

As soon as he'd eaten, John retreated back to his study. His beautiful daydream was shattered. Never had he felt so wretched, so foolish, with every finger pointing at him! Embarrassment burned within him as he thought of what had happened.

He'd prepared such lies but he hadn't been able to use them. The right words hadn't been said. Miss Crowther hadn't answered in the way he'd intended her to, nothing had gone according to plan – and as for Davie's unexpected arrival, and the news he would be in London too! Davie obviously hadn't guessed. He was too stupid, thought John savagely. God, how he hated his brother!

Alone, in the darkness, John brooded. He wanted to go away and hide but he couldn't. He had to go through with it, he had to go to London tomorrow; everyone expected him to.

(iii)

In the privacy of their bedroom Davie asked Charlotte if she didn't consider John's behaviour very odd? Her reply astounded him.

'No, you must be wrong!' he cried, 'It's not possible – not John! What about Mary? And Luke?' He was so upset, Charlotte tried to divert him.

'We must leave things to sort themselves out, dearest. I'm sure nothing will happen, not now. After all, you'll be there with John to look after him. And Mary is far too sensible to let it distress her. Now, while you were in the study, Aunt Armitage came to me with an idea. It concerns Matthew and she wants to tell you herself.'

'Not now,' Davie groaned. 'I'm ready for bed, Charlotte. I've a long day ahead of me tomorrow.' Not to mention the strain of being his brother's keeper. Ten days ago he'd only had himself to worry about; it had filled his mind but now so many other problems had arisen. His son was a thief. There was poor Jane, who wanted to go to London so badly and had surely earned the right to go. Now John . . .

431

'What a terrible situation for Mary,' Davie whispered.

'I'll look after Mary,' said Charlotte firmly. 'Put on your dressing gown and go and speak to Aunt Armitage. I'm sure it will cheer you up.'

Mrs Armitage was wearing an amazing collection of shawls over her *peignoir*. She ushered Davie into her parlour, a rotund bundle of wool, talking volubly despite the hour. She had heard the news, as who had not, but had put her own interpretation on it.

'Mr Davie, how kind to spare the time before your journey to London. And how fortunate Mr McKie is able to accompany you. So comforting to have a companion when one has to visit a medical man. As you know, I have very little faith. Although a friend of Dr Cullen, one can but hope he's well qualified?'

Davie forced himself to smile, to dispel her worried frown, and accepted a ginger nut from the tin, to please her.

'I'm told by Charlotte you've had an idea concerning Matthew?'

'Miss Helen Shields!' Mrs Armitage produced the name like a rabbit out of hat.

'What has Mistress Shields to do with it?'

'She's just the person who should advise you. How many times have I heard you and Mr McKie describe how you relied on her opinion? Should we not invite her down here, to discuss the matter? You and Charlotte have so many other pressures just now.'

Mrs Armitage paused to shake her head at the weight of them. 'Miss Shields could cast her analytical eye.' She looked at him, full of hope.

'You may be right.' Davie was too tired to be enthusiastic.

'The other small idea I had was something I thought might interest Matthew.' Davie waited. Mrs Armitage reached with one mottled hand for his own. She could explain so much better if she held on to it.

'Please don't be upset and hear me out. I know there has been stealing and that it is very, very wrong. But if money interests him, could we not turn that to good use?

'Matthew's very clever at sums – did you know? He can add up so much quicker than Bertha or the other girls in the salon!'

Davie looked at her in a daze. What was she trying to say? That was where Matthew's downfall had begun, stealing tips in the salon. The old lady guessed his thoughts and clung to the hand.

'I thought if at his new school he could be pointed in the right direction, the right books and so forth?'

'What direction is that, Mrs Armitage?'

'Why, to study accountancy, dear. It would give him a purpose. He would know that you and Mr McKie intended him to work in the emporium, perhaps as manager, when you both retire!'

She looked at him triumphantly but Davie wanted to weep, her idea was so idiotic.

'The other dear children all know what they want to do,' Mrs Armitage continued. 'Luke has his medicine, Jane wants to be a dancer, Ted a soldier – '

'He can never be that!'

'No, well, as it's late perhaps we should talk about Ted some other time. But don't you see, Matthew must feel left out.'

'Dear Aunt Armitage, you always see the good side of everyone. For a man to be an accountant, like John, he has to be honest!' And if what Charlotte said was true, his brother was a liar, deceiving his own wife. 'He has to be truthful,' Davie repeated emphatically to push that thought away.

'I know, Mr Davie, and Matthew will have to learn to be truthful and not steal. But if he thought he was to work here eventually, he would lose all incentive to rob, he would wish it to succeed. This', Mrs Armitage waved her flabby elderly arm to indicate the emporium, 'would be his inheritance.'

Davie leaned forward and kissed her impulsively. 'Bless you for having faith in him.'

'Oh, I do. There is good in each one of us, Mr A always said so.'

Convinced Davie had accepted her plan, Mrs Armitage confided in Bertha. 'I shall write to Miss Shields and invite her here. Dear Charlotte and Davie have far too many worries to bother with letters.'

'Excuse me for suggesting it, ma'am, but oughtn't we to ask quicker than that? A letter takes a long time to get up there and Mr and Mrs Davie want to choose a school next week.'

'Oh, yes, Bertha. She must be here as soon as possible!'

'I think we should send a telegram,' said Bertha solidly.

Mrs Armitage was enchanted, she'd never had such an adventure as a visit to a telegraph office. 'Oh, yes!' Mr A had never sent a telegram in his life.

(iv)

They travelled separately; Miss Crowther in the safe seclusion of 'Ladies Only', Davie on the eight o'clock and John one hour later.

John no longer wanted to go but he'd committed himself. He passed a sleepless night, dressed and packed in a state of dejection but went for breakfast because he couldn't think what else to do. Ada served him and brought him the newspaper. He was making a pretence at reading this when the door opened again.

'John, do you still intend travelling to London today?'

'Of course I do, Mary. Why all this fuss?' She ignored the bluster and asked steadily, 'Will you return here tonight?'

'I can't possibly – there's far too much to do – '

'If you do not,' she interrupted, 'Luke and I will not be here when you do.'

'That's absolute nonsense!' but the door had closed behind her.

On the train, he convinced himself it was an empty threat. After all, where could she go? Not Luke! She couldn't deprive him of his son! Of course she would be there tomorrow, just like his carpet slippers.

He'd told his first lie to Mr Richardson. The Quaker looked surprised. 'If you consider you should go to London?' Now, John told himself, there was no retreat: he'd committed himself. What could he do but continue the farce to the end? He was beginning to understand that when a man takes a first dishonest step and hasn't the courage to admit it, his options grow less.

Miss Crowther hadn't been exaggerating when she'd described her day as full. It had begun with visits to garment manufacturers down dirty narrow streets where a lady could not expect civility. This had been a shock the first time; now she was inured.

She'd no hesitation in using her 'class' with hard-faced men who thought businesswomen a joke. In fact nothing stimulated her more than haggling. And after what she saw as humiliation at John's hands, she had a harder edge. Today every penny she managed to shave off was a kind of revenge. Victory brought the same sensation Cecilia formerly experienced out foxhunting.

By lunch-time she was back at her club preparing for the all-important interview. Until that was over, McKie Brothers' business could wait.

On his journey, looking at early wheat, Davie wondered whether he'd be alive to see the harvest. Gone was the conviction that Cullen could be wrong; why send a patient to a specialist? No, there was a sickness within him. Surrounded by strangers on a train, Davie could acknowledge it. There was no one here to see the fear, no one he knew.

He examined the hand resting on his knee, blood, sinew, muscle and skin, still strong in its grip. There was no sign there that his flesh was mortal. Perhaps there was still time? Could this specialist cure him? Please God, let there be that hope at least!

By the end of the journey he'd recovered some of his zest. After all, were not he and John in London at last? Or rather they would be tonight, when John returned to the hotel. They must celebrate – and they'd take Miss Crowther with them!

Davie put aside Charlotte's words; he couldn't believe John could be so cruel to Mary. No, something else was bothering

John. Tonight, on their own, he'd find out what it was. After that, they could put it all behind them and celebrate. 'Hang the expense!' He'd spoken aloud and laughed at the astonished faces. Hang everything! He was in London at last and by God he was going to enjoy himself.

He left a message for John that he'd see him later and began a cheery conversation with the porter. 'I'm from Scotland. I live in Darlington but Scotland's where I hail from.'

'Indeed, sir, you do surprise me.' At Berners Hotel, porters could be relied on for tact.

'I've never been to London before and I want to see the Tower.'

'The – Tower?' Cockney replaced gentility; guests at this hotel rarely went anywhere as vulgar as that. Davie gave his wide, infectious laugh.

'I want to go to the Tower because some of my ancestors were hung, drawn and quartered there – what d'you think of that?'

'Gorblimey!' The porter had to laugh, the chap was so comic. 'Well that's a good enough reason if ever I heard one – here!' He gave a whistle to the rank. A cab pulled up in front of the steps. 'Gentleman to visit the Tower . . . if you don't mind me saying so, sir, it's a fair distance. Would there be anywhere else you want to visit first?'

Davie produced a list. There was a rapid consultation. Porter and cab-driver decided on the route. 'It'll take the best part of a day, sir.'

'Just get me to Harley Street by four o'clock, that's all that matters.'

'Right you are, sir.' A bit of luck this: the driver flicked his horse. And he was a foreigner.

They went to Regent Street. 'A little something for Charlotte' was always the most important item with Davie. As he entered the first shop, the desire to experience everything was strong – it carried him forward on the same wave of laughter. He joked with pale, affected shop assistants, chose the ugliest and declared she'd brightened his day. As they all clustered round, eager to help, he was dazzled by the variety of goods. This was the sort of place John deserved, not the emporium. They should sell up, leave Darlington and start again. He was making plans for the

436

future – what future? Davie laughed helplessly and the girls laughed too, they didn't understand why.

Outside he bought violets from a flower seller. He hadn't anyone to give them to but he hadn't seen a scrap of greenery since the fields through the train window. Suddenly he ached for the wide skies and landscapes of Scotland, ached so much he felt near to tears.

In Piccadilly, traffic hurtled in every direction. He'd never seen such diversity, horse and motor buses, motor taxi-cabs, cars and carriages threading their way through the tumult. Where was everyone going? Were they rushing because life was short for them as well?

Among the slums of Eastcheap, Davie's laughter began to subside. Outside the huge, thick grey walls he was silent. I've seen it, he thought, I've come all this way, the same way they did and I've seen it. But it doesn't mean anything. If that's all legend and history can do, leave me numb, maybe it's all meaningless. 'A pity,' he sighed, 'it would've given me something to hold on to.' He climbed back into the cab.

They stopped briefly for food. The cab-driver apologized for the choice of a coffee shop but it was what Davie wanted; beef stew and rice pudding, fivepence each, men jammed shoulder to shoulder on wooden benches in steamy human warmth. After that there were no excuses left.

'Harley Street.'

Davie was astonished to find he immediately felt such *rapport* with the specialist. Berwick was big and jovial, which came as a surprise. Perhaps as students, he and Cullen had drunk porter together? Davie felt completely at ease. The man examined him thoroughly, probing, finding new areas of pain, then told Davie to dress and sit by the fire.

They swapped yarns, eating muffins, hot and buttery from a silver dish, and Berwick slipped easily into a discussion of his illness as the butter rolled down his beard.

'No cure has been discovered as yet, Mr McKie, but then you had guessed that, I think?'

He had confirmed the sentence of death but Davie found it impossible to bear the man any ill will.

'I'd worked it out. Cullen intended that I should.'

'Yes, he would.' Mr Berwick contemplated for a moment or

437

two. 'There are many palliatives, of course. Some are extremely effective. For a time . . . '

Davie felt compelled to ask the dread question, 'How long . . . ?'

Mr Berwick appeared not to hear. He towelled the butter from his face and hands and went back to his desk. Davie finished his tea and tried not to let the cup rattle in the saucer.

'I was wondering when you could come and see me again,' said Berwick, apparently engrossed in his diary. 'Could you manage to come up to London in, say, three months?' There was a pause.

'How about – six?' The condemned man was begging for a longer reprieve.

'I think three would be wiser. Four – at the outside.'

He accompanied Davie downstairs and into the street. His manner was reminiscent of the men in tweed knickerbockers at the Manse long ago. Davie had passed that examination; this time he hadn't been so lucky. But there was a calm inside where the laughter had been, an exalted state of well-being that enabled him to shake Berwick by the hand and thank him.

'I shall be writing to Cullen of course, suggesting a particular treatment. It should give you relief from those bilious attacks. Excellent chap, William Cullen. Dedicated. You couldn't be in better hands. Come back if things become uncomfortable, otherwise I'll see you in three months.'

Davie was very weary by the time they arrived back at the hotel. But even in this state he didn't forget the children. He treated the cab-driver like a friend; The children's ages were discussed and a crisp white banknote handed over. Yes, the man understood what the gentleman wanted. It would take an hour or two but he'd be back.

'See that you are, mate,' the porter muttered, 'or I'll have your number.'

John wasn't there. In the room originally intended for Miss Crowther Davie considered his future. Three months, and so much to be done. Charlotte mustn't be told, not yet. John would have to know of course. There was everything to arrange for Ted, Jane and Matthew. John would have to be responsible. He'd never see his three bairns grow up!

438

The enormity of the sentence finally reached him and Davie wept.

(vii)

When John arrived in London he decided not to go directly to the hotel. Davie might be there. If he were, questions would follow. John would keep on the move all day if necessary rather than have that happen.

He'd prepared an excuse for this journey, and he'd almost come to believe it, because he wanted to. Some of those shippers in the north-east with whom he did warehouse business had offices in the city. He'd visit and ask for those names that until now had been mere signatures on paper; he'd put faces to them. It would, he convinced himself, enable his letter writing to be more personal in future.

It was a harmless exercise but John hadn't written beforehand. Consequently no one understood why he'd come. At the first office, after surprised greetings, they waited for him to explain. Being the person he was, John wasn't glib enough to conjure up an excuse. After the second try, he gave up.

He had the rest of the day to fill. To be without purpose increased his guilt. Suppose Mary meant what she said . . . ? It didn't occur to him to take a cab as Davie had done, to see all those wonders they'd talked of when they were young. Instead John walked slowly westward past St Paul's, along Holborn, buffeted by those who knew where they were going.

In Oxford Street he became aware of the women every few yards or so along the pavement. Thin, nervy creatures most of them, wary as cats at the suggestion of a police uniform. John tried to ignore them, closing his ears to the plaintive voices that mocked his need. This was the harshest reminder of what his purpose in London had truly been. One young woman touched his arm, stroking his sleeve timidly. John hit out, knocking her into the gutter. There were screeches and cat calls. His pince-nez fell off and he groped for them, intending to help the woman to her feet. A constable appeared and by the time John's vision was restored, they'd all vanished. The young woman had left her hat behind and the constable sneered, 'Want a souvenir,

439

sir?' John shook his head. He waited until the man had strolled on then he followed the way the girl had gone, down an alleyway.

He looked anxiously in each doorway. Plenty of them had come this way and yelled abuse as he went past. He glimpsed the girl standing next to another woman who was examining her bruised arm. 'Here . . . ' He held the money in an outstretched hand for he couldn't bear the thought of her touching him again. 'I'm sorry for what happened, I didn't intend to hit you.' She snatched the money and ran back to her friend before turning to spit at him.

It was dusk and he'd lost his way. Down narrow streets that hid the sun, John had turned south instead of north. He found himself in a garden square. The gate set into the railings was unlocked. Despite the cold, John was so weary he wanted to rest. On the first bench, two men made room for him. They were hunched against the bitter weather. 'Give us a tanner?'

'What?' The man looked round furtively.

'Ssh! All right, a penny then, Guv. You can spare that much. I ain't eaten today.'

'Why don't you work instead of beg?'

The second man sniggered. 'He means it, don't he?' Leaning across he said fiercely, 'For the same reason he ain't. There wasn't no work, not today. Nor yesterday, and I got kids.'

'What do you normally do?'

'Portering down the market. We didn't get picked this morning. If you don't get picked, no work.'

John looked round the square. On each bench there was at least one person; were they all destitute? The men guessed his thoughts. 'There's only us who've got a trade, the rest of them, they're scum.'

And the streets of London were paved with gold, were they? Thank God Luke would be spared this. Luke! The one shining thought he could cling to. Would he be there when John returned? Would Mary take him with her – if she did, what right had he to object? Suddenly John wanted to be in Darlington more than anything else on earth.

He was on his feet, demanding to know directions. 'Half a guinea if you take me as far as Oxford Street, I can find my way from there.' They hustled him, they were so eager. His feet hurt but one of the men gripped his coat, fearful he'd change his mind. 'Here you are, sir, Oxford Circus. You'll find Berners Street's down there.' John handed over the coin.

The first thing John saw in the foyer was Davie, dressed in evening clothes.

'There you are at last, John!'

'I don't think I'll stay – if I hurry I'll catch the last train.'

'Nonsense, of course you're staying. Hurry up and get changed.' Davie was full of a fierce gaiety.

'I want to get back.'

'And I want you to stay. We're celebrating – don't you realize we've never been in London before, you and I? I've found out where the best place is. It's the Trocadero, in Piccadilly. I've booked a table – '

'Oh, no.'

'And I've invited the only pretty woman I know in London to join us, Miss Crowther.'

'No!'

Seizing John Davie said, 'I don't care what you planned to get up to, that's all over and done with. You and Miss Crowther will have to begin to work together again, and the sooner you start the better.'

By the time he had changed and returned to the foyer John had made up his mind he might as well be hung for a sheep as for a lamb. He had probably missed the last train and he needed to eat. It was the thought of being with Miss Crowther that upset him the most. But there was truth in what Davie said. Whatever guilt he felt over Mary, life would continue as before. It had to.

They drove the short distance down Regent Street. John felt nervous but Davie didn't. He swept through the doors on a wave of effervescent laughter, sucking John in his wake.

There were bright lights and palm trees. An orchestra played in the gallery. White linen gleamed, reflecting the gentlemen's starched shirt fronts. They were light years away from the destitute men on those benches. Silver ice buckets filled with bottles of champagne were at every table and wherever he looked, there were beautiful women. Davie took it all in greedily. He turned to John in delight. 'Not one of 'em's a patch on Charlotte!'

They would begin with champagne while they waited for Miss Crowther. Davie had no idea if she'd come, he'd simply sent word they'd be pleased to see her here.

'Oysters and champagne,' Davie decided. 'If Miss Crowther comes why, we can have more oysters and more champagne!' The waiter joined in the merriment, he was a card this one. It was infectious; the whole world was laughing with Davie tonight.

(viii)

It had been an extremely satisfactory day for Miss Crowther. The post of Assistant Manageress in Ladies' Mantles was hers from the date the new store opened next March. Meanwhile, at Mr Selfridge's suggestion, she'd obtained a temporary post with an *Atelier* in Bond Street. She would move to London as soon as she'd worked out her notice.

The WSPU meeting had been stupendous. The movement was a force to be reckoned with now. Mounted police attended their parades, martyrs had been imprisoned, and Cecilia Crowther would soon play her part in it. Her eyes shone as she and Ethel left the hall.

'Only a few more weeks, Ethel.'

'We shall be thankful. We certainly need your share of the rent, Cecilia. Freddie's lost his job again.'

'Oh, no!' Why couldn't he stick at work the way she and Ethel did? Ethel looked so pale and pinched tonight, as though she hadn't been eating properly. 'When I'm assistant Manageress, I'll be on a proper salary again. We'll manage between us, I promise.'

She kissed her goodbye and returned to her club. Nothing could spoil her mood, not even the discovery of Davie's note. After the initial, 'Good Heavens, the very idea!' Cecilia suddenly thought defiantly, 'Why not?' She wanted to enjoy herself, to celebrate, and the invitation had come from Davie. He'd even pinned a bunch of violets to it. If he was there she'd be safe enough from the colourless, stuttering John.

In her best black velvet, Miss Crowther sallied forth. Her driver went into the Trocadero to enquire and returned with Davie. 'How splendid to see you! My brother and I have been so dull. Come and sparkle for us!'

The music was gay, the atmosphere heady. As she sat down amid the splendour, Miss Crowther's conscience caused her disquiet.

'I'm so sorry. I'm here under false pretences.' She had to confess quickly before she lost her nerve. 'As soon as we get back to Darlington, I have to tell you I intend to hand in my notice.'

'Bravo!' cried Davie instantly. 'This must mean you have a better position. What is it, Miss Crowther, what's been happening? Are you at liberty to tell us?' His brain was racing. This was the perfect answer, however hard it was for John. How fortunate it should happen now. 'When will you have to leave us?'

She was startled by the abrupt question. 'Well, when I . . . when it suits you and Mr McKie. When I've worked out my notice.' She and Davie kept their eyes firmly on each other and away from John.

'Would you prefer to leave soon? As soon as Mr Hart and Charlotte have trained someone suitable?' he asked. 'We can decide who that is to be as soon as we return.'

'Yes. Tell me, Mr Davie, are you trying to get rid of me?' Dangerous ground. Half mocking, half laughing, Davie picked his way delicately.

'By no means. We shall be sad to see you go, and we wish you well, don't we John? That goes without saying.' It also went without a pause for an answer. 'Nevertheless, now that buying for this season is complete and before the pressures begin again . . . ' While I still have my strength.

John stared at the napery in front of him. It had all been futile. This was the end of everything and he'd thrown so much away.

'More champagne! Drink up, Miss Crowther, you're a couple of bottles behind us. You must learn to swallow a little faster.' Davie daren't let it flag, he couldn't stop. The treadmill had to keep turning, gaiety must continue otherwise he might crumble.

It was one o'clock before they put Miss Crowther into a cab, tipped the driver well and watched it drive away. 'Shall we walk?' John dreaded being alone with Davie, having to answer questions but he also remembered the pavement creatures. 'We'll ride.'

Effervescence was fast subsiding. Davie hummed the orchestra's melodies but despite his resolve a sadness began to steal over him. He'd almost made up his mind to tell John when his brother spoke first.

'I wish I'd caught that train this evening – I wish I'd never come. Mary told me if I didn't return tonight, she wouldn't be there when I did.'

'Good grief, man!' Davie was genuinely horrified. 'Why didn't you say so before – why did you come? Why do such a thing?'

'It was as though I couldn't help myself, I was so attracted to Miss Crowther. I know that sounds feeble – I couldn't withdraw. Everyone was gossiping, pointing the finger – '

'Because we were so concerned about you and Mary.'

'I couldn't love Mary, not once Miss Crowther was there.'

'And do you really think Miss Crowther would have wanted you?' John shook his head miserably.

'What did you imagine your life would be afterwards?' Davie pressed, inexorably. 'Did you think Miss Crowther would agree to go with you to some hideaway? Live as your fancy woman? Goodness me, John, that doesn't sound like the ambitious young woman we've been entertaining this evening!'

'I had hoped, for once in my life, to love someone.' It sounded humble, not selfish. Davie was filled with pity.

'Do you not realize Mary has loved you from the day you married her?'

'Yes, yes. I feel so humiliated.'

'You feel humiliated! What about her?'

'Please, please, Davie. I think I've lost everything – Mary and Luke. I know I deserve to. I never knew until I was on that train how much they meant to me.' It wasn't self-pity but a force that shook him physically so that he was near collapsing with it.

They were almost at the hotel. Davie flung open the trap and called to the cabbie to drive on.

'Where to, sir?'

'Anywhere. Isn't there a park, a quiet road somewhere?'

444

'This is London, guv. Nearest park's Hyde Park. Over a mile.'

'Well, drive there then.' He couldn't take John into the hotel in this state.

'I've been so besotted with her – '

'Listen, old chap, that's over and done with. You heard her tonight. She's leaving, as soon as we can decently arrange it. You can wipe the slate clean – make a clean breast of it, beg Mary's forgiveness. For God's sake, John, forget your humiliation – think how she must feel! She's the best thing that happened to you.' Davie was not only disgusted, he was angry. Three months was all he had and there was so much to do, so little time. 'You mustn't lose Mary!'

'I know! I'm so sorry. Davie, if when we get back Mary has left me, would you go and speak to her? I don't think she'll listen to me any more.'

More weight to add to Davie's pain, but what could he do? He had to get Mary back for all their sakes. Charlotte would need her to turn to when . . . 'Yes, of course I will. All right, driver, you can turn back now.' Please God, don't let Mary go back to Scotland. I haven't the strength to cope with that.

(ix)

The arch-conspirator, conscious of her extreme wickedness, beamed at Charlotte. 'I think we may have made it sound more urgent than we intended. Bertha and I had to leave out so many words, you see. Most of the explanation in fact. Otherwise it would've been too expensive.'

'I don't think I fully understand, Aunt. You say you sent a message to Miss Shields?'

'We telegraphed. It was so exciting, Charlotte. A very large office and so many pleasant young women. Quite the most genteel situation in which to work.'

'What did you put in the telegram?'

'Why, what I discussed with Davie, dear, concerning Matthew. And about the need for advice. But as I explained, so much had to be left out because of the cost. However I must have made myself clear, here's Miss Shields' reply.' It was produced with a slight anxiety. Charlotte read it.

'I hope I did right, Charlotte?'

'She's coming immediately? In fact she must be already on her way.'

'Yes, arriving tomorrow. Isn't that kind of her? I'm sure you and Davie will find her such a comfort.'

'She asks that we book her in the same hotel she stayed in before.'

'Bertha and I are about to go and do so. Please don't worry, Charlotte, everything will be seen to – I shall ask them to be sure and air the bed.' The conspirator placed a hand on her palpitating bosom to quiet it. So much responsibility, in such a rush! 'You can rely on Bertha and me.'

It wasn't the only communication that morning. The envelope addressed to John lay on the kitchen table where Ada found it. By the time everyone had assembled for breakfast, it was apparent to all of them that neither Mary nor Luke were in the emporium.

CHAPTER SEVENTEEN

Reparation

Before they caught the first train back to Darlington, Davie had been busy. He hadn't slept; he'd catch up with sleep later. There was much to do first, many decisions to be made. In the near quiet of a London dawn Davie deliberated over them.

He was aware of whistling down below in the street, the jingling noise of harnesses in the cab rank, but his thoughts were solely of the tragical farce as seen through Mary's eyes and he felt hot with the shame of her humiliation. There was still a lingering guilt in Davie because he'd tried to prevent her marriage to John. He hadn't been intentionally unkind often in his life. Each event could be recalled, and was regretted. Mary had never complained about that occasion nor said a hard word against him. Perhaps he could now repay her generosity – provided he was granted the gift of time!

It was obvious to Davie that Mary would find Miss Crowther's presence untenable. She must therefore be persuaded to leave immediately rather than work out her notice. She had a position to go to and if he and John were sufficiently generous with their compensation . . . Davie broke off with a wry smile when he considered how much all of this might cost. He'd got three months to re-educate John into spending not saving all of his money – it was probably going to hurt!

Then there was the much more delicate task of persuading Mary to return if she'd already left. If John had to humble himself, Davie was determined that he should. Mary had proved herself the most tolerant of women but she'd suffered enough.

How lucky he had been in life's lottery! Despite his efforts to concentrate, memories of Charlotte flooded Davie's mind. Their life together had been good; she had learned to feel the same passion. What a pity John could not learn the same of Mary. Perhaps there was still time?

How wonderful it had been that night he'd felt such bitter failure over Matthew and Charlotte made him understand none of it mattered, that *he* was all she'd ever wanted! The small hurts over the years, when her affection hadn't matched his in the same degree, all of them were wiped away that night in a great tender wave of loving.

Davie shut his eyes but the wretched tears forced their way through. 'Use the time to advantage,' Berwick had advised gently. Davie brushed the tears away. Three months, possibly four.

Downstairs he was the only one astir. The night porter telephoned ahead, to announce the impending visit at the Ladies' Club. Gentlemen without credentials could expect a cool reception and Davie wanted to be sure he could speak to Miss Crowther. When he arrived, he was relieved to find her dressed and waiting.

Their conversation was in the only area permitted to gentlemen, the front hall. Davie thanked her for receiving him. 'I have a request, Miss Crowther. Much depends on it, including my brother's marriage.'

Miss Crowther flushed angrily and Davie said hurriedly, 'Please, I'm the first to admit John's dilemma is the result of his own foolishness, nothing else. You have always behaved in an exemplary manner. But Mrs McKie has apparently taken exception to this present unnecessary visit to London by John.' He paused to let the words sink in. 'I fear when we return, the situation may be awkward. I therefore believe it would be wise for your employment with us to terminate as soon as possible. By the end of the week, in fact.'

For the first time, Cecilia Crowther began to be frightened. She hadn't nearly enough money saved, especially with Freddie to support. Delight over her own future evaporated; without sufficient means that future might disappear.

'We will repay your generosity if you feel able to comply with my request,' Davie said gently, guessing at her quandary.

Miss Crowther was still uncertain. Could she insist on her 'rights'? But what were they? There had only ever been a verbal contract at McKie's, based on trust. And if Davie were simply offering money, wasn't that an insult to her treasured independence? After all, she'd done nothing wrong.

'I thought eight weeks' pay plus a sum to cover your removal expenses to London.'

My word! thought Cecilia, they do want me out of the way. 'Has Mrs McKie? Has she threatened?'

Davie wasn't prepared to discuss that. Mary had suffered enough. 'It would be better if you could leave as soon as possible,' he replied. 'I will explain to Mr Hart and settle the matter of your room.' Cecilia Crowther shrugged.

'In that case . . . Your offer is very generous. I've already arranged to stay with my brother and his wife. This morning I can visit Bond Street and offer my services at an earlier date.'

'Thank you, Miss Crowther, on behalf of my brother and myself. Now, if you'll excuse me. John and I are returning immediately.'

'Was it Mr McKie's idea that I should leave at once?' She wanted the satisfaction of knowing that.

'Oh no, John doesn't even know I'm here. But it's much the best thing, I'm sure he'll agree.'

As she watched him go it startled Miss Crowther to realize that had it been Davie and not John McKie who'd found her irresistible, circumstances might have turned out differently.

(i)

On the train, because of the early hour, there weren't many travellers. Davie was cold. At last he was weary enough to sleep and pulled his greatcoat round him. John sat opposite with a newspaper which he didn't bother to read. Not even discussion of the proposed Pension Bill could interest him this morning. All his thoughts were directed at his wife and whether she'd be home tonight to welcome him.

How wonderful that Davie had been visiting London after all. Last night in the restaurant when Miss Crowther handed in her notice he'd felt desolate but it was the only solution. Before he could win Mary back, Miss Crowther would have to go. Davie had been beside him, gently urging him to reach that conclusion. John couldn't express his gratitude properly here, in public, but he would soon, he promised himself. As if guessing what was in his mind, Davie said, 'I visited Miss Crowther before breakfast this morning.'

'Oh?'

'I thought it would be best if she left by the end of the week. She agreed. I thanked her and offered eight weeks' wages in lieu of proper notice.'

'Excellent.' John had to force himself. 'Thank you for everything you've done, Davie. I'm most grateful.' Outside over bleak Cambridgeshire fens a late sleet fell. John remembered Davie had a genuine reason for his visit. 'By the bye, was that chap able to suggest anything, that colleague of Cullen's?'

'Not really.' Davie held his breath tightly. Don't let John ask any more questions! But John frowned.

'I thought there'd be a straightfoward explanation of those bilious attacks of yours.' Didn't he have any ideas?' When Davie didn't answer, he asked, 'It's not serious, is it?'

There was one other passenger in the corner seat next to the corridor. He looked as if he were asleep but one couldn't be sure. At any event, Davie spoke quietly in Gaelic. 'I have a cancer of the spine. Between three and six months, I reckon. Charlotte mustn't be told. You're not to tell anyone, not yet.'

In his corner seat the stranger shifted uncomfortably. Grown men weeping in public! Ah. He'd caught a snatch of their conversation. It was in a language he didn't understand: foreigners. That explained everything.

It was a strange deputation that met Helen Shields. Mrs Armitage had come with so many shawls and comforters against the weather, Bertha was laden.

Mrs Armitage was talking before Helen's foot touched the platform, so anxious to establish the *bona fides* of herself and Bertha, inviting Miss Shields to step into a waiting cab and begging her to avail herself of at least one of the rugs against the inclement weather.

Helen managed to collect her wits and her luggage before consenting to be smothered. At the hotel it was obvious Mrs Armitage required a complete inspection before she would permit her guest to accept the room. Helen prodded the mattress dutifully, expressed genuine approval at the newly-installed bathroom and declared herself satisfied. Mrs Armitage was nearly overcome. Such a worry, such a great responsibility, but if Miss Shields was quite, quite sure?

'Some tea?' Helen suggested, desperate to stem the flow. When it came, it astonished her. Hot pikelets and buttered scones, potato cakes and delicate sandwiches, caraway seedcake and Madeira cake.

'I took the liberty,' Mrs Armitage admitted, 'of ordering a small repast to await your arrival.'

'Perhaps', Helen suggested, 'you'd care to join me?' and Mrs Armitage immediately sat, breathless and eager, upon the chaise longue. It had gone exactly as she hoped it would.

During that tea Helen Shields was apprised of all that had happened since her departure from Scotland. Far from being a problem of one small boy's education there had been an upheaval of shattering dimensions. Mrs Armitage had to use both hands to describe the enormity. Dearest Mary and Luke had left home and taken up lodgings with Mrs Fletcher at 18, Coburg Street. Mary had left John a letter. He had taken it to his study to read and had stayed there for hours, refusing to speak to anyone. Charlotte had been rushed off her feet with work, she was quite out of temper. 'Not merely the emporium to see to in Miss Crowther's absence but the kitchen as well! Oh, Mary has been sadly missed!' Jane had added to the upset by asking if she could go to London to study dancing.

'And we could all see that the visit to London hadn't gone well. Poor, dear Davie was so exhausted by it he's taken to his bed. Doctors are responsible for so many of this world's ills, Miss Shields, I think it shameful! There should be a public outcry, do you not think so? Oh, and Miss Crowther is leaving at the end of the week.'

Helen grasped the nettle and began the unravelling process. 'Miss Crowther?'

'Ye-es.' Emotions chased each other across Mrs Armitage's face and she strove to be discreet.

'I fear there may be a *connection* between her and dear Mary's departure. Of course Mary left *before* she knew Miss Crowther would be handing in her notice. So far no one has been able to inform her of it for she refuses to see anyone.'

Mrs Armitage sighed. 'Of course it will mean a heavier load for dear Charlotte but one cannot deny Miss Crowther's departure is a blessing. We've all been so worried about John.'

'Ah!' Helen considered briefly what she should tackle first. The problem of Matthew was negligible compared with the rest. 'Tell me, do John and Davie know I'm here? I had the impression your telegram was – spontaneous? Sent perhaps without their knowledge?'

Mrs Armitage was enraptured Miss Shields should be so clever as to guess. 'Bertha and I managed by ourselves. Dear Charlotte and Davie were so worried about Matthew. I thought with your great experience of boys?'

'Hrmmph.' As far as Helen was concerned another boy needed her attention more. 'Should I call at the emporium this evening?'

'Oh, dear!' Mrs Armitage looked stricken. The kitchen had been in such an upset since Mary's departure. Ada declared she was being put upon, she and Emily Beal weren't speaking to one another. 'Oh, dear! Miss Shields, might I prevail upon you to allow Charlotte and Davie to visit you here? It would save you venturing forth in this bitter weather?'

It suited Helen excellently. The only surprise for Mrs Armitage was that Miss Shields should wish to see John first rather than Davie and Charlotte.

'It would be best, poor Davie not being well, but I don't

know whether John will agree to come.' Mrs Armitage was full of doubt. 'Since his return he's been almost unapproachable! So distressing!' Helen could see that it was. She clasped the mottled hand in her own arthritic one.

'Now, my dear, you've done very well. This room and the tea, they were excellent. It's time for you to have a rest while the rest of us put our heads together. Let Bertha take you home and I'll write a note to give to John.'

Mrs Armitage carried it in the inmost pocket of her reticule. Bertha delivered it with equal solemnity. 'I put it in front of him, told him who it was from and closed the door, ma'am.' After that, they had to wait.

(iii)

The school mistress had invited him to supper. Apprehensive though he was, John went. Surprise gave way to relief when he read her explanation; she was in Darlington to advise on Matthew. Davie would welcome that. Meanwhile, John acknowledged humbly, perhaps she could advise how to plead with Mary. So far his wife had refused him admittance to her lodging and returned the note Katriona had taken round.

'She didn't even open the envelope, Mr John.' Condemnation in Katriona's eyes was tempered, like Davie's, by pity. 'I don't think she'll ever come back. I've heard she's seeking work among the Quakers.'

How long, John wondered, before all Darlington knew of his shame? He bowed his head.

Tonight Helen had arranged for supper to be served in her room. As soon as she saw John, she was thankful she'd done so; he looked so haggard! The joys of matrimony, Helen snorted to herself, she'd been spared those at least. 'John, my dear, come in!' How could she be stern with such a repentant sinner?

'We need something to restore us in this bitter weather,' she told the waiter. 'Whisky for my guest but as I do not care for it, can you suggest an alternative?'

The man gave it as his opinion that hock and seltzer was

enough to suit a lady's constitution. With glasses beside them and relaxed by the warmth, Helen said, 'Now John, suppose you begin at the beginning?'

The relief at being able to talk! He held nothing back, the years of neglect, of turning away from everything Mary had to offer to chase the illusion epitomized by Miss Crowther. 'Like a youth with a bad attack of lust – there's no excusing it.'

Helen waited until he'd finished before asking, 'Does Mary know Miss Crowther is leaving?'

'I don't think so.'

'Then I shall tell her. I intend calling first thing tomorrow. If you have that letter with you, I'll give it to her. I'm sure she'll find it in her heart to forgive – ' but he didn't let her continue.

'Mistress Shields, I wrote not only to beg her for forgiveness but to tell her about Davie. Mary must be told the news as soon as possible. Davie's mortally ill. The doctor in London confirmed it. He's not expected to live above three or four months.'

'Oh, God!' After the first, wild cry, Helen didn't move or speak. She gripped the arms of her chair without noticing the pain. At the sight of her face, John trembled. He shouldn't have told her like that, it was so clumsy. Helen was ashen.

'Tell me – everything,' she whispered at last.

(iv)

The two conspirators waited anxiously for John's return but the later the hour the more satisfied Mrs Armitage became. 'They are having a long, sensible talk, Bertha. Miss Shields is persuading Mr McKie what to do for the best. I think you and I can safely retire. There's bound to be good news tomorrow.'

'We're not quite sure what's happening in the study,' Bertha reported when she arrived with the morning cup of tea. 'Mr Hart's in with Mr John. We think that's about a replacement for Miss Crowther. Mrs Beal's been sent over – she's to take over the cooking until it's sorted about over Mrs Mary. And Dr Cullen has come to see Mr Davie. Mrs Davie's very pleased. She said Dr Cullen will have heard from the London doctor what new medicines Mr Davie ought to have. Now, as it's a bit

454

warmer this morning, would you like me to put out your purple merino?'

(v)

In the small, cold room, Mary looked out at the back yards and alleyways; she had come full circle. The same view, the same room a little farther down the street, from where she'd spent her first night in Darlington. There, memory failed and emotion threatened. She must be sensible! An interview had been arranged later this morning with one of Mrs Richardson's friends, for the position of housekeeper. Would there be a room for Luke? Would the post pay sufficient to cover his school fees? Nothing must interfere with Luke's chances.

There was a tap on her door. Mrs Fletcher was extremely flustered. 'There's someone downstairs, a lady, and I told her what you said to tell everyone but she says she's staying put – and she's not one of the family. Here.' On Helen's card had been written, 'I beg you to see me. It concerns Davie, nothing else. HS.' Mary rose.

'Very well. You may tell her I'll come down.'

'I'll return, for Davie's sake,' Mary said eventually, 'but I cannot live with John. I will move into Mrs Armitage's apartment.'

'Yes, of course.' What did that matter, thought Helen, as long as they were all under one roof again.

'Poor Charlotte! How has she taken the news?'

'Oh, she's not been told, not yet. Davie won't permit it.' But Davie had forgotten to forbid Dr Cullen.

(vi)

Charlotte's reaction was simple: she was furious. A great pulsating storm of anger shook her. Of course, it was based on fear, but she didn't stop to analyse that. How dare fate do this?

455

She needed Davie! How could anyone suggest he might be taken from her – it was monstrous! She paced up and down, terrifying Dr Cullen with her wildness. 'Don't you dare say a thing like that! You're a fool, not a doctor! Davie is recovering! Oh, I can't breathe in here!' She tugged at the neck fastening.

'Mrs Davie, please calm yourself.'

'Calm! You tell me my husband is dying and talk of calm!' Her voice was a high shriek of pain.

When she woke in the morning, wasn't Davie's fond gaze the first thing she saw? During the day, didn't his eyes follow wherever she went? What did it matter if customers noticed it? She couldn't acknowledge his behaviour in public, naturally, that would have been vulgar, but she had no intention of losing it.

'What about curing him?' she shouted, out of control. 'Why not talk to me of that? Davie cannot die – I will not have it!' Charlotte clutched at the mantelpiece, dizzy with anger. Above, the faded cuddy in its frame reminded her only of the marble coldness of her mother. She stared instead at her reflection in the glass, seeing reflected there a fiery determination to fight death every step of the way.

Dr Cullen was given his instructions. A cure must be found. Until it was, every other treatment must be tried. Charlotte would lend Davie her determination to continue. There was nothing she would not do to keep her husband alive.

She began as she intended to continue, and swept into the kitchen. One glance at her face and the quarrelling that had begun with Mary's departure ceased immediately. Neither Ada nor Emily wanted to draw attention to themselves with Charlotte in her present mood. Instead, they fell to with a will.

Davie's intention had been to spare her pain but Charlotte was determined to embrace all of it. She would instill in him the will to live, but first the problem of Matthew had to be dealt with.

She called on Miss Shields the following morning. Helen was unprepared for the new militant spirit. 'Good morning, my dear.'

'Miss Shields, how good of you to travel all this way on our account. I trust my aunt's telegram didn't alarm you unduly?'

Helen was amazed. Charlotte was crisp and elegant; brittle too, perhaps?

'How is Davie?' Helen ventured cautiously.

'Very well indeed. Completely recovered from that exhausting journey to London. He's so much better he's joining us here presently. I wanted to see you first, however, so that you shouldn't be anxious over his appearance. He is thinner because of his illness but he is recovering.'

Helen nodded gravely. 'I see.'

'We made the mistake of holidaying in Biarritz last year – so unhealthy. Then there was an upset with John which worried Davie immensely but that is all over now.' Charlotte was firm. 'Mary is returning today, I'm happy to say. So, with all that behind us, Davie and I can now consult you about Matthew.'

As she rang the bell for more coffee Helen wondered how long the brave front could continue. Only three more months, according to John.

There was a knock, the familiar infectious laughter and Davie stood there furling his umbrella. 'Mistress Shields – how kind of you, how are you?' But as she kissed his cheek Helen experienced the chill fear that Charlotte refused to acknowledge.

If Helen Shields had been dreading their visit, at least Charlotte's attitude made it easier to be businesslike. The list of schools was produced and Helen told them what she knew of their methods. 'There have been so many changes since I first began, new ideas, some of them standing old principles on their heads! We live in such rapidly-changing times, familiar landmarks can vanish overnight.'

Charlotte was already shaking her head. She'd reached the age very early in life when radical thought was to be abhorred. 'Matthew needs stability,' she insisted. 'To be taught right from wrong.' Simple enough, surely, thought Helen.

'What are your plans for his future? Does he have an inclination toward a particular career or is he still too young?'

'He will take over management of the emporium from his father and uncle eventually,' Charlotte replied, having absorbed Aunt Armitage's notion as convenient gospel. Helen turned to Davie and waited. He didn't look up.

'If, in the next few weeks, Matthew could lose any desire to be a thief, that's all I ask,' he said.

It was a relief to Helen that fresh coffee arrived promptly. Letters were sent that day to three of the schools and she agreed to wait for the replies, to assist in the final choice.

She took to visiting the emporium, spending the afternoons in Mrs Armitage's company. Helen Shields had never had a woman friend. In the peninsula there were acquaintances, that was all. It was an odd pairing. Luke and Ted shared the joke that when the two ladies walked abroad, Dignity was accompanied, by Impudence; the stiff, upright figure of the school mistress contrasted oddly with Aunt Armitage pattering beside her.

It was the first time Helen had experienced John's and Davie's world too and it overwhelmed her. So many employees crowding into the dining room at lunchtime and appearing in relays during the afternoon for their tea. John's letters hadn't conveyed the ambiance. Down in the shop it was a fashionable hot-house where intense anxiety could be felt by many people over the set of a sleeve or length of a skirt. Helen Shields wore the same clothes she'd always owned. Each garment was replaced when it became too shabby but for no other reason. When Charlotte suggested tactfully that the school mistress accept a new hat as a gift, Helen declined. Apart from being unfashionably small, her bonnet had been shaped by many winters so that it fitted very comfortably; it would be foolish to part with it. She patted it complacently. The irridescent brooch, still in place, shimmered under her fingers.

Behind the shop, the jumble of rooms devised by Mr Clough intrigued her. Luke took her on a conducted tour one afternoon. 'It's all so compact,' Helen exclaimed. 'You each have a little bit of privacy, somewhere you can escape from the customers and each other. That's good.' She preferred the emptiness of the glen, she'd be stifled living here. Her admiration for Mary and Charlotte increased. To share family life at such close quarters couldn't be easy.

As if to emphasize the difficulty, they reached John's and Mary's domain and Luke said, 'This is Father's room, this is where Mama used to sleep. She's in the room next to Mrs Armitage now. This is the bathroom and here's my room.' The chamber was spare and tidy, like Luke himself. He had plenty of books now, Helen saw. 'You have a proper library.' As she bent to examine the titles, behind her Luke had an odd choke in his voice.

'I've been wanting to thank you, Miss Shields, for arranging some years ago that I should have the requisite number of parents.' Helen straightened up very slowly indeed.

'How long have you known?'

'Since that night in Coburg Street. After she'd run away, Mama was utterly miserable. I think that's why she told me. She said afterwards she regretted it but I'm glad she did.' Luke's eyes were immensely sad. Mary's eyes, thought Helen, in a face that was otherwise, unmistakably young Manners'. 'Mama still cries quite a bit.'

'How much did she tell you?'

'That she left Scotland and you wrote to Father asking him to do his best so he married her.' Helen breathed a little more easily. 'I suppose if he hadn't,' Luke added innocently, 'he might have waited and married Miss Crowther instead?'

'Thank goodness he didn't,' Helen said grimly. 'That would have been disastrous.'

'D'you think so? I'm glad.' Luke was almost cheerful. 'I think Mama's much nicer. Miss Crowther was kind to Jane,' he wanted to be fair, 'but that's because she's a girl. Suffragettes prefer girls.'

'How is your mother, now that you're back here in the emporium?' If it was wrong to question him, Helen couldn't help it. She was responsible for their return and she needed to know.

Luke replied seriously, 'You know we only came back for Uncle Davie's sake? Mama says she will need to help Katriona and Bertha with the nursing when the time comes.'

'It will come then?' said Helen helplessly.

'Oh yes. Poor Aunt Charlotte,' Luke sighed. 'She's going to need a lot of help afterwards, Dr Cullen says.'

Helen nodded. 'Tell me, Luke, now that you know the truth about your parents . . . Has it affected you in any way?'

'I thank God for Father – not the one that "begot" me but my real father. When Miss Crowther has gone I do hope he comes back to us properly, I love him so much.' The simple honesty made her swallow. Then Luke suddenly said, 'You'll meet Miss Crowther tomorrow. She's coming to say goodbye, did you know?'

'No!' Helen looked so horrified, Luke laughed.

'She's awfully pretty and a real lady. That was the trouble, I think. She impressed Father so. Anyway, she's been kind to Jane so we quite like her. I expect Mama will decide to go out for the day until she's finally gone.'

I'm sure she will, thought Helen. All the same, 'tomorrow' took on a horrible fascination.

(vii)

'You promised to help!' Jane was young to be learning that adults often promised what they couldn't perform. Miss Crowther dragged herself reluctantly away from the new leather dressing-case.

'I'm sorry Jane, truly I am.'

'I'll never get away with Father so ill. Mother says nothing will happen to him but Luke says that's not true,' she wailed.

'Jane, listen,' Cecilia was troubled. 'It'll take a little longer, that's all.' She put an arm round the girl's shoulders. 'Remember, you have talent.'

Jane shook the hand off impatiently. 'Nothing happens to talent unless you use it. I'm really sorry about Father and I hope Dr Cullen and Luke are both wrong. But I'm just as sorry for myself.'

'One of the things you learn to accept as you grow older Jane, is disappointment.'

Pompous words were no use at all. 'They're all glad you're going,' Jane told her huffily. 'I'm the only one that stuck up for you but I'm on their side now.' Cecilia smiled sadly. Jane was still very young.

'It was kind of you to speak on my behalf nevertheless. When I promised to help, I should've realized there was little I could do. Are you coming to wish me goodbye?'

They were in the Manageress's cubbyhole. Jane shook her head. As Cecilia picked up the dressing-case, her farewell present from the staff, she thought belatedly of a gift for Jane.

'Here.' Miss Crowther unpinned the WPSU badge. 'This is

460

my proudest possession. I'd like you to have it.' Jane accepted it unenthusiastically. She didn't consider the design very attractive. Miss Crowther's hand was still extended. 'At least wish me luck, Jane. We all need that.' The girl pretended not to notice at first then reached out impulsively to kiss her.

'Thank you for my bird costume. It was heavenly.' She would put the badge in her box with the ridiculous skipping rope the cab driver had bought as a present from Father. Father explained he'd been so tired the man had had to do his shopping for him but fancy a skipping rope when you were nearly grown up!

Miss Crowther braced herself but John wasn't in the study; Davie sat in the desk chair instead and she understood immediately. What a relief!

'A sad day, Miss Crowther.' Davie managed to pull a face to make them both laugh. Tension was banished.

'An inevitable one, perhaps.'

'Quite so.' He slid away from dangerous ground, 'Thank you for all you've done for Jane.'

'She will get her chance, won't she, Mr Davie?'

He fiddled with one of John's pens. 'That's not entirely in my hands. However, it's your future we're thinking of today. Now, you must promise, not too many broken windows. Mr Churchill has a letter in *The Times* today, protesting at WSPU attacks on him.'

'If he supported our cause instead of paying lip service to it, he'd have nothing to fear,' Miss Crowther said with a shrug of her elegant shoulders.

'I refuse to quarrel with you.'

'I'm sorry for what's happened,' she interrupted impulsively. 'I didn't intend your brother should feel the way he did.'

'Yes, well, it couldn't be helped.' Davie was disconcerted. Couldn't it, he wondered? Hadn't she secretly enjoyed John's admiration, preferring to ignore the implications?

'At least when I've gone . . . ' she said.

'Quite.' Davie had recovered his geniality, 'Goodbye, Miss Crowther. Please accept our best wishes, wherever you go.'

'And mine to you. Please convey my sincere regards to Mrs and Mr McKie.'

She made her way through the shop with all the confidence of her class but Davie remembered that first day when a young woman faced penury and had been terrified by the prospect. John had rescued her, but he'd paid a price for it.

(viii)

In the cold, echoing hall Matthew waited to say goodbye. His father was still talking to the form master. Beyond them through the window, the sea pounded against the cliffs. Matthew clenched his hand round the coins in his pocket. Silver and gold, he could tell the difference simply by touching them. They were his talisman against the worst that could happen. Heat from a guinea burned through his skin, warming and circulating heat with blood round his body.

Davie shivered. 'No fires until the first day of October,' the form master boomed. 'It's bracing here, Mr McKie, and our boys don't feel the cold. We keep them on the move. Plenty of sports. Every hour of the day there's some activity or other. Healthy bodies breed even healthier minds.'

Could it be true? Was this the answer and could it make Matthew whole? Davie looked at the bright blue eyes that always managed to hide their real thoughts from him. He stooped to cuddle the thin shoulders. 'Try your best, Matthew. We all love you and want you to do well. I shall be counting the days until you return.'

Matthew wasn't listening. He stared past both men at the sea. 'If a man went out in a boat today, he might drown.'

The master accompanied Davie to the door. 'There are no severe punishments? You promised you will not use a cane or the strap?'

'That is not our way, Mr McKie. We talk to our boys, pray with them to purge their souls of any wickedness. And there are no failures. Your son will walk out of here a man.'

It was designed to reassure and comfort but for no good reason, Davie felt even colder.

It was a week of farewells but Helen Shields kept hers brusque and practical. 'When it's over, bring the children to Scotland. They'll need to get away for a while. There's no privacy here and you'll all need time to recover. Most of all, your father will need you then.'

John nodded sorrowfully.

'Davie's already thought of that. He's doing the thinking for both of us at present. I find it very strange.'

'You shouldn't. When time is short it concentrates the mind wonderfully. Now, where will I find Mary?'

'Wherever I am not,' John answered ruefully. 'She knows my habits. It's not difficult for her to avoid me.'

'If you want her back, you'll have to woo her, John. Davie's never stopped wooing Charlotte and they appear inordinately fond of one another considering they've been married twelve years.' Helen's prim expression banished sorrow temporarily.

'I wish I could be more like my brother, I assure you. I don't believe there's a more popular man in Darlington. Have you seen what happens when he walks out? How many stop him to have a few words with Councillor McKie? It makes me very proud when I see it.'

Helen rose. 'You have the one thing that is denied to him and you mustn't waste it. First you must regain Mary's affection – you will need her guidance. She's more common sense than you and that's a fact. In future I hope you'll listen to her and not go gallivanting.'

John sighed. The school mistress would never trust him again that much was obvious. 'I promise.' He'd given up protesting with Helen Shields.

'I'm glad to hear it. You were never meant to be a philanderer, John.'

Mary was in Mrs Armitage's parlour and the old lady made a tactful withdrawal. 'During my stay here I've had opportunity to consider my past mistakes,' Helen began without preamble, 'in particular as they've applied to you, Mary. If I'd been a compassionate person it might have made a difference fourteen years ago.' Mary flushed but Helen didn't appear to notice. 'I find it difficult to imagine myself otherwise but I might have found a more acceptable solution than John McKie.'

'Miss Shields!'

'You're right. It doesn't do to speculate. What's done is done. As a result you and John are trapped in a loveless marriage.' She paused. Mary didn't deny it but hearing it put so baldly obviously made her uneasy. Helen was satisfied; she'd sown a seed, there might be hope for John despite what he'd done.

'He did not choose me,' Mary said softly, 'He did his duty. And Miss Crowther was extremely – desirable.'

'Yes, she was,' Helen was blunt. 'Thank goodness she's gone. Now it's time to consider your position. You've done what any good Christian woman should do in returning here to care for Davie. However, in future you may have further occasion to want to live elsewhere.' Mary was scarlet but Helen continued as serenely as if she were discussing the weather. 'Lodging in Coburg Street isn't the answer which is why I'm bequeathing you my cottage. It will, I trust, be several years before you enjoy your inheritance. Luke is to have my books, of course.'

'I don't know what to say.'

'There's nothing to say. I happen to know what it is to feel insecure, one can make foolish decisions in consequence. So now you will have a piece of property of your own, eventually. You probably won't want to live in it. I advise you to sell it – and use the money wisely.' She looked at her watch. 'Now, I've precisely five minutes to say goodbye to Davie before my cab arrives.'

She left Mary in a quandary over John, which was what Helen had planned. Far from encouraging her to leave him again, she thought giving Mary security might enable her to take a more charitable view of him. Helen had done all in her power to make amends, now it was up to them.

Davie apologized; he had a small item to add to her luggage. 'A letter which perhaps you wouldn't mind delivering, Mistress Shields. It's not something I'd want Father to read on his own.'

'Very well.' She would not weep!

'And look here . . . ' He spread them out in front of her, 'It occurred to both John and I that as Father couldn't make the journey to England we should send photographs. D'you think these will give him the flavour of Darlington?'

There was even one of the house in Coburg Street. Davie had been thorough. Helen went through the collection; views of the library and St George's, even St Cuthbert's. 'Now he can see where Charlotte and I were married.' There was one of Mrs Armitage taken outside the Establishment. 'You'll explain it all to Father, won't you?' Charlotte and the children were in one group, and John, Mary and Luke were photographed separately, Helen noticed. The last two were of Charlotte in her lace gown with Davie beside her in his kilt, and finally the emporium with John, Davie and all their employees in a line outside.

'My word!'

'Isn't it magnificent!' said Davie modestly. 'I think Father will be proud, even if neither of us did become doctors!' The laughter was forced and he made a performance of pushing the photographs back into the box. 'There's one more request, of a personal nature. Will you come when I send for you?'

She couldn't speak. She picked up the box and made her escape. Mrs Armitage was accompanying her to the station and, fortunately for Helen, was content to chatter without needing any response. It was she who noticed the small parcel on the seat. 'It's Davie's way with gifts, Miss Shields. He's always spoiling Charlotte and me with surprises.'

Helen waited until the train was outside Darlington before opening the package. Inside were two pairs of exquisite silk stockings and a lace handkerchief. Bless the man, when would she ever use such frivolous things!

CHAPTER EIGHTEEN

Losses and Gains

The day Helen left, Mary returned from visiting the Richardsons with an urgent message for John. Mr Richardson had a fever and was in the isolation hospital. In a way the news was almost a relief. For days past the Quaker had absented himself from the warehouse, sending word he was unwell. Now his malady would be cured. All John had to do was carry on with immediate business. But the fever was diagnosed as cholera and that news spread like wildfire. First to summon John was the bank manager.

'Mr McKie, I realize you are not Mr Richardson's business partner. If what I tell you is breaking a confidence, it cannot be helped. Matters have become too serious.' He paused and when he saw John didn't understand, gestured. 'Over there on the table, Mr McKie. Evidence of Mr Richardson's ill-judged philanthropy.'

Balance sheets were spread out for John to examine, each one representing a business supported in its decline, with workers whose skills had been supplanted by new methods. On paper, the businesses represented the Quaker's assets: in reality, their value was almost negligible.

When he grasped their substance, understood how the profits he and others at the warehouse had toiled to amass had been dissipated, John felt numb. 'This is terrible.'

'I did what I could but he wouldn't listen. Now that Mr Richardson is so gravely ill, you and I will have to act. All that property will have to be sold and the workers dismissed if we're to avoid bankruptcy for the Richardson family.'

'Bankruptcy!'

'There's no other way of avoiding it.'

'That cannot be allowed to happen.' The manager's eyebrows rose. 'But for Mr Richardson,' John went on, 'neither Davie nor I would own the emporium. It was the same spirit that guided him in those days, when we were a better investment.'

'Quite so.'

'However, if out of misplaced kindness Mrs Richardson and her family now face ruin?'

'They will, unless we act promptly. All those small businesses.' The manager waved a hand toward the table as if he could conjure them up out of the pieces of paper, 'Who will pay the wages on Friday, for instance?'

'I will.'

'What!'

'I will raise a loan against the emporium. Although I agree we'll have to give notice of closure but everyone, every employee must be given a pension commensurate with his length of service – we might have to sell my Coburg Street properties to do that.'

'Mr McKie!' The manager was scandalized. 'I cannot allow it. I respect your loyalty, sir, and your excellent intentions, but what you suggest – why, it's senseless. Throwing money away for no reason?'

'What would you prefer, Mr Moffat? That those workmen join other beggars on the streets while I have the emporium to support my family?' The manager didn't reply. 'In these times when there are already hungry children out there?' John pointed in the general direction of Tubwell Row but Mr Moffat

467

chose not to look. It was romantic nonsense his client proposed, not financial common sense.

'At least consult your brother, Mr McKie. What you propose will affect him also. But come and see me again soon. We must act before Friday.'

Once outside, John felt strangely elated. So much to be done and he was the only one to do it, provided Mary approved. He couldn't act without her agreement. He found her in the kitchen.

'May I speak to you concerning a business matter? I need your opinion.'

Her gaze was searching.

'Very well,' she said after a pause. 'In the study after supper.'

The balance sheets were spread out as they'd been in the manager's office. John explained their significance slowly so that Mary understood. When he'd finished, she said quietly, 'The news of Mr Richardson isn't good. He's not expected to recover.'

'That makes the situation worse. We must act quickly.' He outlined the choices as he saw them then asked, 'I need you to help me decide, Mary. Davie cannot be troubled. There's no one else I trust.' Another pause. 'It's because of the future. Whatever happens to us,' and he hurried on, not daring to look at her, 'whatever we decide will affect everyone here. Do we take the easy option, or the hard?'

'You cannot put those workmen out on the street and live with your conscience afterwards.'

Elated, even exultant, John said tentatively, 'I cannot manage alone, Mary. I need your strength.'

'What do you want me to do?'

It was a small beginning; he mustn't rush.

'Moffat and I will see to the business side and I shall ask Hart to take charge here, to find ways to cut our expenditure to the bone, but the foremen and their wives of those firms that will have to close have to be visited, Mary. Will you accompany me and help explain? I want them to learn first hand that they need not fear the future.'

468

They shared the nightmare for the next five days. Mr Moffat hadn't exaggerated; the sum required was as much as John could raise. By the end of the week he no longer owned property in Coburg Street and the emporium was heavily mortgaged. On Friday night, he confessed what he'd done to Mary and Mr Hart. He was no longer elated but very frightened indeed.

'I've brought us all to penury because I didn't listen to Moffat.'

'No other decision was open to you,' Mary said firmly.

Mr Hart tried to sound enthusiastic. Privately, he shared John's unease. 'I think, now that we've cut back in every department, and provided we take one step at a time, we should manage.' He wondered whether his two employers were as one now that Miss Crowther had left. From gossip in the shop he knew Mary still occupied a room next to Mrs Armitage.

'Most important of all,' Mary added, 'we've managed to keep it to ourselves. Davie knows nothing about it.' She looked at John, 'Thank Heavens he continues to trust you.'

Her husband flushed crimson. It only occurred to her after she'd left the study, why that was. Well, well . . . she thought, perhaps that's what I should have done all along, given him a scolding occasionally. She gave a smile, the first in days. I shall end up like the school mistress, she thought.

25 April 1908
Dear Miss Shields,
Thank you for your letter. Davie appears to be a little better. He attends another clinic this week, where electrical treatment is available. Charlotte is eager for him to try it and he does so for her sake. His cheerfulness is wonderful to behold and we're so grateful; it gives us all courage.

Luke passed his geography examination with distinction today . . .

3 May 1908

Dear Miss Shields,

You will be pleased to learn the weather was fine for young Ted's birthday celebrations. We all went to Redcar and spent the day on the beach. Davie is much better and can sometimes manage without a stick, which pleases Charlotte.

She declares she is 'rushed off her feet' in the emporium as indeed she is now there are less staff. She is so confident Davie is improving, she has agreed to be on the platform when the new church hall is officially opened next month . . .

Mary's next letter alternated between hope and a darker mood. Helen read it sitting outside, watching an ex-pupil dig manure into her vegetable bed. Davie was well provided he took an hour's rest morning and afternoon. He visited the shop because chatting to the ladies cheered him so, and the latest medical treatment involved sea-water baths.

'Hrmmph . . . ' He could have enjoyed those up here, bathing in the loch. Helen had suggested a visit here. Davie replied apologetically. 'Charlotte prefers that I remain by her side . . . I fear I might not have enough strength for the journey.'

And in ten days' time that wife of his wanted Davie beside her on stage? 'Hrmmph,' thought Helen again. It's to be hoped the English sea water works a miracle so that he can.

(iii)

It was a glorious day. Unlike the concert, the Opening was to be formal. A dignified service of praise to God, not forgetting the efforts of man. As the building had risen so it had lifted Charlotte's hopes. The hall represented Davie's achievement on earth. Surely no Presbyterian God could ignore it?

They entered with the new organ echoing to the roof in a magnificent voluntary. Pews were packed. Ranks of hats on either side were vivid with flowers. As ladies leaned forward excitedly to wave and smile, heady perfumes wafted over them.

470

Davie, hazy with medicine, felt he was in a strange, exotic garden.

The choir sang. Prayers were offered in fervent gratitude and at the end of it all he was exhausted. In the landaulette, hired so that he could stretch out and be comfortable for the short journey home, he interrupted Charlotte's raptures. 'I don't think I shall attend the next ceremony, dearest, when the Tea-House is opened in South Park.'

'But, Davie – you were at the meeting when they decided to build the Tea-House!'

She was so radiant, his wonderful, beautiful Charlotte, surely she could understand?

'All the same, I don't think I will. I'm glad today was perfect.'

(iv)

29 June 1908
Dear Miss Shields,
Pray excuse the urgency of this request. My husband asks if it would be possible for you to visit us in the near future? Dr Cullen has stressed privately that time is short.
Yours faithfully,
CHARLOTTE MCKIE

Telegram to Mrs Davie McKie,
c/o McKie Bros,
Darlington.
Arriving 4.20 PM 2 July stop Helen Shields

(v)

He was content to live from one hour to the next. The quiet talks with John about the future, about what was best for the children, pleased him most. When he'd still been able to joke he'd said, 'For a childless man, you've ended up with a fair number of them, John. I hope they won't prove a burden,' and John had managed to smile.

471

Ted would be dissuaded from joining the army. Davie would maybe talk to him tomorrow. And Jane, she must have her chance if Charlotte could be coaxed to his way of thinking. Meanwhile . . . He tried to drag his attention away from the small bottle on the dressing table; it contained the elixir that kept the pain at bay for shorter and shorter periods.

Jane was stock-taking, checking endless boxes of buttons against an inventory. It was so stuffy in here; the windows couldn't be opened and smells of haberdashery and dust stifled her. It was a rotten job, she reflected, no wonder Matthew, home from school, wanted her to do it. He and Ted had gone to the station to meet Miss Shields. Father had a fancy to see the school teacher again. It was becoming more and more difficult for Father. They took it in turns to sit with him; he wanted to talk, that much was obvious, but the effort was too great. When he grew distressed because the words wouldn't come, Luke would come and give him the medicine. Then there would be peace, for a short while.

Outside someone was calling her name. Noise was strictly forbidden. Jane opened the door and whispered sharply, 'Ted, for goodness sake!'

'She's here. Miss Shields, she's arrived. She took us for an ice cream on the way home from the station. Billy gave his to Blackie – '

'You lucky thing!'

'Would you like my bull's-eye instead?' She was tempted but she could see it had been in his pocket several days.

'No thanks.'

'Tell you what – why don't I ask Mother if you can come with Mat and me to Cocker Beck Fields? One of the chaps in my class is flying his kite there today.'

'I'd better stay, Ted. She'll want me to be in the shop while she's with Miss Shields.' Ted pulled a face and galloped off. Jane watched enviously. It was so much easier if you were a boy!

In the sickroom, the curtains were drawn but some beams managed to penetrate. They made a pattern Davie wanted to caress with his fingers but he couldn't lift his hand, the effort was too great. His bed had been moved so he could see everything: Mrs Armitage sitting reading; Miss Shields beside him in

472

the bedside chair. How long had she been there? The door had opened – yesterday? Last week? Time was a difficult dimension nowadays. All he could recall was his gladness at the sight of her. She'd sat and begun talking as though they'd never been parted, reminding him of the good times, soothing his fears and chasing away any regrets.

'I've let Charlotte down. She wanted me to enter politics.'

'That was never a good idea, Davie. You're too honest. You've achieved more because you weren't selected.' He raised his eyebrows because he didn't believe her, and Helen reminded him instead of all the moments of happiness they'd shared.

Gradually, over a few days, she completed the task she'd set herself when she'd first walked in and seen him: she reconciled Davie to his unfinished life. With Charlotte's help they'd listed the minutiae of small, day-to-day successes; in the end, they'd almost convinced him there had been no need of greatness.

He managed a final lucid talk with John when the women weren't present. He stopped all talk of financial arrangements for the children. 'Sorry, old chap . . . Leave you to see to things . . . Trust you.' John wanted to explain but he could see Davie hadn't much time, the medicine was already making him sleepy again. 'See that Charlotte . . . when she marries again, see to it she chooses a solid sort of fellow. Not another butterfly like me,' Davie whispered.

'Marry!' Despite the lump in his throat, John was scandalized. Davie almost laughed.

'Of course she will. She's only thirty. There's another thing though.'

'Concerning Charlotte?'

'No, you. No more Cecilia Crowthers, John. You've got the best wife but you're a silly, blind old duffer. She'll escape through your fingers if you don't take care. Just you see she doesn't.'

(vi)

Katriona entered pushing a trolley and Helen automatically looked at her watch; the evening ritual had begun. She disap-

473

proved as did Dr Cullen but Davie wouldn't have it any other way. Twice a day, whatever the physical cost, Katriona washed and tidied him so that Charlotte would see her husband at his best. Helen knew that Charlotte would be putting on her own finery, waiting for the summons.

Katriona poured water into the bowl and tested the temperature as if for a baby. 'Would you like me to stay?' Helen asked hesitantly. 'I think Davie's not so well this evening.' Katriona shook her head and picked up the medicine instead. She put an arm round his shoulders and tipped the bottle to his lips. Her touch, gentle though it was, made him cry out unrestrainedly. The monster that gripped his spine with fiery pincers took away all control. Helen was shaken. She watched Katriona. 'Dr Cullen said that the mixture was strong and addictive,' she protested. 'Should you be giving him so much?'

Katriona lowered Davie onto his pillows. 'I don't think we need worry. It's the only thing that helps, we couldn't deny him it. I'll not be long getting him ready, will you warn Mrs Davie for me?'

That night, as they did every evening, they gathered in the dining room and pretended to read. When Charlotte walked in she had Dr Cullen with her. Helen was suddenly aware of an immense tension. Charlotte spoke in the quietest tones she had heard her use.

'You are to visit your father – you too, Luke, to bid him farewell. You will do nothing to distress him. I want no tears tonight, is that clearly understood?' There was a gasp from Jane. Ted stood ramrod straight, his hands clenched at his sides. 'Come along, all of you,' she said softly.

Helen's hand trembled on her book. Mary waited until the door had closed behind them. 'Will you be all right? I must go and warn Bertha and Mrs Armitage.' Helen nodded. Left alone, she waited. Could she maintain her strength of purpose when her turn came? Mercifully it was Dr Cullen and not Charlotte who opened the door and beckoned to her.

'Now, my dear, he's kissed the children. They were brave and now they've gone away to sob their hearts out. Luke is with them. Davie hasn't got long but he'd like you to read him and Charlotte a bit of poetry, that's all.'

'Is John with him?'

'And Mary. I'll be in the passage for when I'm wanted. The thing to remember is that he's content.'

'Have you any idea,' Helen asked unsteadily, 'what it is he wants me to read?'

'It's a piece from the Bible. There's a marker in the place.' As she braced herself outside the door, Dr Cullen whispered encouragingly, 'He's not in any pain, I've seen to that. And I believe he's perfectly happy.'

Helen walked into the bedroom. Charlotte was in the chair beside the bed, holding Davie's hand. In the shadows John stood, his arm round Mary. As he saw Helen, Davie smiled. 'The Minister wanted to come,' he whispered, 'to read the Good Book . . . but he wouldn't approve my choice . . . so you do it.' Helen cleared her throat and began the Song of Solomon. When she reached the words:

> Behold, thou are fair, my love;
> Behold, thou are fair . . .

Davie looked at his love, his heart in his eyes.

CHAPTER NINETEEN

A New Beginning

In the sweet, cool dawn, Helen Shields untangled herself from young Ted's arms, laid him on the bed beside Matthew and Jane and left the nursery in search of John. She found him in the dining room, head on the table, slumbering. Without the pince-nez and made defenceless by sleep he was still the boy she'd first known. Her heart ached to reach out and comfort him as she had the children during the night. Instead she tried to creep away but he was awake. 'It's over . . . He's at peace.'

But she couldn't speak of Davie, not yet.

'John, I'd like to take the children away if you can spare them. Ted was so very distressed last night when his father told him about your grandfather. Something about being executed as a rebel.' John sighed.

'Davie wanted to make Ted understand why he must not go for a soldier. Our grandfather refused to fight for a cause he didn't believe in, that's why he was condemned. We were brought up to honour his memory.'

'But Ted is too young and too vulnerable to understand.

476

There's been too much death. I want to take him and Matthew to Scotland to recover. Luke too, if he'll come. Your father will need them more than ever just now.'

They left immediately after the funeral. As the distance between them and Darlington increased, Helen saw that the sorrow had lessened a fraction. 'There's plenty of work waiting on the croft,' she told them. 'Your grandfather's had no one to help him for some months. Not since the Hamiltons emigrated to Canada.' So many of them gone from the Peninsula, she thought, all the brightest and best.

'Miss Shields, I've been thinking about the spring,' Luke announced unexpectedly. 'It ought to be possible to bring the water supply nearer the croft. Don't you agree, Ted? Between the three of us, we should be able to manage it.' From her corner seat, Helen saw the strained face relax a little.

'Dig a culvert and lay pipes, that sort of thing?' Ted ran a hand through his carroty hair in a way that made her catch her breath. She blew her nose and rummaged in her bag.

'Here you are, pencils and paper. Set to. You should have enough brains between you.' Bless you, Luke, she thought privately.

(i)

It was the first day they'd time to themselves. When he suggested they go out together, Mary didn't demur. He took her to the meeting of the waters and they sat watching the Tees and the Greta sparkle over the pebbles.

The softness of the day stole over them. On the opposite bank there was a sheen of bluebells to gaze at. The only sounds were birdsong and Blackie's lazy munching. Mary listened for a moment or two, thinking how long it was since she'd felt so peaceful. 'I'm so thankful Mrs Armitage persuaded Charlotte to go with her to Harrogate,' she said at last. 'A change of scene was necessary and for Charlotte, a town was much the best place. She needs people to bring her out of her present mood.'

'She never accepted that Davie would die,' John said sadly, 'even at the last.'

477

'I think she did . . . ' Mary considered slowly, 'secretly, but it's against her nature to give in.'

'And they loved each other, so much.' This was dangerous ground.

Mary spoke abruptly. 'Last night as I was helping her pack, Charlotte suddenly asked, "How did I fail?" I tried to reassure her but I'm not sure she believed me. She thinks she could've prevented it a little longer. I wish she didn't rely so heavily on Jane at present. I think we should try and change that, for Jane's sake.'

'Davie told me the children were our responsibility now. He knew Charlotte would need time to recover. He particularly wanted Jane to be a dancer, go to London for her lessons. That means persuading Charlotte to change her mind . . . ' John shook his head at the prospect. 'I've never managed to do that before.'

'Then you'll have to try harder,' Mary said evenly.

'On that last evening, Davie said "It's up to you, John, I know you won't let me down but I'll be there, looking over your shoulder." Thank God he never knew how close we came to disaster.'

'Is it over?' Mary asked calmly, 'Will we survive or will you have to sell the emporium to pay off the loan?'

'I'm not sure. I know there's scarcely anything left. Our only chance is to begin all over again. I cannot do that on my own, Mary!'

She continued to gaze at the bluebells on the opposite bank. It seemed to John an age before she asked, 'Before we met, what sort of girl had you planned to marry?' Her words were so quiet the birdsong almost drowned them. The question caught him unprepared.

'I don't know. I hadn't considered, neither Davie nor I had. Work, nothing but work, filled our lives.'

'And – afterwards? Now you have had time to consider?' He turned to her so full of passion and certainty it burst forth.

'It's taken thirteen years to discover that it could be no other woman but you, Mary. I've made you so unhappy, even more than that other scoundrel, yet now I've brought you here to beg forgiveness. I cannot woo you as Davie did Charlotte, he was a much greater, warmer-hearted man than I but, Mary, I love you

478

with all my heart! I want to give you the world – I can't even offer you this small patch of grass. There's nothing but toil ahead if you stay with me but please, please consent! I swear I'll never again break those vows we once made!' He stumbled across, knelt and took her face in his hands. The tears he'd held in check so long for Davie's sake ran down his cheeks. All the words were finished. He could only wait for her answer.

She didn't speak. She looked at him searchingly before stretching out her arms. And John understood for the first time the reason the birds were singing.

(ii)

The puppy crouched, nose to the ground and sad-eyed because the voice above was sharp. 'You've a lot to learn,' Alex grumbled, 'and I doubt I've the patience nowadays to teach you.' The young dog wanted to obey but instinct alerted him to sounds the old man couldn't hear.

'Is it them?' Alex marvelled, shading his eyes. 'After all this time?' A figure ran out of the haze, full of life, the red hair an aureole set aflame by the sun like another boy long ago. 'We're here, we're all here, Grandfather!' Behind him was Matthew and Luke followed, his arm under Helen's elbow. Ted couldn't keep the news to himself. 'We're going to make a conduit for the spring so you can have water through a tap on the croft – hallo, you've got a new dog.'

'Aye,' the old man managed to whisper, 'one of the new generation.' Ted and the puppy were rolling over joyfully in the dust by the time Helen arrived. There was a brief hug for Alex then Luke gathered both the younger boys and the dog to lead the way to the croft. 'We'll make the tea,' he called, 'it'll be ready when you get there.'

Helen and Alex watched them go. All the way on the train she'd been summoning up her courage but what could she possibly say? Eventually she began by describing the crowds at the funeral who'd come to bid Davie farewell. 'He had so many friends. Even the children couldn't tell me above half the names.'

479

'He took after Jeannie,' Alex nodded, 'she was a warm-hearted lassie.'

'He was a good man. You can be very proud.' It was a long time before either of them spoke after that. Alex said softly, 'Three fine boys, and the wee girl.'

'They are the future. Jane wants to take up dancing. Ted has ideas of being a soldier but John's relying on you to rid him of them.'

'Indeed so!' Shocked out of his sorrow, Alex said sternly, 'You and I must not let that happen. And John?' he asked wistfully, 'Will he come soon?'

'He will. He has some business to attend to then he'll be here.'

'Aye, aye,' he nodded again, satisfied. 'An important businessman in England. And Luke is to be a doctor.' Slowly, and with full hearts, they set off along the path to the croft.